Broken in the Dark

The Alarie Heirs: Book One

Ashley Elizabeth

Content Warnings

This book contains references to abuse, guns, kidnapping, knife play, losing a parent, panic attacks, sex trafficking, sexual assault/rape (depicted off page), violence, and other topics that may be sensitive to some readers, as well as sexually explicit scenes.

Reading is an escape for many of us, so if you feel that the mention of any of the above will upset you, please put this book down.

Your mental health matters.

Prologue

SCARLETT

T ime is merely an inescapable illusion—the only thing I have left in this cold, cruel world.

And I don't want it anymore.

Minutes turn into hours, hours into days, and days into weeks. And before I can do anything about it, all the hope stored inside my slowly failing heart disappears.

Because no one's going to save me.

Besides, even if someone does come for me, I'm past the point of being saved.

I'm broken beyond repair, like a child's toy that was played with too roughly.

I curl my body on the freezing concrete, my bare limbs so cold that a never-ending shiver takes over me. My teeth chatter, and my trembling hands, currently cuffed to the floor, press against my chest, seeking warmth. The sting of the metal digging into my wrists can barely be felt anymore.

I'm numb to everything, including *him*.

A monster with no face.

A demon who haunts my nightmares.

As I close my eyes, drifting off to either sleep or death, a cacophony of gunshots pierces the air in the level above me. I hear men shouting, feet charging, and glass shattering. Thud after thud repeats as if bodies are falling to the floor one by one. Dust floats down from the rickety beams overhead from the impact, spreading over my bruised skin.

"Where the fuck is she?" An animalistic roar thunders through the floorboards.

Fear overcomes me. My body quivers, knowing that this is it. And I'm sad to admit that a tiny part of me is relieved that, one way or another, this will all be over soon.

I hear the wrought iron door swing open at the top of the basement stairs for the first time in days and heavy footsteps quickly descending each one as if on a mission. I try to open my eyes, but my body and mind are too weak. Too exhausted. So I remain frozen, praying death will show me mercy and take me before I have to endure one more moment with him.

"Jesus fucking Christ."

My heart falters.

It's not *him*.

So who is it?

A loud clang beside me startles me, but it's not enough to provide my body with the adrenaline it needs to fight or even open my eyes, for that matter.

The icy metal of the shackles is removed from my wrists as something soft and warm is draped over my practically naked body. The thin floral dress I wore when I arrived here is merely a piece of soiled cloth, barely covering most of me.

"You're safe, Scarlett. We're taking you home."

How does he know my name?

Who is *we*?

And where is home?

My chapped lips slightly part, seeking answers to my questions, but nothing comes out.

Strong, warm arms slide under my body, lifting me easily and cradling me against a muscular chest, taking me up the stairs, away from here. Away from hell.

"Holy shit." I hear a different male voice curse. "Is she alive?"

"Barely," the man whose arms I'm in replies. I feel a pair of soft lips brush against my ear. "I've got you, Firefly. Stay with me." The deep, familiar timbre of his voice pulses within me, awakening a tiny part of my soul, giving me something I thought I had completely lost.

Hope.

"What did he do to her?"

"You already know the answer to that question, brother," a third man's deep voice responds.

"Mom's going to lose it when she sees her like this."

A low-pitched grunt in agreement arises from a fourth man.

The smell of death permeates the air around me, invading my nostrils. I groan as nausea churns my empty stomach.

"We need to go. Now. Burn this place to the fucking ground. I don't want to find anything left of it."

We're moving rapidly. Several pairs of footsteps echo in the space. A door grates open, and a rush of cold air whips at me as we walk...outside? I haven't seen the outside in...I can't remember how long. I try to open my eyes for just a glimpse of the sky, the sun, a tree, anything, but it's futile.

My body has given up even if my mind hasn't.

I use every last bit of strength left to nudge my face into the warm chest. A comforting masculine scent—leather and sandalwood—surrounds me.

"The men have rounded up three survivors we can bring in for *questioning,* but none of them appear to be who we want." There's a slight pause before the man says, "Le Diable's not here… Do you think he knew we were coming?"

"I don't know. But we don't have time to think about that right now. We need to get her to the hospital. And fast." A rough but gentle hand wraps around my wrist, multiple fingers pressing against my skin. "Her pulse is too weak."

"I'll call for an ambulance."

"It'll be faster if I take her." The man's hold on me tightens as a car door opens, and then carefully, he places me on a soft surface, my body melting into the comfort of the cushion beneath me, something I haven't felt in a long time as a thick blanket is placed over me, covering every inch.

"You'll be okay, Scarlett. I need you to be okay. Can you do that for me?"

I try to nod, but I've hit today's last energy ration.

I feel a band wrap around my back, the material pressing against my sensitive flesh, and I whimper from the impact of the pain before a quiet click confirms it's a seat belt.

The car door slams closed, and I hear another door open and then shut. Abruptly, we begin to move.

"We'll be at the hospital in eight minutes. Have the doctors ready for her. And call Mom to tell her we found her," the man snaps into, I assume, his phone before accelerating. "Scarlett, can you hear me? We're almost there. I just need you to fight a little bit longer."

But I don't want to fight any longer.

I'm too tired.

So unbelievably tired.

The car's engine roars, picking up speed and providing a calming white noise effect to my weary mind. And as I let my thoughts wander off to the place I've escaped to for the past who knows how long, I suddenly wonder, who just called me Firefly?

Chapter One

Scarlett

"I'm going to fucking hunt him down and kill him with my god-damn bare hands!"

My mind is lost in a dream amidst the nearby voices floating around me. A dream where four of the most lethal men in the world encircle me, watching over me. Four men who would do anything to keep me safe. Warmth spreads through me as I realize this is the first good dream I've experienced in a long time, and I refuse to wake up.

"Shhh! You're going to wake her. Maybe you boys should go before she comes to. This is all going to be a lot for her."

"Come on, brother, you should get some sleep. You haven't left her side since she's been here."

"I can't leave her! What if he comes back for her?"

"I've stationed guards outside her door. No one will get to her. Besides, Mom's here, and Madeleine's on her way. She stopped by the store to pick up some things to help her feel comfortable."

"Comfortable?" A scoff echoes nearby. "She was just fucking kid-napped and—"

"I must warn you, the presence of men right now could set her off. Especially ones like your—"

"I caution you in how you finish that sentence, Doctor. This woman knows us. She grew up with us. We would never harm her."

"Y-yes, of course. But your mother has told me that it has been years since you have all seen her, and something this traumatic could make her...feel differently toward you. I suggest you keep your distance from her and give her time to heal."

"Keep our distance from her? What the fuck does that mean?"

"Easy, brother. The doctor here is only looking out for her well-being. But he's right. We should go."

Silence fills the space before something rough and warm cups my cheek, a tender, comforting touch on my skin. It feels like my body is slipping beneath a warm bath, every muscle in my body melting into this embrace. A breath caresses my ear. "I'm sorry, Firefly. I'm so fucking sorry. I'm never letting you go again."

The warmth on my cheek disappears, and several seconds later, a soft bang causes my eyes to flutter open, my dream completely dissipating. Adjusting to the bright lights above me, I expect to see the same four musty cement walls I've stared at for the past however long, but instead, I'm met with pristine white walls, scenic framed beach photos, an overwhelming antiseptic smell, foreign-looking machines, and a large window displaying the clear blue sky, the sun shining high above.

The sun. My throat tightens as I take in the sight of something most of us take for granted, not realizing that we may never see it again one day.

A rhythmic beeping stirs my thoughts, my eyes jumping to the machine beside my bed. I'm in a hospital room. Starting to panic, I try to sit up, but it's pointless. My body is too weak, and the needle in my arm, attached to the IV bag beside me, doesn't give me any leeway to move.

"H-help," I try but fail to scream, my hoarse voice unrecognizable.

"Scarlett, it's okay. I'm here." A woman I hadn't noticed in one of the nearby chairs rushes over to me. "Everything is going to be okay, sweetheart. You're safe now."

"S-safe?" I croak. My eyes jump around the room, panicking before landing back on her.

She smiles warmly, her glassy pale blue eyes suddenly appearing familiar even though I know it's been years since I've seen them.

Cecilia Alarie.

"Mrs. Alarie?" She was my mom's best friend before my mom lost her battle with cancer. My mother, father, and I lived on the Alarie Estate in New York for years until one night seven years ago when my father woke me in the middle of my sleep, practically dragging me out of my bed and moving us off their property to Chicago.

He claimed the estate was no longer safe after the murder of the head of the Alarie family, Charles Alarie, and he forbade me from having anything to do with any of them ever again, or there would be grave consequences.

And if you knew how cruel my father could be, you would take his warning and abide by it, too.

"It's me, sweet girl," Mrs. Alarie says, releasing me from my thoughts. She reaches over for a cup on the table beside me and brings it before my mouth. I wrap my lips around the straw, savoring every drop of the cold liquid running down my parched throat. After a few sips, she places the cup back on the table and then reaches toward my face as if wanting to push my hair back, but instead pulls her hand away and tucks the blanket in around me.

"How did I get here?" I try to rack my mind for an answer, but all I remember is clinging to the frozen floor for dear life, seeking warmth.

Confident that I was only seconds away from death.

She shows a small smile. "My boys found you in Chicago. And after a few days at the Chicago hospital, they had you airlifted here to New York."

My boys.

Her sons.

My heart hammers in my chest, an overwhelming urge to cry taking over me as emotions, both good and bad, invade me. The four of them found me. They witnessed me in that basement, chained up like an animal, surrounded by a stench of blood, vomit, and humility. And although I feel thankful they came for me—saved me—a crushing amount of shame washes over me.

Will I ever be able to face them after knowing what they saw? Or from what they can only assume happened to me? A sweat breaks out over my temple, my nails digging into the palms of my hands, causing a faint stab of pain.

"Although, it was Leo who brought you to the first hospital. Too stubborn to wait for an ambulance. He insisted on doing it himself," she muses. "The four of them were just here before I kicked them out to give you some space."

Leonardo Alarie.

My heart thunders madly, and I pray that I'm not hooked up to one of those machines that will alert the whole place of my chaotic pulse.

He's the boy my heart always beat for.

The one I gave myself—I internally shake my head, my throat tightening as the memory of our last moment together flashes before me. Taunting me. A night when I was brave and strong. Young and beautiful. And secretly head over heels in love with a boy named Leo Alarie.

But now...I'm broken.

And I don't have to look into a mirror to know this.

I can feel it.

With every excruciating breath I take.

I shouldn't have survived what I went through.

But somehow, I did.

And life will never be the same.

I don't realize tears are pouring out of my eyes until Mrs. Alarie reaches for a tissue and gently presses it against my skin, wiping the wetness away. "Let it out."

I nod, rolling in my bottom lip, unable to stop the onslaught of tears even if I tried.

Knock. Knock.

The wooden door on the other side of the room creeks open, revealing a pair of bright, blue, familiar eyes that lock onto mine.

Madeleine Alarie.

"Hey, stranger." She takes graceful steps toward me, carrying a weekender bag in one hand and a bouquet of brightly colored flowers in the other.

"Maddy," I whisper, a tiny smile working its way onto my face, tears blurring my vision.

Dropping the bag on the chair, she places the flowers on the table beside me. She rests her hand on the bed next to mine but makes no move to get any closer.

"I just ordered a bunch of clothes and toiletry items for you. Everything will be delivered by the time you come home." She tucks a piece of her long, black hair behind her ear, and a flash in my eye causes me to notice an engagement ring with a massive stone resting on her finger. My chest aches, realizing just how much I've missed in her life over the years.

"Home?" I ask, looking between the two of them, confused. They're sending me back to Chicago. A knot forms in the pit of my stomach, anxiety racing through me at the prospect of being sent back when I just got here after all these years.

"The doctors have requested you stay here for a few more days," Mrs. Alarie starts. "But I will be by your side the whole time." She glances at Maddy and then back at me. "It's your choice, but when they think you're ready to be moved, I'd like to bring you home to the estate in New York. It was always your home, Scarlett." Relief. That's all I feel, knowing I won't be dragged away again. Not this time. "My staff is currently setting up a room in my house for you to recover. We'll have the family doctor on round-the-clock care for you whenever you need him. I just..." She stops herself, choking on her words. "If I had known what was going to happen to you, I never would have let your father take you away from us. I would have... We would have..." She shakes her head. "But with the death of Charles, I wasn't seeing straight. None of us were, and I'm so sorry."

"We all are," Maddy whispers, her eyes dim and downcast.

Tears soak the spot on my hospital gown beneath my chin. "It's not your fault. My father didn't give me a choice. He forced me to leave and stopped me from—" I blink a few times, my eyes scanning the room. "Wait, where is my father? Chicago?"

Maddy's eyes shoot to her mom's, panic evident.

Mrs. Alarie looks down at me with uncertainty in her eyes. "I'm sorry to have to tell you this." She pauses before saying, "But your father didn't survive the fire."

"Fire?" My brows furrow. Why can't I remember a fire? And why do I feel nothing from her words? No pain or loss. Just...nothing.

Maddy tilts her head. "What do you remember from..." She clears her throat. "The day you were taken?"

I bring a hand up to my head, rubbing my temple as I try desperately to recall what happened. "I remember pulling my car into my father's driveway. He had asked me to come over because it had been some time since we had seen one another and he needed to discuss something, but..." What happened next? I pinch my eyes shut, searching my brain for an answer, when a blurry memory comes to me. "But just as I stepped out of my car, I felt a jab in my neck." My fingers travel to that spot on my skin, and a phantom prick from the needle pulses. "Then I woke up in... I woke up in..." I can't get the words out, my chest seizing up.

Oh God.

I clutch the hospital gown over my chest, my breaths coming out too fast and labored as my airways feel on the verge of closing. Every second of that day begins to invade my mind like a disease, and I grip the sides of my head as I gasp for air.

A cement floor. No windows. My wrists were cuffed to the floor. I couldn't move. My head was pounding as if I was hungover. A glass of water and one piece of bread were placed beside me, but I was too scared that they might be poisoned, so I didn't touch them. My dress was ripped up the side, stopping just above my knee. A man, no, a monster, suddenly came down the stairs, appearing as the devil himself with a knife in his hand. The only thing I saw before everything around me went black was his bright green eyes.

"Make it stop!" I scream, my fingers digging into my skull. "Please," I whimper. "Make it stop!"

"Scarlett, you're okay." Mrs. Alarie's soothing voice gradually alleviates my racing heart. "You're okay. You're safe." She smooths out my hair, her calming touch a reprieve from my visions.

"Should I get the doctor?" Maddy asks, fear coating her voice.

"No, no, no!" I shake my head violently. "Please don't." Tears spill down my cheeks. "I don't want to be drugged again."

"We won't call for the doctor." Mrs. Alarie dips a small cloth in the glass pitcher of water on the nearby table and then rings it out. With a tender touch, she places it on my forehead, pressing it back and forth over my skin. The cold water feels refreshing against my overheated skin. "Take a deep breath for me."

I do as she says, my whole body taken over by a slight tremble.

"You're going to be okay," she states firmly but gently. The look in her eyes is one a mother would give her daughter, and for whatever reason, it brings me back to the here and now.

I'm safe.

I'm home.

I'm in the protection of the Alaries.

"I'm sorry," I whisper, my cheeks heating up from embarrassment. I wrap my arms around me, folding into myself. "I don't know what's wrong with me."

"There's not one damn thing wrong with you, Scar." Maddy holds a glass of water before me, allowing me a few sips before she fluffs the back of my pillow. It's quiet for a moment before she asks, "Do you need anything? Another pillow? Food?" She smiles, but her watery eyes give away her true feelings.

I shake my head. "No, I don't need anything."

She nods, her eyes dancing around the room. "I guess I shouldn't have brought flowers, seeing you have enough here to last a lifetime."

Sitting up, I see several vases of pink flowers filling the space by the window and even more on the table beside me. This hospital room could be a cover-up for a florist shop.

"Where did these all come from?" I ask.

Mrs. Alarie walks over to the closest arrangement, admiring them. "Leo had these sent over for you."

He did? But why?

Mrs. Alarie and Maddy share a knowing look, one I try not to decipher.

I snuggle into my pillow, facing the window, and notice that the sun is about to disappear, soon to be replaced by a dark, ominous sky.

But the light in the room is still on, so I'm okay.

As long as the light is on, I'll be okay.

A heavy yawn escapes me, exhaustion weighing down on me.

"We should let you get some sleep," Mrs. Alarie says, noting my demeanor. "Madeleine is going to sleep on the couch if that's okay."

"Of course," I immediately answer, feeling at ease that I won't be alone.

Maddy pats her bag. "Got all the essentials for a sleepover in here. Satin pajamas. Face masks. Chocolate. And some reality shows to binge on my tablet, of course."

My lips faintly curve up, expecting nothing less from her.

Mrs. Alarie points toward the door. "There are guards stationed outside, and I'll be back in the morning." She smiles as she looks between us and then walks over to the light switch, her hand reaching out to flick the switch down.

Panic erupts within me. "Keep the lights on!" I tug the blanket up to my chest, my body shaking uncontrollably.

Her hand freezes mid-air as she quickly turns to face me.

"I'm sorry." Shame washes over me. "It's just that…" I swallow, clutching the blanket harder to my chest. "Bad things happen in the dark."

CHAPTER TWO

Leo

FOUR MONTHS LATER

Darkness comes for you whether you want it to or not. And in my twenty-five years of experience, I've come to find that it's better to embrace it than to run from it.

The gilded *Alarie Estate* plaque comes into view as the gold-tipped iron gates slowly slide open for me. I give a curt nod to the guards on duty and accelerate through the entrance, racing my blacked-out Ducati over the paved roads I know like the back of my hand.

The Alarie Estate is an impenetrable fortress surrounded by miles of ten-foot-high stone walls covered in ivy. A place that no one would venture to without an invitation unless they're prepared to suffer the consequences. A place where my four siblings, my mother, and I call home, along with the many loyal soldiers and workers on our property.

It's filled with memories. Some good. Some bad. And some I try every damn day to forget.

Rounding the corner, I drive along my mother's property, turning onto the narrow driveaway that delves deeper into the shadowy woods before coming upon her home, situated on the water. An almost two-hundred-year-old imposing yet beautiful château that, over the years, has been converted into a home with all the modern-day amenities. It's where I spent my childhood until I was ready to have my own house built on the other side of this lake.

After parking my bike beside the bottom of the stone steps, I pull off my helmet and reach inside the side case, retrieving this week's bouquet of fresh flowers.

An assortment of pink gladioli.

Pink, well, because it's always been Scarlett's favorite color. Even if, now, she hides behind muted tones so as not to stand out. Not to gain any unwanted attention.

And gladioli because they symbolize strength—something she needs now more than ever.

Nudging the front door open, I step inside, looking around, ensuring the coast is clear before I head to Scarlett's bedroom. Opening her bedroom door, I find it empty, just as I expected, knowing she has her virtual therapy session scheduled at this time in my mother's library. I take a few steps toward the vase on her nightstand, noting the lifeless flowers wilting, waiting for their replacement. I switch out the flowers, tossing the old ones in the trash, and quickly head out of the room, ensuring no one knows I was ever here, especially Scarlett.

I suggest you keep your distance from her and give her time to heal.

The doctor's warning from that day in the hospital months ago echoes in my head. The asshole had the nerve to tell me to stay away from her as if he or anyone else could ever tell me what to do.

And as much as I wanted to prove the bastard wrong and show him that Scarlett would be fine when I was by her side, I knew he was right. She's going to need time. Time to heal. And time to move forward.

So, like an obedient dog, I've kept my distance. Only intruding into her space when I know she won't be around or watching her from afar, never letting her see me.

And as my brother Vin keeps reminding me every damn day, it's for the best.

Reaching the dark wooden front door, I wrap my hand around the handle, ready to leave, just as my mother's voice calls out from down the hall.

"Oh, Leo. Perfect timing." I drop my hand and turn, finding her smiling as she approaches me. She pushes back her shoulder-length black hair as she takes her final step toward me.

"Mother." I lean down, placing a kiss on each of her cheeks.

"Come." She motions for me to follow her. "We have some business to discuss."

"If this is about the arms deal with the—"

"No. I don't care to discuss trivial matters right now when I have something more important on my mind."

Trivial? This deal will make the family another hundred million in profits this year, but sure, let's call it trivial.

She opens the door to her study, walking straight toward her desk. As I step inside, spotting several familiar faces already seated around the room, I realize I've walked right into a goddamn trap.

"What the fuck is this?" I ask, grinding my back molars. My eyes scan the room, narrowing in on each of my traitorous siblings.

Each of them, including myself, holds a responsibility within the family—a position we don't take for granted. It's why we are so successful at what we do and why we've become one of the world's most powerful and feared families.

The oldest is Vincenzo, aka Vin, the *family leader* who assumed his role seven years ago after our father's murder. No decision is made without his final say, no business is acquired without his signature, and no killing is committed without a simple nod of his head. He's a wolf in sheep's clothing—or, as I like to say, a beast in a three-piece suit.

Then there's Alessandro, aka Alex, known as the *brains* of the family, able to hack into almost any system in the world. You'll never find his tie crooked or a speck of dust in his home, but don't let his intense desire for cleanliness fool you. One wrong move, and you'll wind up on his bad side, where he'll find great enjoyment in destroying you with just a quick click of his mouse before you even realize a bullet is heading your way.

Next is Mauro, the *muscles*, who hasn't encountered anyone he can't take down. He's a silent slayer who mostly keeps to himself until needed. And he likes it that way.

There's me, the *hunter*, the one my brothers come to when they need someone found or taken out. A deadly predator in the streets of New York who won't stop until I've found my prey.

And finally, Madeleine, the baby of the family, but also the family *financier*. The one responsible for approving significant expenses and keeping all the books clean. But most importantly, she's the one who takes care of the payroll for everyone living on the Alarie Estate, not to mention half the law enforcement in the state who work for us.

We all play a pivotal role.

And we all do it really fucking well.

My mother sits behind her desk, waiting for me to take the seat opposite hers.

I do, reluctantly, my eyes catching on a familiar photo on her desk of her and my father. The one taken of them on the family's private island where they spent their anniversary every year before my father passed. So much love reflects on their faces. It almost makes me laugh knowing that over thirty years ago, no one approved of their marriage, seeing that they came from two rival families.

My father, Charles Alarie, was the eldest son of an extremely wealthy family in southern France. My mother, Cecilia Marchetti, is the youngest daughter of one of the most powerful families in Italy. They met while my mother was studying abroad, fell in love, then moved to America against their families' wishes and created an empire in their own right.

One that no one will ever be able to conquer.

Leaning back in my chair, I look around the room at all of my siblings. "Does someone care to tell me why the fuck I'm being ambushed?"

"Scarlett," my mother says matter-of-factly.

My fingers dig into the arms of the chair, unease flowing through me. Every time I think about what happened to her... I internally shake my head. I can't go down that path right now.

"What about Scarlett?" I feign indifference.

"It's been months since we found her. Since you saved her."

I nod, remembering the whole nightmare like it was yesterday. "Yes, I'm aware."

She clasps her hands together, placing her elbows on her desk and leaning forward, glancing around the room. "I know that you're all doing everything you can to find the man responsible for kidnapping Scarlett, but I'm afraid it's not enough."

I arch a brow, peering at Vin, who shows no emotion. "And what would you propose we do?"

"Marriage."

My eyes whip back to hers. "Marriage?" I lean forward. "Whose marriage?"

"Yours and Scarlett's."

My eyes widen as I look between all my family members again, waiting for them to say, "Gotcha." As seconds tick by, I finally rise from my seat, glaring down at her. "Are you out of your mind?"

She leans back, relaxing into her chair. "I've put a lot of thought into this. And your brothers, sister, and I think the best plan of action is for you to marry her."

"She's right," Madeleine adds. "You know she is."

I shake my head, pinching the bridge of my nose. "Do you hear yourself?" I throw my hands in the air. "You want me to marry the poor girl after everything she went through?"

"That is exactly why we want *you* to marry her," my mother says adamantly.

I accusingly point my index finger at Vin. "You agree with her? With this nonsense?"

"I do." He runs his fingers through his thick black hair. "The man who did this to her has been spending months hiding in the shadows waiting for his moment. But we took what he thought was his, and a marriage might just be the thing to provoke him to come out and play, giving us a chance to find him." He gives a slight shrug, his suit jacket stretching across his broad shoulders. "I know it's not ideal circumstances, but—"

"Ideal circumstances?" My voice raises as I shake my head. They've all lost their minds. "I won't do it." I turn, striding toward the door. "I don't know why you would think that I would be the one—"

"Because you love her." My mother's voice cuts through the room like a bullet piercing a piece of silk.

I freeze, my knuckles turning stark white as they clutch the chrome doorknob with an ungodly strength.

"You love her and blame yourself for what happened to her. Just like you blame yourself for what happened to your father."

I spin on my heels. "Don't." I take two steps, gripping the top of the chair. "Don't bring him into this."

She nods in understanding. "Okay." She looks around the room. "Madeleine, Mauro, and Alessandro, you may leave us now while we discuss details."

The three of them stand, making their way to the door. Madeleine gives me a sheepish smile as she passes me. Mauro clasps my shoulder before walking away, and Alex stands beside me and says, "Just think about it," before stepping out of the room and closing the door behind them.

I look out the glass French doors leading to the gardens in the back-yard. "Why?" I ask, palming the back of my neck.

Mother stands, smoothing out her cream-colored dress before she takes a few steps around her desk, leaning against the wood surface. "Le Diable is still out there."

Hearing those words is like a stab to my heart.

The monster responsible for taking Scarlett is still alive, and every day that goes by without finding him is another day that I've failed her.

"Scarlett lives on the Alarie Estate again, which means she is under our protection," she says. "And I cannot think of a better way to make that message loud and clear to the world than by officially making her one of us. And the only way we can do that is by marriage, of course."

I stare at the floor, shaking my head, before tilting my chin toward my brother. "Why not Vin? He's the oldest. The leader of this family. It would send a more significant message."

Vin shakes his head, rubbing his hand over his dark stubble. "Would you want to break the poor girl's heart even more by marrying her off to someone other than yourself when she's only ever had eyes for you, brother?"

God, I hate it when he's right.

The thought of another man looking at Scarlett sets my mind on murder. I don't even want to think about what I would do if another man were to marry her.

Vin leans back in his chair, resting his hands behind his head, a sinister smile appearing. "Besides, no one is tying this down."

My mother glares at the ceiling. "Lord, give me patience today." She studies me, taking a few steps until she's right in front of me. "It has to be you." Her small hand rests against my cheek. "Out of all of my sons, you are the one who will show her the most patience." Her lips curve up. "As a boy, do you remember watching the sunset? You children would all race to the top of the hill to catch fireflies, and then you'd find a spot, throw down blankets, and lie there waiting. And once the sun finally set, your siblings would get bored and restless, eventually leaving. But not you. You would lie there until complete darkness took over. Eventually, the stars would shine above you, mesmerizing you. You waited because you knew something beautiful would happen and didn't want to miss a single second of it." She lets out a breath. "You thrive in the dark. You always have. And right now, that girl needs someone to help her survive in it... She needs you."

I step away, staring out the window, observing the slight breeze dancing through the trees. "I'm not equipped to help her. I'll probably only make things worse for her."

"You won't."

"How do you know that? How can you be so sure?"

"Because you—"

"Don't say it!" I let out a defeated sigh, knowing this is a war I'll never win. Not when my mother is so set in her ways. "If we do this, it's merely a marriage for her protection. That's all."

She nods. "I've been working with the family lawyers and have had a contract drawn up that includes a clause allowing either of you to get out of the marriage by means of a divorce only after her kidnapper is found."

I run an exasperated hand over my face. Of course, she's already been plotting every detail as if this marriage is actually happening. She knew I would never be able to say no to her. I look over my shoulder when I ask, "How do we even know Scarlett will be okay with this?"

Her smile widens. "Because she already agreed."

Scarlett agreed.

A spot in the center of my chest tightens, a pulse increasing where my heart should be. This feeling is foreign. Strange. And something I haven't felt in seven years. Not since I saw her father's car driving off our property with her in the back seat. The image of her bright blue eyes silently pleading with me to do something as tears fell down her porcelain cheeks has been engraved in my memory, and I will never be able to forget it.

Like a damn fool, I did nothing. Lost in a dangerous haze of grief, I watched the car until it disappeared from view and did not one fucking thing.

I convinced myself that Scarlett was better off away from here.

Away from this dark life.

Away from me.

Where she would be safe.

But I was wrong.

And I'll never be able to forgive myself for it.

I stare at the ground, my mind conflicted with what to do.

My family wants me to marry Scarlett. They think it's what's best for her, but they're wrong.

And that's because not one of them knows our secret.

They don't know the history that Scarlett and I share, the feelings we previously held for one another, or the moment that changed everything between us. I rub at my chest, my heart rate increasing as I remember everything about that night like it was yesterday.

The good and the bad.

Except touching Scarlett is one thing I'll never be able to do again. And I'll have to be okay with that. Because there's nothing I wouldn't do for her.

But I'm also not a fool. And I know that no good will come out of this marriage.

And it's my own fault.

Because over the past seven years, while Scarlett has been gone, I've changed, allowing darkness to consume me. And Scarlett, well, she has always been a ray of sunshine—a beacon of hope. And I refuse to be the one who dims her light.

But I can't ignore the question thundering in my head, demanding an answer.

How will I be able to protect her if she's not mine?

The answer is obvious.

I can't.

Giving up, I drop my hands to my sides and look between them. "When is this happening?"

Vin leans his elbows on his knees, his fingers playing with the family ring on his finger. His deep blue eyes greet mine as he says, "Tomorrow."

Chapter Three

Scarlett

Today's the day most girls spend their lives dreaming about, waiting for their happily ever after to begin. But I've recently learned that happily ever afters are only found in books and movies—never in real life.

At least, not in mine.

The clock on the wall chimes twelve times, alerting me it's time to go, but nerves swarm my stomach like a colony of bees as my feet remain firmly planted on the ground from fear.

Deep breath in. Deep breath out.

Closing my eyes, I repeat this process until I feel a semblance of calm.

I can do this.

I'm just saying, "I do," and then signing my name on the dotted line. It doesn't mean more than that. It's just an arrangement to ensure my safety.

Nothing more.

Nothing less.

And once my tormentor is found, I'll have the choice to end my marriage. To be free. Happy.

But then, why does the thought of ending my marriage before it's even started send another rush of anxiety through me?

Peering in the mirror, I smooth out the front of my dusty rose dress, admiring the floral pattern as it graces the floor around me. The sheer off-shoulder sleeves provide just the right amount of coverage, and seeing that it's not a real wedding anyway—just a town hall ceremony—I chose something simple.

Something that still left me feeling...beautiful? I don't know if that's the right word to describe how I feel, but even I can't help but stare at myself in the mirror—the reflection showing me a tiny glimpse of the girl I barely recognize anymore.

The door creaks open, and Mrs. Alarie sticks her head into the room. "Are you almost re—" Her eyes widen, taking me in. Stepping inside the room, she says, "Scarlett, you are the spitting image of your mother at this age. So beautiful." She wipes at her eyes with a tissue, careful not to ruin her makeup. She's about to place her hand on my shoulder but suddenly stops herself. "I know this isn't the real wedding you deserve, and I'm sorry for—"

I shake my head. "Your family has done more than enough for me. And I appreciate Leo's willingness to..."

I swallow the lump of nerves in my throat.

Leo, the man I will be marrying.

The boy I used to spend my childhood daydreaming about, scribbling his name and mine together in a diary.

The boy who always watched over me, even when he thought I wasn't looking.

The boy I lo—I shove down my emotions, my heart beating rapidly.

Leo was the boy I had always hoped to marry someday.

But not like this.

Not because of an arrangement or a signed contract. But for love. I sigh, gazing back at the mirror—that dream, along with who I used to be, has slowly sailed away out of reach, lost at sea.

"Leo will be kind to you." She rummages inside her clutch, taking out a velvet pouch. "You do not need to worry about what you think he expects or wants from you as his wife. He may be a man many fear, but his walls crumble for you. They always have." She smiles, trying to reassure me of what I'm about to do. Her fingers slip inside the pouch, taking out a delicate silver chain attached to a pear-shaped, blue diamond pendant surrounded by round brilliant diamonds. "This was your mother's. I gave it to her on her wedding day. Before she passed, she asked me to hold on to it for you. I thought it could be your something blue if you would like."

My bottom lip quivers, a rush of sensations coming over me. "It's beautiful." Thinking of my mother sends a tightness rippling through my chest, and I wish she could be here with me today. I don't have many memories with her since she died when I was only a little girl, but the ones I do have, I cherish more than anything. "Thank you," I murmur softly as I scoop up my blonde hair, letting her slide the necklace around my neck and secure the clasp. Without needing or wanting more time to think about things, I don a smile. "I'm ready."

Thirty minutes later, I walk up the stone steps to the town hall entrance with Mrs. Alarie. As we reach the top, I find Maddy waiting. She appears lost in her phone, a frown on her face that disappears as soon as she spots us.

"Scarlett!" She opens her arms, appearing ready to hug me, but then instantly drops them, clutching her hands before her. A bright smile takes over her face. "You make such a beautiful bride."

A slight breeze sweeps my hair over my shoulders. "I'm so glad you're here. I wasn't expecting anyone else."

"Of course. I wouldn't miss this for anything." She checks the time on her phone. "We should probably get inside. The appointment starts in five minutes."

The appointment. Just how every girl dreams of referring to her wedding day.

"Well, I'll head inside and ensure everything is all set," Mrs. Alarie affirms. She looks at me fondly, almost as if I'm not just some girl she's giving away on her wedding day but an actual daughter. "Welcome to the family, Scarlett. Officially." She turns and walks through the large wooden doors, a few people inside quickly moving out of her way, most likely knowing who she is.

"Leo won't be able to take his eyes off you," Maddy remarks, waggling her brows.

I look down at myself, second-guessing my dress. "Maybe it's too much..." My hands pull on the top of the neckline, seeking more coverage. "I should have just worn a simple shirt with pants. I don't want him to get the wrong idea or think—"

"Oh no." She shakes her head. "I didn't mean. Well, what I meant was, Leo won't... He knows... Shit." She pinches the bridge of her nose, taking a few breaths. "Can I be honest with you?"

"Yes."

She drops her hands. "I don't know what I'm allowed to do or say."

My brows furrow. "What do you mean?"

"I mean..." She gazes up at the sky and then back at me, letting out a sigh. "I mean that all I want to do is hug my freakin' best friend on her wedding day, but I don't know if I'm allowed to or not." She gives a slight shrug, her eyes watering.

My eyes mirror her own. After seven years apart, she harbors no grudges and still considers me her best friend. Maybe because she knows I never would have willingly left the Alarie Estate. "I think I could really use a hug right now."

"Yeah?"

I nod. "Yeah."

Without missing a beat, her slender arms surround me, and I wrap mine around her. This is something I've missed. Something my body has been craving—a tender, comforting touch.

"I missed you, Scar," she whispers against my hair.

"I missed you, too, Maddy."

We part, and a genuine smile forms on my face for the first time in a while.

"Don't cry yet." She wipes her thumb under my eyes. "You don't want to mess up your makeup."

I blink a few times, hoping to soak up the moisture. "Do I look okay?"

"You look stunning." She rolls her lips to the side and clears her throat. "I can't wait to officially be able to call you my sister."

"You're going to make me cry again." I fan my face with my hands, making us both laugh.

"Come on." She latches her arm through mine. "Let's get in there before they start without you. Everyone is waiting."

I halt. "Everyone?"

"Just the family."

The family. Soon to be *my* family.

Leo's three brothers: Vincenzo, Alessandro, and Mauro.

Deep breath in. Deep breath out.

We enter the drab building, passing lines of people at the nearby counters. A few people in one area argue over parking tickets, while others are bickering over permits.

She quickly pulls me along, her eyes scanning the numbers above the doors. "I know it's here somewhere... Ah! Here it is." She wraps her fingers around the chrome doorknob.

Suddenly, the reality of the situation hits me like a ton of bricks. I'm about to marry a man I haven't seen in seven years. One feared by anyone and everyone... What the hell am I doing? "Wait, Maddy, I don't think—"

The door swings open, revealing a room full of at least ten people, including four of the most dangerous men in the world. Over the years that I'd been gone, I had heard rumors and rumblings about the Alarie men, their wrath and cruelty, and the power they wielded like a sword, reigning terror down on men they tortured and killed.

And here they stand.

I swallow hard, watching as their familiar eyes land on me. But the only pair of eyes that stand out to me are the dark ones I haven't seen since I stared out of the passenger window in the back seat of my father's car, silently praying he would save me.

"I told you Leo wouldn't be able to take his eyes off you." Maddy drops her arm, taking a step inside the room.

My heart beats violently like a hundred wild horses stampeding in an open field. The boy I gave my heart to all those years ago stands before me, no longer a boy but an unrecognizable man.

His once smooth face appears replaced with a chiseled jaw and stubble. Black ink peeks out at the top of his white shirt by his collar and appears on his hands, which are currently fisted at his sides. His boyish body is no longer lanky but muscular and lean. Muscles stretch under his shirt, and his black pants appear fitted like a glove over his strong thighs. His thick brown hair is trimmed short on the sides with a slightly longer length on the top.

This isn't the boy I remember at all.

No, this man before me exudes power, strength, and respect.

He's a predator in a black suit.

And all I can think is that I've made a terrible mistake.

"I'm sorry," I say in a whispered panic, lifting the hem of my dress. I swiftly leave the room, running across the tiled floor, through the main lobby, and down the twenty steps toward the pavement. I pant as I catch my breath on the sidewalk, spinning on my heels, seeking refuge anywhere. My eyes catch on the woods across the parking lot, where I soon find myself gripping the nearest tree for support, unable to catch my breath.

The sun shining above me suddenly feels too bright.

A coat of sweat drips down my back.

My chest tightens painfully, my breaths coming out in fast pants.

And my poor heart, which has already been through so much, can't slow down no matter what I do.

A panic attack.

That's what my therapist, Dr. Raven, told me I had been experiencing day and night for the past several months. But it seemed they were only getting worse as time passed. Even with all of the tips and tricks I had been practicing.

All of the journal notes I had been writing.

All of the music I had been listening to.

All of the—

"Scarlett."

A deep voice behind me immediately silences my racing thoughts.

Leo.

"We don't have to do this," he says. I watch as his shadow stretches over the stray leaves and grass, dominating over mine. Quickly, I turn to look up and find his eyes watching me, locking in on my every move. "I can call this whole thing off right now. I promise to keep you safe whether you're my wife or not."

"I..." I look around and realize we're alone as I grip the tree bark behind me. A good couple of feet lies between us, and he makes no motion to move closer to me. "I was just overwhelmed." I rest my head against the tree, bringing my hand to my chest and pinching my eyes closed.

"Are you okay?"

I nod shakily. "I just need... I just need a moment."

This will pass.

Think of something that makes you happy.

Chocolate. Pink flowers. Fireflies.

"Do I scare you?"

His question takes me by surprise.

"N-no," I lie.

He doesn't respond, but a rustle of leaves causes my eyes to peek open, and I'm suddenly caught off guard by what I see.

"What are you doing?" I lean forward, my palm on my chest, feeling my heart rate slow down.

He looks up at me from the ground, resting against a nearby tree. "Sitting."

"But..." I look over his outfit. "You'll get dirt on your pants."

He shrugs. "I'm okay with that."

I blink. Why did he put himself on the ground? A clear disadvantage if...

Oh...

I lower my eyes. "You're trying to appear smaller than me."

"Is it working?"

The corners of my lips curve up just slightly. "A little bit."

"I'll take it."

I bend forward, inspecting the bottom of my ruined dress, noting a few pulls and splotches of dirt along the hem. I let out a huff of air. This is not at all what I envisioned for my wedding day. A chuckle leaves me at the insanity of my life, my shoulders shaking from the impact.

Leo's brows furrow as he watches me, and I abruptly clear my throat, trying to appear okay when I'm clearly not. "I'm sorry for...taking off back there." My shoulders fall as I wrap my arms around my stomach. "I guess I just wasn't expecting..." To see the boy of my dreams gone and replaced with a man many fear. But do I fear him? I glance at the lethal predator sitting on the ground like a child in the schoolyard, all so I don't feel intimidated by his presence, and immediately know the answer to that. No, I don't. Not one bit. "To see everyone. I haven't seen anyone except mostly Maddy and your mom these past few months, and I think it just kind of shocked me."

He gradually stands, coming to his full height. "I told my brothers not to come." He rubs his hands over the back of his pants, wiping away dirt. "But they wanted to be here for this. For you," he emphasizes.

I glimpse down at my dress, pulling on a loose thread. "You're right. I'm sorry."

"There's nothing for you to be sorry for." I peek up to find him watching me. "You look..." He squeezes the back of his neck, appearing...nervous? "Well, what I'm trying to say is, you look perfect, Scarlett."

My cheeks heat up. "Thank you." I smooth out my hair, noting how many pieces have fallen out of place, and no matter how many times I push them back, they won't stay put.

Leo lifts his hand. "May I?"

I nod.

His fingers gently push back my loose strands; his touch is so soft that I feel like a piece of delicate china he's trying not to break. Once the pieces are secured behind the barrette, his hand immediately falls to his side, and a sudden chill skates over my skin.

I bite my bottom lip and tip my head toward the town hall. "Do you think... Do you think we can try again?"

"If that is what you want."

He steps away from me, placing his back to me before stilling. Suddenly, his hand reaches out, and I mistakenly let out a small gasp at the sight of the burn on the back of it. Scarred tissue covers the space over his knuckles and down to his wrist, appearing painful. I don't remember him having this when we were younger.

"What happened?" I ask softly, instantly regretting my brazenness.

He quickly flips his hand over, palm up, not saying a word as his jaw clenches. He stares ahead, waiting for me to decide if I want to intertwine my fingers with his. I hesitate a few seconds before slowly placing my hand in his. His rough fingers tenderly wrap around mine, remaining that way as he leads us back inside the brick building, inside the room where everyone remains waiting for us. The officiant begins to speak, but his words blur around me while my attention focuses solely on the fact that Leo keeps my hand in his during the entire ceremony, never once letting go.

After the *appointment*, the seven of us all head to Mrs. Alarie's home for a family dinner outside in her garden. An autumn breeze skates around me, causing the hem of my dress to dance as I look on at the whimsical space.

On a white wooden table lies an extravagant, lavish spread that looks and smells so good. Bottles of champagne chill in metal buckets on each end of the table. Fairy lights are suspended around the flower beds, with white lanterns dangling from nearby tree branches. And for the centerpiece, there's a three-tiered white floral cake.

As I take a step, lost in the sight of the decorations, I trip over a stone step and grab the closest thing to me, which happens to be Mauro's large bicep.

With a heated flush, I recover, standing straight and taking a few steps away. He towers over me by more than a foot. Well, all of the Alarie brothers do. However, where Leo and Alex are lean and muscular, Mauro and Vin are burly with intimidating statures. Clearing my throat, I say, "Sorry. I lost my footing."

Mauro peers down at me with deep brown eyes and merely grunts before heading to one of the free seats around the table. He's the only brother here who is not dressed in a suit, but instead, he opted for what appears to be dark tactical clothing. His dark brown hair is much longer than I remember it being years ago and is tied back in a low knot.

I nibble on my lower lip, worried I might have offended him.

"Come sit by me." Maddy grabs my hand and pulls me to an empty seat beside hers. My hand rests on the back of the chair, and I'm about to pull it out when Leo beats me to it. He drags the chair out and waits for me to sit before pushing me closer to the table. Then, he takes the seat beside mine, scooching his chair a little closer to me than it previously was.

As we all take our seats, Vin taps his crystal glass with his knife and raises it in the air. His eyes catch on me as a warm smile graces his face. "Welcome to the family, Scarlett. I always wanted a sister."

"Hey!" Maddy chides, making me laugh.

"Oops." He throws a wink her way and then glances around at his siblings and mother. "To the Alaries."

"To the Alaries," they all repeat before sipping their drinks.

"Madeleine," Vin states, his voice filled with authority. "Where's Alastor?"

"Oh." She reaches for the glass of wine before her and quickly empties it. "Being the son of an oil tycoon, he's constantly being called away on business and, as we speak, is overseas. In fact, he won't be back until our engagement party."

"What a shame," Alex murmurs, pushing up his glasses. His grey eyes roll as he drags a hand through his light brown hair.

The brothers all share a look, and I can sense Maddy's unease. Maybe they're just being overly protective, but I'm sure being the only daughter in the family comes with enough challenges.

Reaching for her hand, I say, "I can't wait to meet him."

She smiles, but it doesn't reach her eyes.

The next couple of hours are spent enjoying good food while everyone begins to reminisce, laughing over old memories. Some I was a part of, and others I was not. But as time passes, I start to feel myself suffocating in the presence of too many people.

My skin crawls with a familiar coldness I only ever felt as I lay on the basement floor. My wrists lock on the top of my thighs, feeling an invisible heavy weight rest around them. My lungs begin to close up, ready to end my—

"Do you want to get out of here?"

I jolt from my thoughts, meeting Leo's eyes, and quickly nod.

He glances around the room. "We're leaving," he abruptly announces. I guess that's the only farewell he's giving.

All eyes land on me.

"Th-thank you for today," I say so quietly that I'm not sure they even hear me until Mrs. Alarie responds.

"You're a part of this family, Scarlett. You always have been. Now, it's just a little more official." She smiles warmly, and as I look around at the others, I find them doing the same.

Leo stands and extends a hand toward me, which I take, enjoying the overwhelming sense of safety I experience each time he does this.

He leads us out to his black two-door Mercedes. Knowing how much he loved cars and motorcycles when we were younger, I think it's safe to assume it's one of many.

He rushes over to the passenger side and opens the door for me. I slide onto the soft leather seat, dragging the hem of my dress inside the car before Leo shuts the door. Realizing we're about to be alone, encased in this small space together, I start to tremble, so I clasp my hands together just as Leo takes his place behind the steering wheel. The engine purrs to life as we glide out of the driveway and head toward Leo's home.

Or, well, I guess, *our* home.

As I stare at the elegant diamond-coated platinum wedding band, now encircling the fourth finger on my left hand, I try to think of something to say. Anything to say so that the silence between us doesn't feel so stifling. Maybe I could talk about the weather? No. Maybe about his car? But I don't actually know much about cars. How work has been going? I internally cringe, thinking better of it. One, because most of what the Alaries do is illegal, and two, because, as witnessed by the estate we're driving through, business has been quite lucrative while I've been away.

It's evident that for the past seven years, while I've been holed up in a tiny studio apartment, working a minimum wage job at the local bookstore, trying to acquire a sense of independence and freedom...the

Alaries thrived. Becoming even more powerful than one would ever imagine.

Revered by many and feared by all.

So, why did Leo never come find me?

Peeking at his profile, I take in his unreadable expression. A flush spreads up my neck and over my cheeks as I suddenly wonder if he ever thinks about the last time we saw each other. I know I do. How could I not when it filled all the space in my heart, easily becoming my favorite memory? The one I use to get me out of my dark thoughts and horrid dreams. And I question if that moment meant as much to him as it did to me. Should I ask him? My lips part, the question on the tip of my tongue, but embarrassment causes me to slam my lips shut.

Don't be ridiculous. Of course, he doesn't think about that moment between us. Not anymore. Not after everything that happened to me.

I pinch my eyes shut, inhaling deeply.

Strumming my fingers on my knee, I can't take it anymore and spit out the first thing that comes to mind.

"Mauro was quiet tonight. I don't think I heard him say one word." I let the corners of my lips curve up just the slightest bit. "When we were kids, I remember him talking your ear off."

Leo's fingers tighten around the steering wheel. "I forgot you left before...well." He quickly glances at me and then back toward the road. "Mauro can't speak."

"What?" My heart thuds. Did I hear him correctly? "What do you mean?"

"Seven years ago, when the bomb went off at the warehouse, the one that...killed my father." He swallows hard. "Mauro, Dolion, and I were with him, except I was standing by the car when Mauro was right behind him, entering the warehouse." He shakes his head, clearly lost in the memory of that tragic event.

I remember that night so clearly. What had started as the best night of my life soon quickly turned into tragedy as I was dragged out of bed by my father, who told me we needed to leave because the Alarie Estate was under attack and it was no longer a safe place for us. I begged him to let me stay, but my pleas went on deaf ears. So I packed a bag, got in the car, and stared out the window in a fog as we drove one last time through the estate, right out the front gates as we passed...Leo.

That week, the loss of the head of the Alarie family made every headline in the world.

And I wasn't there for them.

For him.

Guilt consumes me.

"The doctors tried everything they could, but his vocal cords were too far damaged," he says. "He can grunt. I've become pretty familiar over the years with what each grunt means, and occasionally, if he really needs to say something, he can whisper one word, but it's painful for him to do so."

"Oh my God." I shake my head, feeling my eyes moisten. "I had no idea. I feel like such an idiot."

Leo reaches for my hand, intertwining our fingers, his thumb gently stroking my skin. "He's okay."

I look out the window beside me, noting the darkness creeping over the landscape. "It must be really lonely."

"What must be?"

"Having no one to talk to," I answer, remembering every moment in that basement that I wished I had someone there with me. Someone to help push me to keep fighting.

"Mom tried to get him to take ASL lessons, and he did for a little while, learning the basics. We all did so we could talk to him. But then, for whatever reason, he just stopped."

I glance at our joined hands, sadness creeping up my chest as I only begin to realize what happened here after my father dragged me away.

My eyes scan the scars on the back of Leo's hand, the one not completely covered in black ink.

"That happened the same day," he reveals, stretching his hand. "I tried to reach for my father when a ball of fire fell on it."

With a magnetic force pulling me, I gently touch his scar, tracing it. He flinches, surprised, but then relaxes, letting me explore. My fingers lightly trail over the scarred tissue, wanting to heal him.

"Does it repulse you?" he asks.

I shake my head. "Not at all. I'm just sorry that this happened to you."

And I silently wonder, in a mixture of anxiety and vulnerability, what he'll think if he ever sees my scars. Will they disgust him? Will he never look at me in the same way? It's one thing for a man in his position to have scars or imperfections, but for women like me, it's something entirely different.

"We never did find who was responsible for that day," he admits so quietly that I'm unsure if he's talking to himself or me. "I should have done something differently. Maybe if I—" He clears his throat, his grip tightening on the wheel. Does he feel guilty for what happened to his father? "If Dolion hadn't pulled me away before the whole place went down, I probably wouldn't be here."

A shiver runs down my spine, and I quickly rid my head of what could have been.

"Dolion?" The name sounds familiar, but I can't put a face to it. "Do I know him?"

"Probably not. He grew up on the property, but mostly kept to himself, training with the other soldiers. He's one of my right-hand men now." He turns down a hidden driveway in the woods. "You'll meet him and the rest of my men soon enough. I want to make sure you...see all of their faces and know who each one of them is."

See all of their faces.

My cheeks heat up, knowing the hidden message.

Because I never saw *his* face.

Only his eyes.

Bright green like a lethal acid.

The car comes to a stop before a giant black stone structure.

I incline forward in my seat to get a better view. "This is your home?" I ask, completely stunned at the enormity.

It's similar to his parents' house in the château style but darker and more intimidating. Vines grow up the side of the house with black flowers peeking through. Grandiose trees stand as tall as the house, surrounding it as if guarding it from the outside world. Flying buttresses extend from the upper portion to a pillar. The whole house carries a medieval aesthetic that sends a shiver down my spine.

"Yes. I had it built a few years ago." He runs his fingers through his hair. "I know it looks a tad bit overwhelming, but it's—"

"Home," I answer for him with a slight smile.

He nods before exiting the car and making his way to my door. The second I stand, I feel a pinch in my toes.

"Ow." I lift my foot, shaking it from side to side. I never was a fan of wearing heels, and it seems my poor feet have swollen in these beautiful death traps.

"Your feet hurt," Leo observes.

"I'm fine," I tell him, even though he's right, and I've been waiting all day to whip these off.

"Let me carry you."

I take a step back, pressing myself directly against the car. "W-what?"

He rubs the back of his neck. "I don't want you to hurt yourself walking in those things for another moment longer."

I look down at my feet, examining the redness displayed on my skin, giving away my agony. I nod, about to take one step toward him, when he fills in the space, wrapping his arms around me and bringing me up to his chest.

Just like he had done months ago.

"Glad to see you've put on some weight," he notes, carefully stepping up the stairs.

"It's rude to comment on a woman's weight," I tease, trying to downplay the nerves swarming inside me at our close proximity.

He laughs. "I only meant...you look like you."

Warmth spreads up my neck as we approach the front door decorated with black-stained windows. "Okay, I can walk now."

"Oh, come on, like I'm not going to take the opportunity to walk you over the threshold."

Butterflies collide in my stomach as he scans the palm of his hand against a black tablet. The solid metal door slowly swings open for us, and he walks us through the entrance, gently placing me before him.

Instantly, I bend down to unlace my shoes, but Leo stops me.

"Let me," he says, kneeling before me. My heart hammers in my chest as he gracefully undoes the first shoe and then slides it off my foot. After he does the same to the second shoe, his fingers linger, and I wonder what it might feel like if he started to rub my feet...

No. I internally shake my head, taking a step back as he stands. I have to tilt my chin up to look at him with my heels no longer on.

"I'll show you around." He walks away, and I follow behind him, my eyes widening at the high ceilings and immense space.

"Down this hall is my office, and the theater room is directly across from it. Over here is the kitchen and the living room." He points across the room to a large door. "That's the formal dining room. It's not used often. Mostly for family gatherings or special events." He turns toward the sliding glass door. "And this is the deck."

As I take a step outside, my mouth falls open.

The stone deck is wrapped in a short glass shield that stands a few feet tall, not obstructing the view of the massive lake before it. Plants line almost every surface, bringing a natural jungle vibe. An infinity pool stretches across the center. Plenty of seating is stationed around a fire pit. And a large swing that looks like a giant bed waits for me to lie on it and gaze up at the stars currently shining brightly.

"This is amazing," I breathe.

"I thought you might like it."

Turning, I find his eyes scanning over the dark lake, appearing almost lost in a memory. Like a beautiful water portrait, the full moon reflects off the water's surface.

He clears his throat, facing me. "It's getting late. Let me show you the bedroom."

My stomach plummets.

I knew what would come at the end of this day.

I knew the wedding night tradition that might be expected of me.

But I wasn't ready then.

And I'm not ready now.

Wrapping my arms around myself, I follow him inside and up the black metal stairs, tension radiating through every pore in my body.

Leo is my husband, who has promised to keep me safe. The least I can do is give myself to him. To the man who saved me.

I can do this.

I can do this.

I can do this.

My heart thuds beneath my chest like a snare drum.

Sweat builds on my forehead.

My body trembles in fear, and my eyes water with unshed tears.

I can't do this, I realize as we approach a large black door.

Clearing my throat, I murmur, "Leo, I don't think—"

"Place your hand on this." Leo points to a steel tablet on the wall next to the door handle, identical to the one on the outside of the house. I do as he says, and the second my skin touches the material, a tiny vibration runs through me, and then it finishes with a low chime.

"This is your room," he states. The door opens, revealing a large space with a white bed, a pink area rug, dark wood floors, and industrial-looking pieces of furniture. It's exactly what I would design for myself. "Only your hand and my hand will open this door with recognition."

"My room?" I ask in confusion.

"Yes."

I'm relieved—in more words than I can say—that he isn't expecting to share a room with me. But I'm also feeling...disappointed?

No. That can't be right.

"There's an en-suite bathroom in the back and a small garden on the attached balcony for you."

I look up at him, trying to think of anything to say, but words have escaped me.

"Well," he starts. "It's been a long day for both of us, so I'm going to bed."

I'm going to bed.

I take a deep breath, knowing the insinuation in his words.

It's time.

He pivots toward the room across the hall, and I follow close behind him, ready to get this over with. As the door to his room opens, he suddenly comes to a stop and turns around to find me directly before him.

"Is something wrong?" he asks, furrowing his brows.

"No." I swallow my nerves down. "I'm ready."

"Ready for what?"

I peer up at him and incline my head toward his room, letting out a rush of air.

His eyes darken, narrowing in on me before he closes them, taking a deep breath. His shoulders, which were tense just seconds ago, drop. "Firefly." My heart does a little flip at the use of my old nickname. The one only he used on me. His eyes open, appearing softer. "We're not sleeping together."

"Oh," I let out, humiliation coursing through my veins. "I'm sorry. I just assumed I was supposed to—"

"I'm not going to touch you." His words come out forceful, engraving themselves on every part of me. "I will never touch you unless..." He shakes his head. "No. I won't touch you. Not like that."

My cheeks flush as I take a step back.

He doesn't want me.

Can't say that I blame him.

But I should feel relieved.

So, why don't I?

Why do I, instead, only feel the sting of rejection?

What's wrong with me?

You're not normal. That's what's wrong with you.

"Of course," I rush out, looking over my shoulder toward my door. "I'm going to bed then. Thank you for today and for this." I gesture around the house as I walk backward. "I-I'm sorry for assuming—"

"You don't have to fear me, Scarlett." He watches me cautiously before he turns and enters his room. Right before his door closes behind him, he looks over his shoulder and adds, "You're probably the only person with that privilege."

CHAPTER FOUR

Leo

I couldn't sleep one goddamn wink last night.

Why? Because for the first time in my life, I don't know what the fuck I'm doing.

My fingers lock behind my head as I stare up at the ceiling, my mind racing with the events of the past twenty-four hours.

I'm married. Married to the girl of my dreams. The one I used to chase around the estate as we stayed up late catching fireflies and stargazing from the safety of being inside the Alarie Estate.

The one I had once envisioned making my wife.

But this is not how I imagined our marriage.

Scarlett deserved a lavish ceremony, one she would remember forever, including wearing a goddamn wedding dress that would elicit one of her heart-stopping smiles. But all I saw as she walked into the dreary cold room was sorrow, fear, and trepidation. It was as if she suddenly realized she was making the biggest mistake of her life by marrying me. And fuck, if that didn't make me feel worse for playing along with my mother's ridiculous scheme.

Sliding my hand down my face in frustration, I pause. Lifting it, I stare at my palm, remembering how it felt holding Scarlett's delicate, tiny hand in mine. Only after my fingers intertwined with hers did her breathing steady and her body relax.

Turning my hand over, I gaze at the distorted flesh on the back of it. The skin never healed from the flames, leaving behind red, angry scarring. I've never once cared about this scar or what others thought of it. Heck, scars are a part of this world. Fought and earned daily. But as Scarlett's fingers leisurely trailed over it, her eyes taking in every inch of it, I worried it would repel her.

Instead, she only gravitated toward it as if a scar of this magnitude was familiar to her.

Although, as far as I know, she has no physical scarring, which is a relief. If she did, I'm sure it would only be a constant reminder to her of what she endured.

I rotate to my side, the blanket falling lower on my bare waist, as I glare at the empty space beside me. The soft black satin calls to me as I rest my hand on the vacant spot where my wife should be sleeping but isn't. Sighing, I clutch the fabric. I used to dream of sweeping Scarlett away for our honeymoon, perhaps to one of the family's private islands, where we would spend weeks soaking in every second wrapped up with each other. Instead, I brought her to my house, gave her a quick tour of her new home, and then showed her to *her* bedroom.

A goddamn wedding night to remember.

Sitting up, I place my legs on the side of the bed, stretching my neck from side to side, when an image from last night pops into my head. The one when Scarlett followed me to my room, her eyes downcast, her fingers anxiously twisting together before her.

She thought I was going to fuck her. She thought I was a cruel monster, expecting her to hand herself over to me, and it shattered my fucking heart.

But she needs to know that, no matter what, I won't touch her. Not anymore. And that's not because I don't want to. In fact, my cock hardens with the mere memory of once being given that privilege. Tasting her. Devouring her. Holding her in my arms as we slept under the stars.

God, it was the best moment of my life. One I constantly find myself thinking about. Dreaming about. Wishing we could repeat.

But I won't do any of that with her again.

I can't.

Because the world may fear me, and I'm okay with that. But not my wife. Never her. If there's even a second in our marriage where she's frightened by me, I'll know I've failed her.

This marriage is her show to run. She's the lead star in our story, and me? Well, I'm merely the supporting character in the background, always there to kill anyone who dares to upset her.

Rays of sunlight begin sneaking across the floor, the sun peeking through the gap between the charcoal drapes. Standing, I twist my body, every muscle coming alive as I head to the shower. Hot water droplets coat my skin, tension releasing from my shoulders. Lathering the shampoo in my hair, I think, *What would a husband do for his wife the morning after their wedding?*

I grin. Probably wake her up by—*No.* I shake my head. *No.*

This isn't a normal marriage.

This is a marriage for her protection.

A marriage with an expiration date. Whenever that might be.

But before our end date, I can at least prove to her she's safe with me. That I'm the same guy I was seven years ago—the one who would do literally anything for her. The only difference is that there are just a few more tattoos, a couple more scars, and a whole lot more muscles.

After getting dressed, I step out of my room, noticing the light on in Scarlett's room, peeking out from under her door. I know it was on all night since I walked through the house three times during the late hours, ensuring all security precautions were taken. Because no one will ever get the chance to lay a hand on her again.

Making my way into the kitchen, I find my loyal companion of the past five years eagerly waiting for me after Madeleine dropped him off this morning.

"Hey, Brutus. You hungry, big guy?"

Brutus wags his short tail against the tiled floor, tilting his head to the side as he awaits this morning's breakfast. I reach into the tin on the counter, scoop out a heaping pile of dog food, and pour it into his silver dish. He sits there waiting...and waiting...and waiting until I finally say the magic word that has him dashing toward his dish in a hurry as if he hasn't eaten anything in days: "Attack!"

I laugh while watching him devour his food. Being an Italian bullmastiff, he looks intimidating as fuck, with his shiny black fur coating his muscular body. But if the truth ever got out that he's really just a giant cuddle monster who sleeps with his favorite toy tucked by his side, it would destroy his reputation. So, it's a secret that remains kept between me and him.

"Maybe Scarlett might like some breakfast. What do you think, Brutus?"

He grunts between his mouthfuls of food, and I take that as a yes. Opening the fridge, I grab the essentials: eggs, bread, bacon, peppers, and potatoes. As I crack the eggs into the skillet, I hear a blood-curdling scream and drop everything. I turn in haste, knocking over the potatoes, and immediately realize Brutus is no longer by his food bowl.

"*Cazzo!*"

I run toward the stairs, taking two at a time, and find Scarlett in the hallway pressed against the wall, her eyes pinched shut and her hands flat against her sides. Big, bad Brutus is sitting in front of her, wagging his tail while giving her a look that says, "Lady, pet me."

I can't help the tiny smirk that appears on my face. "Scarlett." Taking a few steps, I put myself between her and Brutus, my chest just a few inches from hers. But as I look down at her, I notice the tremble passing through her body, and my smirk falls. "It's okay," I say softly. "This is Brutus, my dog. He looks scary, but I assure you that he's a big softy. He won't hurt you. He won't even hurt a damn mouse."

Her eyes hesitantly open, looking right up into mine before she quickly glances around me and directly at Brutus.

"He's just waiting for you to pet him," I add.

"He...he won't bite me?"

"Not unless you try to take his favorite toy away from him."

Her shoulders relax a fraction. "What should I do?"

"Let him smell you. Reach out your hand," I encourage.

She nods and takes a deep breath before slowly holding out her hand, but just as she gets close to him, she rears back. "I'm sorry." She shakes her head, curling in on herself.

"Let me help you."

Her blue irises meet mine, blinking a few times, appearing unsure. But finally, she whispers, "O-okay."

I reach for her hand, holding it gently in mine. My large fingers envelop her small ones, her skin tingling beneath my touch, sending a burst of heat to the center of my chest. She has no clue what she does to me. What she has always done to me.

My eyes find hers. "I won't let anything happen to you."

Now or ever.

Her eyes never leave mine when she says, "I know."

With her hand in mine, I slowly advance toward Brutus and get close enough for him to sniff our joined hands. I cock a brow at him, silently pleading with him to be on his best fucking behavior. His wet nose touches the tips of her fingers, and his tail wags even faster, his butt soon wiggling in excitement.

"He likes you," I note, placing her hand on the top of his head. I move my hand to the side of hers and scratch behind his ear, knowing he loves it when I do that. His head tilts to the side as his jaw slightly opens, thoroughly enjoying the attention. Scarlett moves her fingers, mimicking my motion on the opposite side of his head. His foot taps the floor in pleasure, and she smiles.

She fucking smiles.

And it's not one of the fake ones she throws on when she pretends she's okay, but a genuine, beautiful goddamn smile.

"You really are a good boy, aren't you?" Her eyes sparkle as she watches him in amusement.

I swear Brutus nods as, suddenly, Scarlett gets down on her knees and scratches the side of his stomach. The poor sucker doesn't stand a chance as he plops to the ground, rolls on his side, and stretches his legs out in the air.

"You want a belly rub?" she asks. The palms of her hands glide over his soft black fur until reaching his stomach and rubbing the hell out of him. God, he looks like he's in heaven.

And is it wrong if I admit to being jealous of my damn dog?

Ding. The sound of the doorbell ends our happy little family moment.

Scarlett gives Brutus one more pat before standing beside me. "Who's that?"

"That would be your bodyguard."

Her eyes widen, and her lips part as if she wants to say something, but she quickly closes them, glaring down at the floor.

"What is it?" I ask.

"I thought…" She scrunches her brows, her lips pursing to the side. She looks so fucking adorable. "I thought with me marrying you that you were kind of going to be my bodyguard?" Her cheeks turn a soft shade of pink as she glances up at me.

"I am." I start to reach for a loose strand of her hair, eager to tuck it behind her ear, but stop myself, clasping my hands behind my back. "But you need someone by your side when I'm not with you. Someone who will be able to keep you safe."

She stares off in the distance. "And you trust this man to be left alone with me?"

I see the anxiety tiptoeing across her features. She thinks I assigned some random man to her safety. But I would never do that. Not when her safety is the only thing that's been on my mind day and night for as long as I can remember.

"I trust him with my own life, which is why I'm assigning him to you," I state firmly. "Besides." I take a step toward the stairs. "You already know him."

"I do?" She tilts her head to the side, curiosity evident.

"Come on, Firefly. Let's go say hi to an old friend."

She follows me closely down the stairs, the smell of her floral perfume floating in the space between us. I inhale deeply, the notes of jasmine bringing me right back to seven years ago.

To a time when everything seemed so simple.

My hand twists down on the doorknob, opening it as Scarlett waits behind me, peeking around me to see our guest.

"Leo, long time no see."

Eli Lyon, my oldest friend and the only man I trust with my wife's life who is not family by blood, stands before the threshold.

"It's been too long." I clasp his shoulder and then turn to see Scarlett taking in his appearance, but I know he doesn't appear familiar to her.

"Hey, Scarlett. Remember me?" he asks, his English accent a little thicker than usual since he's been away. It's been years since she's seen him, and the last time she did, he didn't exactly look like this. Muscular. Lean. Powerful. But being in the military for years can do that to a man.

She hesitantly shakes her head, frowning.

"It's Eli," I tell her. The moment I say his name, her eyes widen with recognition.

"Eli?" Her lips curve up as her eyes scan over him. "You look…"

"Not fat," he answers proudly, running his hand over his flat stomach.

She fights the smile tugging on her lips. "I was going to say different." She shakes her head. "I'm sorry. I should have recognized you."

"Yeah, well, I've lost almost sixty pounds and put on all muscle since the last time I saw you. So, can't say I blame you for not remembering the guy who tagged along with the two of you everywhere as kids." His smile grows. "It's good to see you again."

"It's good to see you, too," she responds, her whole body appearing relaxed. "And if I remember correctly, you may have tagged along with us, but I think there was always a certain someone tagging along with you."

Eli clears his throat, appearing slightly rattled as he straightens his jacket, his neck becoming the faintest shade of pink. "I'm sorry I missed your wedding. My flight was delayed, and I didn't arrive until this morning." He glances at me. "But I'm here now, all moved into one of the nearby cottages, and I'm ready for whatever you need me for."

"Good." I nod, motioning for him to follow us inside.

Brutus comes barreling down the stairs the second he sees Eli and tackles him, his paws resting on his chest and his tongue licking his face like a piece of prime rib.

Eli laughs loudly, scratching Brutus's fur. "I missed you too, you big brute."

After Eli regains his stance, we all walk into the living room, where I take a seat in a chair, Scarlett takes the one beside mine, and Eli takes a spot on the sofa across from us. Brutus lies on the floor next to Scarlett's chair, watching her as if ensuring everything is okay before he rests his head on his paws and closes his eyes, drifting to sleep.

I push up my sleeves, stretching my neck. "You know why I asked you here," I begin, looking directly at Eli. "And I appreciate you making it on such short notice. As you know, the matter of Scarlett's safety is of great importance to me. And when I am not here, I want to ensure someone is by her side who would do whatever it takes to keep her safe." I pause, my eyes landing on Scarlett. "There are no rules when it comes to my wife's safety."

Scarlett swallows, looking at me in, I hope, a new light—one where she finally sees what it means to have me as her husband.

Her protector.

Eli nods, sitting forward, his elbows resting on his knees. "Understood. Where she goes, I go."

There's an uneasy disposition passing over Scarlett. Her hands fidget on her lap as her knee bounces rapidly.

"And how do you feel about this?" I ask her.

Her eyes meet mine, her teeth biting down on her bottom lip. A nervous habit she's had even when we were kids.

"Fine," she responds in a soft, flat voice.

"Scarlett," I press.

Pink covers her cheeks. Pushing her hair behind her ear, she glances between me and Eli. "I'm okay with this. I prefer it to being alone with someone I don't know." She looks directly at Eli. "I... I don't mean to sound ungrateful that you're here. For me. Because that's not the case, and I'm so happy to see a familiar face." She shows a tiny smile, slipping her hands under her thighs. "I just... I just have a hard time being around men right now because I never...I never...saw his..."

Her eyes pinch shut, her breaths coming out rapidly. She's going there. The dark place in her mind. The place that's filled with horrific memories that haunt her. The place where she feels broken.

Swiftly, I kneel before her, taking her hands in mine. "Hey." My thumbs rub across her skin. "You're safe, Scarlett. You're here with me." I bring her hands to my lips, pressing a kiss to each one without a second thought. "I won't let anything happen to you."

She opens her eyes, swallowing down all emotions. Tears spill down her cheeks, but she quickly throws on that fake smile everyone has come to know so well.

"I'm sorry...I don't know what that was about."

I rub her hands between my own. "It's okay."

"I think I'm just going to sit outside for a minute and get some fresh air."

"Of course." I help her out of her seat and watch as she walks out to the deck, making herself comfortable on the bed swing, curling her legs beneath her and crossing her arms over her chest as she stares across the lake.

"It's bad, isn't it?" Eli asks.

I turn, plopping back down on my chair. "Yeah. Really fucking bad." Pinching the bridge of my nose, I say, "If she has a panic attack when I'm not here, you need to call and tell me. I don't care if I'm in fucking Siberia in the middle of the biggest deal of our lives; you need to call me and let me know so I can come home to her. I need to be here for her."

"I will."

"And she's scared of the dark. So, always ensure lights are on before entering any rooms."

"Of course." Eli looks outside, overseeing her, observing how she curls into herself, trying to hide from the world. "Did he..." He hesitates before asking, "Did he break her?"

I shake my head. "No, he didn't. But she thinks he did."

"Why didn't you call me sooner?" Eli's eyes land on me.

"Because I know you would have jumped on a plane the second I called you. And after everything you went through last year, I just wanted to give you time. I held off calling you for as long as possible until I knew I had no other option. But we need you." I nudge my head toward the window. "She needs you."

He rests his forearms against his knees as he stares at the floor. "I appreciate that, I do. But that woman"—his eyes turn to Scarlett—"was always a sister to me. And what I witnessed just now was a shell of who she once was. That was a goddamn ghost sitting in that chair beside you, scared of her own shadow." He shakes his head in apparent frustration.

"We need to find who did this to her." His eyes meet mine, the promise of death flashing across them.

"We will." I sit up, watching Scarlett stand and walk over to the balcony, gazing across the water, her long blonde hair dancing over her shoulders as the wind pushes it back. "Because it kills me every second knowing he's out there when he tried to break her." My knuckles grasp the arms of my chair. "After we find him, I need to be the one who breaks him—body and soul. I want to watch the life dissipate from his eyes. I want him to feel pain like no other man has ever felt before."

Eli rolls his neck. "You going to let me have a turn at him, too?"

"What kind of a friend would I be if I didn't?"

The corners of his lips lift but then immediately fall. "What's the game plan?"

I pull the slim hard drive out of my pocket—the one containing every piece of information we've obtained so far, any clue, any whisper of who may have done this or even just been connected to this person.

"And all this time, I just thought you were happy to see me," Eli jokes.

"Funny." Handing it to him, I say, "Months ago, on what I thought was just a normal day, I received an anonymous text that said, 'Now she's mine — Le Diable,' along with a picture of Scarlett unconscious and tied up in the trunk of a car." I shake my head, trying everything not to remember that day. The fury swept through me as I destroyed my office, each of my brothers demanding me to calm down.

As if that would solve anything.

"The devil?" Eli asks, brows drawn together.

I nod. *Le Diable.* The motherfucker gave himself his own stupid nickname.

"Could he be French?"

"Possibly, or just someone fucking with us, knowing we all speak French and Italian fluently." I shrug. "Whoever it is, they knew."

"Knew what?"

I glance toward Scarlett. "They knew how important she is to me and wanted to throw it in my face that they had her."

"Could it be someone from inside?"

I shake my head. "We all thought the same thing, but Alex and his team ran intensive background checks on everyone in the estate when she first went missing, and he found nothing out of the ordinary." I tap my fingers against the arm of the chair. "One of my men, Asher, who had been keeping an eye on Scarlett over the years—"

"Come again?"

I wave my hand dismissively. Unbeknown to Scarlett, did I have guards that kept an eye on her over the years? Yes. And I won't apologize for it when she has always been my top priority. "The point is, as soon as I received the photo of Scarlett, I tried to get in touch with Asher, but my calls kept going straight to voicemail. So my brothers and I took our plane to Chicago straight to her apartment, finding it empty. We then rushed to her father's house, but by the time we made it there, there was nothing left of it. Asher was being checked over by paramedics on sight after being found unconscious on the side of the road. He told us that he had been tailing Scarlett, keeping a five-minute distance between them so as not to be noticed, and as he pulled down the road toward Scarlett's father's house, he saw flames engulfing it. When he stepped out of his car, he saw Scarlett's car and rushed over to it, but as he approached, he was struck from behind and knocked out cold." I twist the wedding band on my finger, looking down at my hand. "Scarlett's father's remains were hardly recognizable. If it weren't for the gold ring on his finger with his family crest, we wouldn't have been able to properly identify him without tests." I rub my temple.

"And Asher doesn't recall anything else? He didn't see a hint or trace of anyone? There were no cameras?"

"The only thing he remembers is hearing a high-pitched laugh as he was losing consciousness. One he said he would never forget. And the feed to the cameras was disconnected the day before, hinting that this was a well-thought-out execution and not just some random target." I sit back, crossing my ankle over my knee. "Alex tried to encrypt the message sent to my phone. To find anything. But all he uncovered was that it was a burner phone purchased from a run-down drugstore in the city with no surveillance."

Eli rubs his chin, deep in thought. "And you're not having any problems with Igor Vasiliev? Or his sons?"

Igor Vasiliev. He thought he was fucking Russian royalty living in his high golden tower in Chicago, constantly trying to interfere with my family's businesses.

On paper, we are among the world's most sought-after real estate moguls. Our diverse investments include hotels, nightclubs, restaurants, and commercial properties. But what really grows the family's profits comes from the less scrupulous deals—the ones pertaining to our hidden casinos and discreet weapon shipments between our overseas partners.

But Igor couldn't touch a hair of our net worth and overall power. It's what he strives for but can never achieve, only infuriating him even more.

He's nothing but a pain in the ass if you ask me.

"Nothing out of the ordinary," I answer. "As far as I'm aware, Igor's sons cut ties with him years ago when they moved back to Russia, wanting nothing to do with him or his business antics. And the only thing Igor would have gained from kidnapping Scarlett was creating an enemy out of the Alarie family. And that includes our extended families in Italy and France. It wouldn't make sense for him to do that. We would destroy him from the inside out."

"Agreed. But it doesn't hurt to look into him." He gives a half shrug as I see his mind working out all the puzzle pieces I'm presenting him with. "How long was she taken for?"

I gaze up at the ceiling, grinding my back molars. "Six weeks."

Eli wipes a hand down his face, looking at Scarlett and seeing her in a new light. "Jesus Christ."

"I know." I rub my temple. "We searched night and day. Fucking everywhere. I was never going to give up on finding her. But then…" I meet Eli's stare. "Six weeks after she had been taken, we got a stroke of luck. You see, Alex had been working tirelessly in the dark web, scouring any bit of information he could get his hands on, including any trace of the name Le Diable. And then it finally happened. One of Le Diable's lackeys sent a text out to someone simply saying, "Le Diable is gone for the weekend. I'm on duty. Meet here, and I'll…" I close my eyes and rush out the last part. "Let you see a glimpse of her." I roll my neck, tension building in my shoulders. "The idiot used Le Diable's name, which sent an alert to Alex, who could then trace the exact location. We were there in a matter of hours, and when we made it there, to the warehouse, well…"

"You found her," Eli replies.

"Yeah. And it was the worst fucking thing I've ever seen in my life." I stare ahead, lost in my mind. "The place was under watch by at least twenty men. We killed all but three that we took back with us to get anything out of them, but they wouldn't speak. The four of us scoured the property, and just as I reached a rusted iron door leading to the basement, I heard the tiniest whimper, causing me to barrel down those stairs." I undo the top two buttons of my shirt, feeling a tightness in my chest. "She was there. Practically lifeless. Nearly naked. Chained to the floor like a goddamn animal."

"Fuck."

I look outside, catching a glimpse of Scarlett. "If we had been there any later, she wouldn't have made it."

I've known this since the moment I saw her motionless form.

If we had waited one more minute before we left…

If I hadn't sped to the hospital like a madman…

If the motherfucker didn't send the text when he did…

She wouldn't be here today.

And a world without my firefly feels too dark, even for me.

"I take it from her admission earlier that she never saw his face?" Eli asks, puzzled. "But how?"

"When she was ready to talk, she told my mother and her therapist everything. The former relayed the information to me. Apparently, this man, like the fucking psychopath that he is, kept her chained in the basement, never letting her see the light of day. Always keeping her in the dark. And when there were moments that she could see him, as the light cast down on his face when he first walked down the steps, she said he wore some kind of devil's mask that completely covered his face, except for his bright green eyes. Besides that, she never saw any hint of who he might be. And he never talked. But she can remember his laugh." I let out a breath. "Her therapist told me that her nightmares have only been getting worse, and in them, she hears his laugh and sees his eyes."

"His laugh?" Eli questions.

"She told her therapist that occasionally, he would laugh uncontrollably like a deranged clown. It's as if he got some sick, twisted pleasure from tormenting her." My fingers press into the arms of the chair, the leather stretching, ready to split.

"Just like the guy Asher heard."

"Exactly."

"Mental illness, perhaps?"

"Highly likely." I pet the top of Brutus's head, trying to calm myself for what I'm about to say. But nothing in the world could calm me in this moment. Well, maybe just the beautiful blonde outside, soaking up that sunlight. I clear my throat. "He kept her down there for weeks. Feeding her scraps. Giving her one glass of water a day. Ra—" My throat dries up, and I fucking lose it as I abruptly stand, striding toward the kitchen island. I grip the edge of the marble counter, my knuckles aching.

A firm grasp on my shoulder stops me from spiraling.

"I know, Leo," Eli says softly. "I know."

"We have to find him," I breathe harshly. My whole body is coiled tightly in tension. "We have a team together, including each of my brothers, searching for him every second of the day, but every time we think we're that much closer to finding him, we come up with dead ends. It's been like this for months. It's like after we found her, he just fucking disappeared. Poof. Gone." I rub the back of my neck, my muscles feeling too tight. "Vin's hopeful that our marriage will entice him into leaving the shadows. That he'll eventually slip up and reveal himself. But I don't know... I don't know what to fucking do anymore. And it's killing me that every day he lives, I'm failing her!" I shake my head. "He tried to break her. He tried to break my fucking firefly!" I roar, my fists shaking as I slam them on the countertop.

Eli pulls over a stool and pushes me down. Then, as if he's been here his whole life, he reaches for a glass in a nearby cupboard and fills it with water before handing it to me. I gulp down the liquid and focus on the counter.

"You asked me to come here to keep her safe," Eli affirms. "And that's exactly what I'll do." He sits on the seat beside mine. "But I'm also here to help you find him. And I plan on doing just that. I'm not leaving until the job is finished. You have my word."

"Thank you, Eli." I lean back, rubbing my chin.

"You're my best mate. Have been since the day you knocked out the two front teeth of that kid in primary school who made fun of my accent."

My lips curve up. "He spoke with a lisp after that day. Such a shame."

Eli grins, clasping my shoulder. "But you're also my brother, Leo. Blood or not." He lets out a deep sigh, tapping the counter with his finger. "We're going to find him. And he'll regret ever fucking with the Alarie family, that's for damn certain."

I nod in agreement. "Vin has a team of our top men working on this, and I've assigned Dolion to his team."

Eli groans, rolling his eyes. "Dolion? As in the motherfucker we knew as kids?"

I arch a brow. "Yes, that Dolion."

He shakes his head, pinching the bridge of his nose.

I try to hide the smirk making its way onto my face, but it's too late. "Does this have anything to do with the fact that as kids, he used to chase you around the property, calling you 'Fat Eli'?"

"No," Eli spits out a little too quickly.

"Well, hate to break it to you, but you're going to need to get along. Especially since you'll most likely be working together on this."

"You really couldn't have picked anyone else?"

I shake my head. "He's been working with my family for years, showing complete loyalty and bravery when needed. He saved my life that night when the bomb went off in our warehouse, pulling me out of the way before the entire building went down." I shrug. "Besides, he recently returned after being gone for months, tending to his dying mother in Greece, so cut him some slack." My lips tilt up. "If you're worried about the name-calling, I can always take him aside and—"

"Fuck you, Leo." Eli stands. "Do I need to remind you that if I wasn't in fucking Iraq, it would have been me going with you that night to the warehouse and saving your life? And not that damn twat!" He smirks, placing his hands on his hips. "What do I have to do? Take a bullet for you to prove my loyalty after all these years?"

"If it pleases you to do so," I answer, grinning.

We laugh, knowing how absurd this conversation is when we'd both take a bullet for the other. No questions asked.

He points toward the glass wall. "I'm doing this for her. Whatever you need me to do, I'll do it. Even if it means working with that arsehole."

My eyes drift to Scarlett, who still appears lost in her own head. "Good." I nod, crossing my arms over my chest, and tilt my head toward the back of the house. "Let's go to my office and talk security logistics. I'm not making a single fucking mistake when it comes to my wife's safety."

CHAPTER FIVE

Scarlett

With Leo and Eli tucked away in the back office discussing business, I take this opportunity to explore Leo's elaborate house. It's dark but inviting.

Cold yet warm.

And as much as it stands to impose and intimidate, I feel an odd sense of ease being here. It's a conundrum, like a haunted house that soothes my fears. But that's probably because everything about this place is Leo.

Black overtakes the walls, both from the inside and out. Even the tiles in the bathroom showers and the counters in the kitchen add a touch of darkness. A few neutral tones are mixed throughout, adding a cozy aura. The grand rock wall surrounding the six-foot-tall fireplace brings an earthy touch indoors. The leather furniture is exquisite and of the finest quality, but it also appears as if it was never used. The kitchen is...you guessed it, black, but with all stainless-steel appliances, appearing like a chef's paradise. The garage turned Batman's cave, housing Leo's luxurious car and bike collection, is a pretty cool touch, if I say so myself.

I grin as my fingers glide over the seat of a fancy blacked-out bike. I'm not sure what the brand is, but I can tell from its condition that it's his prized possession, parked furthest away from all his other toys.

But what really stands out about this place is the panoramic windows at the back of the house. These windows provide a remarkable view of the lake while allowing an abundance of sunlight into each room, softening the shadows where the light meets the dark.

Pushing the wall-high sliding glass door open, I step outside to what I assume will become my favorite place. A slight breeze cascades over my shoulders, and I wrap my arms around my middle.

Fall is in the air. I can feel it.

Taking a few strides closer to the edge, I scan the area, my lips curling up.

I could be happy here.

Peeking over my shoulder, I ensure Leo and Eli are nowhere in sight as I bypass the infinity pool, race over to the bed swing, and jump onto it. I laugh as it begins to rock back and forth smoothly and effortlessly. A small metal button on the arm of the chair catches my notice, and because there's no sign that says, "Don't press me," I press it. Suddenly, protruding from the wall is a transparent plexiglass roof that stretches out, giving me an unobstructed view of the crystal blue sky while protecting me if it were raining.

Wow, I'm never leaving this spot.

I lie back and close my eyes, enjoying the soothing comfort of the back-and-forth motion while listening to the lulling sound of the water moving below. Birds chirp amongst each other in the nearby trees that surround Leo's home. And even though I know Leo's siblings all have a house on this lake, each one is miles and miles away from one another, meaning complete solitude. Silence. Peace.

Humph.

My eyes pop open, my face turning to the side to see Brutus watching me. "Hey, Brutus."

He places his snout beside me on the bed, his big, beautiful eyes trying to work magic over me.

"What do you want, boy?" I roll on my side to scratch the top of his head. He leans into my touch, his little tail wagging back and forth. "Do you just want some attention?" I laugh as his two front paws end up on the edge of the bed, pushing the swing back. He scares himself and takes a few quick steps back. "It's okay." I sit up and bring my feet to the floor, stopping the rocking motion.

He licks my hand, slobber getting all over me. "Yuck. We need to work on your manners." He tilts his head, observing me in confusion. "Come on." I stand, patting the top of his head with my clean hand. "Let's go inside so I can wash up."

Brutus follows me closely as we step into the kitchen. I let the water run over my hands while lathering soap between my palms. "Listen, I think you're really cute. But I'm not a fan of slobber. So how about we make a deal?"

I swear he nods.

"If you promise not to get your drool on me, then I promise to give you daily belly rubs. Deal?"

Woof!

I smirk. "Glad we could come to an agreement."

Brutus turns around and pushes his head into a basket of toys, pulling out a ball and bringing it to me. I toss it into the living room and watch as the massive beast leaps swiftly and gracefully after his ball that stops in the, thankfully, empty fireplace. I wait for him to get it, but he stares at it and then looks over his shoulder, giving me a pointed glare.

I place my hand on my hip, arching a brow. "Are you serious?"

His stare grows impatient as he stomps his front paw, looking like a toddler about to have a tantrum.

"Gee, I guess Leo wasn't kidding when he called you a softy. I didn't take you as the kind of dog who would be scared of anything." I shuffle over, rubbing his head as I pass him and bend down, reaching inside the fireplace to get the damn ball. Just as I toss it in the air, Brutus turns to chase after it, and my eyes catch on a pattern of colors reflecting on the black wall.

Red, blue, green, yellow... But where are they coming from?

Spinning on my heels, I peer around the room until I see it and freeze, my heart beating rapidly. "Is that...?" With a slight tremble in my fingers, I stand on my toes and reach for the object sitting on the mantle but miss it by a few inches.

Quickly, I search the room for anything to stand on and drag the enormous wooden coffee table before the fireplace, using it as a stepping stool. Lifting myself, I come eye level with the object and secure it in my hold, my thumb brushing over the glass.

The worn-out, dusty mason jar, painted in various colors, looks just as it did when I was a child. I clutch it to my chest, tears cascading down my cheeks. He saved it—the mason jar we used as kids to collect fireflies in, painted so that the colors would reflect on a nearby surface when fireflies were inside it.

I wipe the tears away, my heart pounding in my chest.

So many questions run rampant through my head, but as I place the jar back on the mantle, I only wonder... Why?

My fork swirls the fettuccine around my plate, the white sauce eliciting a delicious aroma, but I can't find it within me to take a bite. I glance to my left, getting lost in the lake beside me, wishing I could have one moment where I could jump off the deck and scream as I sail towards the water, letting every horror that plagues my mind out into the universe.

But that's probably not something a *normal person* would dream of doing.

The silence I enjoyed hours earlier now seems almost insufferable, and I'm beginning to feel like an intruder in Leo's space.

"Do you not like it?" Leo asks, sitting across from me at the other end of the table. The distance speaks volumes about how I'm feeling right now.

Alone.

The tall white candles in the center of the table burn brightly, their flames dancing with every breeze that washes over them.

"It's delicious." I give a slight smile. "I'm just not very hungry right now."

I want to ask him why he kept the mason jar. Why did he save it after all these years? But I'm not ready to hear how it means nothing to him. How it's just some trinket he forgot about and placed on his mantle without a second thought.

He nods, wiping the corner of his lip with his napkin. "I can make you something else later if you would like."

I shake my head. "Please, don't burden yourself on my behalf."

His fork falls to his plate, and the high-pitched sound makes me jump. His eyes settle on me, unmoving and unnerving, and his predatory gaze elicits a tiny shiver over my body.

Did I say something wrong?

"You're my wife, Scarlett," he declares firmly. "Nothing I do for you is a burden."

I bite my bottom lip and whisper, "I know it's not real."

"What's not real?"

"This." I motion between us. "Our marriage." I instinctively twist my wedding band. "And that's okay. I appreciate everything you've done for me and continue to do for me. So, I don't expect... Well, what I mean is, I know not to expect more than what it is, a contract with an end date," I say, the last part coming out more defeated sounding than I intended.

He leans forward, steepling his fingers before him. "You think this marriage isn't real?"

I swallow. "I know it's not."

He nods, his jaw tightening. "And what, may I ask, do you think it is?"

I blink. "Well, it's merely a cover for my safety." My shoulders drop. "Nothing more."

His eyes darken. "Married to me or not, your safety would always be my priority. Your signature on a contract wouldn't change that."

My brows furrow in confusion as it suddenly dawns on me... I know what I got out of this marriage. Safety. Protection. Security. But what did Leo get out of marrying me? Why would he go through with this when he gets nothing out of it?

"Ask it," he states as if reading my mind.

I gently place my fork on my plate, my pulse racing. "Ask what?"

He arches a brow. "The question that's sitting on the tip of your tongue."

I look down at my plate and hesitate before quietly asking, "Why did you marry me?" My heart thuds beneath my rib cage as my eyes glance up, catching with his own, seeing past every flaw beneath my surface.

"Because—"

Woof! Brutus approaches us, trotting over to me. He nudges his head onto my lap, giving me his puppy dog eyes. I'm relieved by the distraction but disappointed knowing I won't hear an answer.

"Sorry," I murmur to Brutus, letting my fingers drift through the thick fur on his back. "I don't have anything you can eat."

"Brutus. Come," Leo orders, his eyes leaving me and moving to his dog. Brutus obediently marches toward Leo. "Sit." His butt hits the floor. Leo holds a piece of chicken before him and then tosses it to Brutus, who swallows it whole.

I chuckle, giving Brutus a small clap. "Such a good boy."

Leo's eyes scan across the table, calculating something I don't understand. For a moment, a tender look flashes over his dark irises. One I find myself wishing I could get lost within. A slight pang twists my insides when I suddenly remember that years ago, I did. I got lost in his dark depths, never wanting to resurface, but against my will, I was dragged out of the abyss.

What would things be like for us now if I had never been taken away from here?

I fight the tightness in my throat and the tingle on the tip of my nose, smoothing out the napkin on my lap, and focus on anything other than the man at the other end of the table.

Suddenly, Leo stands, taking his plate in his hands, most likely heading inside for the evening. I lower my gaze, trying my hardest to appear unaffected by this.

When did everything become so awkward between us?

I twist the napkin in my lap, needing something to distract myself with and ground me to the here and now. As my eyes stray toward the lake, Leo moves by me, pulling out the chair beside me.

"There's a better view over here," he remarks as he sits with his back to the lake and his eyes on me. The setting sun casts a warm glow over us.

"But you're not facing it," I muse, confused at what he could be looking at in this direction when the view is behind him.

He leans back in his seat, never looking away from me. "But I am."

Oh. A blush creeps up my neck, the temperature suddenly warmer than it was five minutes ago. I pick up my fork, as does Leo, and the two of us eat in silence. But this time, the silence doesn't feel as stifling. If anything, it feels...nice.

Chapter Six

Leo

Walking into the kitchen, my steps falter as I find Scarlett bent down, searching for something inside the fridge. The goddamn black leggings she's wearing do absolutely nothing to hide that perfect round ass from my ravenous eyes.

Fucking leggings. I adjust my pants and look up at the ceiling.

"Hello," I murmur as I approach the island.

She squeaks before jumping away from the fridge, swatting a hand to her chest. Relief flashes over her eyes as she realizes it's me. "Sorry. I didn't expect it to be you since you're usually out during the day."

True. For the past few weeks, I have kept my distance from Scarlett, giving her space. Specifically from me, knowing it's something she wants but won't say.

During that time, I've been spending my days hunting down any leads I could get my hands on to find Le Diable while also conducting normal business operations. Like tracking down those who have racked up substantial debt in our casinos and then presenting them with what I think to be a pretty fair payment plan.

They pay up now.

Or they die.

Their choice.

And while I've been working during the days, Eli's been on guard, ensuring Scarlett's safety. At night, I come home and secure the premises, not sleeping until I know Scarlett's sound asleep in her room, with the light on.

But today, there's been a little hiccup in the plans, and I've decided to make the best of the situation.

"A little change in plans with today's scheduled meeting." I grab an apple out of the fruit bowl. "Our conference room had a pipe burst last night, flooding the space. So everyone is on their way here now."

"Ev-everyone?" she asks, backing up against the opposite counter.

"I think this would be a good time for you to meet my closest group of men. They live on the property, and it's important for you to see their faces and hear their voices."

She takes a deep breath, processing what will be happening very shortly. A group of unknown men will be coming into our home, her space.

"O-okay." She sounds unsure, and I know I need to put her at ease by reminding her who she married and why.

I walk around the island to her side, gazing down at her. "Who am I?"

She scrunches her brows together. "Leo Alarie."

"No." I shake my head. "Who. Am. I?"

She visibly swallows. "You're my husband."

"Yes, which means I will never let anything happen to you." I take a single step, closing the space between us. "These men won't hurt you. They're helping me with finding the one responsible for…"

"Taking me," she whispers, her eyes solemn. She pushes her blonde strands behind her ear and pulls down on the grey hem of her oversized sweater, ensuring it covers her thighs. Her chin lifts, a faux smile gracing her face. "I'll be fine."

My lips turn down. "That's your fake smile."

Her lips part. "My what?"

"Boss." I look over to see Eli entering the room. "They're here. Are you ready for me to let them in?"

"Send them in." I notice a slight tremble take over Scarlett, and after dropping the apple on the counter, I hold out my hand for her. "Come with me." Her fingers intertwine with mine as I lead us to the kitchen entryway. My grip on her hand remains firm as several pairs of footsteps head our way. Leaning down, I brush my lips against her ear and whisper, "You can do this."

She nods, sucking in her bottom lip.

I wish I could hide her from the world and keep her safe in a goddamn golden tower. But that's not a life anyone should live. And I'll be damned if my firefly doesn't start living her life to the fullest again, which we'll do by taking little steps every day. Starting right now.

Dolion is the first to enter, and Scarlett inches closer to my side. The warmth of her body seeps through the fabric of my shirt. I don't move in fear of scaring her; instead, I let her decide how close she's comfortable getting to me. She drops my hand but quickly clutches my shirt, pressing her side to mine. The tremor in her fingers doesn't go unnoticed, and slowly, I bring my hand to her lower back, needing her to know I'm here. *She's safe.* She flinches at my touch, her eyes jumping to mine.

"Okay?" I ask.

She eases her back against my hand. "Okay."

Asher, Nico, and Sergio come up behind him. The four of them stand shoulder to shoulder, clasping their hands behind their backs. Intimidating motherfuckers in their own right.

Most importantly, though, they all have brown eyes, hopefully reassuring Scarlett.

"Gentlemen, I'd like to introduce you to my wife, Scarlett. Scarlett." I jerk my head toward them. "This is Dolion, Asher, Nico, and Sergio."

She gives a polite smile, grasping herself tighter to my side. "It's lovely to meet you."

Dolion bows his head and smiles. "It's a pleasure to officially meet you." His hand reaches out for her free one, but I don't give him a chance to touch her as I step between them, placing my body before hers.

"I'm afraid no one is allowed to touch my wife but me."

Dolion gives a knowing smirks as he steps back. "Of course, sir."

Taking my place back by her side, she immediately grabs my shirt again, gluing herself to me. And damn, I could get used to this.

The remaining three dip their heads and reply with polite greetings, knowing nothing more is allowed than that.

Scarlett looks up at me, and I see it in her eyes—a woman seeking assurance from her husband that she did a good job.

"You did so good, Firefly." Before I realize what I'm doing, I lean down, gently pressing my lips to her temple. Is it a simple gesture to claim her in front of my men, ensuring they know who she belongs to? Probably. Unfortunately, she freezes, and I instantly draw back to give her space. Her vibrant blue eyes widen as a slight blush spreads over her cheeks. "We should be done in a few hours. Eli will be just outside if you need anything," I declare as I let my hand drop from her back and lead my men toward my office.

Sitting behind my desk, I watch as all four of my men take their places on the other side. Leaning forward, I steeple my fingers in front of me. "Before we begin, I want to make one thing abundantly clear." My eyes narrow in on each of them, and the severity in my voice rings out through the room. "No one is to touch my fucking wife, no one is to be within five feet of my wife, and no one is to even look at her the wrong way, or I will cut out your eyeballs and sever each one of your fingers one by one so you will never be able to see or touch anything ever again." Sergio loosens his tie, a bead of sweat rolling down his temple. "Capisce?"

"Understood, boss," Dolion responds with a stern dip of his head.

"Good." I lean back in my seat, the sight of fear in their eyes reassuring me. "Now, what have you found out?"

Asher clears his throat. "I recently received some intel from an informant in the black market pertaining to the Vasiliev family, specifically the head of the family, Igor. Word is, he's entering into a sex-trafficking business with a silent partner, and they have a new club opening fairly soon. One specifically used for high-end auctions." He leans forward, raking his fingers through his dark hair. "He also mentioned that there's a third man involved, responsible for collecting the girls for these auctions."

I raise a brow. *Sex trafficking?* That's not something my family would ever dabble in. It goes against everything we stand for. But Igor? Well, that doesn't seem too far off.

"Has anyone confirmed this?" Dolion asks.

Asher shakes his head. "Merely whispers."

"And we are to believe whispers now?" Dolion asks incredulously.

"We are to respond accordingly to anything that might help find this so-called Le Diable," Asher replies.

I pinch the bridge of my nose. "Are his sons involved?"

"There was no mention of them," Asher says. "Only Igor. Apparently, after losing a decent sum of money in their investments last year, he's been looking for a quick way to make it all back."

"Sex trafficking does sound like something that would appeal to Igor," Nico surmises, rubbing his chin. "He's a man with no conscience."

"I don't understand what this would have to do with Scarlett." Dolion taps a finger on the arm of his chair, deep in thought. "This feels like another dead end to prevent us from finding the asshole."

Sergio gives a half shrug. "I think it's worth investigating."

Asher lets out a breath, staring at the floor. When his eyes glance up, landing on me, I know whatever he's about to say will not be good. "I think there could be a connection between the sex trafficking and—"

"Scarlett," I answer, bolting upright.

"The fact that she was kept in the basement of a warehouse seemed odd to me," Asher says. "It's like she was being held there with a purpose. Like they kept her there waiting for something."

Tension lines my shoulders as I roll my neck. All at once, a missing puzzle piece clicks into place. "The purpose to sell," I grind out.

This isn't fucking good at all.

"I think... I think Le Diable could be the third man," Asher states. "The one responsible for collecting the girls for the auctions."

I stand, taking a few steps toward the closest window, gripping the frame. I reach into my pocket and pull out my phone, dialing Vin.

"What's up, little brother," he answers on the first ring. "I'm a little busy." I hear a female giggle in the background.

"We have a fucking problem."

"What's going on?" His voice deepens, all playfulness gone. I hear his feet shuffle and a door close shut. "Is Scarlett okay?"

I let out a deep breath. "Scarlett's safe." I hear a sigh of relief on the other end. "Sex trafficking," I spit out.

"What about—"

"Igor Vasiliev is getting involved in sex trafficking with a fucking silent partner right under our noses!"

"Okay..." There's a few seconds of silence before he asks, "Do you want me to kill him?"

I grind my back molars. "How did we not see it? They were all in fucking Chicago!"

"See what?"

My shoulders heave, my hand tightening around my phone. "They wanted to sell her."

Understanding registers in Vin when he says, "Le Diable wanted to sell Scarlett."

"He was holding her there to wait her turn." I know it. I know it with everything inside me, and I feel like I'm about to be sick, knowing how much worse it was about to be for her if we didn't find her. "They kept her there with Le Diable until they were ready for her. And if Igor's getting involved in trafficking, it only makes sense that they would have been working together."

"Fuck," Vin breathes. "I'm coming home." I hear the fly of his zipper go up. "I can be there in the morning." The line goes dead.

I completely forgot he's in Germany for business with Alex, working on acquiring a shipment of metal needed for our suppliers, who are responsible for creating some of the most high-tech weapons anyone has ever seen. I'm hopeful him leaving early won't fuck up the deal. But at the same time, I know why he wouldn't hesitate to depart.

Family.

And whether Scarlett realizes it or not, she's a part of this family. She's a sister, a daughter, and a wife. And there's not one thing one of us wouldn't do for her.

As bickering continues behind me, I open the security app on my phone, needing to see Scarlett with my own damn eyes. *I need to know she's safe.* But when I find her on the tiled floor in the kitchen with her knees tucked up against her chest, shaking, I lose it.

"Nobody leaves this room!"

Running out of my office, I slam the door behind me and make it to the kitchen in a few strides, her quiet sob the only sound I register around me. Sitting on the floor beside her, I lift her onto my lap. "What happened?" I brush her hair out of her eyes, running a hand down her trembling back. "Talk to me."

"I...I..." She gasps for air, clutching at her chest, on the verge of a panic attack.

"Breathe, Firefly." Her quivering fingers reach out to me, gripping my shirt tightly as she closes her eyes and takes a deep breath. "That's it. Just like that. You're doing such a good job." She does it again and again until she slowly reins in her sobbing and molds into my chest, her head resting on my shoulder. "What brought this on?"

She tilts her head back, and her glossy eyes meet mine. "I was cutting vegetables for my salad, and then...I nicked my finger." She lifts her shaking hand, showing me the droplets of blood sliding down her index finger. It's not a deep cut and nothing that should bring someone to this level of terror. But seeing blood on her causes an overwhelming need within me to protect her. Maybe that golden tower isn't such a bad idea after all. "And when I saw the blood, I had a flashback. I-I was back in that basement, and he was..." She stops herself, closing her eyes, tears slipping out.

"Open your eyes, Scarlett."

She does, looking right into mine. There's so much pain, too much pain, and I wish I could take it all away from her.

"You're here with me." I cup her cheek, my thumb brushing away every tear that escapes. "It's just you and me. And I won't let anything happen to you."

The palm of my hand rubs circles over her spine. She lets out a breath, her shoulders dropping just a fraction as she looks away from me. "He liked to use a knife on me," she admits softly.

Everything around me blurs. My chest tightens. My fury boils on the precipice of leaking out. "What did he do to you?" I ask calmly, suddenly needing to know every detail of what this monster did to her.

She looks away, pushing herself from me.

I loosen my grip on her. "Please, Scarlett... Talk to me."

She stops, hauling herself back into my arms. Her legs straddle me, gripping me to her. She swallows, looking up at the ceiling before saying flatly, "He liked to mark how many times he..." Her eyes lower, the insinuation hanging heavy between us. "I can't say it."

It takes all of my control to remain calm. To not show an ounce of my wrath to her in fear of scaring her.

"Where?" My voice practically shakes with fury.

She closes her eyes. "On my lower back."

My hand on her back freezes as a fire erupts inside me. I take a deep breath, reining in every quivering muscle, ready to explode in terror upon every single person who has ever done harm to my wife.

"I promise you, I will find him. I will hunt for him in the shadows and find him in the darkness. And when I do, I will make him suffer for everything he did to you. I won't stop, even when he begs for mercy." I press our foreheads together, her labored breaths mirroring mine.

For a moment, I'm worried my words will terrify her. That she'll leap from my grasp and run as far away from me as she can. Instead, she shoves her face into the crook of my neck, her arms forcefully wrapping around me. A broken sob escapes her, her body convulsing in my arms. Tears pour out of her eyes, wetting my neck. On impulse, my hands tighten around her body, never wanting to let her go. And knowing deep within my heart I'll never be able to.

We sit like this for a few minutes, my hands carefully placed at the top of her back, moving in a soothing touch. "Thank you," she whispers, her body slowly calming down.

I twist my head and press a gentle but firm kiss to her temple, knowing words are not enough right now. I'm relieved she doesn't flinch and, instead, melts against me, her body relaxing into my grip.

Abruptly, a gasp leaves her, and she pushes back slightly. "Oh my God. I got blood on your shirt." She rubs at it with her other hand as if it can be wiped clean, but the stain only becomes bigger. "I'm so sorry."

"It's just a little blood, Firefly." I reach for her hand and inspect her finger. "Let's get you cleaned up." She moves to get up, but before she can, I lift her in my arms and stand, bringing her to the island and placing her beside the sink. I walk away from her, the loss of her body against mine sending a foreign shiver through me, and I find a Band-Aid in the cabinet. Turning around, I catch her staring at her finger. The blood dribbles over her porcelain skin. I gently take her hand in mine, turn on the cold water, and place her finger under it.

"I remember you did this for me when we were kids," she muses, a tiny smile trying to appear.

"Oh, yeah?" I pretend not to remember that day when there's not a single thing I've ever forgotten pertaining to her.

"Yeah. When I cut my knees on some rocks after falling off my bike. You carried me inside and took me to the bathroom to clean me up. And then you kissed each knee to make them feel better." She shakes her head, laughing. "I was so embarrassed because..." Her words trail off, her eyes looking like she regrets what she said.

"Because?"

She hesitates before saying, "Because I had the biggest crush on you." She bites her bottom lip, looking down at her lap.

I take two fingers and lift her chin. "The feeling was mutual."

We both stare at each other, unsure what to say or do.

Every instinct inside me wants to kiss her. Hold her in my arms and taste her until she can't take anymore.

But logic and reason keep me frozen. I know what she's been through. Not to mention, I promised her I would never touch her in that way. And I will never break that promise.

Pulling her finger out of the water, pleased to see it's no longer bleeding, I pat it dry and wrap the Band-Aid protectively around it. And just like old times, I bring her finger to my lips and gently kiss the part surrounded by the Band-Aid, lifting my eyes to find her lips parted as she watches me.

"All better," I say huskily.

"Thanks," she gets out, her voice a little softer. Her eyes blink, and she shakes her head. "I'm so tired. I think I should just head to bed for the night. You can go back to your meeting." She tucks her hair behind her ear. "I'm fine."

"Having a panic attack uses a lot of energy." I place the palms of my hands on the counter beside her. "I'll carry you."

She nods in approval. Her legs wrap around me, and her cheek rests against my shoulder as I take each step up the stairs and head toward her room. I position my hand on the scanner, allowing her door to pop open. As I place her on the side of her bed, I notice she's fallen asleep in my arms.

I tuck the blankets around her and run a hand through my hair as I briefly glance down at her before quickly leaving, giving her space.

Opening the door to my office, I find several pairs of eyes widening in horror as I enter the room. "What?"

"Why do you have blood all over your shirt?" Nico asks.

Glancing down, I find splotches of blood covering my white shirt. "There was an accident, but everything was taken care of." I approach my desk and lift the gold paperweight from a pile of neatly stacked papers, playing with it in my hands, Scarlett's words echoing in my ears.

"He liked to mark how many times he... I can't say it."

"Now, where were we?" I question. "Ah, yes. Finding the son of a bitch who dared to touch my wife so I can kill him with my bare fucking hands!"

The gold paperweight crashes through the nearest window, glass shattering to the ground below. My hands rest on my hips as I wait for the fury to subside, but with each passing second, it merely intensifies.

"Dolion?"

"Yes, sir?"

"Get me a meeting with Igor Vasiliev." I roll up my shirt sleeves before sitting in my seat, every eye in the room on me. "It's time I pay him a visit."

CHAPTER SEVEN

Scarlett

A streak of sunlight cascades through the slight gap in the wall-sized curtains, aiming directly at my face. I wince, stretching my arms and legs. Sitting up and rubbing my eyes, I blink, suddenly noticing a vase of fresh pink flowers. I reach out, gently grazing the soft petals between my fingers. *They're beautiful.*

Leaning forward, I inhale their pleasant aroma and uncover a note placed partially beneath the vase.

Firefly,
I didn't want to wake you.
I'm meeting with my brothers this morning.
I'll be back in the afternoon.
Please eat something.
Eli is stationed outside the house.
Yours, Leo

I bite my bottom lip, holding back the smile taking over as butterflies swarm my stomach.

Opening the bedroom door, I'm greeted by my second favorite pair of eyes that elicit an automatic grin as his butt wiggles back and forth. "Are you hungry, big guy?" Brutus's dancing picks up, and his head nudges my leg, slobber making its way onto my leggings. "Okay. Okay." I laugh. "Let's go get some breakfast."

He follows me, matching my stride as we walk through the hall, down the stairs, and into the kitchen. I grab his dish and fill it with a scoop of dry dog food, but it feels like it's missing something. He couldn't possibly enjoy eating this every day, right? Maybe some green beans or carrots might add some flavor.

My eyes dart to the fridge, unease creeping up my spine.

But that would involve using a knife…

A tremor runs down my spine. I don't know if I'm ready for that right now.

Unease fills me at the thought of having another panic attack with Leo not here to help me through it.

A slight whimper from Brutus pauses my thoughts as I look back at him patiently waiting for me.

"You're right. I'm sorry. I can do this." I straighten my shoulders and let out a breath just as I open the fridge door. "I can do this. I'm just cutting some vegetables. It's not a big… What the—"

An assortment of labeled containers, big and small, line the shelves, stacked on top of one another.

Mushrooms, strawberries, pineapple, celery, chicken, carrots…

Everything is cut. Diced. Chopped. Sliced. Peeled.

I blink a few times, my knuckles tightening on the handle. My heart thuds beneath my chest, knowing who did this.

Woof!

I shake my head. "Sorry, boy. I got distracted." Reaching inside, I grab the container labeled mixed vegetables and add a scoop to Brutus's bowl, who happily gobbles up every last bite.

Leaning against the counter, I play with the hem of my shirt, twisting it around my finger as my mind tries to decipher what this means.

Some people might look at chopped vegetables and think I'm crazy for thinking it means anything, but it does. I know it does. Those containers prove to me he really will do anything to keep me safe, both mentally and physically, and that thought sends warmth through me.

Gripping the handle to the fridge door, I open it to get one more look at the perfectly stocked shelves. My heart swells, and the corners of my lips curve up.

He did this...for me.

———

A chill in the air cascades over my shoulders. The thin cotton fabric of my T-shirt does little to protect me from the elements, and I instantly regret not bringing my coat. My eyes scan the sky, noting the ominous presence of threatening grey clouds above, following me, taunting me.

This should only take a minute, I think, as I swing the old, rusty iron gate open and follow the stone path up the hill covered by an abundance of red and yellow leaves. I glance over my shoulder, seeing Eli waiting in the car for me just like I asked him to, and continue moving toward the numerous graves that align this space. Workers, family members, friends... This is where they reside. This is where they are laid to rest. In a private cemetery meant only for the people who were either loved or loyal to the Alarie family.

Which is why I'm here now, seeking out my father's grave.

Months ago, when I first arrived at the Alarie Estate, Mrs. Alarie informed me that they had brought my father's remains here. Even though he fled this place seven years ago, clearly displaying a lack of loyalty to the family, they did it believing it would comfort me to know he was here with me.

They did it for me, and I didn't have the heart to tell them that his presence only terrifies me.

Alive or dead.

I thought I might have a hard time finding his burial place, but the shininess of the new stone and the way the grass hasn't fully grown through the dirt are clear indicators of who this plot belongs to.

A heaviness weighs down on me with each step I take, a sudden unease sweeping over me the closer I get. Rain slowly descends from the clouds above as my feet come to a stop inches from his grave. "Anthony Balcom. A devoted husband and caring father," I read out loud, scoffing at this false statement.

Devoted husband? Caring father?

My hands clench by my sides as I pinch my eyes shut. So much anger swirls through me. Anger at myself for thinking that coming here would be a good idea. And anger at the monster buried six feet beneath the ground, who instilled fear and submission into me with just a lift of his hand or the raising of his voice.

My eyes open, blurry with unshed tears.

"Why?" I whisper, years of pent-up frustration scratching at the surface. "Why did you treat me as if I was nothing? As if I held no value to you?" A tear escapes, traveling down my cheek, and falls from the tip of my chin right onto the soil that covers his casket. "My whole life, you made me feel like I did something wrong. Like I was never enough. But I was your daughter! Your only child, and I loved you!" More tears slide down my cheeks, coating my skin. "I loved you even when you hit me and when you lashed out at me with your vicious words. Because I thought... I thought someday you would finally love me back."

A flashback from one of the nights that tainted my vision of my father appears before me.

"Look at you," my father sneers, his gaze roaming over me. "Foolish girl, you were out with that Alarie boy again, weren't you? After I specifically forbade you from doing so."

My bottom lip trembles, knowing there is no right answer to this question. If I say yes, he'll be mad. And if I say no, he'll be furious at me for lying. So, instead, with as much confidence as I can muster, I say, "I don't understand. Why can't I see them anymore? They're my friends, and we live on their property. Besides, I'm almost eighteen, I can—" I should have expected it, but the sting from his hand across my cheek catches me off guard, and I end up biting the inside of my lip.

"You stupid, stupid girl." He towers over me. "I prayed for a son. One that would make me proud. But instead, I was given a whore." He spits on the ground in front of me.

I step around him, needing to get out of here. Maybe I can stay the night in Maddy's room. Although, I don't know how I'll be able to hide the red mark on my face, which I'm certain is only getting worse.

Suddenly, I'm pulled back and thrown against the wall. My father's hands encircle my throat, holding me in place as I try to fight him. Unfortunately, with a lack of oxygen, I give up and become docile beneath his hold.

"Where the fuck do you think you're going?" he roars in my face.

"Anywhere...from...here," I gasp out. My vision begins to blur as tiny black dots appear in my periphery. "Let me go!"

He laughs menacingly. "Never. Because someday, you may hold value to me."

I'm beginning to lose consciousness, my body going limp. He removes his hands from me and lets me crash to the floor, where I gulp for air.

"You are never to go near that boy again, or any of them for that matter, and if I find out you do..." His lips curve up in a sinister smile. "Well, let's just say I know plenty of ways to kill a man without anyone knowing."

I drop to my knees, not caring that the ground is damp and muddy. "I hate you!" My breaths come out hard and fast, so much fury building inside me. "And you want to know why?" A bitter laugh escapes me. "It's not because of your coldness toward me. No." I shake my head, my wet hair clinging to my face. "It's because I feel guilty for being relieved that you're dead." I roll in my bottom lip. "You're dead. You can no longer hold any power over me, but somehow, you do, making me hate you even more." I pick up a red leaf, curling my fingers around it. "But I guess it's better to feel something than nothing." I open my fist, letting the leaf float to the ground, and angrily bow my head. "I should thank you because if you hadn't died or if I hadn't been..." I clear my throat, shaking my head. "I never would have ended up back where I belong...*home*, at the Alarie Estate." I sit back, enjoying the feeling of rain against my skin. "I'm finally home again."

I even my breathing, focusing on the rush of getting out these words for the first time. He raised me to be his meek daughter who took only what he gave her: pain, fear, and insecurities. Never love. No, definitely not that. And although my dream was someday to say all of these things to his face, I still obtain pleasure knowing I said them above him, with six feet of dirt between us.

I don't know how much time passes when I feel a familiar presence around me, wrapping his leather jacket over my shoulders.

"You'll catch a cold."

I stare up at Leo, feeling a thousand different emotions warring inside me. But the second my eyes latch onto his, calmness overtakes me. He holds his hand out for me, and I take it, letting him pull my body up against his. *Safe.* It's what I feel every time I'm beside him. It consumes me in a way I've never experienced. It's like I no longer have to look over my shoulder or sleep with an eye open. Because he's here.

His fingers tenderly smooth back my wet strands as his other hand slides around my waist, binding me to his chest.

Looking deep into the dark depths of his eyes, I ask, "Does it make me a bad person that I find comfort in my father's death?"

A muscle ticks in his jaw. "Was he cruel to you, Firefly?"

I nod, unable to voice everything he put me through over the years. Especially after I lost the safety of being on the Alarie Estate.

He wipes the raindrops from my cheeks, the tender touch enough to make my knees buckle. But his arm around my waist only tightens. "Why didn't you ever tell me?"

"I couldn't," I breathe. "When I lived on the estate, he would threaten each of you if I ever told anyone about what he did to me, knowing how much you all meant to me. It was the only leverage he had over me." A sob escapes, warm tears mixing with cold raindrops. "And when he dragged me away from here, he forbade me to have anything to do with you all. And it killed me. Because every day I wanted to come back here. But I couldn't risk it. If he hurt your family, it would have been my fault, and I never would have been able to live with myself if something happened to"—*you*—"any one of you."

His hand rests on my cheek, causing my eyes to fall shut. "Your father was never a match for the Alaries."

"I know that now," I whisper, opening my eyes. "But I was terrified and also so in..." *Love.* I stop myself, lowering my eyes. I can't admit that. Not now. And not ever. Leo has made his feelings clear to me, and I must respect that.

He doesn't want to touch me.

Not anymore.

Not like he once used to.

Once, the lust in his eyes for me used to make me weak in the knees. It made my heart pitter-patter in anticipation whenever I was around him.

Nevertheless, I've never seen that look since we've been married. Not once. And it's time to stop expecting more from him when I shouldn't even want more in the first place. Right?

"I wish he were alive," he says matter-of-factly. My eyes widen at his admission, abruptly taken aback. "Only so that I could kill him for everything he ever did to you."

I rest my forehead against his chest. His white T-shirt is practically see-through from how drenched it is, revealing a sea of black ink, more than what was there years ago. On the spot above his heart, a small object catches my eye. It has a variety of colors, but it's hard to make out what it truly is without his shirt off. I bite my lower lip, the thought sending my heart racing.

"Let's get you home." His hands move soothingly up and down my back. "I'll run a warm bath for you and get a fire going."

I smile. A warm bath and a cozy fire to cuddle in front of with a book in my hands sounds like a nice way to end this day.

I take a step back, certain that he'll want to put some space between us, but he closes his hand over mine and leads me down the hill toward his car, Eli's vehicle long gone.

As we pull into the driveway, the rain unexpectedly stops. I take a step out of the car just as the sun peeks through the clouds, shining over the house.

"We're home," Leo says, taking my hand.

I admire the house before me—dark, solid, beautiful—and for the first time, it hits me: *This is my home, too.*

"We're home," I repeat softly, seeing everything a little differently.

But what I don't voice to Leo is that being with him has always felt like home.

Chapter Eight

Leo

"When are you taking your wife on a goddamn date?"

I choke on my water. My fist pounds on my chest as I regain a breath, using the back of my arm to wipe off the water dribbling down my chin. "What are you talking about?" I ask, narrowing my eyes on Vin.

His hand moves smoothly over the steering wheel, turning us onto the highway. "A date. It's when two people who like each other go out—"

I scowl. "I know what the fuck a date is."

"Then why the fuck have you not taken your wife on one?" His brows raise in question.

I shake my head. "It's not like that with us."

"Not like what?"

I rub my temple, looking out the window. "That's not what Scarlett wants."

Vin scoffs, causing my head to jerk in his direction. "You sure about that?"

"Yes. I think I know Scarlett a little better than you do, and I know a date with me is the last thing she wants." I place my water in the middle console. "Trust me when I say this marriage is just a safety net for her."

Vin rolls his eyes. "If you say so."

As we continue driving, my mind wanders, mulling over his words. Would Scarlett go on a date with me if I asked her to? Would she even want to? I never did have a chance to take her on a proper date all those years ago. Maybe going on one might bring us closer together. *Or maybe*, I think, with dread filling my stomach, *it would only make things worse*. Sighing, I rest my head against the headrest, closing my eyes.

"We're here," Vin murmurs, slowing down the car as we roll up to the Vasiliev Tower. I reach inside my jacket, ensuring my gun is secure, and glance out the window. "Now remember, stay calm while we're here. We don't need a war to start today when it's only the two of us."

Igor Vasiliev doesn't just own the penthouse or even a few floors, for that matter, but the whole fucking skyscraper. It's his impenetrable fortress where no one comes or goes without his approval.

I glare at him. "It seems to me that the pot is calling the kettle black."

"I'm calm." He loosens his tie. "I just get a little antsy when we're outnumbered."

My eyes assess the scene outside of the car, where I count four men coming toward our vehicle with their hands on their holsters, ready to draw their weapons in a split second if needed.

"They certainly know how to give a warm welcome," Vin remarks, putting the SUV in park. "Come on. The sooner we get inside, the sooner we can leave."

We walk side by side, imposing figures as we approach the guards.

"Gentlemen," Vin announces with a wide grin. "Happy to see us?"

"Can't say that we are," one of them sneers. He's bulky but short. I could probably kill him in ten seconds. Maybe seven.

Vin *tsks*. "Is that any way to greet a guest?"

"Guest?" He scoffs. "You two aren't anything, but—"

"Vincenzo. Leonardo." Our heads turn toward the man, appearing behind his guards. *Igor Vasiliev*. A snake in a wrinkled suit. His broad smile widens, hiding his cold, cruel personality. His fingers push back his greasy white hair. "Shall we go to my office?"

Vin's lips curl up. "Gladly." He stands before the bulky guard. "Take note. That's how you greet a guest."

The man merely leers at us as we follow behind Igor. He walks steadily through the heavily guarded lobby, not stopping until we approach a desk with another guard behind it.

"Weapons," the guard states.

Vin and I peer at Igor.

"Just a precaution," Igor answers. "Can never be too vigilant."

"Of course," Vin replies. I arch a brow, boring my eyes into Vin, not wanting to part with my gun, but as Vin unloads his weapon into the container pushed before us, I follow his lead.

We step into the nearby elevator, the three of us, plus another guard, standing in silence. Just as the elevator music grates on my last nerve, we stop at the top level, the doors parting.

Gaudy. That's my first thought as my eyes scan over the atrociously decorated space, enveloped in gold everywhere the eye can see.

"Love what you've done with the place," Vin mutters, giving me a side-eye and mouthing *fucking tacky* for only my eyes to see.

"Isn't it exquisite? It was just redone last year." Igor proudly scans the space, leading us farther away from the elevator and down a hallway.

"Sir." A guard appears before Igor.

"What is it?" Igor asks, rubbing his temple.

"We've received word that your daughter has run away. She's left her devices behind, leaving no way to track her...this time."

Igor has a daughter?

Igor's hands clench into fists at his sides. "That spoiled fucking brat!" He seethes. "If she ruins this deal for me, I will end her."

Vin glances at me, arching a brow.

Igor smooths out his tie. "No matter. I expect you to find her and bring her back here before the day is over, and if you don't, well...I don't think you want to find out what will happen."

The guard visibly swallows. "Yes, sir." He turns and quickly hurries away.

"Children," Igor muses with an eerie smile. "Sorry for the interruption. My daughter apparently doesn't understand her place in the world yet, but soon will." Coming to the end of the hall, he opens a large door, gesturing for us to step inside. As he sits behind his desk, he takes a long look between us as we sit opposite him. "Now, what is it you'd like to discuss? I was told it was quite urgent."

"It is." I lean forward, ready to get straight to the point. "Were you aware my wife was kidnapped?"

He frowns. "Was she your wife when that took place?"

I narrow my eyes. "She's my wife now."

He gives a slight shrug. "I don't see what this has to do with me."

"Were you aware?" Vin repeats for me, his voice deepening.

Igor flicks his wrist. "I heard rumblings." His eyes land on me, his lips curving up. "Rumors have swirled of the terrors she endured."

I grip the arms of my chair, my knuckles turning white. It takes everything in me not to jump from my seat and strangle the son of a bitch.

"Such a shame to have happened to such a pretty girl," he continues. "Wasted goods now, it would seem."

I snap, lunging for him without a second thought, but before I get the chance to wrap my fingers around his neck, Vin shoves me back down.

I catch a malicious smile appearing on Igor's face. "Oh my, have I touched a nerve?"

I roll my neck, my heart beating madly. I feel like a caged animal stuck in a room with my prey that I'm not allowed to hunt. Pure fucking torture.

"And you know nothing of her kidnapper? Le Diable?" Vin asks, appearing calm.

"Le Diable? What an interesting name." Igor hums in amusement but shakes his head. "I'm afraid I've never heard of him."

Vin nods, steepling his fingers before him. "You know what is interesting is that the warehouse she was found in is located on the same route as one of your loading docks. A coincidence? No?"

Igor presses a hand to his chest in mock offense. "You think I would have anything to do with her kidnapping?"

"I wouldn't put it past you," I spit out with venom laced in each word.

His eyes darken, a cold smile forming. "Careful, boy. One might think you were disrespecting me in my own home."

"We mean no disrespect, Igor." Vin leans back, his body filling out the seat as he narrows his eyes on Igor. "But you can understand how we might think this has something to do with you after what we've recently heard."

"And pray tell, what would that be?"

"Sex trafficking," Vin says candidly. My eyes catch a quick twitch in Igor's jaw and a hard swallow before he leans back, smoothing out his jacket. "You wouldn't be having a hand in that nasty business, would you?"

"Sex trafficking?" He scoffs. "Why would I involve myself in that when I can get pussy wherever and whenever I want."

"Isn't the answer always the same?" Vin wipes a piece of lint from his jacket. "Money."

Igor laughs. "Money?" His arms open wide. "As you can see for yourselves, I have plenty of that."

"Not according to our intel."

Igor's face reddens. Little does he know, Alex took a peek into Igor's assets just this morning, noticing a substantial amount of money disappearing throughout the year, leaving him with, well, not enough to be owning a fucking gold tower in the middle of Chicago.

"You insult me after I welcomed you into my home, telling me you've been having me looked into," he yells, slamming his fist on his desk. "What right do you have?"

"The right to know who the fuck took Scarlett!" Vin roars, rising from his seat. "You think you can hide in the shadows like Le Diable." Vin spits on the floor, his body tight with tension. "But you've forgotten who you let into your home. We are the Alaries, and we have eyes and ears everywhere. If I so much as find out you had anything to do with Scarlett's disappearance, then I will hunt you down myself, you sorry sac of balls. You will regret ever fucking with us because Scarlett is one of us, which means if you messed with her, then you messed with me, and that means a goddamn war that you will not win, old man!"

The door bangs open, revealing two guards with their weapons drawn.

Igor smiles cruelly, slicking back his hair. "It appears our time is up. Shame, as I was very much enjoying our conversation." He stands, straightening his tie. "Always a pleasure, gentlemen. I do hope you find this"—his hand waves in the air—"so-called Le Diable." He chuckles, gesturing for us to depart.

My eyes bore into him, my feet refusing to move. Vin's hand clasps my shoulder, and begrudgingly, I walk out of Igor's office, knowing that this will not be the last time I see him.

And the next time I do, I have a feeling there won't be so much life left behind those cold grey eyes.

The guards guide us toward the elevator and send us down to the bottom floor. After retrieving our weapons and returning to our car to head to our private plane, I glance at Vin.

"Thank you for having my back with this," I say.

Vin loses his tie, throwing it to the back seat. "I would do anything for our family. And Scarlett is a part of this family."

My lips twitch. "You did a good job at keeping your cool back there."

He lets out a boisterous laugh. "Do you think he'll invite us to the Christmas party this year?"

"Not unless it's to hang your balls as mistletoe." I smirk. The car stops at a light, and I glance at the crowded sidewalk where men in suits are glued to their phones as they meander through the Financial District, presumably heading to their mundane jobs. "Do you think he knows more than he let on?"

He runs his fingers through his dark hair. "Of course I do. And I also know for a fact he was lying to us and is very much involved in sex trafficking."

My brow arches. "Enlighten me."

He pulls out a business card from his pocket. "Well, while I kept my cool...I snatched this from his desk. He was too distracted trying not to piss his pants to notice."

The all-black card appears merely just that until you turn it in the light, revealing a name: *Blue Velvet Fantasies*.

My brows draw together. "What the hell is this?"

Vin grips the wheel, his fingers tightening. "It's an underground sex club. But it's more than that." I stare at him, waiting for him to continue. "Before Dad died, I went with him there. Or at least, another club with the same name."

I scratch the back of my neck, feeling incredibly confused. "A little father-son bonding?"

"You could say that. But it's not what you're thinking." His smile falls as he looks straight ahead. "It was used as the place where sex auctions took place on women and..." He stiffens, shaking his head. "Minors."

"What?" I rear back. "Then why the fuck were you there?"

The light turns green, and the vehicle accelerates. "We went to shut the place down. Dad had a team of men with him, and, as the oldest, I went with him to see everything firsthand. He never told me who it belonged to, but he was furious. I had never seen him that way before." He looks lost in thought before saying, "Men came to bid on women who had been drugged and were brought there against their will." His jaw clenches. "It was a place of true horrors. We got in, freed the woman and children, and then lit the place on fire, leaving the perverted bastards inside to die."

"Jesus Christ."

"Yeah." The car comes to a stop beside the flight of stairs leading up to the plane entrance. "I hope I'm not right, but if I am, if this is a duplicate of the same club from seven years ago, then there's going to be a lot more women kidnapped." He undoes his top button. "We need to find it fast. We need to burn it to the ground, along with every one of those sick fucks."

I rub my chin, taking in everything he just said, when something occurs to me. "Did you say seven years ago?"

"Yeah," he answers. "It was a few days before Dad died." He gets out of the car and grabs his bag from the trunk.

I sit for a moment. Something doesn't feel right about the timeline. Vin's light tap on the window beside me causes me to open my door.

As Vin takes the first step up the stairs, I ask, "Do you think they're related?"

Vin stops and turns. "Is what related?"

"All of this." I place my hands on my hips, looking in the distance at nearby planes taking off. "Dad's murder. Scarlett's kidnapping. The sex club. Igor. Le Diable. Fucking all of it."

Vin takes a step toward me, letting out a sigh. His eyes darken as he runs a hand over his stubble. "If it is, then shit just got a lot more fucked up."

Shutting the door behind me, I lean against it and pinch my eyes closed, dread weighing down on me.

Everything just got a whole lot more complicated.

Pushing off, I walk toward the kitchen, needing a drink, when my eyes spot Scarlett asleep on the couch. I pivot toward her and sit on the side, the cushion dipping slightly, but Scarlett doesn't stir.

I glide my knuckles across her porcelain cheek, my fingers pushing back her long blonde strands over her shoulder. The blanket that probably once covered her body now lies between her and the couch. Her T-shirt has ridden up, revealing her lower back, and my hand freezes midair, evolving into a fist that comes down hard on a nearby pillow.

Fury engulfs me. My blood turns molten as my vision goes red. It feels as if there's no oxygen in the room, my chest heaving steadily. My eyes remain fixed on every single one of Scarlett's scars. Every deep gash. Every thick line. And I feel seconds away from losing all of my self-control.

To torture myself, I try to count them. I try to see just how many times he marked her. But the lines all blur together, with no end and no beginning, becoming one colossal scar.

Without warning, something happens to me that I haven't experienced since my father's death. I bring my hand up to my cheek, pulling back to see wetness on the pads of my fingers. Tears gather in my eyes, my throat tightening painfully.

If I could make one wish in this life, it would be that I could take all her pain away. Physical and mental. I wish I could carry it for her so she would never experience it again.

How could someone do something like this to her?

How could they try to break something so valuable?

With a slight tremble, my fingers lightly graze the raised skin.

Lowering my head in shame, I think about how I failed her. I let this happen to her. I let a monster torture her because I didn't run after her when she was taken from here.

Taken from me.

I let her go, thinking it was safer for her to be as far away as possible from this life. But I was wrong. And because of that, she faced the consequences of my actions.

But I'm going to make things right.

Starting right damn now.

Soothingly, I run my knuckles across her cheek. "Scarlett."

She rouses, stretching her body and rolling onto her back, her eyes blinking up at me. "Leo? What's wrong?" She sits up, panic evident in her eyes.

"Nothing." I cup her cheek and relish how she instantly melts into my touch, no longer flinching. "Nothing at all. There's just something I want to ask you." She waits, a little yawn escaping her. "Well, you see, I was just thinking." I squeeze the back of my neck. "Or, I guess, what I'm trying to say is…" I let out a deep breath. What is wrong with me? I'm an Alarie for God's sake! Asking my wife out on a date shouldn't be this difficult. Her eyes soften as an adorable smile forms on her face, and that's all the encouragement I need. "Would you like to go to dinner with me tomorrow night?"

She bites her bottom lip. "Like a date?"

"Yes…"

"A date with…me?" Her brows scrunch together.

My lips tilt up. "Yes, Firefly. A date with you."

Her smile widens, and she nods.

"Yeah?" I ask, my thumb brushing over her soft skin.

"Yeah. I'd like that a lot," she answers as a soft shade of pink caresses her skin.

Relief swarms through me, and my muscles relax.

"Well." She lets out another little yawn. "I should probably head up to bed." She swings her legs over the side, rubbing her eyes.

Before she can stand, I stop her.

"Let me." Standing, I hook both of my arms underneath her and hold her against my chest. She presses her head into the crook of my neck as I walk up the stairs and bring her to her room. After turning on the light, I place her on her bed, pull the blanket around her, and tuck her in. "Good night, Scarlett." I lean down and press a featherlight kiss to her forehead.

"Good night, Leo." She turns on her side and closes her eyes, quickly drifting to sleep as if I never woke her.

I head for the door, ready to turn the light off, when I immediately stop myself, knowing it'll terrify her if she wakes up alone in the dark. The harsh light casts an angry glow over the space as if it knows it shouldn't be on at this time of night. If only there were something else that could help her sleep soundly. Something that—

That's it.

I close the door behind me and pull out my phone, swiftly pressing it to my ear.

"Mr. Alarie?" A yawn stretches across the line. "Is everything okay?"

"Felix, I need something made and with a quick turnaround time." There's silence on the other end. "Felix?"

"You know it's one in the morning, right?"

I grind my back molars. "Is this a bad time?" I ask with a hint of authority in my voice. He shouldn't be questioning when I call upon him for what we pay him.

"Of course not, sir." He clears his throat, and I hear him stumbling out of bed. "As the Alarie family jeweler, I am privileged to create anything you desire. What is it you are looking for?"

Walking into my room, I ask, "How familiar are you with fireflies?"

CHAPTER NINE

Scarlett

My knee bounces uncontrollably beneath the table. I swallow hard as I reach for the glass of water before me, bringing it to my lips and savoring the liquid as it slides down my dry throat.

Nervous doesn't even begin to describe how I feel right now as I contemplate the fact that I'm on a first date with my husband.

I must have changed at least ten times before we left the house, over-thinking every little thing. From the length of my hemline, the tightness of the fabric, the openness of my neckline, and even the color choice in fear that it would draw too much attention to myself. I finally opted for a black A-line dress with a boat neck and sheer sleeves, the length ending just above my knees, and paired with black flats and a silver chain belt to complete the look.

Before we left the house, I glanced in the mirror, giving a little twirl, thinking I looked nice. However, as my eyes travel around the opulent room with women dining beside their significant others in gorgeous six-inch heels and body-hugging dresses that leave little to the imagination, I'm starting to second-guess myself.

Leo deserves a woman like one of them. One who isn't fearful of showing off her legs or a hint of cleavage. A woman who's confident in her skin, owning her true worth. One that matches him in power and appearances.

And that's not me.

Leo's fingers clasp around my hand, bringing it to his lips. "You look perfect." His soft lips brush the back of my hand, sending a shiver through me.

"Thank you," I murmur, my cheeks heating up under his gaze. He returns my hand to the table but keeps his hand firmly fastened around it.

"What are you thinking about?" he asks.

A boisterous laugh to my left catches my attention. It's a beautiful couple, dripping in elegance and sex appeal. The woman is wearing a red skintight dress with her ample cleavage out in almost full display for the man beside her to admire as he slides his chair closer to her, grazing his finger across her collarbone. He leans forward, pressing his lips to her neck, his tongue poking out for a taste. She seems to enjoy it as she arches her neck to the side, giving him sufficient room to explore.

God, do I feel out of place here.

"Scarlett?"

I shake my head, turning my attention to Leo. "Sorry. I was just thinking about how beautiful this restaurant is."

He leans forward, bracing his elbows on the table. Probably not the etiquette on par with a place like this, but I would love to see any person in here tell him otherwise. His white button-down shirt, tucked into his black pants, fits nicely against his chiseled chest. His sleeves are rolled up, exposing the ink on his veiny forearms and hands, sending a foreign feeling to the pit of my stomach. My heart picks up speed as I suddenly have the urge to trace every single one of his tattoos, maybe not with my fingers, but with my ton—

No! I internally shake my head. What is wrong with me?

His hardened gaze narrows in on me as his lips curve the slightest bit, a cruel but handsome smile on display only for my eyes.

He's a man that everyone fears.

Everyone, that is, except me.

"You're lying, Firefly."

My lips part as I shake my head. "N-no. I—"

He suddenly stands, lifting his chair and relocating it beside mine. Sitting, he shifts toward me, his eyes studying me. "Was this a bad idea for a first date?" He tugs at his collar, a touch of red skimming up his neck.

And I realize something that calms my racing heart. He's nervous. Just like me.

I smile, placing my hand over his, and suddenly recognize it's the first time I've initiated contact between us. But it doesn't feel wrong. If anything, it feels right. More than right, actually. Because I don't have the urge to run or cry. No. When I touch him, I simply exist in his promise of safety. A bubble of bliss that I never want to leave. And I like this feeling. I like this feeling...a lot.

"No." I shake my head. "Not at all. This was a great idea, and I'm glad we're here. I'm just feeling a little nervous."

"With me?"

"No." I watch as I let my finger trace the ink over the back of his hand. The slight tremble in my touch dies down the longer I explore. He doesn't move or say anything; he just watches me curiously. "Never nervous with you. Just nervous that I'll mess this up." I give a slight shrug. "In case you haven't noticed, I don't exactly fit in with the crowd of women here." My eyes travel around the room, taking in the beauty before landing back on the white tablecloth. "They all look like supermodels, and I look...well, I'm pretty sure I look like I haven't slept in years." I give a timid smile. "I guess I don't really feel like myself right now."

His eyes darken, his hand flipping over, intertwining our fingers. He moves in so close that his knees press against the outside of my thigh, sending a slight pulse in my core. "Do you think I care what any other woman in this place looks like?" His lips ghost over my ear. "Do you think my eyes have strayed once while we've been here?"

I swallow down the flutter of butterflies in my stomach trying to escape. The warmth of his breath cascades over my neck, and I suddenly wish I was the woman at the nearby table who was having her neck sampled like an appetizer. "I'm...I'm not sure."

He takes my hand and places it on his chest. "You are the only one in here my eyes are drinking in. The only one making my heart beat faster than it should be." I feel the thump of his heart matching my own. I find myself wanting to curl my fingers into him. To tear apart his shirt and feel his defined muscles under my touch. But I shouldn't feel this way.

A slight panic snakes through me, and for the second time tonight, I question what the hell is wrong with me.

I was kidnapped and tortured by a faceless man.

A monster.

I shouldn't ever want to be touched again, not after everything I went through.

But God, I want Leo to touch me more than I've wanted anything in my entire life. And that scares me more than I care to admit.

My breaths come out faster, my heart on the verge of cardiac arrest. This is wrong. Everything about this is wrong.

But he's your protector...

Your first love...

Your husband...

"Scarlett, you are the only one who—"

"Well, if it isn't Leonardo Alarie." A high-pitched voice has us both turning our heads to the side, where I find a tall, slender brunette in a stunning blue satin dress approaching our table.

Leo drops my hand and sits back in his seat while I quickly compose myself, placing my hands on my lap and staring at the woman before us.

I'm the only one who…what? I wonder.

"Natasha," Leo murmurs, stretching his neck to the side.

"You look just as delicious as ever," she practically purrs as she bats her long lashes at him. Her eyes rake over his body, undressing my husband before my very eyes. She either doesn't care that I'm here or is too lost in her X-rated daydream to notice my presence. "Why haven't you returned any of my calls?" She pouts and rests her hand on Leo's forearm.

Everything around me stills as my eyes focus on where her fingers graze his skin with a familiar touch.

They've been intimate with each other.

My heart pounds.

My vision goes blurry.

I want to scream at her for touching what's mine.

I want to shove her away from Leo and watch as she stumbles backward with pure shock on her overly-painted face.

I clench my hands into fists, my breaths accelerating. But as I blink back the tears forming, I suddenly see this woman in a new light.

This is who Leo wants.

Dark hair. Long legs. Brown eyes. Confident. Sexy.

She's everything I'm not.

I look down at my lap, hating myself for getting caught up in the dream that this date meant that Leo was starting to see me in the same light as he had years before. But why would he ever want me again when he's been with someone like her?

A sharp stab of jealousy slices right through my wildly beating heart. *I feel so stupid.*

"Please remove your hand before I have to do it for you." Leo's deep, authoritative voice sends a chill over my skin.

My eyes dart to him, his face exemplifying a wrath I've never seen. Natasha chuckles, probably assuming he's joking, but she removes her fingers just the same. Leo leans toward me, his eyes only on me as he speaks. "Natasha, have you met my wife, Scarlett?" He reaches for my hand on my lap and brings it to his lips, kissing my wedding band. I stare wide-eyed, warmth spreading throughout my chest. "She is the only woman allowed to touch me."

Leo turns his eyes to Natasha and watches her cheeks turn bright red. She murmurs, "Congratulations," before quickly spinning on her heels and heading toward the back of the restaurant, swiftly disappearing out of sight.

Leo's dark eyes connect with mine. He doesn't hesitate to say, "It was one time. A few years ago."

I shake my head, take a deep breath, and attempt to compose myself. Within minutes, I went from being turned on to fighting off a panic attack and experiencing jealousy for the first time in my life. The thought of Leo with another woman is not something I want to ponder all that closely. Not at all, in fact.

"I didn't expect you to be celibate for all those years. We both had our own lives." I reach for my glass of water, quickly taking a few sips. "Besides, I can't say that I blame you. She's stunning."

Leo releases a deep, throaty laugh, and I find myself taken aback. "Something funny?" I ask, crossing my arms over my chest.

"Don't you see?"

"See what?"

"She's the exact opposite of you."

Hurt spreads in my chest as my arms drop to my sides and my eyes lower. "Yes. I have eyes." If she's who he wants, why doesn't he just run after her then?

His face morphs into that of a deadly killer. A stone-cold expression takes over as he catches my hand, not releasing it even when I try to yank it away. Sitting forward, he ends up right in my face, his lips only inches from mine. "She's cold and cruel. Greedy and bitter. A fake, money-hungry gold digger who only wants me for the power I come with. I've never been attracted to her. Not once. And I only slept with her because she's the exact opposite of you in both looks and everything else." His eyes soften, his thumb gently caressing my hand. "She's everything I don't want."

"W-what?" My heart thunders so loudly that I'm not sure I'll be able to hear anymore.

He presses our foreheads together, the palms of his hands cupping the sides of my face. "I've only ever wanted—"

A clearing of a throat causes me to jump back. The waiter, who tugs on his collar, appearing very uncomfortable, stands before us. "Your dinner is served." He dips his chin, walks backward, and two other waiters appear, quickly serving our plates.

After they walk away, Leo reaches over and begins cutting my steak into bite-size pieces. Knowing he's doing it so I don't have to pick up a knife causes my eyes to mist over.

"Thank you." I place my napkin on my lap, smoothing out the fabric. "And thank you for the flowers today. They're different than what you've normally gotten me but very beautiful. I placed them on my nightstand."

Leo freezes mid-cut, suddenly turning his stealthy gaze on me. "What flowers?"

I arch a brow, remembering the card that came with it with the words *Always mine* on it. A blush spreads over my cheeks as I internally shake my head. "The black dahlias you had delivered to the house today."

Leo rolls his neck, his jaw working back and forth as he drops the knife. He suddenly reaches for his jacket and stands, holding out his hand for me to take. "We're leaving. Now." His eyes jump around the room, narrowing in on each patron as if they might be unsuspecting prey in his next hunt. His other hand reaches into his pocket and comes out with a wad of bills that he throws onto the table.

Taking his hand, he pulls me along, and I do my best to keep up, but it's hard when he's well over a foot taller than me.

"Leo," I huff, trying to catch my breath. "I don't understand what's going on."

He throws a deathly glare at the valet, who bolts out the door in pursuit of his car.

The restaurant manager rushes over to us, smoothing his hand over his bald head. "Mr. and Mrs. Alarie, I apologize if everything was not up to your standards. We can—"

"Everything was excellent." Leo rushes us out the door. "But it's time for us to leave," he throws over his shoulder.

Just as we take a step outside, his car appears. The valet jumps out of the driver's seat and tosses Leo his keys.

Everything's happening too fast.

"Leo, wait!" I pull on his hand, causing him to stop in his tracks. Once again, his eyes examine our surroundings before landing on me. "Will you please tell me what's going on?"

He looks down at me as he opens the passenger door, waiting for me to step inside. "We need to go."

I shake my head, holding my ground as I cross my arms over my chest. "I'm not getting in the damn car until you tell me why!"

I internally gape at my insolence. Shit... What did I just do?

Something like admiration flashes in Leo's eyes. "As pleased as I am that you feel comfortable enough with me to defy me, now is not the time." He removes the handgun from the inside of his jacket, turning the safety off before he looks into my eyes and says, "We're leaving because I didn't have any fucking flowers delivered to the house today."

CHAPTER TEN

Leaning back in my leather chair, I swivel to the side, glancing out the window. The sun is just beginning to set, alerting me that I should be leaving, heading home to my wife, but instead, I'm stuck here dealing with a stubborn motherfucker who apparently doesn't realize he's dying whether he talks or not. And if he would just give us what we're looking for instead of prolonging the inevitable, then I could give him the promise of a quick and painless death. But the longer he holds out on us, the longer we'll drag out his painful demise.

And what the fucker also doesn't comprehend is that I'll wait all goddamn day for him to speak if I have to.

"Are you Le Diable?" Vin roars with intensity as his fist connects with the smug asshole's jaw over and over again. The man hangs in chains wrapped around his wrists, his feet unable to touch the ground. Mauro stands to the side, arms crossed over his defined chest as he watches silently, impatiently waiting for his turn.

"If you keep doing that, he won't be able to give you an answer," Alex muses, typing furiously on his keyboard across from me.

After Scarlett and I raced home, I stormed into her bedroom and handled disposing of the flowers myself, bringing them out to the firepit and watching them turn to ash one by one. I then bid Scarlett good night and shut myself in my office to contact my brothers and Eli, ensuring we figured out who sent these fucking flowers to her.

It didn't take long for Alex to hack into the security system of the local florist from which the flowers came. He then ran face recognition on each customer who entered the store, narrowing the culprit down to one felon with a mile-long rap sheet.

Michael Thatcher. Thirty-six. Single. Unemployed. Current residence is located in a mobile home about an hour from here. Drug smuggling, grand theft auto, rape, kidnapping, and armed robbery, were just a few things on this man's record that made him stand out.

We're doing the world a service today by getting rid of him.

Vin and Mauro picked him up a couple of hours ago while he was taking a piss in his trailer and brought him back here for some...*questioning.* After Eli came to the house to keep an eye on Scarlett, I made my way over to our warehouse, hungry for vengeance.

Is he Le Diable?

Did we finally get lucky and catch the monster?

Well, honestly, I'm not too optimistic, but that's what we're here to find out.

Although, we've been at it for a while now, and I'm getting antsy the longer I'm away from Scarlett.

"I'm not telling you shit." The guy spits blood onto Vin's pristine white shirt.

Vin rolls his shoulders, cracking his neck from side to side. "This was my favorite shirt, fucker. How am I going to get all this blood out?"

"Oh, I know how to get it out," Alex starts. "First, you need to soak it in—"

"I wasn't fucking serious!" Vin pinches the bridge of his nose.

Mauro's lips curve up in amusement, a silent chuckle escaping him.

Alex keeps his attention on his laptop. "Well, sorry for trying to be helpful."

"Enough." I stand and roll up my shirt sleeves to my elbows. Approaching the bastard, I circle him, enjoying the familiar scent of fear permeating the air. "Do you know who we are?" I stand directly before him, crossing my arms over my chest.

Michael smirks as blood trails down his face. "Nobody. You're nothing." His swollen eyes move around the room. "The whole lot of you are nothing but worthless pieces of shit."

My fist connects with his jaw, and a loud crunch echoes in the room. "Now, that's no way to talk to your hosts. Is it, Michael?"

His head lulls to the side. "Fuck you." My fist slams into his stomach, a gurgling noise leaving his throat.

"Let's try this again." I grip his thick neck, squeezing just enough to play the role of God as I control how much air I allow him. "We already know it was you who ordered the flowers for my wife. So are you or are you not Le Diable?"

A blue tint takes over his lips as he faintly shakes his head.

"Good. Now we're getting somewhere." Disappointment eases through me, knowing this isn't the man we want. But I know he has something he can share with us. Something that will lead us that much closer to finding Le Diable. I snatch the handwritten note from my pocket with my free hand, holding it before his bulging eyes. *Always mine.* The fucker had the audacity to write that for my wife to see. "Who gave you this to include with the flowers?"

After his eyes catch on the card, I crush it in my hand and then toss it to the floor, bringing my other hand around his neck.

Michael gasps for air, his eyes beginning to bulge. I slightly loosen my grip, allowing him the gift of oxygen.

"No...one."

I squeeze harder, watching as he struggles. "You have two options. One, you refuse to tell us anything, and we drag this interrogation out for as long as we can until your body eventually gives out on you. Or two, you tell us who sent you to order the flowers, and we end this now." Seconds tick by, and I glance over at Mauro. "Get me the pliers. If he's not going to talk, then I guess he doesn't need a tongue."

Michael suddenly squirms to life beneath my hold, ferociously shaking his head.

"Having a change of heart?" I loosen my grip. He gulps down air as I back away, giving him my back. "Talk."

"Le." *Cough.* "Diable." *Cough.*

Every vein in my body runs like a river of ice. My hands at my sides clench into painful fists. "I hope, for your sake, you can do better than that. We want a real name. Now."

His voice comes out hoarse. "I...don't have another name."

I spin on the balls of my feet, reaching my hands out to strangle him.

"Wait...wait!" He coughs up blood, his breaths growing shallow. "I have an address."

"An address?" My arms drop to my sides.

He nods frantically. "Yes! Yes! It's where he told me to meet him on Friday, right before midnight, for my payment. I never saw him. He...called me on an unknown number. Told me he missed his girl and just wanted to remind her who she belongs to."

His girl?

Who she belongs to?

My vision grows darker, black and red spots outlining this fucker. "And you took the job just like that?"

He chuckles before choking on blood. "Would you say no to a grand just for ordering some stupid flowers?"

Wow. This guy really is a moron if he thought he was going to ever see his money.

"Where were you meeting him?"

"Over at the old docks in the Bronx, off of route ninety-five past the abandoned warehouses." He spits to the side. "He said he'd meet me there on his boat with my payment."

We have a place, a date, and a time.

Bingo.

"You going to let me go now?" He grins triumphantly.

Humor fills me, a laugh escaping me. "Oh, Michael." I grip his chin. "Not a chance in hell."

His eyes widen as his wrists tug on the chains. "But, but, you...you said you would end this now if I spoke."

I nod, wiping my bloody hands on his shirt. "I did say that. And being a man of my word, I swear that's what we'll do. End this." It's almost humorous watching his shoulders sag with relief as if we are going to let him walk out of here like a free man. I nudge my head toward Mauro. "Have at it, big guy."

Mauro grins as he strides over to him, a frightening beast to those who deserve it. A gentle giant to others. He grabs the baseball bat by the corner, and his smile widens.

The poor fucker pisses his pants, a damp spot growing between his legs. "Please, no. No!"

I drown out the screaming as I wash my hands and then plop myself on the closest chair, letting out a heavy breath.

Vin saddles up on the seat beside me. "Guessing we have a date at the docks on Friday?"

"We do." I lean toward the bar cabinet, pulling out a glass and a bottle of whiskey.

"Interesting," Alex murmurs, staring intently at his screen.

After pouring the amber liquid into the glass, I give it a quick swirl and then shoot it back, enjoying the pleasant burn.

"What?" I ask.

Alex turns his screen, pointing at an image of the black dahlia, the flower I burned to nothing more than embers. "It says here the black dahlia is a symbol of betrayal." He looks lost in thought. "Do you think..." His eyes meet mine. "Do you think Le Diable feels betrayed by Scarlett because she married you?"

Betrayed?

Vin leans forward, resting his elbows on his knees. "He's mad. But this is good."

"Good?" I question incredulously. "How the fuck is this good? He sent flowers to my wife."

His hand clasps my shoulder. "He's coming out to play now. He's getting brazen and no longer hiding in the shadows. This is a good thing. It finally gives us a chance to find him." He takes the bottle from my hand and pours himself a glass. "We can't catch a ghost, brother. This is what we've been waiting for." He looks over at the dangling corpse. "Looks like the fucker got what he deserved." He makes his way toward Mauro, helping him unchain the man.

I lean back in my chair, resting my head as I gaze up at the ceiling.

He's right, of course.

But it doesn't mean I fucking like it.

Not when it involves Scarlett.

Speaking of... I glance at my watch. She should have started her virtual therapy session a few minutes ago. I drum my fingers along the arm of my chair as I pull out my phone from my pocket and stare at it.

Would it be invading her privacy if I was only trying to learn more, to gain better insight into what's inside my wife's head, to help her heal, to...

Fuck it.

My index finger slides across the screen, turning it on. I discreetly glance at Alex to my left, but he's too lost in his computer to notice as I enter my house's security system. I pull up the live feed until I find the one that focuses on Scarlett. She sits on the sectional with the laptop placed on the coffee table. Her shoulders are hunched, her arms are wrapped around herself, and her knee bounces, informing me of her distress.

My fingers dig into the arm of the chair. Maybe therapy isn't good for her if it's making her this upset.

What could this so-called psychologist, Dr. Raven, be saying to her to make her this uncomfortable?

Without a second thought, I reach for one of my earbuds in my pocket and insert it into my ear, immediately pulling in the voices through the feed.

"Last time we met, you mentioned your nightmares weren't occurring as often as usual. Is that still the case?" Dr. Raven asks.

Scarlett nods, visibly swallowing. "Yes. I've been... I've been sleeping much better." She rakes her hands through her hair, twisting the ends.

"Still with the light on?"

"Yes." Scarlett dips her chin, embarrassment washing over her features.

"You appear upset. Is something on your mind you'd like to discuss?"

Scarlett shakes her head, twisting her fingers together on her lap. "I'm... It's just..." She looks down, rubbing her hands over her face. "I think something's wrong with me."

She thinks there's something wrong with her?

There's absolutely nothing wrong with her.

She's perfect.

"Why do you say that?"

Scarlett takes a deep breath, closing her eyes. "The things I'm dreaming about..." She glances at the screen. "They're not thoughts that someone like me should be having."

"Someone like you?"

"Someone broken!" Scarlett's eyes widen from her outburst. She wraps her arms around her torso, rocking back and forth. "I'm...sorry. I shouldn't have shouted."

"Scarlett, this is a safe space. This is your time to talk so we can unpack everything together."

Scarlett nods, deep in thought.

"Can you tell me what these dreams are about?"

Scarlett's knee stops bouncing as she runs her hands back and forth on her thighs. "They're usually about...my husband."

I freeze. Did I hear her correctly?

She said she dreams about...me?

"And why is this upsetting you?"

"Someone like me shouldn't have thoughts of..."

"Thoughts of?"

Thoughts of what I almost scream out loud.

A blush spreads over Scarlett's porcelain cheeks. "Sex."

Sex.

I mold back into the chair, my body suddenly feeling heavy. My wife is dreaming about sex with me.

Suddenly, my pants feel about one size too small, and I quickly adjust my position.

"There is absolutely nothing to be embarrassed about. Sex is a completely normal and healthy way of expressing our emotions. Especially toward a loved one like your husband."

"You don't understand... After everything that happened to me... After what *he* did to me, I shouldn't be having these thoughts. I shouldn't want to be touched or kissed or..." She swallows nervously. "But with Leo, I get these feelings that I haven't felt in years... Urges. And I don't know what to do. I don't know if I should act on them or ignore them. It's...overwhelming. Sometimes, I wake up in the middle of the night from a dream with him in it, and all I want to do is go to him. Run to his room. But I stop myself." She shakes her head; tears slowly run down her cheeks.

My heart cracks at her admission.

She's needed me, but she's been too scared to tell me.

"And why don't you?" Dr. Raven asks.

She bites her bottom lip. "I just...can't."

"Why not?"

She rubs her temple, her fingers digging into her scalp. "He doesn't want to touch me." She lets out a resigned sigh. "He told me so. On our wedding night, when we came home, he told me he wouldn't touch me. And he's stuck true to his word. Only doing so when necessary. Holding my hand, pressing kisses to my forehead, but nothing more than that. And why would he want to after what I went through? I can't blame him. I probably disgust him." She wipes at her eyes. "We went out to dinner last night, and someone who knows Leo...intimately came up to our table. She was stunning. And it killed me to know that she had been with my husband in that way." She shakes her head. "I can't help but feel like I'm not enough for him. Like I'm not good enough for him. Maybe once I was, but now... Well, I don't think he wants me in that way anymore. Not like he used to. And I'm trying to be okay with that." Tears stream down her cheeks. "I don't understand what he's getting out of this marriage with me," she whispers that last part, sounding so utterly defeated.

And it breaks me. It fucking shreds my heart to pieces.

My fist slams down on the arm of the chair.

I'm fucking stupid.

The only reason I told her I wouldn't touch her was so she knew she didn't have to fear me. After everything she went through, I assumed she would need space and be repulsed by my touch. But maybe if she knew how I'd spent every night for years thinking of her and only her, she would know that disgust is the furthest thing from my mind when she's in it.

"Scarlett, you have confided in me that, seven years ago, you were intimate with this man. You expressed that you felt safe with him. Close with him. Cared for by him. Perhaps, after living through so much trauma, you're unknowingly seeking that same feeling you experienced with him previously because it's comforting and familiar to you," Dr. Raven states.

Scarlett holds her head in her hands. "Maybe." She drops her hands, fidgeting with the hem of her shirt. "I'm just so confused about the physical part of our marriage. And to be honest..." Her gaze returns to the screen. "I'm scared."

"Then talk to him. Tell him everything you've been telling me. Take time to sit down with him and let him know how you're feeling about all of it. He could feel just as confused as you are, but neither of you will know unless you talk things out in an open dialogue. A relationship won't succeed if there isn't communication."

I turn off my phone and slide it into my pocket, having heard everything I needed to hear. Loud and fucking clear.

Scarlett needs me.

My wife needs me.

I jump up from the chair, throwing my jacket on as I stride outside toward my bike.

"Where are you going?" I hear Vin yell behind me, but I don't stop.

Not when only one woman has ever taken up all the space in my cold, dark, beating heart.

And it's about damn time she knows the damn truth.

Scarlett Alarie is mine, and there wasn't a moment in the past seven years when she wasn't.

Shoving through the front door, I glance around, unbuttoning the top buttons on my shirt, my chest feeling too tight. My eyes immediately spot Scarlett through the glass wall on the deck, enjoying her favorite swinging chair with a book in her hands.

It kills me to know that I've filled her head with insecurities and doubts. Ones that are entirely inaccurate to the narrative of our story, and I'll be damned if I let them fester inside her for a second longer.

It's time she knows the damn truth.

I slide the glass door open with too much force, the wall reverberating beside me.

Scarlett drops the book in her lap with a small gasp, her hand slamming against her chest. She lets out a relieved sigh once she sees me, a beautiful smile tugging up on her lips. "Leo, you're—" Her smile falters as she stands, her eyes scouring over my predatory stance. "What's wrong?"

My chest heaves with each passing second. I'm ashamed I let it get this far. Boring my sight into her sapphire irises, I say, "You need to know."

Her brows furrow. She rolls in her bottom lip, confusion written all over her face. "Know what?"

"My heart has only ever broken once in my life." I point toward the north side of the property, directly toward the entrance at the front of the estate. "And it was when I was forced to watch you leave through the front gates, unable to do a goddamn thing about it. I watched you leave, and it nearly killed me, Scarlett. I was in such a bad place mentally after my father's death, lost in a cloud of darkness. A darkness that has only grown throughout the years... But the moment you left..." My heart thumps wildly in my chest, coming to life for the first time in years. "That was the moment I lost all the light in my life."

Her lips part, her shining eyes widening from my admission. "What..." She bites down on her bottom lip, blinking back tears. "What are you saying?"

"I'm saying..." I pace toward her, realizing what I'm about to do should have been done the second she was back in my sight. I stand before her, our chests grazing as she looks up at me with something I haven't seen in years floating across her eyes. "That you were always mine. Even when you left, you were still mine, Firefly."

Reaching into my pocket, I pull out the folded document I've been holding on to—our marriage contract. The one giving us an out in this marriage. An end date to us. But there will never be an end between me and her.

As I shred it before her, letting the pieces float to the ground between us, her beautiful eyes lock onto mine, relief and longing swirling in her blue orbs.

It's at this moment I know that I should have never promised not to touch her.

"Fuck it," I breathe. My lips land hard on hers as I taste her for the first time in years. I wait for her to pull away or push at my chest. I'm ready to stop the second she needs me to, but instead, she fists the fabric of my shirt, pulling me closer to her as if every part of her has been waiting for this moment as much as I have. Her lips part, allowing me access, my tongue sweeping over hers. I wrap my arms around her waist as she moans into our kiss.

With reluctance, I pull away, pressing our foreheads together. "I want you, Scarlett. I want you so fucking badly it physically hurts. And I'm sorry if I ever gave you a reason to think I didn't. But I didn't want to scare you. I didn't want you to fear me." My thumb runs under her eyes, brushing away the loose tears. "It would destroy me to cause you any more pain. More heartache." I brush my lips against hers, savoring her sweetness. "Our time together under the stars was the best moment of my life. A memory I'll cherish until my last breath on this earth. So don't, for one minute, ever doubt my feelings for you when I've only ever wanted you. Only you."

She clutches my shirt, pressing her face into my chest. "I needed to hear that."

"I know, baby." I smooth out her hair, kissing the top of her head. "I'm so fucking sorry. I should have told you sooner." She sobs into my shirt, holding on to me for dear life. "I've got you, Scarlett. I've always got you."

After a few minutes of holding her tightly in my arms and never wanting to let go, she leans away and looks up at me. "I take it this means you heard everything I said in therapy today?" The playful grin she shows confirms she's not mad at me.

"Yeah. But I needed to know what was going on in here." I cup her cheeks, kissing the top of her head.

"I'm sorry. I should have told you. I just didn't know how to bring it up or what to say." She rests her hands on my chest. "I've been very confused. Feeling things when I'm with you that I'm not entirely sure I should be feeling." She shakes her head, a few loose strands falling out of place, framing her face. "I want to...do things with you. I just don't know what I'm ready for or how much I can handle. But I'd like to try." She looks downcast, defeat weighing heavily on her. "My mind is just all over the place."

I reach out, lightly gripping her chin with two fingers. She softens into my hold as I tilt her head toward me. "I will give you whatever you desire. All you need to do is tell me what you want and how you want it. We play by your rules. You control the speed of our marriage. You run the show. Not me. You."

Her features relax as her eyes meet mine. "Thank you for being so patient with me. I'm sorry that you got coerced into this marriage."

"Coerced?" I question. "Is that what you think?"

She nods, glancing down.

I sweep her hair back, tucking it behind her ear. "Remember when you asked me why I married you?"

"Yeah." She bites her bottom lip. "I still don't understand why you did when you gained nothing from it."

I place my hands on her cheeks, bracing her face before me. My eyes bore into hers, my lips curving up. "I've got you, Firefly." I press a kiss on her forehead, a foreign sense of warmth forming in the center of my chest. "I've got you."

CHAPTER ELEVEN

Scarlett

A knock at the front door causes me to drop my book in my lap. Brutus, previously sound asleep, jumps up beside me, growling. A second later, I hear the door swing open, my heart racing, even knowing Eli is stationed outside and won't let anything happen to me.

"Hello?"

My body relaxes from the familiar, sweet voice of Mrs. Alarie.

"There you are." She smiles as she saunters over to me, appearing elegant as ever in a navy shift dress.

I stand, smiling. "To what do I owe this surprise visit?"

"Oh, I hope you don't mind that I stopped by unannounced, but I was just on my way to pick up Madeleine to join me on a visit to the St. Elizabeth Jean's Center for Women and Children when she, unfortunately, had to cancel. I have so much to bring over there that I was wondering if you might be available to help me?" Her hand finds the top of Brutus's head as he angles it for scratches behind his ear.

"Oh, umm..." I tuck my hair behind my ear, my gaze darting to the ground. Why would a place like that want someone like me to step inside their doors? I'm sure the neon sign above my head, blinking *broken*, would probably deter everyone from me.

"It'll be a quick drop-off. Back before you even know it," she says, arching a brow while giving me her best smile. A smile that no one would ever be able to say no to. Least of all me.

The corners of my lips tug up. "Sure. Let me grab my bag." I place my bookmark in my book and then give Brutus a quick scratch on his head. "I'll make sure to give you extra tummy rubs when I get home."

Her hands clasp together. "Oh, wonderful!" She looks down at Brutus, scratching his chin. "Are you okay if I borrow her from you for a little?"

He barks once, making us both laugh.

Thirty minutes later, we pull up to a large brick building. My stomach tightens at the sight. Cement blocks surround the structure, making it look almost like a prison with no signs of any plants or colors. I step out of the car that Eli drove us in and meet Mrs. Alarie by the SUV trunk.

"I can help with those," Eli offers.

"I'm sorry, Eli, but I'm going to have to ask you to stay outside." Mrs. Alarie frowns. Eli's face scrunches together as he shakes his head, appearing ready to disagree. "Most women in here are not comfortable with the presence of a man. You may scare them without even intending to."

He squeezes the back of his neck, examining the sidewalk. "I understand. I'll wait right outside the front door. Is there any other entrance to this building?"

"I believe there is a back exit."

"Okay." He pulls out his phone. "I'll have Alex hack into the camera system to keep an eye on the back."

Mrs. Alarie smiles. "Great." She turns toward me. "Shall we?"

I follow closely behind her as we approach the front door and step inside the small vestibule. An older woman with pure white hair, sitting behind the plexiglass window, looks up from her paperwork.

Sliding open the window, she says, "Mrs. Alarie, I didn't realize you would be joining us today."

"Oh, I just had some things I've been meaning to drop off." Her eyes glance over to me. "I've brought my daughter-in-law here with me today for some assistance. Scarlett, this is Mrs. Webber."

"It's a pleasure to meet you, Mrs. Webber."

A wide grin pulls at her face. "Just call me Betty, child." She presses a button on the wall beside her, and the door at the end of the hall unlocks. She meets us on the other side, holding the door open for us. As we step through, my eyes take in the lively room filled with vibrant colors and plants, appearing nothing like the mundane display outside.

"Welcome to St. Elizabeth Jean's Center for Women and Children," Betty says, taking a few bags from my hands and leaving me with only one small one. "Follow me this way. Do you two have time for a little tour?"

"Oh, I'm not—"

"Of course," Mrs. Alarie remarks, answering for the both of us.

I suppose a short little tour won't hurt.

Betty begins walking through the room, pointing things out on the way. "Over here, we have the game room. On Tuesdays, we run a bingo night that can get pretty crazy. Prizes range from a five-dollar coffee gift card all the way up to a toaster oven." She chuckles to herself as we continue walking. "In this section, we have the mental health rooms where a nearby therapist comes several times a week for appointments or walk-in visits. Many women here need someone to talk to, and we pride ourselves on always making this an available resource for our residents." My free arm wraps around my mid-section, knowing how much it's helped me to have someone like Dr. Raven to talk to. I couldn't imagine not having that resource available. We pass a few people who Betty works with and introduces us to. She seems to know every face in the place. "Down that hall leads to the apartments."

"Apartments?" I ask.

Betty nods. "Many women and children who come here need a warm bed and a roof over their head. Some come because they can't afford anywhere else. Some come seeking refuge from an abusive partner. And many simply come because they have nowhere else to turn in a time of need." She looks sorrowfully down at the bags in her hands. "Unfortunately, it's just not possible to have enough rooms for everyone who needs one, but we do the best we can to get the women the help they need so that they're able to use these units as a source of transitional housing before heading on their way. A quicker turnaround makes it possible for us to help more people. The more resources we can offer, the better chance of getting someone a new start on the right foot." She gives a big smile, and the optimism radiating off her feels pretty contagious.

"What kinds of resources are offered here?" I ask, curious as this is not at all what I had been envisioning.

She blows out a breath of air as we come to a stop. "Where to start? Well, besides the mental health rooms, we also offer assistance for those who may be struggling with drug or substance addiction. We offer affordable healthcare resources with an onsite doctor. We have counselors ready to assist with the transition from living in temporary housing to finding a permanent home. We have career counselors who aid in job advancement and help with anything from setting up a resume to landing an interview. We provide financial support to as many residents as possible who would like to attend college courses. We provide three meals a day served through our food pantry. Much of the food is locally produced or donated from neighboring restaurants and grocery stores." She looks out of breath when she turns to me with a big smile. "Should I keep going?"

My lips part in shock. I had no idea all of that would take place somewhere like this. "That's amazing that you guys are able to do so much for the people here."

"We do what we can with what we have. We're always grateful for people like you two who take the time to come here and spread your generosity. We wouldn't be the place we are today without people like that." She points a finger at Mrs. Alarie. "Especially this one."

"Oh, stop." Mrs. Alarie waves a dismissive hand. "I just do what I can."

"Betty! I'm so glad I found you." A petite woman wearing a hairnet rushes up to us. "We're short-staffed in the cafeteria today. Is there any way you might be able to lend a hand?"

Betty shakes her head. "I have to get up to the front desk for coverage. It's just Debra up there now." Her brows scrunch together, deep in thought.

"If you need help," Mrs. Alarie starts, "Scarlett and I can lend a hand."

Anxiety spears me. I've never cooked a damn thing in my life. Sure, I can throw together a salad or boil spaghetti until cooked al dente. But this? I rub my wedding band nervously. What if I fail at this? What if I let everyone down?

Betty shakes her head. "I couldn't ask you to do that."

"Well, if you can't," the other woman begins to say, "I can. Any chance you two wouldn't mind getting dirty in some elbow grease and helping a poor old lady like me serve up some lunch?"

Betty scoffs. "You're younger than me."

"I didn't say you weren't old either."

The two of them chuckle at that.

Mrs. Alarie looks at me. "What do you say, Scarlett?"

I suck in my bottom lip, glancing around before saying, "Sure."

A few minutes later, I find myself donning a hairnet and sporting an apron tied around my waist. Clutching a silver serving spoon, I prepare to serve mac and cheese on people's trays.

Deep breath in. I've got this. I can do this. I will be the best mac and cheese server this place has ever seen. Deep breath out.

"Yay! I love mac and cheese," a little girl squeals as she reaches my station. The woman beside her, who I assume is her mother, beams, looking down at her as if she's her whole world.

And I suddenly understand that she probably is.

The woman's fading blue bruise around her eye catches my attention, but I quickly drop my gaze before she notices me staring and glimpse down at the girl. "Want to know a secret?"

The girl nods her head eagerly.

"I love mac and cheese, too."

The girl's mouth opens wide. "No way!"

"Yes way." I grin, scooping a healthy portion onto her plate.

"Even as an adult?"

I chuckle. "Even as an adult."

After the line is served, Mrs. Alarie walks over to me, and it's a sight to behold. Her navy shift dress is hidden behind a giant neon pink apron. Her dark hair is pushed back behind a hairnet. And her hands are completely covered in bright yellow gloves. "Well, I think I just gave those dishes a run for their money." She smiles as she removes the hairnet, her perfectly coiffed hair falling back into its original place.

"If anyone can pull off this look, it's you," I tease.

She examines her reflection on the giant stainless-steel fridge's surface. "It is quite the look." She removes the gloves from her hands and rests her hip against the counter. "What do you think?"

I peer over the room; many people are still enjoying their meals. A sense of pride fills me, knowing I helped with this. "It's pretty amazing what they're doing here."

"It is." Her hands reach behind her, untying the apron. "I try to get over here as much as I can, but I'm ashamed to admit that it's been a while since my last visit."

"I heard you two were the dream team over here." Betty walks up to us with a glass of water in her hands for both of us. "If only there were more people out there who'd be willing to help out like this."

I remove the hairnet, tucking my hair behind both ears. "You know, I was thinking, I have time on my hands if you need help with anything. I don't know what I could be good for, but..." I give a slight shrug. "I'm available."

Betty beams. "Well, isn't that something? We were just saying upfront that we need someone to come and read to the children on Mondays and Wednesdays in the afternoon. Is that something you might be interested in?"

"Yeah." I nod enthusiastically. "I would love that."

"Then it's settled." Mrs. Alarie smooths out her skirt. "Sign me up for whatever you need, Betty. I'll come with Scarlett on those days."

Betty pulls out her phone. "Let's get the schedule figured out."

"Excuse me?" I peek over the display case to find the same little girl from earlier. "Do you happen to have any more mac and cheese? I'm extra hungry today. My mom says I'm going through a growth spurt."

I laugh. "You're in luck because I do." I scoop a serving into a bowl for her and hand it over.

"Would you want to come have lunch with us?" she asks.

"Oh, I don't know if I'm allowed—"

"Go on," Betty says. "We'll figure out the schedule in the back room."

I look back at the little girl and say, "Lead the way." I scoop myself a small bowl of mac and cheese and walk over to the table where her mom waits. "Is it okay if I sit here?"

"Of course." She gestures to the seat across from her.

"I'm Scarlett," I tell them as I sit.

"I'm Willow," the little girl points to herself. "And this is my mom."

Her mom laughs. "You can call me Celeste."

"It's nice to meet you," I respond before taking a bite of my food.

"Mommy doesn't have any friends here. So I thought if you ate with us, you could be friends."

Willow's words cause her mom's cheeks to heat up, and her gaze travels down to her plate.

"I don't have many friends either." I give a slight shrug. "Friends are hard to make as adults."

Willow looks sad. "They are?"

I nod. "So it was good that you asked me to sit with you, or I wouldn't have had anyone to eat my lunch with."

Celeste smiles at me and then looks at her daughter. "Hey, Willow, isn't that Amber over in the corner playing in the princess's dream house?" Willow's eyes widen, an excited smile lighting up her face. "Go on," Celeste says with a grin.

Willow jumps from her seat and scurries over to the other child.

Celeste gives a slight chuckle. "Sorry, my daughter has this lovely habit of just saying whatever is on her mind to anyone."

I wave a hand dismissively. "Don't worry. She's adorable, really."

"Thank you." She cuts a piece of her meatloaf, and my eyes catch on the knife. The metal glimmers under the lights above, and I swallow down my nervous energy. Quickly, my eyes move to hers. "So, did you just arrive here for temporary housing or...?"

"Oh no." I shake my head, placing my fork down. "I came with my mother-in-law to help her drop some things off. But it looks like I also just signed myself up for visits to read to the children."

She nods, her brows furrowing. "So, you're married?"

"Yes." I instinctively twist the wedding band on my finger.

"And he's good to you?"

I blink a few times, a little taken aback by her question. "He's—"

"Sorry." She runs her fingers through her brown hair. "That was completely inappropriate of me to ask." She taps the table, giving a half smile. "I guess you see where my daughter gets it from."

I smile. "No. It's fine." I lift my fork, twirling it through my bowl. "My husband is very good to me."

She nods. "You're lucky." She points to her eye, the one with the fading bruise. "I've never been able to say that before."

"I'm sorry," I immediately reply. An ache extends across my chest, wishing there was more that I could say or offer than those two words. A phantom-like stab slashes me across the back, and I realize Celeste and I might have more in common than she realizes.

She just can't see my scars like I can see hers.

"Don't be." She sits back in her chair, folding her arms over her chest. "I should have known better. But we're here, and we're safe. And that's all that matters now." Her eyes search across the room, hooking onto her daughter. "I will do whatever it takes to keep her safe. Even if that, unfortunately, means keeping her away from her father."

"Scarlett, dear," Mrs. Alarie calls over. "Are you ready to get going?"

I look back at Celeste. "Will you be here next week?"

"I'm not sure. We just arrived here three days ago and started going through the motions of everything."

"Well, if you are," I start, "I'd love to have lunch with you again."

She smiles, and I notice a slight glimmer in her eyes. "I'd like that a lot."

"Great." I stand, removing my apron. "It was really nice to meet you. Hopefully, we'll see each other again." I turn and make my way toward Mrs. Alarie.

"Everything okay?" she asks.

"It is." I gather my hair together, twisting it into a loose bun on the top of my head. "Thank you for inviting me today. I think I needed this."

She smiles warmly. "Then it's a good thing you were available to help me today."

I side-eye her, crossing my arms over my chest. "You were never bringing Madeleine here with you, were you?"

She grins, looping her arm through mine as we walk out. "I guess you'll never know."

Walking through the front door, I gravitate toward Leo's office, knowing that's where I'll find him. I knock on the wooden door, slightly pushing it open, revealing him sitting behind his desk, looking out the window, deep in thought.

His face softens as soon as he sees me, his tired eyes shining slightly brighter.

I walk over to him, needing to be near him. Needing to be in his arms. The place I have always felt safest.

"Hey, how did everything go with—"

I cut his words off when I take him by surprise, sitting on his lap, wrapping my arms around his neck, and crashing my lips to his.

For the first time in our marriage, I initiate a kiss.

And I instantly regret not doing this sooner.

He's tense beneath me, but only for a moment. Once he relaxes, his arms wrap around me, pulling me closer to him. The taste of his lips instantly calms me. It soothes the aches within me. The pain that no one can ever see from the outside.

After a moment, we separate, and I stare into his eyes, getting lost in the darkness.

"Not that I didn't love that, but what was that for?" He brushes my hair down my back and then kisses the tip of my nose. "Is everything okay?"

I lift a shoulder and then let it drop. "I missed my husband."

His eyes darken. "Say that again." His voice comes out husky and deep, desire laced in each word.

The corners of my lips lift. "I." I kiss the tip of his nose. "Missed." I kiss each one of his cheeks. "My." I lean up, kissing his forehead. "Husband." My lips press to his, and I part them, welcoming his eager tongue. His hand grips the back of my head, his thumb massaging my scalp as we take a moment to explore and taste. When he sucks on my bottom lip, I find myself letting out a whimper. His lips travel down my neck, spreading goose bumps all over my body like an electric current that can't be shut off. I feel my nipples harden against my bra, and wetness pools between my legs.

"I could spend all day kissing you," he breathes against my neck as he kisses, nips, and sucks every inch.

In a haze, I start to grind against him, seeking friction, and then suddenly freeze, my whole body going tense. My eyes blink open, and as if Leo knows my body better than I do, he stops his ministrations and cups my cheek.

"Hey, are you okay?"

"Yeah." I swallow. "I think I was just getting carried away."

He shakes his head. "There's no such thing as getting carried away with me." His lips turn down, noticing my reluctance. "Remember, we play by your rules. Not mine." He kisses my chin. "You run the show. Not me."

I relax in his hold, resting my head on his shoulder. "You make everything so easy for me."

He laughs. "Is that a bad thing?"

"No." I glance up at him. "Sometimes being married to you doesn't feel real." He smooths out my hair, twirling a piece around his finger. "When I was out with your mom at the women and children's center today… Well, there were a lot of women there. Women who had nowhere else to go. Women who were…"

"Abused," he answers for me.

I nod. "I had lunch with this woman who had a bruise on her face. And I just knew right away what it was from." A single tear escapes, and before I have a chance to wipe it away, Leo does it for me. "It's hard for me to wrap my head around the fact that there are men out there who feel it's okay to abuse women."

"Those men are not men at all. They're weak cowards who prey on innocent targets. They get a power high, bringing down those who are physically weaker than them. They're monsters."

His arms tighten around me as if protecting me from outside forces.

"And then there's you," I say softly, my eyes meeting his. My heart pumps in my chest as I look at the man before me who would do anything for me. "You'd burn the world down for me if I asked you. Wouldn't you?"

His lips graze my temple. "I'd burn it to ash and await your next request." He places the palm of my hand over his heart. I can feel his mirroring my own. "My heart may beat beneath my chest, but it's you who owns it. It's yours to do with whatever you please."

Without hesitation, his lips land hard on mine, consuming me whole, and I find myself unable to get enough of him, but also not knowing how far to take this. As if sensing my internal conflict, Leo pulls back and rolls our foreheads together. His breaths come out fast and hot as his hands grip my waist, reining in his control.

His hand slides up my back, a gentle caress with each stroke.

"I wish you didn't have to leave tomorrow," I whisper.

He informed me last night he needed to leave for a few days to take care of some business without giving me any details. But I know, in my gut, who it has to do with: the monster in my nightmares. So, I don't question him for specifics, especially knowing Leo probably wouldn't even tell me them anyway, not wanting to cause me any fear. But since our marriage, this will be the first time he's spent a night away from me. And although we don't share a bed, it still leaves me feeling slightly more alone than usual. I tuck my head into the crook of his neck, inhaling his familiar, comforting scent—leather and sandalwood.

His nose nestles over my hair, his lips peppering the top of my head with kisses. "I'll be back as soon as I can. Eli and Mauro will both be here for you, switching shifts. If you need me for anything, call me. Okay?"

"Okay." I brush my lips against his neck. "Promise you'll come back for me."

"I promise, Firefly. I'll always come back for you."

CHAPTER TWELVE

Leo

"Anything?"

"Nothing," Vin answers, holding his custom AK-47 tucked against his right shoulder as he peers through the night scope. "Not a single damn boat in the vicinity."

Alex pushes his night vision goggles to the top of his head. "I don't get it." He holds up his wrist, checking his watch. "It's after midnight. He was supposed to be here by now."

"Patience, grasshopper," Vin murmurs.

"Don't give me that grasshopper bullshit." Alex rubs his hands together. "Something doesn't feel right."

"You're just uneasy because your shirt is wrinkled." Vin looks away from the scope and smirks.

"Fuck you!" Alex smooths out the front of his shirt. "It's not my fault that I actually care about how I present myself. I mean, look at you." He waves his hand at him incredulously. "You look like you just rolled around in the mud with the pigs."

"It's called camouflage. And I'll have you know I paid a pretty penny for this shit." His eyes zoom in on Alex's shirt. "Is that a mustard stain?"

"What? Where?" Alex frantically pulls at the fabric, twisting it from side to side.

Vin hunches over, laughing, clutching the gun to his chest. "It's too easy."

I pinch the bridge of my nose. "Fucking hell. You two are the worst. Please explain to me why I got stuck here with Tweedledee and Tweedledum?"

"You were the one who asked Mauro to babysit for you," Vin remarks, wiping tears from his eyes.

I grit my teeth. "He's not fucking babysitting. He's running opposite shifts with Eli since I can't be there."

Vin shrugs. "Whatever you want to call it."

Alex clasps my shoulder. "As much as we joke around, you know we won't let you down. Scarlett's our family."

I nod. "I know."

As we wait, Vin gets back in position, aiming his rifle directly at the docks. "So." He cracks his neck. "How are things between you and the wife?"

Alex throws a rag over an old milk crate and sits on it.

"Good," I offer, leaning on the windowsill.

"Good?" Vin repeats. "Ice cream is good. Money is good. But I'm asking you, how is your marriage?"

I squeeze the back of my neck. "It's a one-day-at-a-time thing. All I can do is be patient and be there for her, which I think is helping. But sometimes I feel like I have no fucking clue what I'm doing and that I'm just going to make everything worse for her." I turn and lean back, folding my arms over my chest. "I took her out on a date the other night. To the White Table, thinking that's what she would want. But she seemed intimidated by everyone there. And then…" I tilt my head up to stare at the ceiling that appears ready to collapse at any moment.

"What?' Alex asks.

I rub a hand down my face. "Natasha was there."

"Fucking Natasha." Vin groans. "She certainly knows how to ruin a night."

I sigh. "You could say that. But actually, I think it might have helped."

"What do you mean?" Alex swipes at some dirt on his pants.

"Scarlett thought I wasn't into her. She got this idea in her head that she repulsed me, which was most definitely my fault, and I sort of heard her tell her therapist this and well..." I glance at my brothers. "It gave me the kick in the ass that I needed to tell her how I feel."

Vin nods in understanding. "Sometimes we need a little kick in the ass to see things the right way."

"Do you love her?" Alex asks, no humor on his face.

The question should take me aback. I should feel uncomfortable even talking about emotions and feelings amongst my brothers like a couple of teenage girls, but instead, I answer truthfully. There's no use denying it any longer.

"I never stopped."

Vin takes a step toward me and clasps my shoulder. "I'm happy for you. For both of you. You deserve each other. Things will take time after everything she's been through, but when the time is right, everything will fall into place as it should be."

I run my fingers through my hair. "She deserves the whole world. I just don't know how to give it to her."

"You could start with a redo of that first date," Alex offers. "Scarlett's never been into that fancy shit, and you know it. She likes simple things."

"Simple things," I repeat, taking in his suggestion. My mind slowly churns a plan in my head. One I think Scarlett may actually enjoy this time. "You're right."

Static comes through the handheld transceiver.

"We have a visual on an approaching vessel." Sergio's voice comes in muffled.

I bring the device to my lips. "Remember, stand down until we give the word. We don't want to risk missing our shot or scaring him off."

"Yes, boss."

"Where's Dolion?"

"His gun jammed, so he went back to the vehicle to get a new weapon, but that was about fifteen minutes ago. I haven't seen him since— Never mind, sir. He's entering the building now."

"Good. Give him my message."

The line goes silent as we all line up at the window, waiting. Vin tightens his grip on his gun as he patiently watches the spot right around the bend. It's the only opening for a boat to come in and out of, which means we won't miss him. Alex has the transponder in his hand, ready to transmit the signal to the bombs he had mounted under the docks earlier today. And I wait to give the orders, with blood boiling beneath my skin, ready to end this motherfucker once and for all.

"The boat is coming in slowly, heading directly toward the dock." Vin redirects his scope, his sight narrowing in on the hooded figure driving the boat. "Wait a minute." Vin looks at me with concern etched in his features. "We have a problem."

"What do you mean?" I ask, lowering my gun.

He puts the handgun in my free hand so I can look into the scope. I zoom in on the figure. "*Cazzo!*"

Shoving the gun back into Vin's chest, I turn to Alex. "Don't fucking hit that button."

"What?" Alex removes his goggles. "Why?"

"Because that's not Le Diable on the boat. It's a dead guy taped down to the steering wheel." I grip the radio, watching as the boat veers off course, heading straight toward the warehouse where Dolion and Sergio are positioned. "Get out of the warehouse now!" I roar.

There's no answer from Sergio or Dolion.

"I repeat, get the fuck out of the warehouse!"

"Sir," Sergio starts. "It's—"

I watch in stunned silence as the boat launches in the air, careening right into the warehouse. The second it makes contact, a ball of fire explodes around everything. Half of the building catches fire, while the other half crumbles under the weight, transforming into tattered pieces of debris.

My entire being freezes as if I'm reliving the same nightmare from seven years ago.

The SUV stops in front of our warehouse, where my father arrives to inspect the latest shipment of weapons delivered hours earlier. The moon shines down, casting an eerie glow around the building. Mauro and my father stride to the main door of the warehouse as both Dolion and I step out of the car and lean against it.

I glance down at my phone. My thumb hovers over Scarlett's name. I should call her and make sure she got home safely. She wouldn't let me bring her home, insisting she could get there herself, but it still didn't feel right to me.

Pressing send, I clutch the phone to my ear, waiting to hear her sweet voice, but it immediately goes to voicemail. Strange. I try again, but the same thing happens. Maybe she's sleeping, too exhausted from tonight's activities. A smile pulls at my lips, remembering every second of our time together. How smooth her skin felt under the rough pads of my fingers. Her soft whimpers of pleasure. The way her eyes bore into mine as she came around my cock, screaming my name.

The trust she gave me.

At that moment, I felt like her protector.

And I knew I would never let anything happen to her.

I will always keep her safe.

Because she's mine.

Sliding my phone into my pocket, I look up and see my father enter the building with Mauro right behind him.

Boom!

I'm knocked off my feet, a red-hot force like I've never felt before shoving me against the car that's now rolled over on its side. A ringing in my ears is all I hear as I grip the metal behind me, my vision blurry. I reach a hand to my head and bring it before my eyes, seeing blood coating my skin. I blink a few times, shaking my head, hoping to regain my focus, but it only makes it worse. Taking a step, I wobble at first before taking a few more. My eyes scan the scene before me, seeking out my brother and father.

"Dad! Mauro!" I scream.

Fire surrounds me as I panic, searching for them, until finally, my eyes land on Mauro. I run to him with a slight limp. As I approach, I notice the massive amount of blood surrounding him.

"Mauro!" His eyes blink. "I'm going to get you out of here." I lift him under his arms and drag him toward the car, placing him beside it. Ripping off my shirt, I press it to the deep cut in his throat, which seems to have the most damage. With a shaky hand, I pull out my phone, press one, and hold it to my ear.

Vin picks up after the first ring. "What the hell is taking you guys so long? I want to go—"

"We've been attacked," I rush out. "Send help, now!" I end the call, not giving him a chance to respond. He has our locations on his phone, and I know help will be available in a matter of minutes. I take Mauro's hand in mine and clasp it over the material that is quickly soaking up the blood. His skin is ghostly white, his lips transforming to a shade of blue. "Hold this. I'll be right back. I need to find Dad."

I jump to my feet, running back toward the building.

"Dad!" I roar, my eyes frantically scanning everywhere.

"Here!" His voice comes from inside the quickly burning warehouse. Relief immediately fills me.

He's alive.

My dad's alive.

But as I make it to the entrance, I find burning beams blocking the path. "Cazzo!" I pace the side, looking for another way inside, but there are no windows and nothing I can scale to gain access.

I make it back to the front. "Dad! Where are you?"

"Over here!"

I lean over the beams, seeing my father's form hunched over about ten feet away. There's a cascade of blood gushing down the side of his head. I reach my arm over the debris. "Come on, Dad. We need to get you out of here." I look up at the remaining building, seeming ready to fall at any second. My father tries to stand but immediately falls to the ground, coughing up a storm through the thick black smoke.

"My foot. It's broken," he gets out, gasping for air.

A loud creak above us fills my stomach with dread. "Dad, get up. Now." My throat tightens painfully, my eyes misting over. "Please, Dad. I need you... I need you to get up." We both hear a second groan from the beams above, preparing to give out.

A small ball of fire falls from the rafters, landing directly on my hand. "Shit!" I shake my hand and wipe it across my pants, not caring what the damage is. The only thing I care about is getting my father out of here. Right the fuck now.

"Dad. Please." The ball of emotions lodges in my throat. "Please fight. Fight for your family. We need you." I try to lift the beam, fighting through the pain of heat seeping over my skin, but it's useless. It must weigh at least half a ton, if not more.

The sound of tires screeching to a halt nearby lifts my spirits.

Help has arrived.

We'll be okay.

"Help is here. We'll get you out, Dad." I rub the back of my forearm across my face. As my arms drop to my side, my eyes catch with his, and at that exact moment, a beam directly above him begins to splinter.

"I've always been so proud of you, Leo." He smiles, his eyes filling with tears. "You'll be okay. I know you will be." A cough attack overtakes him before he says, "Tell everyone how much…how much I love them."

"Dad, no!"

The weight of the roof collapses on top of my father just as I'm pulled away, Dolion appearing behind me, tugging me back to ensure I'm out of harm's way.

"Dad!" I roar, dropping to my knees.

As Mauro was transported to the nearest hospital by helicopter with Alex by his side, and Vin raced home to tell Mom and put the family in lockdown as the new head of the family, I sat there through all the chaos, watching as men watered down the burning rubble until they doused every last flame.

My father's remains were nothing more than wet ash.

A black car drove by me.

Blue eyes pleaded with me to save her.

But I was too consumed with grief.

So I let her go.

All the light became lost within me.

Only darkness remained.

"Holy shit," Alex breathes, waking me from my trance.

I internally shake my head. "We need to get over there!"

The three of us immediately race out, heading directly to the scene.

"Sergio! Dolion!" I yell over and over again. My eyes scan the surroundings, but there's too much smoke to see much of anything.

"Over here!" Vin points at a body crawling out from under debris.

Dolion.

Vin grabs him underneath his arms and drags his body away from the building. He coughs up a storm as he sits up, wiping his forehead with the back of his arm.

"Are you okay?" Vin asks.

"I'm fine." He shakes his head. "The boat wouldn't stop. It came directly for us as if on an automated course."

"Where's Sergio?" I ask, dread already pooling in my gut.

Dolion's eyes look downcast. "He didn't make it."

My fist connects with a splintered piece of wood beside me as I roar into the night. Blood trails down my cracked knuckles as pain overtakes me.

Sergio died.

He died under my watch.

Under my protection.

Alex clasps my shoulder. "We should get out of here."

"Yeah." I look around, hearing sirens in the distance, when something occurs to me. "How did he know we would be here?"

Vin scratches his temple, looking off at the water. "Maybe there was something we missed." He glances back at me. "He's playing games with us. And we need to quickly learn how to outplay him."

I roll my neck, every muscle bunched up in tension. "Let's go." I stride hastily, wanting to get the fuck out of here.

"Hey." Vin stops me, pulling on my arm as Alex and Dolion continue toward the SUV. "This is a part of the job—a part of our world. And Sergio knew that. He always knew that, but he did it anyway because he was loyal to our family."

"It doesn't make it any better."

"I know." He shrugs. "But his death isn't on you, Leo. And neither was Dad's."

My heart stops as my eyes jump to his face. "Don't—"

"I fucking will." Vin crosses his arms over his chest. "I saw your eyes when the boat hit this place. But you weren't in the here and now; you saw the warehouse from seven years ago burning down." He sighs, dropping his arms. "You had no way of getting to Dad. If you had somehow managed to get inside that warehouse, it would have fallen on top of you, too, and you know it. And this family would have lost two members that day instead of one." His features soften. "The only person who blames you for Dad's death is you."

"You don't understand." I grip the ends of my hair. "Maybe if I had been faster. Or if I had tried to—"

"No, Leo. Nothing you would have done would have saved him." He watches me, his shoulders dropping.

My hand grips the back of my neck, squeezing hard. I tilt my head up, closing my eyes. "I miss him every fucking day."

"I do, too." I open my eyes to see him running his fingers through his hair. "But he wouldn't want you to be holding on to this guilt. Especially when it's not your guilt to bear. Someone planned our father's murder. And hopefully, someday, we'll gain closure by finding the culprit responsible and killing him using the only suitable method: fire."

I drop my arms, letting out a breath. "What do we do now?"

"Now..." He rubs the side of his jaw, deep in thought. "We get you home to your wife. And tomorrow...tomorrow we regroup. Go over everything we have on this fucker, and look for the missing piece. And Leo?"

"Yeah?"

"We will find him. We have to. Because we can't let Dad down." He points to the sky. "The big guy is always looking out for us, and right now, he's with us more than you realize."

CHAPTER THIRTEEN

Scarlett

With an exhausted sigh, I open my bedroom door, ready for another sleepless night. Sleeping alone in this massive house for the past few nights has left my nerves fried. And I know Leo told me to call him for anything, but I don't want to bother him with this. Admitting to him at twenty-four years old that I'm scared of the dark would make me feel embarrassed and weak. Maybe even a touch pathetic.

Rubbing my eyes, I stare at the light switch and reach my hand toward it, knowing I should turn it off. To be a normal human being and sleep in the dark. But I can't. I just...can't.

"What is wrong with me?" I murmur, defeated, dropping my hand to my side.

My phone vibrates in my pocket.

Mauro

A gift for you from Leo was just dropped off. Would you like me to bring it inside?

A gift? I step toward my window and draw back the curtain to see a shiny black SUV pulling away.

Scarlett

I'll meet you at the front door.

As I take the last step down the stairs, Mauro strides inside. He gives me a curt nod and holds out a small black box wrapped with a white ribbon. I hesitantly reach for it, remembering that the last thing delivered to me was not from Leo as I thought it had been.

"Is this really from Leo this time?"

He pulls out his phone with his free hand and quickly types before turning it toward me.

Mauro

The man who dropped it off is in charge of the jewelry for the whole family. He is trusted and very loyal to our family.

My eyes widen. Jewelry?

I take the box from him, holding it carefully in my grasp. "Well…" I hike my thumb over my shoulder. "I'm going to head to bed." He nods in understanding, halfway turned out the door when I say, "I'm sorry you have to spend your night babysitting me."

He shakes his head and types on his phone.

Mauro

You're a sister to me, Scarlett. Always have been. We will all do whatever it takes to keep you safe.

I roll my bottom lip in, feeling my throat tighten. "Thanks, Mauro." He smiles and turns out the door, leaving me to return to my room.

Sitting on the edge of my bed, I suddenly feel like a kid on my birthday as I stare at the wrapped box. I cradle it in the palm of my hands, unsure of what's hiding inside. Why would Leo have gotten me a gift? Christmas is a few months away, and my birthday is even further than that. Curiosity wins as I delicately pull the end of the ribbon and watch as it comes apart, tumbling gracefully to the floor. I glide my finger around the top of the box, carefully lifting the cover. Peeking inside, my eyes catch on an array of vibrant stones glinting beautifully.

Completely removing the lid, I find a... "Oh my God," I breathe.

I place the box beside me and gently pull out the contents, examining it before me. It's a firefly—a crystal firefly adorned with a kaleidoscope of blue, pink, purple, and green gems. The wings are designed in translucent stones and on the back... I freeze, my heart crashing against my rib cage.

With shaking fingers, I turn the firefly over just as a quiet gasp leaves my throat.

"It's...a nightlight," I whisper, my finger trailing around the bulb attached to the back. A single tear slides down my cheek as the corners of my lips lift. "He got me a nightlight."

A soft laugh escapes me. Most women in my position might expect diamond necklaces, red-bottom shoes, or luxury cars. But this gift... I shake my head in a mix of disbelief and gratitude. This gift, this simple nightlight, means more to me than any material possession ever could.

With an unstable hand, I reach toward the closest outlet by my bed and plug in my gift. Then, with a little "I can do this" mantra and a deep breath, I shut off the bedroom light. My eyes are met with a treat as the stones shine over the room, eliciting a rainbow of colors.

Tears fill my eyes. I lie back on my bed, my head resting on my pillow, pulling the covers over my legs. I stare at the ceiling, getting lost in a beautiful sea of colors. For the first time in months, I don't feel so scared of the darkness surrounding me as I drift off to sleep, escaping to my favorite memory.

SEVEN YEARS AGO

A summer breeze rolls in as the sun begins its daily descent, producing a sky of soft pinks that put any painting to shame. I smooth out the blanket beside me, hoping he might come tonight. It's been weeks since I've seen him, and the last time I did, we were surrounded by everyone we know, pretending we haven't been sneaking around with each other behind their backs with secret kisses, rushed glances, and hidden touches.

But tonight, he'll come. I can feel it in my heart.

Leo Alarie will always come for me.

As children, we came here with the others to catch fireflies, have water balloon fights, or take an afternoon dip in the lake. But as we all grew, fewer people started venturing this far out until it dwindled to only me and him. Not that I would ever complain about that.

This place became my escape. Somewhere, I would spend my nights hiding from the world with a good book on my lap, particularly on nights when my father would come home in a frightening mood. I never wanted to be home on those nights.

A shiver of terror runs through me just from thinking about his brute strength.

A few days ago was a perfect example of this. It was probably the angriest I've ever witnessed him. After he started destroying furniture and wishing he weren't stuck with a worthless daughter like me, I snuck up to my room, out the window, down the terrace, and began my hike to this spot where I spent the night curled up against this tree, not leaving until the sun rose.

I check the time on my phone, and disappointment fills me. Maybe he's not coming tonight. I let out a frustrated sigh, staring up at the night sky. Darkness sweeps over the land, with only the stars and the moon providing any light source.

I lean against the tree, close my eyes, and listen to the crickets and the soothing resonance of the little waterfall in the nearby creek. A snap of a twig opens my eyes, landing on the man I've been waiting for. A heart-breaking smile appears on his face, sending warmth flowing through me.

A smile pulls at the corners of my lips. "You came."

He walks closer and then sits on the spot beside me. I notice this time that something feels different. There's a shift in the air as his thigh touches mine, and he makes no motion to move away.

"I came, Firefly."

"You know, being referred to as an insect isn't very romantic."

He smirks. "I think it fits you perfectly." His hand reaches out, tucking a loose strand of hair behind my ear. A slight tremble rolls through me at his touch. The proximity between us feels almost too close, but at the same time, not close enough.

I swallow nervously as his fingers trail down my neck. "I wasn't sure you were going to come tonight."

He leans closer, his nose brushing against my cheek. "Why?"

My breaths become soft pants as his lips press against my skin, gliding down my neck. "It's just been a while since I've seen you. I thought maybe you got bored with me or something." The moment the words leave my mouth, I instantly regret how pitiful I sound.

He stills and pulls back, boring his dark whiskey eyes into mine. "I'm sorry for making you second-guess things. My father has been keeping me busy teaching me the ways of the family business." His fingers loop around the ends of my hair, rubbing it between his fingers. "You have it wrong, Firefly. Life is boring without you. Not the other way around."

Although his words ease my mind, I suddenly realize how exhausted he looks, adding a whole new set of worries to my thoughts. My fingers reach out, and my thumb traces the dark circles under his eyes. "Is everything okay?"

"Yes and no." He slides his arm behind me, and I curl into his side. "We've been dealing with more problems than usual this week. My father took Vin and a few men with him somewhere a few nights ago, and when they came back, well, I've never seen them so lost in their heads." He stares up at the sky. "Neither of them has spoken of what happened, but I know it wasn't good. And in a few hours, Mauro and I need to go with him to our warehouse to check on a shipment of weapons that was delivered. My father received an anonymous tip that it may have been tampered with."

My brows scrunch together. "Who would tamper with it?"

"No clue. Maybe he's just being overly cautious. But he's taking the threat seriously." He shakes his head. "I don't know how to explain it, but something has felt off recently. It's like he hasn't told us what's really been going on. And I can't help but think that something big is coming."

A shiver rolls through me, and Leo's grip around me tightens.

I look up at him, worry eating away at me. "If something were to happen to you..."

"It won't." He tries to give me a reassuring smile, but it doesn't ease my nerves. I glance down at my lap, nervous he'll see right through me. To be a part of this life, you need to be strong. Something I'm not feeling at this moment. "Hey." He hooks a finger under my chin, tilting my face up toward him. "You're scared for me, aren't you?"

I solemnly nod, feeling my eyes mist over. "I can't lose you."

He leans closer, his lips only an inch away from mine.

God, how I've missed this.

"Then it's a good thing I'm not going anywhere." His lips press down on my temple and then brush across my skin. "I was thinking tomorrow, we could let everyone know about us."

My heart hammers in my chest as butterflies overrun my stomach. "You...you mean, like, make it official?"

"Yeah." His thumb glides back and forth across my bottom lip, his eyes darkening. "I think we've kept this secret for long enough. It's time everyone knows that you're mine."

"Yours," I breathe. "I like the sound of that."

His lips crash down on mine, demanding entry as he consumes me. Body and soul. His hand cups the back of my head as his other hand finds my waist, tugging me against his body. My arms wrap around his neck as I greedily devour him.

One kiss is never enough. I always need more and more. He's like a drug I never want to quit—my secret addiction.

His hands slide down my waist to my bare thighs, his fingers skimming under my pink dress.

"Leo," I say breathlessly.

He pulls back, his eyes searching my face. "Should I stop?"

I quickly shake my head. "Please don't."

His lips return to mine, his hand sliding further up my leg. We've never done more than kiss, and he's always seemed content with that, but right now, he needs more.

And so do I.

The pads of his fingers graze the lace fabric between my thighs, and on instinct, I spread my legs, allowing him access to all of me for the first time.

Leo groans in satisfaction as his fingers travel down my center and press against the damp fabric. "So wet for me." His lips glide across my neck, nipping and sucking a path to my collarbone as he tugs my panties to the side. A slight breeze hits me, and a pounding grows in my core. A whimper leaves my throat as his index finger slowly slides between my slit, back and forth.

"Have you ever been touched, Firefly?"

I shake my head, unable to form words, and drown in a haze of desire. Leo appears pleased by my answer, and suddenly, I feel the tip of his finger breach my entrance, swirling slowly inside me. It's not a lot of pressure. Nothing I can't handle, but it's enough to make me moan. My whole body burns with unbridled need beneath his touch, and I revel in the intense pleasure overcoming me.

"Spread those legs wider for me, baby."

Without hesitation, I do, seeking to please him. His finger dives inside me, catching me off guard. "Leo!" I grip his shoulders, my nails digging into his white T-shirt. The feeling building between my legs is unlike anything I've ever experienced before. The palm of his hand rests over my clit, gently providing just the right amount of pressure I need, driving me closer and closer to the brink of eruption.

But I want more.

I need more.

I want all of him.

"Leo," I pant.

"Yes?"

"I want you." He pumps faster, and I can barely think straight. "I want...all of you."

His hand freezes as he stills above me. I instantly miss his ministrations, feeling the orgasm drifting away. My chest heaves, and my eyes lock with his, waiting. Every second passing makes me feel a little more vulnerable than before. Maybe this was a bad idea. Maybe I shouldn't have asked for more...

"Are you sure that's what you want?" He cups my cheek, staring intently into my eyes.

And just as I'm on the verge of getting lost in them, I nod. "I've never wanted anything more."

He kisses my temple. "I'll always give you whatever you want. You know that."

My heart pitter-patters, a mixture of nerves and excitement filling me.

"It might hurt a little," he says softly. "I need you to tell me if you need me to stop. Okay?"

"Okay." I bite down on my bottom lip as a flush spreads over my cheeks.

He presses his lips to mine with so much tenderness I melt beneath him. My fingers grip the hem of his T-shirt, sliding it up his torso, and I watch as he tugs the rest of it off, revealing a finely tuned masterpiece. Reaching out, I trace the tattoos on his chest, admiring his body like a beautiful painting. My fingers glide lower, traveling over every rugged ridge and contour on his stomach, pausing when I reach the denim waistband.

He smiles and leans down. "Someone has no patience."

I lick my lips. "I just..." I let out a rush of air; courage fills me as I splay my hand over the bulge between his legs. He's hard. So goddamn hard. And big. Leo groans as I inch my hand around, taking note of his thickness. Yep, definitely big. "I feel like I've wanted this forever. And now it's finally happening."

He brushes his lips over mine, slightly hissing when I apply just the right amount of pressure. "You aren't the only one feeling this way."

"Really?"

He grabs the hem of my dress and begins to slide it up my body. "Really."

I sit up, lifting my arms in the air as he pulls the dress off of my body, leaving me in just my pink matching panties and bra. His eyes wander appreciatively over every square inch of me, seeming ready to devour me.

With shaky fingers, I reach behind me and unclasp my bra, letting the straps slide down my arms. His eyes darken. A muscle in his jaw ticks. And before I lose my courage, I reach down toward my panties, but he stops me.

"Let me." The palm of his hand softly presses into my stomach as he gently pushes me back onto the blanket. I lie and wait as he settles between my legs, anticipation mounting in my core. A steady pulse vibrates between my legs, my body craving everything he's about to give me. With both of his hands, he tucks his index fingers under the lace that resides over my hips and then slowly slides it down my legs.

Lying here utterly naked before him, I feel every nerve ending heightened. I feel every spot his eyes engrave into his memory. I feel every breeze caress my skin. I feel wetness drip down my thighs.

I feel every goddamn thing.

"You are a sight to treasure, Scarlett. One I truly don't deserve."

Not knowing what I'm supposed to do, I remain still, my chest heaving as my heart spins out of control. I watch him stand with so much control, his eyes never leaving me as he unbuttons his jeans and then lets them and his underwear fall to his ankles, stepping out of them.

A small gasp escapes me. He's thick and long. Hard and veiny. My mouth waters. My pussy flutters. The only problem is that there is no way it's going to fit.

It's physically not possible.

He immediately takes in my worried features and lies beside me, soothingly gliding his hand over my stomach. "If you want to stop, we can."

I shake my head. "No. I want this. I'm just...nervous."

He gives me an affectionate smile, his finger circling my belly button. "I'm nervous, too."

"You are?" Knowing this, I instantly feel relieved that I'm not alone in this.

"Of course." He slides his hand up my stomach, through the valley of my breasts, and up to my cheek. "I want to make you feel good." His thumb skates across my cheek. "I want to make your first time perfect."

"You are," I reply. "Because the thing that's making this perfect is that it's with you."

He kisses my lips and suddenly freezes, panic in his eyes. "Shit."

"What?" I sit up in alarm, worried someone might be coming.

"I don't have a condom." He looks up at the night sky with disappointment flashing over his features.

"Leo." I press my hand to his chest, feeling his heart pound steadily. "I'm on the pill. If you're okay with not using a condom, then so am I."

He hooks a finger beneath my chin, tilting my face up. "We'll go slow, okay?"

I nod, feeling every muscle in my body tense up, anticipating what's to come.

Our lips mold together, and I follow his lead, lying back. He positions himself on top of me between my legs. Every cell of blood in my body burns under his touch, wanting, no, needing more.

He reaches between us, clasping his hand around his hardened length and positioning it right above my entrance. He rests his weight on his elbows, looking down at me, and brushes a few loose tendrils of my hair out of my face.

"Relax, baby. It will help this not hurt so much for you."

"I'll try." I close my eyes and take a deep breath, waiting for my muscles to release all the tension within me. When I open my eyes to Leo's, I give a slight nod, and he slowly slides inside me.

Oh God. It's too much. The stretch is causing me too much pain. I grip the blanket with one hand and clasp onto his shoulder firmly with the other. Tears fill my eyes, but I swallow down my pleas for him to stop.

I can do this. I want this. I want him.

"Should I stop?" he asks, concern in his tone.

I shake my head, biting down on my bottom lip.

"You're doing so good, Scarlett." His thumb swipes under my eyes. "Your pussy is taking my cock so well, baby."

I melt under his praise, feeling relaxed and ready to take more of him.

He continues sliding inside. "Just a few more inches."

I inhale through my nose and exhale through my mouth. The pain becomes almost bearable. Fully seated inside me, Leo stills, giving my body a moment to adjust.

"I'm going to start moving now, okay?"

"Okay." I show him a tiny smile as he starts a slow rhythm, in and out. The pain becomes a distant, dull memory as something else takes over with each thrust. *Pleasure.*

He leans his head forward, kissing my lips as his hand moves up to my breast, and he begins to pinch my nipple, twisting and tugging on it lightly. A zap of electricity shoots to my core, and I moan into his kiss. He does it again and again until I'm trembling beneath him.

"More," I beg.

His pace increases as he slides all the way out and then sinks fully back in. I stare up into his eyes and notice his jaw clench with each thrust. He's holding back, reining in his strength so he doesn't hurt me. But he won't. I know he won't. I wrap my legs around his hips, digging my heels into his ass, urging him on.

"Don't hold back."

He shakes his head. "I don't want to hurt you."

"I can take it," I say, pressing a kiss to his neck. "Promise."

He hesitates. I see the internal conflict in his eyes.

"Please," I breathe.

His control implodes. His thrusts grow faster and harder. I cling to him, taking everything he's giving me, and it doesn't take long for the all-consuming pleasure to build inside me.

"I'm so close," I murmur, getting lost in the haze.

Suddenly, his hand slips between us, his skilled fingers rubbing over my clit, giving me just the right amount of pressure my body needs for a release.

"Oh God, Leo." My eyes roll back as I grip his shoulders, on the verge of unraveling.

"You're so beautiful, Scarlett. So goddamn perfect."

"Leo...I think...I'm going to..."

"Come for me, Scarlett."

I shatter beneath him, the orgasm washing over me like a tidal wave I can't escape. My vision goes black as I get swept under, lost in a sea of bliss.

Leo's movements become jerky before his body stills over me, and I feel him pulse inside me, warmth spilling within me. A groan leaves him, my name on his lips, as he buries his face in the crook of my neck, his lips pressing to my skin.

My heart races. My mind clears. Everything around me blurs in tranquility.

And as I come to, seeing nothing but the stars above me, and feel Leo wrapped around my body, my heart swells with so much tenderness I think I might burst.

This was better than any dream I could have ever had.

Because this... This was real.

Leo sits up, looking down at me. "Are you okay?" His hand rests on my stomach, worries consuming his eyes. "Did I hurt you?"

I shake my head, a smile tugging on my lips. "I feel the happiest I've ever felt in my life."

Relief washes over him as he lies beside me and pulls me into his side, my head resting on his solid chest.

"Leo?"

"Yes?"

"Just so you know, that was a perfect first time for me."

His knuckles stroke my jaw, his eyes taking me in as if trying to remember everything about this moment. "This is the best night of my life. I'm never going to forget it."

I snuggle against his chest, closing my eyes, wishing for more nights like this under the stars with him. When he falls asleep, breathing steady and quiet, I bring my lips to his ear and whisper, "I can't wait to marry you someday, Leo Alarie."

CHAPTER FOURTEEN

Aﬀter stopping in the driveaway, I remove my helmet, peering up at the front door where Eli stands on guard.

All seems as it should be.

And it's as if the weighted blanket suffocating me these past few days finally dissolves into the wind.

Eli gives a low whistle. "When did you get a Ducati Superleggera?" he asks, eyeing my bike. "I thought they only made a few hundred of those. And definitely not in that finish."

I shrug. "It's custom."

"Of course it is." Eli smirks, shaking his head. I informed him and Mauro of the failed mission last night, ensuring they kept extra vigilance around the estate.

Le Diable may have escaped our wrath this time, but we'll be ready for him next time.

We don't have a choice.

As I reach the top step, I clasp Eli's shoulder. "I take it everything has gone smoothly while I've been away. Nothing to report?"

"No." He shakes his head but pauses, brows furrowing. "Well..."

My pulse races. "What is it?"

He scratches the side of his head. "She hasn't left the house."

"Today? But it's only noon. I'm sure—"

"No." He runs his fingers through his hair, letting out a breath. "She hasn't left the whole time you've been gone."

"But I've been gone for almost four days."

"I know. I asked her several times if she would even just like to go for a drive to get out of the house, but she didn't want to leave."

"I see." I rub the back of my neck, deep in thought. Opening the front door, I look back at Eli. "Thank you for letting me know."

"Of course."

"You may depart early. I'll be with her for the rest of the day."

"You got it, boss." He strolls down the driveway toward his awaiting SUV.

I lock the door behind me and walk directly toward where I know I'll find Scarlett residing on the swinging bench.

I force open the glass door, startling her.

"Leo!" She drops the book in her hands beside her, her feet moving from beneath her to the ground. A warm smile graces her face. "You're home early."

"I couldn't take another day being away from"—*you*—"home."

She tucks a loose piece of hair behind her ear. "Well, I'm glad you're home."

"You are, huh?" I lean on the metal post, crossing my arms over my chest. She bites her bottom lip, giving me a very playful expression. "Come here, Firefly," I tell her, opening my arms wide.

She immediately stands and walks over to me, melting into my hold. With her in my arms, any and all traces of tension in my body dissipate.

"I missed you," she breathes against my chest. She tilts her head to lock eyes with me.

I cup the back of her neck, brushing my thumb against her skin, leaning closer to her lips. "The feeling is mutual."

Her palm rests against my chest. "And Leo?"

"Yes?"

"Thank you for the nightlight. Or well, what I mean is..." She takes a deep breath, stands on her toes, and brushes her lips against mine. "Thank you for making the dark a less frightening place for me."

I can't hold back a second longer. I press my lips to hers, hungry for her taste. Her hands grip my shirt as if trying to anchor herself to me. I slide my tongue past the opening of her lips, exploring and tasting. God, she's so fucking sweet. So delectable. I suck on her bottom lip, letting it out with a pop before grazing the tip of my nose against hers. "I'll always help you find the light within you."

She presses her face into my chest, and we stand there for a few minutes, enjoying each other's embrace. I tighten my arms around her, never wanting to let her go.

Because when she's in my arms, I know she's safe from the whole goddamn world.

Something wet touches my arm, and when I look down, I see Brutus standing beside me with Scarlett's book in his mouth, thinking it's a fucking chew toy. "No, Brutus." I take the book from him, holding it out of reach.

"Oh, Brutus." Scarlett laughs, taking the book from me and wiping the drool off the cover with a nearby towel. "You owe me a new book." She playfully nudges the top of his head.

I eye the cover of the book, noting a man and a woman in a passionate embrace with only a bunch of damn sheets wrapped around them. *Hmm.*

"Were you reading anything interesting?"

She blushes the prettiest shade of pink, indicating what kind of book it is. I suddenly have the urge to read to her. I want to know what parts are her favorite and what makes her cheeks turn a deep shade of crimson.

"It's just one of my favorites. I've had it for as long as I can remember."

"A romance?"

She nods, bashfully playing with a piece of her hair. "They help me escape when things get to be a little too much up here." She points to the side of her head with a slight shrug.

I frown. "Should I get Dr. Raven for you?"

She shakes her head. "No. I'm good. I just needed a story to get lost in for a little bit."

I notice the yellowing pages and bent cover as if the book has been read hundreds of times. "Is that the only book you have?"

"That and two more up in my room."

I squeeze the back of my neck. How did I not think to stock up on her favorite items in my house? She's loved to read her whole life. And to find out she uses them as an escape and only has three fucking books to read in this entire house... This is unacceptable. "I'll buy you more."

She shakes her head, grinning. "I don't need more."

I arch a brow. "You're married to one of the richest men in the world. The least I can do is buy you some books."

"I don't need your money. Besides, you've done plenty for me already. You gave me a place to call home. A place where I feel..." She stops, her lips closing shut.

I grip her chin, waiting for her eyes to meet mine. "A place where you feel what?"

"Safe." She smiles. "A place where I feel safe."

My heart squeezes. Her bright blue eyes hypnotize me under her spell, almost making me forget what I have planned for us tonight. I loop my arm around her and quickly glimpse at my watch.

"Let's go for a ride."

She tilts her head. "You mean...

I tap her nose and wink. "Yes." Reaching for her hand, I lead her outside to my bike.

She stares at it with wide, unsure eyes.

"I won't fall off?" Her voice comes out unsure.

"You won't fall off."

"And you promise not to crash?"

I sign a cross over my heart. "On my life, I will not crash." I throw my leg over the seat and reach for the helmet. I'll have to get a personalized one for her, but for now, this will do. "Put this on."

She hesitantly takes it from me and then secures it around her head. "Now what?"

"Bring your right leg over the seat."

She does as I say, her thighs wrapping around mine. "And now?"

I reach behind me for her hands and place them firmly against my stomach. "Hold on tight."

Her hands clutch my shirt, gripping on for dear life as I rev the engine and then, more slowly than I usually would, retreat down the driveway, away from our home, and toward a place I haven't been to in a very long time.

Scarlett rests her head against my back, and I suddenly worry that this might have been a bad idea.

"Are you okay back there?" I yell over the roar of the engine.

I feel her nod, and she replies, "This is amazing!"

My lips curve up as we travel through the estate, passing the darkened forests, and finally arrive at our special place.

Coming to a stop, I hear Scarlett gasp. "Is this...?"

"Yes." I slide off my bike and hold a hand out for her to take.

We stroll toward the giant maple tree with only the moon and the fairy lights I had a few guards string around the area, guiding us. Beside the tree, a blanket on the ground holds Scarlett's favorite foods in to-go containers, safely protected from the outdoor elements.

To some, these woods would cause a sense of fear and impending doom. But to us, these woods hold precious memories that overshadow the darkness surrounding us.

"You did all of this?" she asks in awe as we walk side by side.

"With a little help," I admit. "I thought we could have a redo of our first date."

She looks over everything and then tilts her head back, her eyes taking in the night sky. A pristine black canvas covered in billions of bright stars glowing a little extra brightly. "This is perfect." She spins around with a wide, beautiful smile on her face. "Thank you."

I sit against the tree, spread my legs before me, and pat the space beside me. She sits, her denim-covered legs tucked beneath her as her eyes look over the several containers.

"Are you hungry?" I ask her.

"Famished," she answers, placing a hand over her stomach.

I hand her the one closest to her and watch as she opens it, revealing spring rolls. "Oh, wow." She looks up at me under those long dark lashes. "You did good."

I laugh as I reach for the container of fried rice. "It's good to know I can satisfy my wife with food."

She blushes, tucking a loose strand of hair behind her ear before taking her first bite, moaning in appreciation.

And fuck, I would do anything to hear that beautiful, delicious sound again.

We eat our dinner in comfortable silence, the only noise coming from the nearby creek and crickets. With a full stomach, I place my containers to the side and relax against the tree, gazing up at the stars.

Scarlett settles in beside me, resting her head on my shoulder. "Thank you for bringing me here. I always wondered if it still felt the same."

"Yeah, I wondered that too," I confess.

She glances up at me, brows furrowed.

I shrug. "I couldn't find it in me to make it up here...without you."

She looks down, rolling in her bottom lip. "So the last time you were here was when..."

Her words trail off, but I know exactly what night she's referring to. The one mixed with so many emotions. It was the night Scarlett and I spent tangled together under the stars. But only hours later, it was the same night I lost my dad. An old ache awakens in my chest, and I absentmindedly rub the spot.

"Yeah. That night, Firefly." I stretch out my arm, casually inspecting my watch, before I drape it across her shoulders and hold her in my embrace. Only a few minutes until showtime. She snuggles against me, her long blonde hair tumbling over my chest. "Did you have a nice time while I was away?"

"Me?" She peeks up at me. "Of course."

"Hmm." I thread my fingers through her silky strands, twirling the ends. "Go anywhere interesting?"

She looks off to the side. "I umm..." She bites down on that pillowy soft lip, appearing unsure.

"Talk to me, Scarlett."

She rubs the top of her thighs back and forth, biting her bottom lip as she stares down at her lap. "I didn't go anywhere." Glancing up, she asks, "Did Eli tell you?"

"It's his job to report on your well-being."

She huffs. "I feel like an animal in captivity."

I lift her chin. "Hey, that's not what this is."

"No. I know. I'm sorry." She hides her face behind her hands, her breathing picking up pace. "I just wish things were how they were be-fore...he took me," she whispers, dropping her hands to her sides.

My heart splinters at how defeated she sounds. I shift, cupping her face, and look down at her. "They will be. Maybe not today or tomorrow, but they will be. It's just going to take some time." I press a kiss to her forehead, inhaling her jasmine scent. Pulling back, I hook two fingers under her chin, tipping her face up. "Why didn't you leave the house while I was away?"

She rolls in her bottom lip, her eyes watering, but she's not letting the tears out.

"Do you not feel safe with Eli?" My hand slides down her face to her neck, my thumb running over her pulse point.

"No, no," she rushes out. "Of course, I feel safe with him. It's just, well, I don't know." Her shoulders slump. "I wanted to go out for a coffee one of the days, but then I decided just to make it at home. Maddy had asked me to come over for dinner one night, but I told her I wasn't feeling up to it. I changed my schedule at the women and children's center, which made me feel horrible, but I didn't think I could handle going. Then I thought about going out to look for a dress to wear to Maddy's engagement party, but when I put my hand on the doorknob, all ready to leave, I kind of freaked out and spent the rest of the day watching movies on the couch." She shakes her head, her eyes downcast. "I guess the truth is, I only feel truly safe when...I'm with you."

My heart swells with pride.

She feels safe with me.

I should be ecstatic to hear this.

But I hate that she feels this way.

Because as much as I love being her protector and will do anything and everything to keep her safe, I want her to reach a point where she feels safe with or without me by her side.

But she won't.

Not until Le Diable is gone for good, no longer walking this Earth.

She sniffles, still fighting back the tears. "And I had become so used to you being home or on the property that when you left, I didn't know what to do with myself. I was scared. And I hate that I was. I hate it so much." The first tear slides down her cheek. My thumb stretches up to catch it, wiping it away. "I hate that I'm fearful of my own shadow. I hate that every man I meet makes my skin crawl in fear. I hate that I can't just go out and grab a coffee without thinking this is the moment I'll be kidnapped again. I hate that I lost my independence." She sucks in her bottom lip, her eyes closing shut. "I hate that he broke me."

My heart completely shatters.

A violent sob overtakes her, and I quickly pull her onto my lap, binding my arms around her.

"The last thing you are is broken." I brush my lips across the top of her head, my hands gliding up and down her back. "You are one of the strongest women I know."

"I don't think I am."

"You are, Scarlett. You fought every day you were in that basement. And you survived. You wouldn't be here right now if it weren't for the strength inside you." I gently rock her, rolling our foreheads together. "You aren't broken. Not even close. But you're hurting and scared. You went through something so traumatic. Something most people could never comprehend. And it's going to take time to heal. Maybe more time than you want, but it's what you need. Mentally and physically. But know this, Scarlett, you don't need to go through this alone. Not when I'm here. And I'll be by your side during this whole journey because it's you and me until our days end." Her fingers slide up my chest, resting right over my heart. "It kills me every day that Le Diable's still alive because I know how much he terrifies you. But I promise, Firefly, I won't rest until I find him. I won't stop until he's six feet beneath the ground and only after he's endured unimaginable pain."

She sniffs, wiping her face. "Promise?"

"I promise." I kiss her temple. "And believe me when I say Eli wouldn't let anything happen to you either. He looks at you as his sister, and it would destroy him if something happened to you while under his watch. Not to mention you have three other big brothers that would slit anyone's throat if they even looked at you the wrong way. Even Madeleine can be pretty feisty when provoked."

She lets out a little chuckle. "I guess you're right." She pulls back, looking away. "I'm sorry that I'm such a mess right now." She runs her thumbs under her eyes, stopping a fresh trail of tears. "You brought us here for a nice moment, and I've ruined it."

"You haven't ruined anything. Besides." I lift my wrist and look at my watch. "The night is not over yet. In fact, it's beginning in three...two...one..."

Boom! Boom! Boom!

She jumps in my arms, pinching her eyes shut and burying her head into my chest.

I place my lips beside her ear. "If you stay like that, you'll miss the show."

She peeks up, staring at me questionably.

I nudge my head toward the sky, and she glances over just as another boom echoes around us.

Her eyes widen as she leans forward. "Leo!" She turns toward me, excitement dancing across her eyes. "There're fireworks!" Her eyes dart back toward the sky as she watches an array of colors splashing across the blackness above us.

I smile, an unfamiliar feeling filling me as I watch happiness spread over her features.

"There are." I trail my fingers down her spine. When I reach her lower back, I let my thumb travel in gentle, soothing circles.

She leans back into my touch, lost in the sea of colors around us. A moment passes before she asks, "Did you plan these?"

"I did."

She faces me, blue shadowing her features as a giant firework bursts overhead. "You did this for me?"

My knuckles stroke across her cheek. "I would do anything for you." She closes her eyes and leans into the palm of my hand. "You know, while I was away, I realized something."

"What?" she asks softly.

I let out a breath, entranced by her in more ways than she'll ever know. "How goddamn much I missed my wife."

My lips land on hers, a jolt of electricity slicing through my entire body. She parts her lips, letting my tongue inside, giving me a better taste. She moans into the kiss as her arms wrap around my neck, pulling me closer to her. She straddles my lap, her pussy stationed right over my throbbing cock. All she would have to do is move just a tiny bit to give herself—

She slowly, almost unnoticeably, grinds against me. A whimper escapes her. "Leo," she pleads in a whisper. "I don't know what to do. I don't... I'm not sure..."

"Use me, Scarlett. Listen to what your body needs." I position my hands firmly on the ground beside me. "I won't touch you." She regards my hands, her chest heaving, her pulse thrumming beneath her collarbone. I press my lips to hers. "I know you need the release, baby. So, use me to get off."

An internal war rages inside her head. I can see the very thoughts crossing over her blue irises as she battles against herself. I shake my head. "Don't think about it, Scarlett. Don't think about anything. It's just you and me. Right here. Right now. So, take what you want from me. Take what you need."

Her eyes blink, guilt overtaking them.

"I'm your husband, Firefly. You always have my permission to use me however you please."

She bites her bottom lip, her hands gripping my shoulder for support as she adjusts herself, suddenly shifting her hips over my thigh. She rocks forward slowly and then pauses, looking at me for assurance.

"Just like that, baby."

I watch with rapt fascination as she begins to move fluidly back and forth, seeking her pleasure from me. Even if I'm not actually doing anything.

She's the one in control.

This is all her.

"Does that feel good?"

She closes her eyes, her hips moving quicker. "Y-yes." She hangs her head back, her tits pressing against her top.

"Fuck, you're so beautiful, Scarlett. So fucking perfect."

I wish I could do more for her.

I wish I could tear those damn pants right off her and bury my face between her legs, giving her pleasure like she's never imagined. Tasting her sweet-as-sin pussy with long leisurely strokes from my tongue as she squirms beneath me, wanting, no, begging for more.

But I can't.

Not right now.

This is just step one in our journey.

So with all the restraint I can muster, I keep my hands plastered firmly to the blanket, my cock hardening painfully beneath my pants.

"Leo," she moans. "I'm so... I'm so close." Her speed picks up as her nails dig into my shirt. A pretty flush spreads over her cheeks and neck. Her lips part. Her eyes fall shut.

She's consumed by desire and on the brink of an orgasm.

Fireworks continue shimmering above us as I place my lips against her ear. "Let me see you come all over your husband's leg."

She screams out my name as she unravels beautifully on top of me. Her chest heaves as she arches into me, and I capture her lips in a kiss, her movements faltering. She pants hard, her skin rosy and her eyelids heavy as she comes to a complete stop, holding on to my shoulders for support.

I gently coax her against my chest, scattering kisses to her hair as she snuggles her face into my neck. "You did so fucking good, baby." She relaxes in my hold, my hands smoothing up and down her back. I know how much courage it took for her to do what she did. She reined in her fears, owning her pleasure like a true queen, and I'll never take the trust she gave me in that moment for granted. "I'm so proud of you," I murmur against her ear.

And all I can think is...

That's my goddamn wife.

CHAPTER FIFTEEN

Scarlett

I'm an imposter.

A fake.

A phony.

All of the above.

Standing in front of the floor-length mirror in my bedroom, I slide my palms over the black satin fabric hugging my hips and feel everything except the one thing I should feel: beautiful.

My hair, styled in waves, cascades over my off-shoulder sleeves and down my back, while my makeup is done so flawlessly that no one would ever notice the deep bags beneath my eyes. My four-inch heels match the silver clutch on my nightstand. My skin has been buffed and polished to perfection. And the scars on my back are hidden beneath the backing of my dress, concealing all evidence of my past trauma.

At least, in the physical sense, that is.

But as I stare at the woman before me, I don't recognize her.

I only pity her.

Grabbing my clutch, I exit my room and slowly descend the stairs, careful not to trip and fall. Just as I take the last step, Leo appears in an all-black suit, looking the part of my black knight in shining armor.

His eyes, burning with evident desire, sweep over every square inch of me. "You look perfect."

I fight the urge to shy away and instead stand tall, reveling under his intense gaze. "Thank you." I wish I could see myself through his eyes. Maybe then I would feel better about tonight—more confident and assured, less fearful and uncertain.

But tonight is not about me.

It's for Madeleine.

And I won't miss another important event in her life—especially not her engagement party.

Not now, when I'm here.

Leo holds a black shawl for me, wrapping it over my shoulders. His hand finds mine, our fingers intertwining, before guiding us out the front door to the waiting car. A driver stationed by the front of it opens the door.

With every inch the car drives beyond the safety of the solid stone walls surrounding the Alarie Estate, the more rapidly my heart pulses with apprehension.

Leo reaches for my hand residing on my lap. "Nervous?"

I nod, unable to speak.

"Don't be." He brings my hand to his lips and kisses the back of it tenderly. "I won't let anything happen to you."

I relax the tiniest bit, knowing this is true.

Knowing he will always do whatever it takes to keep me safe.

The rest of the drive goes by in comfortable silence until we reach the venue, an Alarie establishment, and I see groups of people walking through the entrance.

That tiny pulse of nerves within the center of my chest turns into a full-blown thunder at the thought of being in a room filled with so many unfamiliar faces.

"Maybe...maybe this was a bad idea," I say, gazing up at Leo, who frowns. And the thought that I might be disappointing him upsets me more than I care to admit.

"It's up to you, Scarlett. I would never force you to do something that would make you uncomfortable. But I think it's a good idea to get back out there again. Slowly. With me by your side." His hand cups my cheek, his thumb stroking my skin back and forth. "We'll have guards with us tonight, including Eli, and as promised, I won't let anything happen to you."

I nod. He's right. Of course, he is.

"Besides, Madeleine will give me absolute hell if you don't make an appearance. She'll probably key one of my cars." He smirks, twirling a tendril of my hair.

I let out a small chuckle. That is precisely something Madeleine would do. "You're right. I'm sorry."

He lightly grips my chin, tilting my face up. "You have nothing to be sorry for. This is a lot. And I would understand if you want to turn this car around and go home. But I'm giving you the choice to decide."

I peer out the window to my side, spotting several women and men dressed to the nines, laughing and conversing. They look happy and normal.

And that's all I want.

To feel normal again.

"I want to do this for Madeleine," I murmur, facing him. "This is a big night for her, and I've missed so much over the years. I don't want to miss anymore."

"Are you sure?"

"Yes."

His grin grows. "That's my girl." His rough voice awakens the butterflies in my stomach. "But if it becomes too much for you and you need to leave at any point, let me know. Okay? We'll take it one step at a time."

I nod, taking a deep breath.

Leo exits the car, and after I slide across the seat, he holds out his hand for me. Wrapping my shawl tighter around my shoulders, I place my hand in his, stepping out into the cool night air.

The second the car door shuts behind me, several pairs of curious eyes stare at us in probably both awe and fear. It's expected, seeing that I'm standing hand in hand with one of the world's most feared men. But it feels a little more intense than I anticipated.

Eli and a few other men appear and walk closely behind us before Leo signals to the other men to disperse throughout the property.

Hushed whispers float through the space as we bypass the crowd waiting outside. Once we make it inside to the top floor where the party is taking place, I feel a slight weight lift.

Step one feels completed.

"Okay?" Leo asks, leaning closely to my side.

I turn into him, his familiar scent comforting my unease. "Why was everyone staring?"

This gets him to smile. "I've never been seen in public with a date." He bends down, brushing his lips over the side of my neck. "But tonight, the whole world will know you're my wife." He lifts my hand, pressing his lips directly on the wedding band.

My wife.

"I'm going to sweep the room, boss," Eli declares before taking off, preparing for anything that might go wrong.

Like someone trying to kidnap me...*again.* I swallow the lump in my throat, my eyes wearily traveling over the room. Could *he* be here tonight?

Leo presses a kiss against my temple, sending a pleasant shiver down my spine, instantly distracting me from my thoughts.

"Cold?" he asks, noticing my slight tremble.

"Just a little," I lie, knowing he sees straight through it.

He brushes his lips against the shell of my ear. "Shall I warm you properly when we leave here?" My lips part, a quiet gasp escaping me. My core burns with need from the insinuation of his words. And having a repeat of the other night, the one when I came apart in his arms, sounds exactly like what I need right now. But maybe more.

"I think—"

"Scarlett!" Maddy approaches, stunning in an off-the-shoulder ivory strapless gown that flows to the floor. A thigh-high slit appears on her left side as she takes a step.

I smile, reaching out to embrace her. "You look amazing."

"Me?" she questions, looking me up and down. "What about you? This dress is stunning."

My cheeks heat up from the attention.

"So, where's the man of the hour?" Leo asks, brows raised as his gaze sweeps the room. "He is here, correct?"

Maddy bites her bottom lip, nodding. "Oh, he's somewhere—"

"I'm right here, sweetness." A tall man with slicked-back blond hair appears by her side, seizing his arm tightly around her waist. His smile appears slightly too big as he takes in Leo and me. More so me, his eyes focused on parts of my body I wish he would avoid.

Leo adjusts his stance, tucking me slightly beneath his hold. "Alastor."

"Leo," Alastor responds before his eyes move back onto me, traveling up and down my body. "And who do we have here?"

"My wife," Leo answers for me, his voice deepening. "Scarlett Alarie." He enunciates my new last name with possessiveness. And it does something to me.

Alastor's creepy smile grows. "Ahh. So you're the girl who was kidnapped."

Suddenly, Leo steps before me, his back muscles beneath his jacket tensing as he forces himself into Alastor's face. "Do you think that's funny?"

"Not at all," Alastor replies calmly, putting his hands up in mock surrender. "Merely stating a fact."

Leo sneers down at him. "Keep your mouth shut if you know what's best for you."

"Noted." Alastor's expression remains neutral.

A thick tension swarms the air around us, the silence almost suffocating.

"Come on, boys." Maddy gives a nervous chuckle. "Let's all play nice tonight."

"Of course, darling." Alastor leans down, pressing a kiss to the top of her head. Is it my imagination, or did Maddy just cringe? "Wouldn't want anything to stop us from becoming husband and wife now, would we?"

She shakes her head, her expression turning serious. "Of course not."

"Alastor!" a woman nearby shouts for his attention.

"Excuse me." Alastor dips his head before slipping away. The eerie smirk on his face, thankfully, disappears from view.

Leo tenses beside me, pinching the bridge of his nose. His free arm loops around my waist, tugging me against his side. "What the fuck, Madeleine?"

"What?" she asks, peeking around the impressive room. She brings her polished fingers to her mouth and chews on her thumb's nail—a nervous habit she's had since we were children.

"You had to pick the biggest asshole in the room to fall in love with?" Leo's tone drips with disgust.

"It's not..." She shakes her head, dropping her shoulders. "You don't understand."

"Then why don't you try to ex—"

"I have to go to the bathroom!" Maddy rushes out. She turns toward me, smiling, but her tired, melancholy eyes tell me a different story. "I'm so glad you're here. I'll come find you later!"

"Of course." I watch as she turns and walks away, her steps rushed. After meeting Alastor for, at most, two minutes, I can't help but wonder what she sees in him. He doesn't seem like the kind of man she used to go after. In fact, as Eli approaches, I realize that Alastor is the exact opposite of Eli in every way. The man Maddy spent her teenage years crushing on. And crushing hard.

But I guess those days have passed, seeing that she's happily engaged to someone else.

"Everything's cleared," Eli informs Leo.

"Good. Now go find my sister." He jerks his head toward where Maddy disappeared. "And try to find out what the hell is going on with her." Leo gives Eli a cautious look, one that causes Eli's expression to turn stone cold before he nods and takes off after her.

"I take it you're not a fan of her fiancé?"

"You could say that." He runs his hand through his hair, blowing out a frustrated breath. "Don't ever find yourself alone with him. I don't trust him for as far as my eye can see."

I frown. "But you trust him to marry your sister?"

"Oh." He shakes his head, chuckling, a mischievous glint in his eye. "Their wedding is not happening."

"What—"

"There you two are." Mrs. Alarie approaches, appearing elegant in a deep blue cape gown. "I just saw Madeleine storming off down the hall. Is everything all right?"

"It will be." Leo's cold gaze is focused on the back of Alastor's head.

Mrs. Alarie nods, perfecting her smile as guests begin to fill the space. "And where are your brothers?"

"Vin and Alex will be arriving shortly. They were held up at the casino. And Mauro wasn't planning on coming. You know these things are difficult for him to—"

"He's here," I interject, noticing the hulk-sized man walking through the room. Mauro appears entirely out of place in a suit that looks a tad bit too small for his burly frame. His finger pulls at his collar as he approaches, a few strands of hair escaping from the neat bun.

"Mauro." His mother beams. "You look so handsome."

He grunts in response, a light shade of pink spreading up his neck. He's uncomfortable, feeling out of place amongst those who don't understand him.

Just like me.

It pulls at my heartstrings to know that even though he appears solid and unbreakable from the outside, he's hurting on the inside.

Fragile.

Without thinking it through, I find myself wrapping my arms around him, my cheek pressing against his chest. "I'm glad you're here."

His body freezes beneath my hold, and I wonder if I crossed a line I shouldn't have. Have I made this worse for him?

"You know, you can hug her back," Leo quietly remarks.

Mauro's arms slowly curl around me, and I feel his body relax. I want to tell him that I see him. That I know the pain he feels. But I stop myself because maybe I don't. Maybe we all feel pain at different levels. What may cause one person only a little heartache or grief may cause someone else more pain than they may be able to handle. Either way, I want him to know that I'm here. That we're all here.

He awkwardly pats my back a few times before we part, showing a slight smile as Leo heaves me back to his side.

"Madeleine will be so glad you came," Mrs. Alarie says softly, her eyes glassy with unshed tears.

He nods and examines the room, his eyes hopping from person to person as if seeking out someone in particular.

A quartet in the corner of the room starts playing music as the wide French doors open, signaling to guests that dinner is ready. Leo leads us inside the room, nodding to familiar faces as we find our table. Fancy embroidered name cards distinguish everyone's seats, and as I attempt to take mine, Leo squeezes my hand and shakes his head. He swiftly switches our nameplates, placing me to his right. Our hands part so that he can pull out the chair for me, and I sit as I lift the hem of my dress.

Leo doesn't appreciate the distance of his chair from mine, so he inches his chair closer and sits, shoulders straightened, eyes on alert, glancing around the room as his hand lands firmly on my thigh, his thumb slipping beneath the slit, finding my bare skin to dance back and forth across.

It's his way of ensuring everyone in the room knows I'm his.

My attention slides to my right as the chair at the head of the table moves.

"Ah! Leo, I'm so pleased you brought your beautiful wife tonight. I thought you planned to hide her behind that fortress forever." An older gentleman with a French accent chuckles, smiling warmly.

"Not at all." Leo turns toward the man, his hand moving from my thigh to the back of my neck, his thumb stroking my skin in a calming gesture he knows my body craves. "It is an honor to introduce you to my wife, Scarlett. Scarlett, this is Uncle Claude, my father's eldest brother."

I turn toward Claude, holding out my hand. "It is a pleasure to meet you."

"The pleasure is all mine." He takes my hand and leans down to kiss the back of it. I know this man means no harm. One could sense his warmth and kindness from a mile away. But Leo knows me. He knows my discomfort of being touched by anyone beside him, so he immediately stops it.

His hand jumps across, yanking mine toward him.

"I must warn you, Claude; Scarlett is mine, which means only my lips touch her skin."

A shudder runs through me at the thought.

Claude smooths a hand over his salt-and-pepper hair. "He was always the possessive type. Even toward an old man like me. But I'm flattered you consider me competition." He takes a sip from the glass before him, appearing unbothered.

Leo's hand moves back to my thigh, slipping under the slit and then sneaking about an inch higher up my leg. The rough pads of his fingers gently squeeze before slowly caressing my skin.

I let out a deep breath, my insides turning molten beneath his touch. A familiar ache begins to grow between my legs, and to distract myself, I glance around the room, studying all the well-dressed couples taking their places at their tables.

Madeleine and Alastor are seated at the closest table to ours at the head of the room. Vin and Alex arrive, taking their seats across from us beside Mauro, while Mrs. Alarie sits between a few women I don't recognize, chatting away. The room is packed with faces I don't know, but my eyes snag on a man in particular, one well-dressed just like everyone else in the room, sitting at a table with a few other men at the other end of the room, and who is...staring at me.

I freeze. His eyes watch me. Study me. Violate me. An overwhelming surge of fear engulfs me as his lips curl into a menacing smile. His hazel eyes reveal that he's not Le Diable, but then, who is he?

Leo squeezes my thigh, bringing my attention to him.

"Is everything okay?" he asks, his eyes most likely noting every trace of anxiety on my face.

I clear my throat and throw on a smile, not wanting him to know I'm overreacting to the sight of a man I don't even know. "I'm fine."

He leans in and brushes his lips against mine. "Just say the word, and we can go."

"Not yet." I pick up my fork and stab a piece of the salad. "I can do this."

"I know you can."

At around the third course, I feel myself going into an overdrive of nerves and paranoia.

I keep catching the man blatantly staring at me. But every time Leo's head turns in his direction, the man innocently shoots his eyes to his plate.

There's shrill laughter and deafening conversations. Knives and forks scratching against plates. Chairs scrape across the floor as people come and go. Music wafts through the enormous room.

And the cherry on top of my oversensitive mind is Leo's hand crawling deliciously closer to the danger zone. His thumb grazes my skin, subtly inching nearer as he leans in to converse with Claude.

I feel...everything.

And it's all too overstimulating.

Too goddamn much.

Abruptly, I push myself away from the table, my gold cloth napkin falling to the floor as I stand, nearby watchful eyes landing on me.

Leo stands, towering over me. "What's wrong?"

"Nothing." I scratch the side of my neck; my skin feels too tight. "I-I need to use the restroom."

"I'll go with you."

I place my hand on his chest, trying to subdue my trembling. "I'll be right back. I saw where it was when we walked in. Besides, it's not like you can go in the ladies' room, anyway," I tease, trying to assure him I'm fine when I know I'm not.

"You're sure?"

I nod. "I'll be back before dessert. Promise."

He appears hesitant before leaning closer. "You have five minutes. If you're not back by then, I'll come find you."

"I expect nothing less." I place a kiss on his cheek and turn, smoothing out my dress as I exit the room.

I need air.

And I need it now.

Bypassing the restroom, I continue walking straight ahead through the deserted hall toward the balcony doors. The moment I swing the glass doors open and step outside, a rush of cool air cascades over my bare skin in a welcomed embrace. I close my eyes, letting out a deep breath.

I'm safe.

I'm safe.

I'm safe.

I repeat the mantra as I open my eyes and advance toward the railing, taking in the view of the city before me.

I've never been much of a city girl, but even I can admit this is pretty extraordinary, especially from so high up. The lights twinkle around every building and lamppost beneath us, reminding me of tiny fireflies, which causes a smile to form on my face.

Still, nothing rivals the beauty found on the Alarie Estate. A place I'm itching to get back to.

Just a few more hours.

I don't want to disappoint, Leo.

I can do this.

"I would imagine this view is quite different from what one might find chained up in a cellar with no windows."

Every muscle in my body stiffens as terror descends upon me. My fingers, clutching the railing, tremble as the stranger's presence inches closer to my body.

"You are so very pretty, Scarlett." A deep Russian accent assaults my ears. His breath trails across my exposed neck, and I take a step away, moving on shaky legs out of his reach, inadvertently cornering myself.

My eyes widen. "Y-you?"

He smiles, the same creepy smile he gave me only an hour ago from across the room. "My apologies for not properly introducing myself." He dips his head. "Many call me Fedya."

"And why are you here?" I place my hand between us to keep a semblance of distance. "I assume you're not here for either the bride or the groom."

"No." He shakes his head. "I'm here on behalf of my employer."

"And who do you work for?" Unease fills me, certain I know the answer to this question.

His smile grows. "Now, Scarlett, you're a smart girl. You know the answer to that."

No. This isn't happening. I internally shake my head, waiting for the man to disappear with no such luck. This is just one of the regularly occurring nightmares I have. It has to be. My pulse thunders in my ears as every brain cell I have yells at me to run.

Quickly, I step to my right, but he blocks my path, caging me against the stone banister. Fisting my hands at my sides, I grit out as calmly as I can, "Get out of my way."

"You know I can't do that." He steps closer to me, all the space between us vanishing. "I'm afraid you'll be leaving with me tonight."

All-encompassing terror sideswipes me as I grip the railing tighter for support, my knees on the verge of giving out.

"My husband won't let that happen!"

The man looks around, laughing. "Where is he? He won't even notice I've taken you until it's too late. And once I have, I assure you, he'll never be able to find you." His gaze hardens. "Not this time."

Tears streak down my cheeks. Is he right? Will Leo not even notice that I'm missing?

No! He's wrong! He doesn't know the things Leo would do to keep me safe. He would burn down the whole goddamn world to find me.

"You're going to make him a lot of money." The man raises his hand, appearing ready to wipe the tears from my face. "You're so young. So beautiful. So fragile—"

Boom!

CHAPTER SIXTEEN

T his brazen motherfucker thought he was about to touch my wife.

My wife.

When I noticed Fedya, aka Igor's loyal dog, missing from his seat when Scarlett disappeared to the bathroom, I knew we had a problem on our hands because he was the same man who hadn't been able to take his eyes off my wife the entire night since we sat down for dinner. Darting his eyes toward his plate every time that I tried to catch him in the act. Fucking coward.

So, imagine my surprise when I opened the door to the balcony with Eli and Mauro right behind me and found my wife cornered like prey while the asshole's hand was raised in the air attempting to touch her.

Therefore, I was given no choice.

I shot his hand.

No one touches my wife.

"You shot my fucking hand!" Fedya turns toward me, crying like a baby, as he holds his blood-soaked hand to his chest. A perfect shot to the center of his palm eases my fury just a fraction. Eli strides toward him to apprehend him while I rush to a trembling Scarlett.

"Get him out of my sight, Eli," I shout as my arms lock around my wife, bringing her flush against my chest. "Take him to the warehouse."

"You got it, boss." Eli pushes him out the door with help from Mauro. Crimson blood trails across the marble-tiled flooring.

"Firefly, I'm here. You're safe." I remove my jacket, placing it on her shoulders. Her big blue eyes look up at me with so much vulnerability flashing through them.

"You...you didn't let him t-touch me," she stammers disbelievingly, her teeth chattering.

I palm her cheek, running my fingers down to her neck where I feel her pulse point racing too fast. "No one touches you but me." She blinks a few times, my words registering deep within her. "But I need to get you out of here before you go into shock."

She slowly nods, about to take a step when I lift her in the air, securing her to my body with one arm under her thighs and the other across her back.

She's safe. She's safe. She's safe. I repeat the mantra, urgently trying to ease my fury.

She clutches my shirt, nuzzling her face into the crook of my neck, deeply inhaling.

"We're going home," I tell her.

"Home," she repeats quietly.

With ferocity and haste, I make it to the waiting car before anyone has a chance to notice our absence. I place Scarlett on her seat, close the door behind her, and walk around to my side, quickly getting in next to her. After I alert the driver to bring us home, Scarlett climbs onto my lap, burrowing herself into my embrace.

I gently smooth her hair as I brush my lips across her temple. "I never should have let you out of my sight." Feeling her shiver against me, I adjust the heat setting to full blast.

She shakes her head. "Y-you can't be with me twenty-four-seven. He would have gotten to me one way or another tonight."

"No, he wouldn't have if—" Then it dawns on me. "Firefly." I tilt her chin toward me, her eyes resting on mine. "What did he say to you?"

Her eyes water. Tears escape, dribbling down her cheeks, and they break my fucking heart. The fear. The pain. The helplessness. None of it should be there. But it is. And I can't wait for the day when I can annihilate the monster who put it there.

She blinks, looking out the window beside her. "He said that...he was going to take me tonight but that you wouldn't be able to find me this time." Her eyes jump back to me, her bottom lip trembling. "And that I'm going to make *him* a lot of money. But I don't understand what that means."

The goddamn sex auction. I grind my jaw. Fedya's words confirm my greatest fear. Scarlett was being held for a sex auction. One that has yet to happen and one that, if they had brought her to, I don't know if I ever would have been able to find her.

And that scares the living fuck out of me.

I brush her blonde strands out of her face, tucking it behind her ear. "No one will ever take you from me. No one. Because you're mine, Firefly, and I promise you that I have been and will continue to kill every person involved with your kidnapping. Every person who has so much as touched a hair on your head will pay for their crimes by my hands. I will make them suffer. I will watch them lose their goddamn dignity as they beg for death. But I will not give it to them because death is too easy. Too kind. And I will not be their salvation. Only their damnation. They will regret ever coming anywhere near you. My wife."

I push the steel door open; Mauro, Vin, and Alex are hot on my trail. Tied to a chair in the center of the room is my prey.

My blood boils.

My skin burns.

All with the desire to maim the motherfucker who tried to touch my wife last night.

A vicious smile spreads across my face as my eyes take in his ragged appearance. There's sweat coating his temple, his dark hair is disheveled, his three-piece suit is a rumpled mess, and I'm pretty sure there's an old piss stain on the front of his pants.

But being left here all night tied to a chair, awaiting your judgment day, can do that to a man.

"Good morning, Fedya." I pull up a chair and sit across from him. My brothers stand closely behind me, their eyes drilling into him.

He sneers at me before spitting on the ground between us.

I roll my neck from side to side, my index finger tapping madly on my thigh as I try to calm my murderous thoughts.

"What were you doing at Madeleine and Alastor's engagement party last night?" Vin asks, leaning against the wall, his arms crossed over his chest. He appears calm, cool, and collected, but I know him. He's far from it. Not only was this creep trying to take Scarlett, but he was also on Alarie property.

That's two strikes against him.

Fedya smirks. "My employer sent me to bring back his *asset*."

I snap. My fingers wrap around his throat, strangling the life out of him. Vin taps me on the shoulder.

"If you do that, we find out nothing."

Fuck, he's right. Before Fedya loses consciousness, I release him. He gasps for air, gulping it down as fast as he can, taking only a moment to regain his composure.

"By employer, you mean Igor Vasiliev?" Alex brushes off a piece of lint from his jacket. "We already know you're one of his cronies. So why did he send you?"

Fedya shakes his head, laughing. "Igor did not know I was coming here last night. Although, he would approve of my actions." He *tsks*. "You really pissed him off by meddling in his business."

"Meddling?" Vin scoffs. "If you mean interfering with trafficking, then yeah, we're going to fucking meddle in his business."

"Ah. But you see, it's not just his business." His grin widens.

"What the fuck do you mean?" Vin's brows tug together, a muscle ticking in his jaw.

Alex tilts his head to the side, observing him, seeing something the rest of us don't. "Check his pockets."

"Gladly," Vin affirms. He was already cleared of all weapons, but Vin pats him down, emptying his pockets of trash and miscellaneous items until he holds a familiar black card before us.

Blue Velvet Fantasies.

"Why the fuck do you have this?" Vin grips the card, his knuckles turning stark white.

"My employer gave it to me." Fedya shrugs his shoulders, appearing too relaxed for someone about to have his last moment on earth. "He's the owner of this prestigious club."

"Igor?" Vin questions, pinching the bridge of his nose with force. He looks about ready to combust any second.

Fedya shakes his head. "No. He is an investor, yes, of course. Such a lucrative investment. But he is not the owner."

"Then who is?" I ask, losing all of my patience.

Enjoyment flickers across his features as he says, "A ghost."

Vin grabs him by the collar, bringing them face to face. "We're not playing your games. So tell us, who fucking owns this club?"

Fedya merely states again, "A ghost."

Vin pushes him down and takes a few steps away, placing his hands on his hips. "Can we just kill him already?"

"No." I shake my head, determined to get something useful out of this fucker. "If you're not going to tell us who owns it, then you can determine how quickly we kill you by how you answer this next question. But either way, you're not walking out of here alive."

Vin rubs his temple. "You're not going to get anything out of him when he's getting off on playing games with us."

"Then let's play it my way." I grab my knife and hold it under Fedya's chin, digging it into his skin. "Who is Le Diable?"

He looks around timidly, and something new passes over his features. *Fear.* "He..."

"Answer my fucking question." I press the tip into his skin and droplets of blood roll down his neck.

"H-he'll kill me if I tell you."

"Well, I'm going to kill you, anyway, so might as well get it off your chest."

His eyes dance across the room, trepidation stopping him.

"Why are you acting as if he's here now?" Alex asks, cautiously peering around. His hand tightens on his gun as his eyes scope out the space.

"Because he's everywhere," he whispers as if fearing someone might hear, but we're the only ones here. "H-Halloween night."

I narrow my eyes. "What about Halloween night?"

"That's when the next shipment of girls is coming in, and that's...that's when you'll find him there. He's responsible for collecting the girls and bringing them in for the auctions."

"Find him where?" I demand, the knife now coated in a sheen of blood.

His eyes seem lost. "He's bloodthirsty crazy. The things he's done..." A shiver runs through him. A vehicle approaching outside causes Fedya's eyes to widen. Footsteps crunch on the gravel outside.

"Where?" I roar.

"I've said too much." His eyes meet mine, a warning glimmering across them. "Trust no one."

Before I can stop him, he slams his neck down on the knife. Blood spurts all over my hand and clothes. Fedya chokes on his blood, gurgling noises filling the space for only seconds before his body goes limp.

"Fuck!" I remove my knife, dropping it to the floor.

"Do we believe him?" Vin pulls out his phone, most likely texting the cleaning crew.

"There was no reason for him to lie about Halloween," Alex muses, handing me a towel. "Especially if he was going to kill himself."

I nod. Halloween is only weeks away. Hopefully, it's enough time for us to find this place and stop anything from happening.

Mauro holds out his phone toward me. *Now what?*

"I don't know." I toss the towel to the floor.

Alex paces the room. "At least we have a date. That's something we can work with. I can set alerts in my system based on the date."

Vin frowns. "That's hardly anything to work off of." He pinches the bridge of his nose. "We need to find the location. Once we have that, we'll have Le Diable in our clutches. Not to mention, we'll be able to destroy this sex club. We'll be able to kill two birds with one stone."

"When you went with Dad, do you remember anything about what the club looked like from the outside?" I ask.

He shakes his head. "I was so overwhelmed. I—" His voice trails off.

"What is it?"

"I remember, when we pulled up to the place, it just looked like an ordinary warehouse. It didn't appear as anything special—especially not a club. If anything, it looked worn down, ready to collapse at any moment. I think that's why they chose it. To hide in the dark instead of standing out. They keep their establishment hidden from prying eyes."

I nod. "That's something we can use."

The steel door slides open, revealing Asher and Dolion. Dolion strides closer, inspecting the body. He rubs his eyes and shakes his head. "That ended quicker than I assumed it would."

I look back at the lifeless body. "He took matters into his own hands."

Asher places his hands in his pockets. "By the looks on your faces, I'm guessing you didn't get much out of him?"

I stand, zipping my leather jacket. "Nothing of importance." I head toward the door, stepping outside. A fall breeze caresses me as three words whisper around me.

Trust no one.

Chapter Seventeen

Scarlett

The front door opens, and my body tenses before I hear the familiar deep timbre of Leo's voice.

"I'm home."

I jump up from the swing and step inside, observing several takeout bags in his hands. Brutus rushes to the bags, his nose inspecting tonight's dinner. He thinks he'll get something out of one of them, and knowing how easily I give in to his big brown eyes, he's probably right.

"I picked up Italian for dinner," Leo says. "I hope that's okay."

I smile. "I would expect nothing less."

His lips curve up as he enters the living room, heading directly toward me. With only inches between us and the bags still in his hands, he leans down, capturing my lips in a tantalizing kiss, leaving me weak in the knees, wanting more.

"Did you have a nice day?" he asks, pressing our foreheads together.

"I spent my morning with Maddy, and then I went to the women and children's center to read to the kids in the afternoon." I softly press my lips to his. "But this right here is my favorite part of my day."

"Mine too." He brushes his lips across my temple and then places the bags of food on the coffee table in front of the sectional.

Pulling a large treat out of his pocket, he throws it to the other side of the room, where Brutus makes himself comfortable.

"Are we eating in the living room tonight?" I inspect the spotless space. It's not a room we've used very often; even Brutus keeps his slobber far away from it.

He gives a half shrug as he removes his leather jacket, placing it on the back of one of the chairs. "Thought we could enjoy dinner and a movie tonight if you're up for it."

A delicious warmth spreads through me.

Dinner and a movie.

Something normal people do.

"I'd like that." I sit on the end of the sectional, tucking my legs beneath me.

Could this be our new life? Would we eventually fall into this comfortable routine together? Leo would spend his days negotiating deals and interrogating those who got in his family's way. And I would... Well, what would I do? Or, more like, what could I do, especially when I had a difficult enough time leaving the safety of the Alarie Estate?

I enjoyed the ease of being around Leo. The familiar closeness we once shared has become more apparent each day, although maybe we aren't as close physically as we once were...

An alluring chill ghosts over my skin as I remember our intimate moment together seven years ago. A beautiful memory that got me through so many dark days. Saving me. But could we find our way to that place again with each other? Or would Leo eventually lose patience with me, ending this marriage after Le Diable is found, expecting me to move on and forget about our time together? Our marriage. Him. All of it.

I mean, a man can probably only go so long without sex. They have needs. Desires. Cravings. As far as I know, Leo isn't getting any of those things met by anyone else. Or is he? God, I hope not. Is it even fair for me to be upset if he is when I haven't given him what he needs?

This is too deep for a Friday night.

"Good." Leo's voice releases me from my thoughts. He removes the containers from the bags and sits on the sectional. Reaching for the remote, he asks, "What would you like to watch?" He rolls up his sleeves, revealing his veiny muscular forearms covered in black ink. My eyes travel over each intricate design, watching the way they curve around every ridge.

"Scarlett?"

Shit. "Hmm?" What did he ask me? And how can something as trivial as a forearm cause me to lose all train of thought?

Because you know what that hand attached to his forearm is capable of doing...

He grins as if knowing what I was just thinking about. "What would you like to watch?"

"Oh, right." I shove my fork into a familiar pasta dish, twirling the noodles. "Actually..." I clear my throat. "I was hoping I could talk to you about something first."

"Of course." He turns all of his attention on me.

"I umm..." I scratch my neck. I can do this. I had been thinking a lot about it recently, and it was time to come out with it. "What happened at Maddy's engagement party made me think about things. And you see, I was thinking..." I swallow down my nerves. *Out with it, Scarlett!* "I was thinking I could take some self-defense classes," I rush out in one breath.

Leo runs his fingers through his hair, deep in thought. "Well, fuck."

Was this a bad idea? I thought he would approve, but maybe I overstepped my boundaries. A sweat breaks out on the back of my neck, and I shove my hands beneath my thighs.

"I should have thought of that," he admits.

Relief washes over me.

"You're not mad?"

"Mad?" His brows furrow. "Of course not." He leans against the back of the couch, rubbing his chin. "Would you be opposed to one of my brothers training you?"

My lips open and close. "Your brothers? I was kind of hoping it would be you who trains me..."

He studies me, his eyes focused as he leans forward, his elbows resting on his knees. "I would love nothing more than to help you with this, but I feel like I would hold back because I would be scared of hurting you." His eyes soften. "And that's the last thing I ever want to do."

I nod, understanding. "Then who?"

"Mauro," he says matter-of-factly. "He trains all of our men in hand-to-hand combat. He will be the one to train you. I'll reach out to him tonight about this."

"Okay." My shoulders drop. Is this a good idea? I've been thinking about it a lot recently. Convincing myself that it would help if I knew some basics. However, maybe this would turn out to be a disaster, especially if I were to train with someone other than Leo. But I understand his reasoning and know why he wants it to be Mauro.

After all, with Mauro being the unofficial enforcer for the family, he's probably the most skilled on the property and can teach me everything he knows.

God, listen to me. I sound like someone getting ready for battle when I'm just looking to learn the basics. Things I should have learned years ago.

"Is there anything else you wanted to discuss?" Leo asks, his head tilted to the side.

I shake my head, pulling myself out of my thoughts. "No."

He hesitates as if he can tell there's more on my mind but picks up the remote instead, giving me space. "So, what should we watch?"

"Something a little lighthearted?"

"You got it." He scrolls through the streaming services until we narrow our options and pick one we agree on.

About halfway through the movie, when the friends who are fake dating realize they have actual feelings for each other, I sulk against the cushion, rubbing my tummy. "I ate too much."

"Me too." Leo pushes his containers to the side and lies on the sofa, bringing a blanket over his body.

He looks comfy.

He looks warm.

He looks—

"Want to join?" he asks me.

I bite my bottom lip, my heart beating a little faster.

He holds up the blanket, revealing a good amount of space beside him. "The offer only lasts for another ten seconds." He slowly starts bringing the blanket down. "Ten...nine...eight..."

He's giving me a choice.

But do I want to join?

Yes, of course I do. But am I ready to join?

It's just a cuddle.

Basically, it's one giant hug.

A giant hug with my husband.

The same man who cut up all my fruits and vegetables so I wouldn't have to. The same man who purchased a custom nightlight for me. And the same man who restrained himself while I rode his thigh, seeking my pleasure.

"Three...two..."

"Okay." A smile tugs at my lips as I scoot across the couch.

I burrow myself into the space beside him, aligning my back to his front. My head rests on his bicep, and he brings the blanket down, cocooning us in warmth. His other hand rests on my waist, his sock-covered feet tangling around mine.

"Is this okay?"

"Y-yes."

His thumb, resting on my waist where my shirt has ridden up, caresses my skin back and forth, and my breathing increases.

"You're not trapped here. You have the freedom to leave at any time," he assures me.

"I know." I reach for his hand by my head, intertwining our fingers, instantly relaxing me. "I never feel trapped with you. It just takes my body a moment to realize I'm safe."

His body relaxes against me. "I understand."

Gazing up at the screen, I observe the two main characters in a heated embrace. The man has the woman pushed up against the wall as she moans out in pleasure, tugging on his hair. Suddenly, the man drops down to his knees before her, hauling up the hem of her dress, revealing her underwear.

A slight throb takes over my center as I watch with bated breath for what's to come.

Does the woman want the man to do this?

Does she have a choice in what's going on?

But as the man pushes aside her panties and buries his face between her legs, she screams, "More!"

I realize...she's the one in control of this moment.

She wants this.

And I suddenly find myself squirming, wondering what something like that might feel like. Would I like that? Would Leo even want to do that to me?

"Does that feel good for her?" I ask in a whisper before I can stop myself. My cheeks blaze in heat. Why did I ask that?

Leo's body stiffens for only a second before his head leans closer to mine, his hand sliding to the front of my stomach.

"It does." His warm breath caresses my ear, sending a shiver down my spine. "When done right, it can be the most pleasure a woman feels." His fingers trace my skin, heightening my impending arousal. "See the way the man can't stop. He can't get enough of her. Of her taste. Of her smell. Of her desires."

I can't breathe as I watch the screen before me. The man's hands grip the woman's thighs as he continues his ministrations, the woman grasping his hair, holding him hostage to her core as her back starts to arch and her mouth forms a perfect circle. And then, finally, a scream fills the room. But I realize then that it's not a scream produced by pain. One I had become so accustomed to leaving my throat months ago. But instead, it's a scream released from her overwhelming stimulation. It's a good kind of scream.

"Because providing her pleasure gives him pleasure in return," Leo murmurs, his hard body molding right up against mine.

I swallow hard; my whole body is engulfed with pulses of need shooting throughout every vein.

I want that.

I want to be in control of my pleasure. My body. My needs.

The night outside with Leo by the tree, when I straddled his thigh, was a small step in that direction. But watching this scene unfold before me makes me recognize it wasn't enough for me.

And I need more.

I tilt my head to the side, my eyes catching with Leo's.

"Do you want that, wife?" he asks, as if reading my mind. His nose grazes my cheek, his lips peppering kisses on my skin. "Do you want your husband to make you feel good by licking your sweet pussy until you come just like she did?"

My lips part in both shock and longing from his words. "Please," I breathe.

"All I want to do is worship you." His eyes lock with mine. "Tell me you want that too."

I nod.

"I need to hear you say it, Scarlett."

"I want that." A tremble rolls through me as his eyes darken with hunger. "But I'm...scared."

He leans over me, gently pushing my shoulder down so that I'm lying flat on my back. His hand finds my cheek, his thumb gently stroking my skin.

"Are you scared of me?" For the first time I can ever recall, I note a hint of fear in his eyes as he waits for my answer.

"No." I shake my head adamantly. "You don't scare me. You're the one person I trust most in this world."

His face softens, all hints of fear vanishing from his eyes. "Then what are you scared of?"

I swallow, closing my eyes, emotions I worked so hard to keep at bay, deciding to come out and play. "I'm scared of having a flashback," I admit. My eyes blur with tears. "I'm scared that being with you in that way will bring me right back to those days where I was..." *Locked up like an animal. Used. Left to die.* A tear slides down my cheek. "Broken," I whisper. "But I want to try. I want to feel a semblance of control over my life again."

Leo's lips brush against mine. Softly and tenderly. "I'm going to prove to you that he didn't break you, Firefly." He backs away, watching me. "If you let me, I can remind you what it feels like to be intimate with someone you trust. Someone who only wants to make you feel good, to bring the light back into your eyes." He wipes my tears with his thumb and then presses a kiss to the same spot. "As your husband, I want nothing more than to bring you immense pleasure. I want to take care of all your needs. And I want you to know that you are always the one in control when you're with me. I bow down to only you, wife."

A whoosh of air leaves my lungs as my heart pounds behind my rib cage. "Remind me, Leo. Please," I say softly, almost begging.

"I will," he promises. "But you need to do two things for me."

"What?"

"The first thing is I need your eyes on me the whole time. I want you to see who is bringing you pleasure. I want you to be present in this moment with me. Only me, Scarlett. I don't want you getting lost in your head."

I let out a breath. "Okay."

"The second thing is that if you want me to stop, you tell me to stop. It's that simple."

"I can do that."

"Good." He leans down, pressing his lips to mine. A kiss that starts slow and sweet but quickly turns hungry and consuming. I wrap my hands around his neck, tugging him into me as my tongue slides against his, tasting, exploring, savoring. He slowly parts, a mischievous glint in his eyes as he slides down my body. "Tell me one more time that you want this. Let me hear you say it."

My heart rate increases, but it's not from nerves or fear. It's from pure excitement. "I want this."

He lifts the edge of my shirt, revealing my belly button. His lips land on my skin over and over again. A fire erupts in my stomach as my fingers clutch the blanket; anticipation, as I've never felt, builds within me.

He continues slowly sliding down my body, taking his sweet time. Sending me into a haze of unrelenting lust. His fingers find the zipper on my pants, and he looks up at me. "I'm going to take these off. Okay?"

"Okay." I stare at the ceiling, my heart thrashing recklessly.

"Scarlett."

"Yes?"

"What did I say?"

What did he say? I rack my mind. Did I already do something wrong? Am I messing this—

"Look at me, beautiful girl." My eyes meet his. "I want you to watch everything I'm about to do to you. I want you in this moment with me and only me. Are you here with me?"

"I'm here," I breathe.

He slides my pants over my thighs, and I lift my legs as he continues to pull them down until they're entirely off me and tossed to the floor. Nerves rattle through me as he stares at my black panties, his gaze unwavering. His thumbs slide under the edge of my underwear. "Now, I'm going to take these off. Okay?"

"Y-yes."

He slips the fabric gently down my legs. A cold gust of air hits me as I lie here with my bottom half bare to him. His eyes ignite with a primal fire, desire and longing taking over him. But he clears his throat and, ever so slowly, lowers himself between my legs, his face right above my most intimate area. The pounding between my legs intensifies to an unbearable level as I tighten my thighs together.

"Spread your legs for me, baby. Let me see all of you."

Letting out a breath, I widen my legs, allowing him full access to my center.

His tongue comes out, licking his lips, his eyes taking me in. "Such a good girl." Slowly, he lowers his mouth with his eyes on mine as he sticks out his tongue, flattens it against me, and takes one long, leisurely stroke.

"Ohhh," I gasp at the unfamiliar but satisfying touch.

"I'm going to make you come now, wife." He reaches his hand for mine, gently squeezing. "Don't forget, eyes on me."

And with that, he buries his face between my legs, lapping up my center like it's his favorite meal, not leaving a single crumb on the plate.

"Leo," I pant, squirming with pleasure.

This feeling is indescribable.

It feels good. Really good.

But it also feels like too much.

Like a part of me might explode at any moment.

But I want to unravel.

I want to lose control.

With my husband's head between my legs.

I begin to close my eyes, getting lost in this all-consuming pleasure trip, but Leo stops everything, and before panicking, I quickly remember his words.

I want you to watch everything I'm about to do to you. I want you in this moment with me and only me.

So my eyes pop open, noticing him smirk before he goes back to worshiping me.

"Oh, Leo... It feels so good," I moan.

My words only motivate him to work harder and faster. His tongue swirls inside me and then over me before landing on my most sensitive part.

"You taste so fucking sweet."

I squeeze Leo's hand as incoherent words leave my mouth.

"Oh yes... I'm almost... I'm about to..." My back arches off the couch, and my thighs begin to quiver. His fingers dig into my hip, holding me in place while his other hand tightens around my hand. His lips slide up my slit, sucking hard on my clit, and I unravel, falling down a dark abyss as I collapse back onto the couch, spent and completely drained, panting fast and hard. Leo pulls every last bit of the orgasm out of me before he slightly pulls away, leaning over me.

Wow. Just...wow.

I had no idea it could be like this.

That it could be so freeing and empowering all at the same time.

His eyes never break from mine as he moves up my body, positioning himself over me.

"Are you okay?" he asks softly, his hand cradling my cheek.

I blink back tears, a small smile breaking free. "I'm more than okay." As the lust fog dissipates, I come to my senses and realize I'm probably expected to do something for him in return. I swallow down the lump in my throat. "Do you... Do you want me to—"

"No," he rushes out, his face softening as he kisses my lips tenderly. "Making you feel good makes me feel good. It's that simple, Firefly." He slides onto his side beside me and wraps an arm around my waist, pulling me alongside him. I snuggle my face against his chest as he wraps the blanket around us.

"Thank you, Leo," I whisper. "For being patient with me and making me feel not so..." *Alone*. But I stop myself before admitting this out loud. "Well, what I mean is I don't think I could get through any of this without you."

His lips glide across my forehead, his grip around me strengthening. "Those seven years I went without you was a life not worth living, and now that I have you again, I won't risk losing you. Never again. The price is too damn high because you're worth everything to me." He presses his lips to my skin as warmth cascades over every inch of me. "Everything."

CHAPTER EIGHTEEN

Leo

A scream of death rings out, piercing me straight in the chest and abruptly waking me. Blinking a few times, I wonder if it was just a dream until I hear Brutus barking beside my bed followed by a blood-curdling scream ascending from across the hall.

Scarlett.

I leap out of bed with stealth as I reach inside my nightstand for my gun, bypass Brutus, and shove open my door. Scarlett's door is secured shut, not showing any malicious attempt by someone entering. I slap my hand on the scanner and wait the two point five seconds for it to recognize me. The mere seconds feel like an eternity as the screaming continues to assault me from the other side of the door. At the exact second the door unlatches, I storm inside like a bull seeing red. My eyes survey the dark room, the only source of light coming from the nightlight, casting a glow directly onto the bed, revealing only Scarlett.

My hammering heart begins to settle at the realization there's no intruder. Nor any person causing physical harm to her.

As I approach the bed, watching Scarlett toss and turn with tears running down both cheeks, she screams, "No, please don't!"

My chest tightens painfully from her plea. A plea I'm sure she used several times.

I sit beside her and place my gun on her nightstand, the bed creaking beneath my weight. Leaning over her, I run my knuckles along her jaw.

"Scarlett, wake up. You're okay, baby."

"No. No. Please don't!" She sobs, kicking the blankets off her body.

I can't bear the sight of her in so much distress, so I reach for her shoulders, gently giving her a little shake. "Scarlett!"

Her eyes pop open, her chest heaving from exertion. She blinks back tears, appearing lost in a trance as flashes of horrific images dance across her irises.

"It was just a dream. You're safe." I remove my hands from her, unsure if my touch is too much for her to handle right now after what I can only assume she dreamed about.

But as abruptly as my hands leave her, she jumps up and plasters her tiny body onto my lap. Her legs wrap around my torso like a vice, and her arms wrap around my neck, hauling herself into me. She buries her head into the crook of my neck, her tears dampening my skin.

"It felt so real. I couldn't make it stop," she sobs. "He tried... He tried to..."

"Shhhh." I stroke my fingers through her hair while my other hand wraps around her trembling body, holding her protectively to me. "I know, baby. I'm here. You're safe. I won't let anyone ever hurt you again."

She relaxes the tiniest bit in my hold, her cries slowly dying out.

We sit like this for a few minutes, and I'm struggling with the thought of having to let her go. Having to leave her alone in her room after the pleas I heard her scream out in terror.

I'm certain she's fallen asleep until her soft voice breaks the silence surrounding us. "Can I..." She stops herself, pressing her forehead against my chest.

"Can you what?"

She lets out a deep breath. "Can I stay with you tonight?" she asks softly, her voice laced with vulnerability.

"Of course, baby." I move my hand over her back, noticing how damp her T-shirt is. "Do you want to walk, or are you okay if I carry you?"

"Carry me," she whispers.

My hands move under her thighs, holding her to me as I stand and exit her room. Walking into my room, I find Brutus pacing beside the window. He hurries over to me, his nose anxiously sniffing Scarlett. "She's okay," I tell him as I head straight to the bed. Noting that I've got it handled, he pivots toward his bed and plops down, curling into a ball. "Let me get you a new shirt to wear." I settle Scarlett down onto the mattress, pulling the blankets over her bare legs. I turn to my dresser and pull out a simple black T-shirt. As I approach the bed, I notice her eyes gazing over my body, wandering over every tattoo with a tilt of her head, and I realize this is the first time in years that she's seen me without a shirt on. "Would you be more comfortable if I put something on?"

She shakes her head as a delicate blush creeps up her neck.

The blush is a good sign.

It means she's feeling something other than fear.

I hold the shirt out for her, but she remains frozen.

"Do you want help?"

Her eyes meet mine, and she doesn't need to say anything for me to know what she wants.

"Hands up," I tell her.

She reaches her shaking hands in the air, waiting for me to remove her T-shirt. My fingers grip the hem of her shirt, carefully pulling it up and over her body. My eyes stay glued to her eyes the whole time. As much as there is a part of me wanting to trail over every goddamn beautiful inch of her body, there's a bigger part of me that won't allow my eyes that privilege.

Not until she allows me.

After replacing her shirt with the new one, she snuggles her body into the mattress beneath the comforter. "Thank you."

I sit on the bed beside her, my hand cupping her cheek as I stroke her skin with my thumb. "Do you want to talk about it?"

She shakes her head. "I just want to forget about it."

I nod in understanding. Reaching into my nightstand, I pull out a bottle of pills the family's doctor, Dr. Hayes, gave me for her to take in situations like these.

"Do you want to take one of the pills Dr. Hayes prescribed you? He said it would help—"

"No." She sits up, clutching my forearm. "Please don't make me take it. I can't. It will only make things worse. Please don't," she begs, sounding fearful.

"Hey." I embrace her, pulling her into me. "I would never make you do anything." Her body relaxes, her head resting on my shoulder.

I glance at the container in my hand, reading the label. *Take one as needed every twelve hours*. It seems like a regular prescription to me. "Out of curiosity, why don't you want one of these?"

She stares at the bottle. "When I take one, I still have nightmares. I just can't wake up. I can't scream. I can't move. It puts me into a state of sleep paralysis."

I arch a brow. Sleep paralysis? I remove the cap, peering at the thirty or so pills in it. What the fuck is this shit? "Does Dr. Hayes know this?"

She pinches her eyes shut and nods. "I told him what happens when I take one, but he told me I should continue to take them so I wouldn't..." She swallows hard. "Disturb you."

My body becomes rigid. *That son of a bitch.*

"I'm sorry for waking you. Really, I am. I didn't mean—"

"You didn't wake me. I was already up," I lie, rubbing her back.

She appears relieved. "I don't know how easy it will be for me to fall back to sleep."

"Is there anything that might help?"

She ponders my question, her eyes appearing unsure.

"Tell me what you need, and I'll do it."

She bites her bottom lip. "Can we cuddle?"

I tip my head and kiss her temple. "Lie down."

She rolls in her bottom lip, trying to hide a smile breaking free. It's so goddamn cute, too. I watch as she lies down before I get up and round the bed, sliding in beside her. My fingers clutch the blanket, dragging it up and over our bodies. Once settled, I slide my bicep under her head to use as a pillow. She inches closer, resting her shaking hand against my chest, and I wrap my other arm around her waist, my hand splaying out over her back. I feel her body ease against me, her feet tangling with mine.

"Leo?"

"Yes?"

She lets out a little yawn, melting into the mattress. "When did you get the firefly tattoo?" Her hand reaches up, pressing flat against my heart, right over the design.

My lips tug up. I wasn't sure she caught the sight of it in the dark. "Years ago," I answer. "When I knew there was only ever going to be one woman who owned my heart."

She peeks up at me under her lashes. Neither of us says anything as we lock eyes, and she leans up, pressing her lips to mine. "My heart is yours," she whispers, closing her eyes. "It always has been."

The sound of rain bouncing off the glass pane windows echoes in the room like a calming lullaby. It doesn't take long for Scarlett's breathing to even out and for her hand against my chest to fall slack.

I nestle my lips over the top of her head, inhaling her floral aroma, my hold on her strengthening. "I will kill the man responsible for haunting your dreams, Scarlett. But not until I break him as he tried, but failed, to do to you. That is my vow to you."

My fingers strum along the edge of my desk as I lean back in my chair, waiting for the man of the hour to arrive.

The only thing keeping me calm is the memory of waking up with Scarlett wrapped around me, sound asleep. Her blonde strands were splayed around my chest. Her pink, sultry lips were slightly parted, looking more tempting than ever. Her long, smooth legs were encircling mine. And me? Well, I had to lie perfectly still with a fucking hard-on, not wanting to scare her away by risking her finding out the effect she had on me.

The effect she's always had on me.

And I decided at that moment that she's never sleeping anywhere else but in my bed. *Our bed*.

It's settled.

The door to my office creaks open, and my mother walks in with furrowed brows. "What's with the emergency meeting?" she asks, taking one of the seats across from me.

"All in due time," I respond, checking my Rolex on my wrist. I have a meeting with the family contractor in an hour, so the son of a bitch better have his ass in my office right the fuck—"

"Good morning." Dr. Hayes enters my office with a broad smile. One that I can't wait to wipe off his smug face.

I return the smile with a terse one of my own. "Please, take a seat." I motion toward the only free chair left in my office.

"Well, what a pleasant surprise, Harold," my mother says, glancing between us. "I didn't know you'd be joining us."

"I got a text that I was needed urgently." He straightens his tie, looking at me. "Is everything okay, sir?"

I sit up, steepling my fingers under my chin. "You've been the family's doctor for a long time now, wouldn't you say?"

He mulls it over. "Yes, I believe almost twenty years."

I drop my hands before me. "And all those years, you've been loyal to my family. Some might even say, you've become a part of this family."

He nervously pulls on the sleeve of his jacket. "Yes, I would like to think that."

I nod. "That would be why I'm terminating you instead of killing you."

The doctor's face blanches. "I beg your pardon."

My mother gasps. "Leo, what is this about?"

I reach inside my jacket pocket, pulling out the bottle of sleeping pills. "Did you, or did you not, prescribe these to my wife, knowing they would put her in a sleep paralysis?"

The doctor's mouth opens and closes like a fish out of water. I'd find it amusing if I weren't on the verge of murdering him. "Well, yes, but—"

"And did you, or did you not, tell my wife to take these so she wouldn't disturb me?"

"Oh, Harold." My mother rubs her temple. "Please tell me you didn't."

He clears his throat. "I was doing this with you in mind, sir. I just thought her nightmares may become too much for you to have to endure."

A deep laugh rings out in the room. "You thought it would be too much for me to endure?" My fist slams on my desk as I stand, towering over him. "What about my wife, who has to live through her trauma in her dreams every fucking night? Did you stop to think that maybe that would be too much for her to endure?" I clench my jaw, rolling my neck. "Every night, she dreams of what that man did to her over and over again. But when she takes one of these pills, she can't move. She can't even make a fucking sound. So I have no idea that she needs me to save her from her nightmares!"

A bead of sweat rolls down the doctor's brow. "I'm sorry. I was just trying to find a way to silence the screams she—"

"No one silences my wife!" The severity of my words thunders around us.

"I...a-apologize, sir." Dr. Hayes smooths out his tie with a trembling hand. "It won't happen again."

"No, it won't because you're done working for my family. Dr. Rose will be your replacement. I'll have a severance package sent your way for all the years you've worked for us, but that's as far as my kindness extends. I expect you moved out and off our property within the day."

"But—"

"Out!" I roar.

Dr. Hayes rears back, almost falling out of his chair as he abruptly stands, tipping his head down. "Yes, sir."

Once the door closes behind him, I feel an immense satisfaction flow through my veins.

My mother lets out a whoosh of air. "So, I assume that's why you needed me here."

I sit, running my fingers through my hair, pushing it back. "I knew you'd need to hear it for yourself."

She nods, leaning forward. "So, your wife, is it?" An elated grin erupts from ear to ear on her face.

I roll my eyes. "Don't you have somewhere to be? Another sibling to bother?"

"As a matter of fact, I do." She stands and steps toward the door.

"Wait. There's one last thing I want to discuss with you."

She turns, gripping the top of the chair, giving me her attention.

"Anthony Balcom's grave."

She arches a brow. "What about it?"

"I'm having him moved off the property," I state with certainty. "I don't care where he goes, but he's not welcome on Alarie soil. Vin is making other arrangements for him, but I just wanted you to be aware."

"He's dead," she drawls, confused. "What could he have possibly done to piss you off while six feet under?"

"Apparently, he was a cruel father. I didn't push Scarlett for details, but I could see all the pain he caused her in her eyes. She admitted that he would threaten one of us if she ever spoke out against him, so she never said anything. She was more worried for our safety than hers. And I won't allow him the privilege of being buried here. This is Scarlett's home now. Not his."

She shakes her head in disbelief. "I had no idea. He always seemed kind enough. Maybe a little rough around the edges, but what man in our world isn't?" Her eyes pool with tears. "Your father would have done something about it. He would have handled this if he had known."

"I'm handling it now."

"That poor girl has been through so much. Too much." She dabs her eyes, looking out the closest window. "I wish I had known."

"None of us did." I lean back, tapping a finger on the arm of my chair. "But I suppose *sometimes* you never truly know someone until it's too late, no matter how close to the person you think you are."

Chapter Nineteen

Scarlett

Forcing open the door to the gym, I'm assaulted with an abundance of nerves. Nerves over having someone so close to me who isn't my husband. Nerves that I'm not mentally or physically strong enough to do this. And above all, I'm just plain old nervous that I'm going to fail.

But this is Mauro. My brother-in-law. Someone I've always felt safe with. And someone who, the second Leo texted him a week ago about this, quickly created a schedule and a game plan for us.

One we would be starting today.

Immediately, I spot the intimidating presence of Mauro, going at it in the ring with another man. His muscular body is coated in a sheen of sweat as he steps from side to side, almost as if in a dance with his opponent. His hair is pulled back in a low bun with a few loose strands that have escaped, swaying before his eyes. Clear, determined focus covers his features as he swings his right arm, landing a punch right into the man's jaw, now spinning on his heels.

The man raises his hands in surrender, and the two of them come to a stop.

"Fuck, you got me good." The man rubs his jaw, moving it back and forth. "Guess I better practice my ducking." He smirks as Mauro grunts and nods in response. He grasps Mauro's shoulder. "Same time next week." He then bends under the ring ropes, walking toward the locker room.

Mauro turns, his eyes landing on me.

I give a meek wave, and he jerks his chin, indicating that I should come on up. I swallow hard as I pull down on my T-shirt, well, Leo's T-shirt, over my leggings. My hands grip the rope as I lift my leg and awkwardly climb onto the mat, sliding up on my stomach until my whole body is on and finally pushing myself into a standing position. The strap on my bag begins to slide down my arm, so I drop it beside me.

I glance around the room. There are other men here working out, minding their own business. But to me, it feels as if all eyes are on me. I cross my arms over my stomach and step to the side, my back hitting the post.

"I didn't realize how many people work out here." I give a tepid smile. "I guess I should have assumed." Suddenly, more men walk inside, joking and laughing with one another as they make their way to the nearby weights. They're harmless. Not even giving me an ounce of attention. But as my eyes dance around the room, noting how many men are in here versus women, aka me, I begin to panic, feeling weak and no longer ready for this. I pull at the hem of my shirt, shaking my head as I pick up my bag, securing the strap over my shoulder. "Maybe this was a bad idea. I'm sorry for wasting your time, Mauro."

Mauro tilts his head, observing me. Just as I make a motion to leave, he suddenly turns and walks away.

Great. He probably hates me.

He reaches into his bag and pulls out an airhorn, letting off the noise for five seconds as he twirls his index finger in the air for everyone in the place to see. Only a few seconds go by before everyone drops what they're doing and makes their way to the closest exit, leaving only me and Mauro inside.

"Oh." I rub the back of my neck, embarrassed. "You didn't have to do that for me."

He faces me, pulls out a small notepad and pen, and quickly scribbles on it. When he turns it towards me, I read, *I want you to feel comfortable.*

I drop my shoulders and again let my bag fall to the floor. "I appreciate that."

He scribbles again and then flips it around for me to see. *Today, we will work on a few basic self-defense moves. First, the ready stance, then the palm-heel strike, the front kick to the groin, and finally, the hammer fist punch.*

I nod. "Are these things that someone like me can do?"

He nods. Jumping out of the ring, he grabs a dummy on a stand and then drags it up on the mat, standing it in the center. He signals with two fingers to his eyes and then points to his chest, which I assume means *watch me.*

Focusing on Mauro, I observe how he stands before the dummy, his feet shoulder-width apart and his hands by his side. He takes a slight step with his left leg and then somewhat bends both knees. Elevating his back heel, he brings his hands up about a foot from his face, palms facing forward. He then tucks his chin and faintly shrugs his shoulders.

His eyes catch on me, widening as he gives a thumbs-up.

I nod. "Yeah. I think I got it." I mimic him, or at least I think I do, but he steps up, gesturing toward my left leg. I shake my head, not understanding what he wants me to do with it. "I don't understand."

He reaches down to my leg, and on impulse, I jump back, tripping over my bag and falling directly onto my ass. "Ow," I groan as I roll over. My pride hurt more than anything. "I'm sorry. I didn't mean to—"

He crouches beside me, showing me his notepad. *I won't hurt you. I want to help you. I want to make sure you can defend yourself.*

I shake my head with a little pathetic chuckle. "I'm a mess, right? My brother-in-law, a guy I trust with my life, goes to touch me when he's just trying to help me, and I freak out." I bend my knees, wrapping my arms around myself.

He presses his lips together, jots down some words, and turns the paper toward me. *You're not a mess. You're a fucking badass.*

He grins, and I laugh, a genuine no-holds-back kind of laugh. "Thanks for the vote of confidence."

He shows me his notepad. *Ready to try again?*

"Yeah. I'm ready."

He stands and extends his hand for me to take, bringing me back to my feet. He returns to his ready stance and points at me to follow suit, which I do. He scratches his chin as he examines my posture. He motions toward my leg, silently asking permission, and I nod. He gently moves my left leg further ahead and out, giving me more balance and stability. I don't freeze under his touch or jump back as if my ass is on fire. I let him do what he needs to, and as his hand returns to his side, I feel proud of myself. Looking at me, he arches a brow, waiting for me to acknowledge my stance.

I slightly rock on the balls of my feet, evenly distributing my weight between the two as something I'm not used to blooms inside me: confidence.

For the first time in a long time, I feel confident and ready to move forward with not only today's lesson but also with life itself.

Because, as Mauro himself said, I'm a badass.

And it's about damn time I start acting like one.

———

After spending the morning with Mauro training and feeling a little more confident in my abilities to protect myself, I went to the women and children's center, where I spent the afternoon reading to a room full of children and helping serve lunch. I ended my day at Maddy's, binging the latest reality show with Chinese food containers on our laps until it was way past my bedtime.

Leo

I'm outside.

I smile as I slide my phone back inside my pocket, exhaustion weighing down on me, but also excitement from knowing how the night will end. In Leo's bed...most likely with his head between my legs.

It had been a week since my nightmare woke Leo, and every night since then, I've slept in his room. In his bed. No questions asked. And every night, he's made me come with his head between my thighs, not stopping until he's pulled every ounce of a delicious orgasm out of me before I promptly fall asleep with my head on his chest and his arms wrapped around me.

And I've never slept better in my life. But maybe I've overstayed my welcome, and he wants his space back? Maybe I should sleep in my own room tonight?

No. You need to talk to your husband and not just assume. If therapy has taught you anything, it's how important communication is in a relationship.

"I have to go," I tell Maddy.

She rolls her eyes. "Is your warden here?"

"Yes." I yawn, stretching my arms above my head. "But honestly, I'm so tired. I can't wait to fall into my bed." Well, Leo's bed.

"Go." She waves me off. "Go be adorable with your husband."

I chuckle, making my way to the front door. As soon as it swings open, I find Leo on the top step waiting for me.

He smiles when he sees me. "Ready to go home?"

"With you? Always." I lean up and press a soft kiss to his lips. "I missed you."

He runs his fingers through my hair, cupping the back of my head. "There isn't a second that goes by that I don't miss you, Firefly." His hand slides down my side, reaching for my hand. "How did training go with Mauro? He texted me earlier to let me know he was very impressed."

A slight blush creeps up my neck. "I think he's exaggerating, but I appreciate him helping me." I give a slight shrug. "I enjoyed it, and honestly, I'm looking forward to working with him more."

He leads me to the car, and as we make our descent home, I get a whiff of something unfamiliar. "Don't take this the wrong way, but...what's that smell?" I sniff the air, my nose inching closer to him. "Why do you smell like paint?"

He grins. "I have a surprise for you."

My eyebrows shoot up. "You do?"

He nods.

"Why?"

He reaches over, clasping my hand in his and bringing the back of it to his lips. "I don't need a reason to spoil my wife."

Goose bumps spread over me, a fire blazing in my core. I quickly shut my thighs together, trying but failing to dissipate the need between my legs.

"But what does the smell have to do with it?"

"You'll see."

We pull into the driveway, where I find a dumpster and a storage unit.

"What's all this?" I was only gone for the day... What could he have possibly accomplished in a day?

"Come on." He gives me a mischievous smile as he slides out of his seat and then makes his way over to my side of the car. As he takes my hand in his, we walk up the front steps, reaching the door, but before we enter, I stop him.

It's now or never.

"Leo, there's something I want to talk to you about."

He takes a step down, so I'm not at such a height disadvantage. But let's face it, I still have to crane my neck back to look up at him.

"What is it?" he asks, concern etched in his dark eyes.

I straighten my shoulders, tilting my chin up. "As you know, for the past week, I've been sleeping in your room. In your...bed."

He grins. "Yes, I'm aware."

"And, well." My shoulders drop, my heart fluttering nervously. "I was wondering... Well, you see, the thing is—"

"Will you move into my room?"

"I..." My lips part, no words coming out.

His grin widens as he leans forward and brushes his lips against my ear. "Make me the happiest man in the world by making it *our* room."

"Our room," I breathe, a smile forming.

"Is that a yes?"

"It's a definite yes."

He picks me up and swings me in a circle, both of us laughing like little kids.

"You can change anything you want about it. Make it something you like."

I shake my head as he places my feet back on the ground. "I like it the way it is, especially because it feels like you. The smell. The colors. The atmosphere. It's all you. And it relaxes me."

He kisses my lips. "At least add a pillow or something to make it yours too."

"I'll think about it."

He opens the front door. "Come on, Firefly. Or have you already forgotten you have a surprise waiting for you?"

I bite down on my bottom lip, holding in a squeal of excitement as we pass through the living room and kitchen and then head up the stairs.

As we reach the top step, he stops and looks at me, running his fingers through his hair. "If you don't like it, I can change it back."

My eyebrows scrunch together. "Don't like what?"

He looks lost in thought and maybe a little nervous before lightly squeezing my hand and walking us to my bedroom door. Or, I guess, my former bedroom door.

"Do you trust me?"

I don't hesitate when I say, "Of course I do."

"Close your eyes."

"Wh—" I shut my lips, stopping myself from questioning him, and do as he asks, pinching my eyes closed.

I hear the scanner give a quiet beep, allowing the door to open. Leo guides me inside the room with him, and that paint aroma that was in the car is in here, too, but more potent.

We come to a stop where I'm confident the bed should be, but there's nothing in my way. Leo drops my hands and steps away.

"Open your eyes, Scarlett."

I do, hesitantly, unsure what to expect. A new dress? Maybe a necklace? Peeking open my eyes, I see...

"Oh my God," I whisper. My heart thrashes in my chest as oxygen leaves my lungs. "What... How... When..." I spin in a circle, my eyes dancing around the room in amazement until finally landing back on Leo. "You... You built me a library?"

Every wall is submerged in dark wood shelves completely filled with books. A gold rolling ladder is positioned by the door, with a track that leads it around the entire room. Plush leather chairs and couches sit before a faux fireplace that roars to life. Flowers of all different shades are placed throughout the room, providing just the right amount of color to this beautiful yet dark space.

I'm stunned into silence. Overcome with emotions and overwhelmed by his generosity in something so significant.

"Well, I can't take all the credit. I only paid for everything and worked with our family contractor on the design. But a team of thirty guys spent the day here to get everything done in a day so it would be ready before you came home. And I might have picked up a paintbrush to help, hence the smell." Leo hesitantly approaches me. "Do you like it?"

"Like it?" I shake my head, my eyes watering. "I love it." I take a step toward him as his arms open wide for me and crash against his chest. "Thank you," I say softly. "Thank you so much."

His hand smooths down my back. "I did some research and found that reading can be a healthy coping mechanism, especially for trauma survivors."

I swallow hard, my throat tightening. "Really?"

He brushes a tendril of my hair back. "Studies have found that reading helps reduce stress, anxiety, and even depression. But not only that." He looks pensive regarding his following words. "They found that reading someone's similar experience can help with feeling less alone."

Alone. The one word I've been feeling for months, even when surrounded by people.

I roll in my quivering bottom lip. "How did you know?"

"Because I know you, Firefly. I see the pain you've been carrying in your eyes for months, and it breaks my heart." A tear escapes, sliding down my cheek. "When things become too much for you up here..." He presses his lips to the top of my head. "I want you to be able to use this space as your escape. A place filled with grand stories, epic love tales, and adventures. A place that may help you feel less alone each time you pick up a new book."

"You thought of everything." I sniffle, more tears escaping down my cheeks. I can't process a single one of my thoughts. This is so much. Too much. It doesn't feel real. "I feel like I'm dreaming."

He smiles. "You haven't even seen the best part yet."

I pull back. "There's more?"

His eyes gaze up at the ceiling.

With a deep breath, I mirror his motion and let out a gasp. "Leo."

The once pure white ceiling above me is now painted, portraying a starry night sky. It's beautiful. Perfect. It looks exactly like it did on the night when...

"Did you know there's a company that will send you an image of what the night looked like at a certain place and day?" Leo asks.

I shake my head, my eyes filling with tears, knowing where this is going.

"Do you know what night this is from, Scarlett?" His voice comes out like a soft caress floating over me.

I roll in my bottom lip and nod, pressing my face into his chest. This man did this for me. He did all of this...for me. "It's from our first night together." A sob escapes me as I cling to his shirt. "I don't deserve you."

He grips my chin, tilting my head until our eyes meet. "You deserve everything and so much more. You deserve the moon and the stars. I only wish I could catch them for you and place them at your feet." He kisses my temple. "There's nothing, absolutely nothing, I wouldn't do for you."

And I know that.

Deep down, I've always known that.

These past few months, he's surrounded me in a blanket of safety. He's pre-cut every single thing in the fridge, so I never have to pick up a knife. He had a custom nightlight created for me because he knows I'm scared of the dark. He's been patient with me, giving me whatever my body is ready to receive, never asking me for anything in return. And now this...

I'm simply lost for words. My heart feels two sizes too big, pleading for me to release three words into the air.

Three little words that hold so much power.

But as I rest my head against his chest, listening to his heart flutter as fast as mine, I know saying those words won't be enough. They won't truly capture the emotions storming inside me. They won't adequately express how much all of this means to me. And they won't do justice to my heart.

The one currently beating for him.

But I don't have to tell him with words.

Not when there are other ways to let him know.

To show him.

By giving him...

Me.

CHAPTER TWENTY

Leo

Advancing up the front steps, my eyes graze the area for any sight of Eli but come up empty. Unease fills me. Something feels off.

It's not until I reach the door that I find a note taped to the stained glass.

What the fuck is this? A note from Le Diable? Fury sweeps over me as my fingers rip the paper from the door, hastily tearing it open. My eyes scan the paper, and my breathing becomes more manageable as my body relaxes at the sight of the familiar handwriting.

Meet me at our spot.
-Your firefly

My lips curve up as I turn around, promptly walk down the steps, and swing a leg over the seat of my bike. Feeling like a predator on a chase to catch his prey, I lower my body closer to the handlebars and accelerate, zipping through the estate, until I come upon a familiar black SUV with Eli sitting in the driver's seat.

After catching my eye, he gives me a salute and a smirk as he drives away. I park my bike and eagerly take my first step down the hill, not stopping until I see her.

My firefly.

"You're here." Her smile grows, her whole demeanor radiating like there's a goddamn halo around her.

And knowing her, there probably is.

Fuck, I really don't deserve her.

But I'm a selfish man, and I will *never* give her up.

She tucks a piece of hair behind her ear, her cheeks tinting a shade of pink. She's wearing a loose, short pink dress that sways in the breeze, and my heart tightens at the sight. Not only because of how beautiful she looks but also because the dress symbolizes how safe she feels with me.

And it does something to me.

My eyes wander over the space. She's standing in the center of a thick blanket beside a tree with pillows on one end, a bottle of champagne chilling on the other, and the full moon above us casts an ambient glow over everything.

"Was this a bad idea?" she asks softly.

"No." I adamantly shake my head.

Her forehead furrows. "Then why won't you come closer?"

"Because I'm too goddamn scared that I'll take one step toward you and wake up from my dream."

She smiles. "You're not dreaming."

"I don't deserve you, Scarlett." I stand my ground, not wanting to spook her by moving closer. "You're everything good in this world. You're..." My source of light in the dark. You always have been. "Too good for me." I rake my fingers through my hair, a tremble taking over me. "But you have no idea how much I want you. How badly I want to worship every perfect inch of your body as it was always meant to be worshiped." I let out a harsh breath. "I need you, wife. I've needed you every day for the last seven years. And I don't think I can wait one more goddamn second for you."

She bites down on her bottom lip, her smile turning seductive. Looking at me under her long lashes, she says, "Then why don't you come here and take me."

I don't stop to think. I won't wait for another confirmation. I don't even fucking breathe. I just move. I stride toward her, grasping her in my arms as our lips collide. She melts under my touch, molding against my body, her fingers clutching my shirt. Her lips part for me as my tongue slips inside, tasting and exploring.

Slowly, we both kneel on the blanket, intertwined with one another. My hands cup her face, my thumbs tenderly stroking her skin. She winds her arms around my neck, tugging me closer. Her breasts press against my chest, her hardened nipples rubbing against me. I curl an arm around her waist and carefully guide her body to the blanket beneath mine.

Her legs encircle my torso, binding me to her. Warmth shoots through me when she lifts her hips, pressing her pussy against my hardened cock.

Suddenly, she pauses, pulling back from our kiss, panting as she peers up at me with her sapphire eyes.

I push her hair away from her face. "Are you okay?"

Her eyes blink a few times, her face softening as she reaches up and places the palm of her hand on my face. I turn into it, pressing a kiss to her skin. "I've never been better." She leans up, capturing my lips with hers. "I want this. I want you."

An animalistic need takes over me.

My wife needs me.

And I'm about to officially make her mine. *Again.*

My fingers skim down her thighs, not stopping until they find the hem of her dress. I scrunch the fabric in my hand, pulling it higher, past her hips and over her waist. She lifts her ass as I drag the fabric over her head, leaving her in nothing but a black lace bra with matching underwear.

"Goddamn," I breathe, holding myself up on an elbow, admiring her. "You're so perfect." I ghost my lips across her collarbone and then over the swell of her breasts. The pads of my fingers skim down her stomach, circling her belly button, and then venture lower until I hit the edge of the lace. A breath escapes her as my eyes glimpse up, catching hers. All I need to see is the little nod she gives me before I tear the fabric to shreds with an unrestrained desire, leaving her pussy bare.

And fuck is it a sight I never want to forget.

My hands slide between the insides of her thighs, spreading her legs open for me. A sinfully sweet flush embraces her body, and her arousal is evident. Leaning down, I press a kiss to her mound, inhaling her intoxicating scent. My fingers slip between her slit, finding her soaking wet for me. My cock hardens almost painfully. "You're so wet for me, baby."

A soft moan floats through her luscious lips as two of my fingers glide back and forth, swirling over her entrance and dipping slightly inside.

"More," she pants.

Circling my thumb over her clit, I apply just the right amount of pressure to distract her as I slide my fingers all the way inside. I can feel her tighten around me and watch as her fingers grip the blanket, her back slightly arching. Her legs widen, seeking more from me. I press a hungry kiss to her lips, greedily taking everything she'll give me. Pulling back, I hover over her as I continue to thrust in and out, watching her face for any indication that this might be too much for her. But it's not. She's relishing in her pleasure.

And I feel like a goddamn caveman as I watch my woman beneath me get closer and closer to ecstasy.

My lips land on her neck, trailing down to her breasts, her nipples peeking out the edge of her bra cups. I push down the fabric and suck on one, latching onto it. She writhes in pleasure, and with each nip I take, I feel her pussy arousal pool around my fingers.

"That's it, baby. You're doing so fucking good. You're so close. I can feel it."

My thrusts become faster, her breaths quicker.

"Oh God. I'm going... I'm going to..."

I rub my thumb over her clit, providing a vibration as I move it swiftly back and forth. "Come for me, Scarlett."

She shatters. Her raw beauty captures me in a trance, and everything around me blurs except her. Her eyes pinch closed, her cheeks stain pink, her lips part wide, a silent scream trying to escape. Her body heaves and thrashes before finally collapsing onto the blanket beneath her.

I gently remove my fingers, licking each one clean, savoring her taste as if she were my personal aphrodisiac.

My knuckles stroke the side of her face. "You did so well, Firefly." Pressing my lips to hers, she lets out a content sigh, stretching her body like a cat just waking. She sits up, her disheveled hair falling over her shoulders.

She truly is a sight to behold.

Her fingers reach for the hem of my black T-shirt. I lift my arms in the air and wait as she pulls it up and over my head, tossing it beside us. Her eyes run over my chest, staring at the firefly over my heart.

Slowly, she leans forward, pressing her soft lips to my skin. "Make me yours," she breathes, peering up at me.

I hook a finger under her chin, tilting her head so our eyes meet. "You're sure?"

"I'm ready," she says steadily. "I want to be yours again. Only yours." There's not a drop of fear or hesitation in her voice. No uncertainty in this moment between us. And it's the sexiest fucking thing I've ever seen.

She watches as I unzip my jeans and yank them, along with my briefs, off my legs. Her eyes widen, not in fear but in appreciation. And more importantly, in lust.

Leaning my back against the tree, I stretch my legs in front of me. "Come here."

She eagerly crawls her way over to me until she's sitting on my thighs, my cock jutting out and rubbing her stomach. I reach around her, unhooking her bra, and watch in awe as the straps slowly fall down her arms, revealing the most perfect pair of breasts I've ever seen. I cup them both, my thumbs circling her nipples, and she moans, grinding her wet pussy against me.

"Ride me, baby."

Her eyes blink. "I… I've never… I don't know what to do." A hint of defeat crosses over her features, which won't do.

"Yes, you do." I grip her hips, helping her get into position. "I want you in control tonight. This is a big moment. You're offering me everything I've ever wanted on a silver platter, and I am forever grateful. But I want you to listen to what your body wants tonight. To what you need. If you want to go faster, I'll match your pace. If you want to stop, we'll stop." I sweep her hair off her shoulder, placing a kiss on her soft skin. "We have a lifetime together. Endless nights to make up for. Ones I can't wait to take the lead on." I wink, and she looks down, a flush creeping up her cheeks. "But tonight is your night, baby."

I know she meant it when she said she was ready for tonight. But I don't want to rush headfirst into this, destroying all the progress she's made. So, by having her on top, riding me, I'm giving her the reins to control everything about this. The pace. The speed. The intensity. She's the driver. The one with the power to accelerate or stop.

She grips my shoulders as she sits up and adjusts her hips, aligning her entrance with my cock. Slowly, she lowers herself. My tip nudges inside her, and fucking hell, this is better than I remember.

She's so tight.

So wet.

So goddamn perfect.

Her fingers clamp down as she reaches my shaft. A loud moan leaves her as her eyes pinch shit, her lips parting. I can see both pain and pleasure mixed in her features, so I caress my hands over her back in soothing circles.

Her ass grazes my balls, and I let out a guttural groan.

She stills. "Did I hurt you?"

I shake my head, laughing. "No, baby. You didn't hurt me. It just feels so fucking good being inside you again."

She blushes. "I'm sorry for making you wait."

"Don't apologize for that." Pushing back her hair, I say, "I would have waited forever if you needed me to."

"I know. That's why I couldn't wait anymore."

Her eyes bore into mine, shining brightly under the starlight. Pleasure erupts around my cock as she begins to rock her hips up and down, finding a rhythm she's comfortable with. A speed she can control. I hold her tightly, letting my eyes wander over her, cherishing every second of this moment, but above all, treasuring the woman in my arms who seems so free, owning her body.

Tilting my head down, I nuzzle my lips in the valley between her breasts and lick my way over to her nipple. I suck hard, listening to the whimpers and gasps that escape her. Her nails drag down my shoulders, her thighs tensing. She's on the verge of her orgasm. I can feel it.

"Leo... I need more," she pleads.

Bringing my hands back to her hips, I grip her and start moving her faster and harder, giving her what her body needs. Her head rolls back as she moans out in pleasure.

"Ohhh... Yes! Just like that..."

Her chest flushes as her thighs begin to tremble. Suddenly she clings to me, holding on tightly as she unravels in my arms, burying her head in the crook of my neck, releasing a scream. I keep thrusting inside her, so close to my peak of pleasure. A moment later, a groan escapes me as my balls tighten almost painfully, and then, finally, I fill her up with my warmth.

We both hold on to each other as if we are one and at this moment, that's exactly how I feel.

I burrow my nose into her hair, inhaling her familiar jasmine scent. "Are you okay?" I press my lips to the side of her neck, feeling her pulse beat wildly.

She nods against me. Her body slowly relaxes in my arms, and I reach for one of the blankets nearby, wrapping it around her. She softens against my chest, placing her palm over my heart. "Don't let go of me."

My arms tighten around her, and my lips find the top of her head. "I never will."

CHAPTER TWENTY-ONE

Scarlett

The Escalade stops before an iron gate at the Alarie family manor in The Hamptons, and Leo sticks his hand out, scanning it before the entrance slowly slides open. He drives the SUV down the long driveway and stops by the stone stairs that lead to the massive doorway. As I open my door, the smell of the nearby ocean crashes over me, eliciting a smile.

The dark double doors of the house open, revealing an elated Maddy stepping outside. "Who's ready to party?" She double-fists two bottles of champagne, a genuine smile spreading across her face. I step out of the car as she suffocates me in a bear hug. "I'm so glad you came!"

"I wouldn't miss this." I center the pendant on my silver chain, falling flat over the white square-neck tank top I paired with navy abstract knotted wide-leg trousers. I figured I would at least try to look The Hamptons' part today.

Eli rounds the back of the vehicle, and Maddy's smile falters. The bottles of champagne are lowered to her sides beside her white and deep blue boho-chic dress.

"And may I ask what you're doing here? This is a girls' weekend," she grits out. "I only allowed Leo to come because he'll go into anaphylactic shock if he's not by Scarlett's side."

She sounds murderous, and I look between them, feeling a wall of tension. Did I miss something?

Eli smirks, jerking his head toward me. "Where she goes, I go. Boss's order."

Sorry, I mouth with a slight shrug. If I had known his presence would be a problem, I might have asked Leo to let Eli stay home. But I assumed Maddy would have been excited to see his familiar face.

Judging by her tight features...I was very wrong.

She plasters her smile back onto her face, feigning indifference. "No bother. Two boys won't ruin—" Her words die out as a familiar black G-wagon pulls up behind our Escalade. "You have to be shitting me."

The driver's door opens, and Vin steps out, removing his designer sunglasses. He nods his head in greeting to some of the guards on patrol and then looks around at all of us. "The party has finally arrived."

The passenger door opens next, quickly revealing a disgruntled-looking Mauro.

"Don't mind him," Vin starts, approaching him. "He wasn't too keen on coming this weekend, but I insisted a weekend away with his siblings was just what he needed." He displays a broad smile as he squeezes Mauro's shoulder. "Unfortunately, Alex had some work to take care of and won't be joining us."

"No, no, no, no, no!" Maddy drops the bottles of champagne on a nearby table and storms up to her brothers, shoving a finger into Vin's chest. "This is supposed to be a girls' weekend! My last weekend of fun before I have to tie the knot!" she complains with a stomp of her wedge.

"Have to?" Eli asks curiously.

She waves her hands around dismissively. "Have to. Want to. Same difference."

Vin rubs his knuckles over the top of her head, clearly pissing her off more as she shoves him away, smoothing down her hair. "Don't worry, little sister. We came here to have fun, too. Isn't that right, Mauro?"

Mauro grunts, shaking his head.

Leo whispers in my ear, "That grunt means *I was forced here against my will.*"

I chuckle, clasping my hands over my mouth.

"Hey, guys!" A beautiful brunette walks out the front door in a figure-hugging deep purple dress. She smiles, pushing up her black-framed glasses.

Wait a second... Is that?

"Hey, Scarlett." She walks up to me, wrapping her arms around me as I stand there stiff as a board. "I'm so sorry. I wanted to come see you sooner, but I've been swamped with classes and couldn't get away until now."

"Alina?" I ask, pulling back to get a better look at her. Alina Fowler lived on the Alarie Estate when we were kids because her father was Charles Alarie's right-hand man. Maddy told me that before Mr. Fowler retired, he helped Vin transition into the family leader after their father died. But this can't possibly be the same scrawny girl I remember from childhood with wire-rimmed glasses and acne, who would spend all her free time in the local library. This woman has long brown hair that flows past her waist, big brown eyes that look like they belong to a princess, and a golden tan on her skin that practically sparkles. This can't be her, can it?

"I know, it's been too long." She pulls away, tucking a piece of hair behind her ear. "Unfortunately, I'm only here for the weekend. I have to go back to school on Monday." She frowns before looking over at the rest of the men.

"Good to see you again, Alina," Leo says.

"Couldn't stay away from us, could you?" Vin teases with a wink.

She smiles until her eyes land on Mauro, and the second she sees him, it's like no one else in the world exists.

She swallows hard and then smooths down her dress. "Hey, Mauro," she says while also...signing?

Mauro's eyes widen as he realizes what she just did.

Does Alina know ASL?

Maddy's arm winds around Alina's shoulders, pulling her to her side. "Well, for better or worse, let's get this *girls'* weekend started. Shall we?"

The music pumps throughout the entryway as we bypass the line and enter the newest club on the island, Red Eleven. The only reason the men even considered letting us come here without any complaints is because it's one of the many clubs they own.

"Are you sure you're okay coming here? Because we can leave right now," Leo tells me as we sit at a red booth in the VIP section. His eyes travel around the space, ensuring there are no threats.

I place my hand on Leo's thigh. "I'm okay." It's not a total lie. I can't say I was as eager as Maddy and Alina were to come here. I would have been completely fine with a glass of wine by the outdoor fire pit, but Maddy was adamant about having a girls' weekend. So here I am. At a nightclub. Surrounded by people.

Okay, maybe I'm not as fine as I wish I were, but I'm trying.

And besides, I'm here with four of the scariest men I know. There's no way I could be any safer than I am right now.

My eyes wander around the room, stopping on girls dancing in cages like trapped birds. They're wearing very little as they move their bodies. Men beneath them stare up in pure lust. But it's the restraints wrapped around their ankles that make me pause. Are they trapped and held there against their will? My breathing picks up, my pulse booming.

"They're professional dancers who come on their own free will to work here. We pay them better than anywhere else in the area would." Leo's words soothe the anxiety building inside me.

"But..." I look back at the girl closest to me. "What about the chains around her ankles?" My voice comes out so quietly as I get lost in a memory.

The metal digs into my wrists as I pace. The long chain drags behind me as I walk back and forth, trying to think of a way to escape this nightmare. Suddenly, I hear the familiar creak of the metal door at the top of the stairs swing open. All hope vanishes within me.

No. No. No.

I quickly run to the corner, the chain pulling me back, causing me to stumble to the cement ground. My knee scrapes against the rough floor, and my teeth bite down on my lower lip to hold in the scream. As I look up, I find him *standing before me, staring down at me with his poisonous green eyes. His masked face tilts from side to side as he silently observes me. He reaches into his back pocket, pulling out his knife—the one he enjoys using on me.*

"Please, don't," I beg in a whisper, tears falling down my cheeks. But he doesn't listen to my pleas. He never does. He lowers the knife to my skin, and I let out a blood-curdling scream that echoes across the room.

"They're just an illusion." Leo's voice cuts through my vision. Reaching for a glass of water before me, I gulp down a few sips. "The cuffs aren't locked, and they're not real metal. They're plastic and only worn for show."

"Oh," I get out, barely remembering what I had asked. The restraints. Right. "That... That's good, then."

His gaze on me hardens. I can feel him dissecting every tremble I try to mask. "Maybe this is too much for you, Firefly."

I shake my head adamantly, feeling anger engulf me. "No. I said I'm fine, so I'm fine. Just drop it," I grit out. My eyes suddenly widen, surprised by my temper. *Shit.* I should not have just done that. I lower my eyes, inching away.

"You spoke back to me." He wraps his hand around my jaw, forcing my eyes on him.

"I-I'm sorry. I shouldn't have—"

"About damn time."

My lips part. "What?"

"You're my wife. Putting me in my place is kind of your job." He smirks. "And not going to lie." He reaches for my hand, placing it on the hard bulge between his legs. "It was a turn-on."

"Me, talking back to you was a turn-on?" I ask, confused, my fingers massaging over his length beneath the table.

He shakes his head, laughing. "No, you, standing up for yourself is what made me hard."

I bite down on my bottom lip. "Good to know," I admit, unable to remove my hand.

His lips ghost over my ear. "Do you like knowing your effect on me, wife?"

I nod, feeling his length pulse in my grip. God, why is this so hot?

"As much as I love your fascination with my cock, how about we save this for inside the bedroom tonight when we're not at a table with my siblings?" He shows a playful grin, and I suddenly feel my cheeks flush, remembering where we are.

"Oops," I whisper in embarrassment, removing my hand. Thankfully, when I look around, everyone else is too wrapped up in their own conversations to notice us.

"Tonight." He presses a kiss to my lips.

"Tonight," I repeat, anticipation growing between my legs.

He throws an arm behind me and then motions for the cocktail waitress, who strolls over excitedly at the prospect of taking our order. Drinks are ordered and served fairly quickly. As the liquid slides down my throat, I feel any previous doubts float away. I let my guard down, genuinely enjoying myself.

"Did you guys receive the invitation to the governor's dinner?" Vin scoffs, looking between his brothers. "Like I would ever go to that stuffy, boring night of elitists comparing their most recent stock transactions."

Mauro raises his glass in agreement.

"Yeah, not a chance in hell," Leo concurs. "He can find his investments from someone else."

"I heard he has." Vin eyes Leo over his drink.

"You don't mean..." Leo's brow arches.

Vin simply nods.

"Why the fuck would he get involved with him?"

I'm clearly missing something.

Vin shrugs. "Heard they share a similar interest."

Leo's hand on the table clenches into a fist, and without a second thought, I reach for it. He turns it palm up, tangling our fingers together. His body relaxes under my touch, and I marvel at the power he's given me.

"Let's dance!" Maddy nudges Eli's shoulder, who begrudgingly gets up so that she can squeeze past him. I don't miss the way her hand carefully brushes over his that's resting on the table or her eyes that quickly peek up, locking with his for only the briefest moment before they both look in opposite directions.

What was that?

Maddy stands. Her short black dress molds to her hips, the ones she is resting her hands on. "Come on, ladies!"

Alina downs the rest of her drink and then, taking a very rigid Mauro by surprise, slides herself over his lap. "Excuse me," she murmurs as his hands land on her waist, helping her across. She jumps out of the booth, settles on her heels, and stands beside Maddy, who is waiting for me.

"Do you want to dance?" Leo's warm breath cascades over my ear, his nose nuzzling my neck.

My eyes dart around the place, waiting for a man in a mask to jump out and yell, "Surprise," ruining the night, but I won't let him. Not even in my vivid imagination.

I nod, so Leo slides out of the booth, allowing me to exit. Maddy grabs my hand. "Girls only!" She drags me and Alina behind her to the center of the dance floor.

It's easy for the two of them to move their hips with the music, matching the beat as if they wrote this song. But for me, it's a struggle.

Maddy squeezes my hand. "You can do this, Scar. Pretend we're in my room like when we were kids, and we used to blast Britney Spears and dance until the early hours."

I close my eyes and wait for the moment when everything clicks. When it does, my hips begin to sway softly, feeling the rhythm pulsing beneath my skin.

"That's it!" Alina urges.

I open my eyes and see the two of them smiling encouragingly as the three of us join hands and start dancing in our private circle.

I can feel Leo's eyes burn on my back, and I know that no man in this place will be able to get within a few feet of me, which brings me peace.

After a few songs, sweat begins to drip down my back. I run my fingers through my hair and can tell by the rough texture that it's not going to be a pretty sight. "I'll be right back," I yell over the music. "I'm just going to the bathroom." I point to the black door with the restroom sign above it at the back of the room.

"Want me to come with you?" Maddy asks.

"No. I'm fine. Actually, no, I'm great. I just need to throw my hair up. I'll be back in two minutes!"

"We'll be here!"

Making my way to the bathroom, I have to squeeze past a few people, but eventually, I get to the door and am relieved to find no line. I walk into the single-use room and lock the door behind me. I groan at the sight of my frizzy hair and mascara smudged under my eyes but immediately begin fixing it with what I have. Reaching inside my bag, I pull out a hair tie, and my phone falls to the floor.

"Shit."

When I pick it up, I tap the screen to ensure it still works, and that's when I see I have a new message from an unknown number. *Hmm.*

I swipe the screen and go into my messages.

My stomach drops as I let my phone slip between my shaky fingers, plummeting to the ground.

All the air leaves my lungs as I collapse to the floor, clawing at my chest for a breath.

It's him.

CHAPTER TWENTY-TWO

Leo

It all happened so fast.

One second I'm watching Scarlett move gracefully and sensually on the dance floor, my cock straining against my pants as she sways her hips to the beat of the music in that skin-hugging pink dress. In the following second, I glance at Vin as he disappears down a dark hallway with a woman at his side. And in the third and final second, when I look back to where Scarlett was dancing, she's gone.

"What the fuck?" I jump up from the table and make my way over to my sister, grabbing her arm. "Where the fuck is Scarlett?"

"Calm down, Caveman." She pushes my hand away. "She just went to the bathroom."

"You know she can't be alone." I narrow my eyes at her. "Why didn't you go with her?"

She stops dancing, placing her hands on her hips, displeasure written all over her face. "One, I offered to go with her, but she didn't want any company, so I respected her wishes. And two." She focuses her eyes on me as she pokes her index finger in my chest. "You need to give her space,

Leo. She needs to breathe, and not with you breathing down her neck all the damn time. You'll make her feel like a prisoner all over again."

I grind my back teeth. "You have no fucking idea what she's been through."

"Don't I, though?" she snaps back at me, her face paling as remorse spreads across her features.

"What's that supposed to mean?"

"N-nothing." She pushes her hair behind her ear, and I can't help but notice a tiny tremble in her fingers. She clears her throat, straightening her shoulders. "Nothing." Her hand, now clear of any nerves, motions toward the back of the room. "The bathroom is that way." She turns around, giving me her back as she makes her way toward Alina.

I shake my head in frustration. I don't have time to play fucking games. Storming off toward the bathroom, I push past a few bystanders until I find myself in front of the door.

Knock. Knock. "Scarlett, it's Leo."

Nothing.

My hand pulls down on the doorknob, but it's locked.

Knock! Knock! Knock! "Scarlett. Open the door, baby."

One second...two seconds...three seconds...

Fuck this.

I rotate my neck and then roll my shoulders before lifting my right leg and putting all my force behind a kick that blasts the door wide open.

My eyes jump around the dark space before immediately landing on Scarlett, curled in a ball next to the vanity. Tears stream down her cheeks as she trembles like a leaf. Her wide-open eyes are glossed over, lost in another world.

In two strides, I'm standing before her, kneeling. My hands cup her cheeks, turning her face toward mine. "What happened?"

She says nothing, her eyes looking at me but not seeing me.

She's in shock.

"Scarlett. Look at me, baby." I brush my lips across hers as one of my hands slides around her neck. My thumb rests on her pulse point, beating out of control. As I pull back, her dazed eyes blink a few times, the ghosts of her past slowly disappearing from view. "Good girl." I swipe back her hair. "I'm here. You're safe." I run my hands down her arms, gliding my fingers up and down, hoping my touch will bring her back to me. "Tell me what happened."

Her lips part, but no sound comes out. Hesitantly, her hand lifts, and with a shaking finger, she points to her phone lying on the floor across from us.

I reach for it, swiping across the screen until I see what has her in this state of panic.

Unknown Number

Always mine.

I clench the phone between my fingers as fury sweeps through me. Engulfing me until I'm practically seeing red.

This fucking bastard.

Shoving her phone in my back pocket, I don't wait a second before lifting her in my arms and carrying her out of the bathroom. She tucks her head against my chest, the shivering in her body intensifying as we move through the club. Her fingers grip my shirt as tight as she can, holding on to me as if I might disappear from her grasp.

I make it to the table, where I find Eli and Mauro, hands on their concealed weapons tucked into their pants, ready for an imminent attack.

"Get the girls and find Vin," I order them. "We're leaving now. And get a hold of Alex. Tell him we got a new message. But this time, it went to Scarlett's phone."

I don't wait for their responses as I turn and exit, barreling out of the building like a bull with a taste of freedom for the first time.

We make it to the house in minutes, and after carrying Scarlett to our room, I place her on the bed, noticing that her shaking has subsided, but not entirely. I wrap a blanket around her shoulders and then head to the bathroom, turning on the faucet to the cast iron clawfoot tub. My fingers swirl in the water, ensuring it's the perfect temperature. Searching in the cabinets, I find a bottle of lavender bubble bath and pour some of it in the water.

Going back to Scarlett, I pause in the doorway.

She looks lost. Scared. Helpless. And it breaks me.

It fucking breaks me.

I take a few steps until I stand before her and place my hand on her cheek. She melts into my touch as if needing my strength.

"We need to get you into a warm bath. Okay, baby?"

She nods, staring off. Her mind is clearly lost in a dark place. And I'm not sure what she's seeing, but it's scaring the fuck out of me.

Carefully, I lift her, slowly walking back into the bathroom and dimming the harsh lights to a mere glow. I stand her before the tub, the blanket falling to the floor around her.

"I'm going to take your clothes off. Okay?"

She nods.

"I need to hear you say it's okay, Scarlett."

Her lips part. "I-it's o-okay."

I reach behind her and slowly unzip her dress. Not in a sensual way filled with lust. But in a way that won't have her scared of my touch. That won't erase all the progress we've made with each other. A way that tells her I want to help her. I want to make her feel better.

As the dress falls to her feet, she steps out of it. My eyes graze over her, loving every piece of her before me. I unclasp her bra, and she wiggles her arms, letting it fall to the floor as well. Kneeling, I glide my thumbs on each side of her underwear and slip it down her thighs and calves. As I reach her ankles, she steps out of those as well, her hand reaching out to me, gripping my shoulder for support.

Standing, I hold a hand out for her, letting her know it's time to step into the tub. She takes my hand, gripping my fingers as she slowly lowers herself, bubbles surrounding her. She bends her knees, resting her head on them as she wraps her arms around her legs, keeping her eyes closed.

Just as I'm about to sit on the floor—because I'm not leaving her goddamn sight—her whisper fills the space between us.

"Can you...come in with me?"

I don't hesitate. I strip myself bare, kicking my clothes to the corner before sliding in behind her. She slowly leans against me, and I take that as an invitation to wrap my arms around her, holding her against my chest.

She fits perfectly in my arms.

But the contrast between us doesn't go unnoticed. Besides our significant scars—her back and my hand—we have more differences than similarities. Where her skin is smooth, mine is rough. Her body is like a piece of porcelain; mine is a tattoo-plagued being. Her hair is a soft blonde cascading smoothly down her shoulders, but mine is dark and messy.

Yet somehow, we work, blending light and dark together, creating a space where only we fit.

She reaches hesitantly for the closest bottle of shampoo, but I stop her, wrapping my fingers tenderly around her wrist. "Let me." She nods, shifting forward just the tiniest bit. I grab the spray nozzle and turn on the water, my other hand reaching in front of her to tilt her head back as I soak her hair. I then take the shampoo and pop the lid, inhaling the sweet scent of peaches and apples. My hands rub a dollop amount together between my palms before I lather it in her hair, massaging her scalp.

She lets out a soft moan, relishing my touch. I rinse the shampoo and do the same thing with the conditioner.

When I've finished, she turns in my arms, facing me. Her blue eyes no longer appear lost but clear and beautiful. Present. "Thank you."

I press my lips to her shoulder. "Is this helping?"

"Yes." I feel her body relax in my hold as she closes her eyes and snuggles her face into my chest. One of my hands rests on her stomach, my thumb gliding back and forth across her smooth skin as my other hand rests on her thigh.

Silence fills the room as we lose track of time and stay just like this, neither of us wanting to move.

As Scarlett falls asleep in my arms and peace surrounds us, I stare out the French doors beside the tub, overlooking the ocean. I think about all of the things I'm going to do to Le Diable once I get my hands on him before I kill him and then kill him again and again and again.

Because I may not be God, but I hold the power to bring that motherfucker back to life over and over again simply so I can kill him in every single imaginative way I can think of.

I won't stop until he breaks.

CHAPTER TWENTY-THREE
Scarlett

Air fills my lungs as I take a deep breath, hold my head high, and enter the indoor pool room.

"Scarlett!" Maddy jumps from her lounge chair, nearly tripping over her bag as she runs over to me. "I'm so sorry!" She wraps her arms around me, squeezing hard.

"What for?" I ask, pulling back.

"I should have gone with you to the bathroom. Leo was right." Her eyes look downcast. Does she blame herself for what happened last night? "I shouldn't have let you go alone. I just thought you needed some space and—"

"Maddy." My lips curve up. "You didn't do anything wrong. Besides, it was a solo stall. Were you going to stand in the corner facing the wall while I peed?"

She laughs, shaking her head. "You're right." She shrugs. "I'm trying to do everything right, and I think I'm sucking at it."

I purse my lips to the side, taking in her slumped shoulders. "Honestly, you're the only one treating me like everything is normal. Like I'm normal. And that's all I want."

She gives a sad smile. "You are normal, Scar."

I let out a breath of air, looking away. *So badly, I wish she was right.* The beach lies less than a hundred feet from the house, and with a nearby window open, I listen to the comforting sound of the crashing waves. "What did you have planned for us today?" I ask, hoping she'll get my hint to change the subject.

"Oh!" She grabs my hand, pulling me to the free lounger beside hers. "I have a full spa day planned for us. The manicurist will be here any minute."

I sit back on the lounger, dropping my bag to the ground. "That sounds like my kind of day."

She plops back down on her chaise. "Alina went for a walk on the beach but should be here any—"

"Hey, guys!" Alina strolls toward us from the other side of the room, her hair wild from the cool ocean breeze. She sits at the end of my chair, looking at me when she asks, "How are you feeling?"

I lift my shoulders. "Honestly, more embarrassed than anything."

"Don't be," they both say in unison.

I shake my head. "I don't know. One minute, I was fine, and then I saw..." I pause, swallowing down the terror that tries to sneak up inside me. "The text...and then it's like I just blacked out. I don't remember much of anything after that."

Except I do.

I remember the way Leo carried me in his arms to safety.

I remember the warm bath and his willingness to join me when I asked him to.

And I remember feeling complete tranquility before falling asleep in his arms.

Maddy reaches for my hand. "Vin updated me, so I told Alina what was happening. I hope that was okay?"

"I was a little...concerned," Alina admits. "So I kind of forced it out of Maddy."

I worry my bottom lip between my teeth. "I'm sorry if I—"

"Oh no. Don't be sorry." Alina unzips her purple puffer vest and drops it to the side, revealing her black athleisure wear. "I just wanted to make sure you were okay."

I show a small, appreciative smile. "I am."

Maddy squeezes my hand. "They're going to find him, Scar. I know they will."

"I know." I feel the familiar tightness in my chest whenever someone mentions him. "Can we talk about something else? Anything else?"

Alina bites her bottom lip, stifling a smile. "How about how your husband stormed out of the club carrying you in his arms like he was on the cover of some Harlequin romance novel." She fans herself. "Now, that is a man."

My cheeks heat up, and I can't help the laugh that slips through my lips.

"God, you think the whole world is one never-ending romance book," Maddy teases with a smirk. She sits up, removes her bathing suit cover-up, and adjusts the red straps on her bikini.

Alina shrugs. "I can't help it. Sometimes fictional worlds are better than the real thing." She looks lost in thought before saying, "Besides, look at you, living the fairy-tale life. Marrying your knight in shining armor."

Maddy's smile falls, her expression turning into stone.

I look to Alina, who gives me an *I have no idea what's happening* expression before turning back to Maddy.

"Maddy?" I ask, snapping my fingers in front of her face.

She shakes her head, blinking. "Sorry." She throws on her perfect smile. "Just distracted."

I lean toward her. "Is everything okay—"

But before I finish, a few women walk through the door with the head guard on duty.

Maddy claps her hands together. "Perfect timing." She jumps up, striding toward the team of women, telling them where to set up.

I watch her carefully, observing the mask she wears so perfectly in front of everyone and knowing that for just a moment, it almost slipped, revealing more than she was willing to share.

And I'm worried about her.

I sit on the edge of the bed, twisting my hands together on my lap, practicing breathing in and out. "Why can't I just be normal?" I pathetically ask myself. My shoulders slump as I drop my head, frustrated tears filling my eyes.

Knock. Knock.

Looking up, I spot Leo standing in the doorway.

"Hey, I thought you would be with…" His smile falters. "What's wrong?" In a mere second, he's over by my side, sitting beside me, wrapping a protective arm around my waist.

"Oh, nothing." I hastily wipe at my damn traitorous eyes, throwing on a smile.

"You're giving me your fake smile."

My smile falls. "How do you know the difference between my smiles?"

"Because I *know* you." He brushes my hair back. "Talk to me." His hand trails down my spine in soothing motions, paying a little extra attention to my lower back.

I glimpse down at my lap, embarrassment filling me. How do I explain to him what I'm feeling? Or more like, what I'm not feeling?

"Weren't you supposed to be having a spa day with Madeleine and Alina?"

"We were." I squeeze my hands together. "And everything was fine. We got manicures and pedicures. And then…"

They started setting up three tables with blankets on them. I instantly knew what it was for, and I panicked, telling Maddy I was tired and needed to go inside for a nap.

"They were preparing to give us body massages." My body tenses at the mere thought. God, how pathetic am I? "And I... I couldn't stand the idea of someone touching me in that way. I mean, I could barely hold it together for the manicure and pedicure. But the thought of someone's hands on my body..." I shake my head. "I...I couldn't do it." I cover my face with my hands. "When will I be normal again?" I whisper, defeat laced in my voice.

Leo gently pulls my hands away from my face, bringing them to his chest.

"What is normal?" he asks.

I glance away, not in the mood for this. "You know what I mean."

"No. I don't think I do." I look back at him, my eyes narrowing. "Let's see," he starts. "Madeleine puts ketchup on everything, including eggs." He grimaces. "Mauro has a fear of small spaces. Alex won't let his food groups touch each other on his plate; if they do, he won't eat it. Vin names each and every single one of his cars. And me, well, I prefer to know the ending to a movie before I watch it. Don't care much for surprises." He shrugs. "Everyone has something about them that makes them different. Maybe even a little special." He gives a slight smile. "The word *normal* means conforming to a standard of what is expected. But if we all did what was expected, the world would be a little boring, don't you think?"

I let out a heavy sigh. "I guess you're right."

"No one is normal, Firefly. Least of all, this crazy family you're a part of." He softly presses his lips to mine.

"Leo, I..." *I love you.* The words sit on the tip of my tongue, begging me to release them. But for whatever reason, I just can't. "I don't know what I would do without you."

"Well, you'll never have to find out because I will always be here." He kisses my temple, his hand resuming a circular motion on my lower back, right over the scars he knows are there. "And just so you know, woman or man, no one is allowed to touch you. Not even a fucking masseuse. Wait until I see Madeleine."

I laugh at his threat. "She just wanted to do something nice for us. I know it was supposed to be her weekend, but I have a feeling she did all this for me. It was her way of helping me have some normalcy, and I really appreciate that."

He sighs. "You're right. She did do this for you. She begged me for weeks to make this happen."

"Really?"

"Yeah. She missed you while you were gone. I think she's trying to make up for all the lost time now."

"I missed her too." I look up into his eyes when I say, "I'm worried about her."

His forehead furrows. "Why?"

"I don't know. Call it a gut feeling, but something doesn't feel right between her and Alastor. He doesn't seem her type." I don't mention that Eli was the only guy I ever knew to be her type.

I'm not sure how much he would love to hear that his baby sister had the hots for his best friend.

He presses his lips to mine. "I don't want you to worry about it. Everything will be taken care of."

"What does that mean?"

He looks down at me thoughtfully. "It means the Alaries will never let anything happen to one of our own."

I pause, assessing his response. Words he said to me at Maddy's engagement party echo in my head. *Their wedding is not happening.* "At Maddy's engagement party, you told me their wedding wouldn't be happening, but I didn't think you were serious... But you were, weren't you?"

He smiles, pressing his lips to my forehead, the only answer I receive.

CHAPTER TWENTY-FOUR

Leo

I unwind from Scarlett's naked, sleeping body and sit up, my mind racing with unanswered questions. Grabbing a pair of grey sweatpants and a T-shirt, I lock the door behind me and head outside, where I find Mauro and Vin around the fire pit with Cuban cigars between their fingers.

I sit in the free chair beside Mauro and shake my head when Vin offers me a cigar. I never did care for them.

"Suit yourself," he answers, stretching his legs before him.

Mauro pulls the cigar from his lips and blows a thick puff of smoke toward the sky.

"Can't sleep?" Vin asks.

"Too many unanswered questions plaguing me." I lean forward, staring into the fire. The orange, blue, and yellow hues blend, mesmerizing my weary mind.

"We'll find—" Vin stops speaking as he pulls out his phone from his pocket. "It's Alex." He accepts the call, putting him on speakerphone. "Alex, did you find anything from the text?"

The first thing we hear is Alex's fingers tapping away on a keyboard. "No," Alex answers, letting out a defeated sigh. "My team and I have been working on it all day, but we can't pinpoint a location. He's fixed it so the phone's location changes every five minutes, leaving us nothing to go off of."

"Shit." Vin smooths his hand over his stubble. "Well, I take it you called us for something else then?"

The clacking on the keyboard pauses. "Igor slipped up."

"What do you mean?" I ask, angling closer to the phone.

"I'll let you hear for yourself." Alex taps a few buttons, and then suddenly…

"What are you doing calling me?" Igor's chilly tone floats through the phone. "I told you our conversations have to happen in person. There're too many eyes and ears watching and listening."

"Yes, well, this couldn't wait. Thanks to your employee, Le Diable, I am now facing quite a bit of heat and need things fixed now!"

I still. His employee? My hand clenches into a tight fist. That motherfucker does know Le Diable and lied to our fucking faces. "Whose voice is that?" I ask, cracking my knuckles.

"Governor Garrett Johnson's," Alex answers.

Vin and I share a look.

Igor laughs. "It's funny if you think I can tell that monster what to do." He pauses. "Besides, he doesn't work for me."

"It's not funny!" Garrett spits out. "He's making things very difficult for me."

Igor sighs. "What's the problem, Garrett?"

"The problem is that there are too many missing girls in my state. And the blame is being directed at me for not doing enough about it," he hisses. "It's an election year, and I cannot risk things falling apart!"

"Listen," Igor starts. "You knew what was needed when I presented you with our plan. And I believe you were quite happy to learn of the cut you would be receiving."

"Yes, but that was before I had the voters breathing down my neck seeking answers!" He lets out a breath. "Why can't he collect girls from other parts of the country?"

"His current employer is in New York, so that's where he must stay...for now."

Garrett huffs. "And the owner of this club, your partner... Are the rumors true?"

"They are," Igor states. "He's back from the dead." A deep, satisfied laugh fills the line. "And he's very much looking forward to your discretion while allowing him access to your...lovely state."

Mauro's brows furrow in confusion, all of us feeling the same way. Who the fuck could he be talking about?

"Yeah. Yeah," Garrett adds. "Just as long as no one forgets my portion of the profits. I'm going to need it to buy off extra voters this year because of all this shit."

"Of course. You'll be compensated quite fairly."

"And the auction... When is that happening?"

"You mean the biggest auction of the year? Well, two weeks from today," he says matter-of-factly. "Why? Will you be bidding?"

Garrett chuckles. "If I can make it into the city without anyone noticing, then I'll be there."

The city.

"Good," Igor drawls.

"Will you be running the show?"

"I'll be there, ensuring all guests get exactly what they came for."

"And Le Diable?"

"He'll be there to deliver the inventory."

"Ahh, I'll finally see the face of this so-called Le Diable," Garrett muses. "And the location?"

"That is private information and you must wait until I see you in person at your governor's dinner next week. I've said too much over the phone as it is. Who knows who could be listening?"

"Fine. And the problem with the missing girls?"

"I can guarantee you that there will be no more issues after the night of the auction."

"How can you be so sure?"

"Because there will be a new ruler in your— Did you hear something?"

"No."

There's a rustling sound.

"I must go. We'll speak soon."

The conversation ends, and silence fills the space between us, with only the ocean's crashing waves beside us.

"Le Diable is here in New York," I say through clenched teeth.

"And the biggest auction of the year will be held two weeks from today on Halloween," Alex muses.

"And Le Diable will be there." Vin leans forward, steepling his fingers under his chin. "You know what this means, don't you?"

Mauro glances between the two of us, not comprehending.

I lean back in my chair, staring up at the pitch-black sky. "It means we're going to the fucking governor's dinner to get the details on the location."

Alex groans just as Mauro lets out an exasperated grunt of displeasure.

Vin clasps Mauro's shoulder. "You and me both, big guy. But remember who we're doing this for."

Mauro nods in understanding. He turns to me, placing his hand on his chest, right over his heart. "Scar...lett," he manages in a hoarse whisper.

"Alex?" Vin lets out a puff of smoke.

"Yeah?"

"Can you get us a way to listen to Igor at the dinner?"

"Of course," he answers. "Piece of cake."

"Good." I run my fingers through my hair, pushing it back. "Once we obtain the location, we'll have the last piece of the puzzle."

"Looks like we have a plan," Vin surmises.

"We have a plan," Alex repeats.

I stand, looking off at the dark water. We're so close to catching Le Diable. I can feel it in my grasp. He's been just out of reach this whole time, always finding a way out of our clutches. But not this fucking time. We've got him right where we want him. "Le Diable is going to regret ever fucking with the Alaries."

It's a lesson he'll learn.

Slowly.

Painfully.

Until his dying breath.

My lips curve up, pleasure surging through my veins for what I plan on doing to him.

Chapter Twenty-Five

Scarlett

A whimsical chime sounds as my hand drops to my side.

"Eli, can you wait out here?" I ask, shifting uncomfortably.

Eli's brows furrow. "Why?"

"Well, for whatever reason, it's clear that Maddy can't particularly stand to...be around you." I give a sheepish smile and shrug. "So, it might be better not to come inside." I'm still not sure why she's insisted on giving him the cold shoulder recently, but it's obvious something happened between them while I wasn't living here.

Something she hasn't felt the need to share with me yet.

He grunts in agreement, rolling his eyes. "I'll wait right here," he states as the door swings open.

Maddy appears in a soft grey sweatsuit with a beaming smile. That is, until her eyes catch on the man standing to my right, and her smile completely vanishes.

"I didn't know you were bringing your babysitter with you." She purses her lips to the side and arches a brow.

"The only one who needs babysitting around here is you," Eli quips, his jaw tensing.

"In case you haven't noticed, I can take care of myself. I've been doing it just fine for years, creating a wonderful life for myself." She gestures toward everything around her: the tennis court, the expensive cars, and even the massive boat docked in the lake.

And maybe if someone didn't know her, they may think that's the case. That she's living her best life. But I know her better than most. She doesn't care about things. She never has. She only ever wanted something when she was feeling down. Instead of being an emotional eater, I always considered her an emotional shopper.

Buying something merely to give herself a dose of dopamine. And when it wore off, she'd do it again and again—like a drug addict seeking their next hit.

Glancing around at all the expensive things surrounding her, I'd say she's in a downward spiral that she isn't ready to acknowledge just yet.

And from the barely there dark circles under her eyes, I know in my gut that something isn't right.

"Wonderful?" Eli lets out a quick, deep laugh. "Now, isn't that the biggest joke of the year."

Her hand by her side transforms into a shaking fist. "You goddamn bast—"

"Okay!" I interject, looking between the two of them. "I didn't come here for you two to butt heads. I came bearing gifts." I raise the quart of cookie blast ice cream, Maddy's favorite.

Her smile returns. "In that case, come in. But leave the trash outside." She tosses her long dark hair over her slender shoulder and strolls away, leaving the door wide open.

I'm sorry, I mouth to Eli.

He shrugs, displaying a playful grin. "Don't worry about it. She's more bark than bite. Nothing I can't handle."

"I hope you're right," I say over my shoulder as I walk inside her house, closing the door behind me.

My eyes travel around the open, bright space as we walk through the foyer, past the grand dining room, and into the kitchen. Everything's spotless. Exactly where it belongs. But that's Maddy. She likes everything in order.

Perfect.

She reaches into a cabinet, pulls out two wineglasses, and then retrieves a bottle of wine from the hidden fridge built into her kitchen island. A deep sigh leaves her as she pours the almost clear liquid into each glass. I sit on one of the counter stools as she pushes a glass my way.

"Bowls or spoons?"

I smile. "Spoons."

She extends the drawer beside her and grabs two perfectly polished silver spoons. I remove the lid from the ice cream, and without missing a beat, we shove our spoons inside, bringing a hefty bite of sugary sweetness to our lips.

"Bottoms up," she muses before her lips wrap around the spoon. A small moan escapes her as her eyes close. "God, I love ice cream," she says through a mouthful of it. "You always know the way to my heart."

I lick my spoon clean, savoring the chocolatey chunks. "I like to think I know my best friend pretty well. Even if we did spend some time apart."

The corners of her lips slightly curve up. "Time apart only made us love each other more."

"True." I dip my spoon in the container. "And speaking of being best friends..."

She arches a brow, waiting for me to continue.

"I'm worried about you."

Her eyebrows furrow as she bites her bottom lip. "Worried about me?"

"Yes." I grab a napkin and place my spoon on top of it. "I want to make sure everything is okay."

"Why wouldn't it be?" she asks with some defense in her tone.

I shrug, popping a brow. "You tell me."

She rests her spoon on the counter, her palms flat on the marble surface as she closes her eyes. "Everything will be... I mean." Her eyes pop open. "Is fine. Everything is fine." She lets out a deep breath. "I think I'm just stressed with the wedding planning. That's all."

I bite my bottom lip, not knowing how to ask the real question on my mind. If I press her too much, she'll shut down, so I tread carefully as I say, "And Alastor..." I trail off, glancing toward the ice cream. "He's the one?"

A thick silence fills the space between us.

She swallows hard, and right before she puts her spoon back into the container, I swear I see her eyes mist over.

"He's the one," she repeats in a monotone voice.

Lie.

"He's good to you?"

"The best."

Lie.

"He doesn't hurt you?"

"Never."

Lie.

"You love him?"

She pauses, her lips parting. "Of course."

The biggest lie of all.

"Okay." My hand reaches across the counter for hers. "But you know, if you need to talk to me or need...help, I'm here. Right?"

A tight smile shows on her face as she nods. She clears her throat, turning toward the fridge. "You know what we're missing? Toppings!" She opens the fridge door and digs inside, obviously ready to change the topic.

And as her best friend, I know she'll talk to me when she's ready. And right now, she's not.

"This reminds me of when we were kids," I say.

She turns toward me with whipped cream, cherries, and chocolate sauce in her arms. "You mean when we used to have sleepovers at my parents' house and sneak downstairs in the middle of the night to eat ice cream in the butler's closet?"

We laugh and then freeze, our eyes connecting.

"You don't think?"

"Should we?"

We speak simultaneously, making us laugh even louder as we race toward the stairs, the quart of ice cream in Maddy's clutches.

Ten minutes later, matching in satin pajamas, courtesy of Maddy, we both find ourselves lounging on the floor in the butler's closet, scarfing down ice cream as we laugh and reminisce about childhood memories.

And God, it feels so good.

So *normal.*

"Remember that one time when Leo and Vin were tubing on the lake, and Vin saw a snake and screamed like a little girl before he fell off his tube and lost his shorts?" Maddy laughs hysterically, falling on her side. "God, that was priceless."

I wipe the tears falling from the corners of my eyes. "I think Eli was the only one brave enough to remove the snake."

Maddy's laughter fades as she sits up, wiping her eyes. "Yeah. I forgot about that."

She becomes quiet and pours some chocolate sauce into her mouth. Then, reaching for the bottle of sauvignon blanc beside her, she guzzles it down. Clearly, we've come to the portion of the evening where wine glasses are unnecessary.

"Can I ask you something?" I lean against the cupboard, crossing my legs in front of me.

She places the bottle beside her and arches a brow, waiting.

"Are you ever going to tell me what happened between you and Eli?"

She rests her head against the wall, staring up at the ceiling. "There's nothing to tell." Her eyes glance toward me.

I arch a brow in challenge.

She sighs, rolling her eyes. "I really hate how well you know me."

I smirk, licking some sauce off my spoon.

She shrugs, giving in. "Maybe someday."

"Someday," I repeat, reaching for a cherry.

"And what about you?"

"What about me?"

"Are you ever going to plan a proper wedding?" She nudges my foot with hers. "I remember the wedding scrapbook you used to have as a kid. Don't deny it."

I feel my cheeks heat as my shoulders drop. "I don't know. Maybe someday. If Leo wants to, I guess."

She scoffs. "Are you kidding? He'd do anything for you. If you tell him you want a wedding, he'd probably rent out the Taj Mahal for you."

I chuckle. "You're probably right."

She looks at me, a tender smile on her face. "He really loves you."

I roll in my bottom lip, looking down. "I know. I mean, I think I know."

"You think?" she asks incredulously.

"Well, it's just we haven't exactly said those words to each other yet." I drop my spoon on a napkin and, out of habit, twist the wedding band on my finger.

"And what are you waiting for?"

"I just..." I let out a heavy sigh. "We went into this marriage knowing there was an end date. Our contract stated that we were free to divorce when the time came. And even though things have changed between us, and it feels a hell of a lot more than just a contract, I just want to wait to know that he'll still feel the same way about me even after..."

"After what?" Maddy asks.

"After..." My words trail off as my throat tightens.

"After they find Le Diable," Maddy whispers in understanding.

I nod. "I feel like Cinderella waiting for the bell to strike midnight, and I want to know that when it does, he'll still be here. He'll still feel the same way I feel about him." I lift one shoulder. "It's stupid, I know. Especially after everything Leo has done for me, but I don't want him to feel stuck with me. I want him to have an out."

Maddy's hand finds mine and gently squeezes it. "I understand. I do. But I know my brother, and he's not going anywhere. Especially not after he tore apart the whole world searching for you." Her eyes glance down at our hands and then land back on me. "He's only ever loved you, Scar. So, don't be scared of putting your heart on the line with him. Cause all he'll do is handle it with care." She leans back, her eyes lost in thought. "Few people in this world are lucky enough to find their true love." Her lips curve up. "And that's exactly what you and Leo are to each other."

I give a half smile. "I'm sure you and Alastor are that—"

"Don't," she rushes out, defeat crossing her eyes. "We both know that's not true." She takes another sip from the bottle and then places it between her legs, her finger tracing the label. And my heart breaks for her. I want Maddy to be with someone who makes her happy and treats her like the center of his universe, exactly the way Leo treats me. But as far as I can tell, Alastor is never around. Never by her side at family functions. Never sending her flowers or gifts while he's away. But maybe that's how she wants things to be between them.

"So." She clears her throat, wiping at her eyes. "Do you know what you plan on wearing to the governor's dinner next week? If you ask me, I'm not looking forward to another stuffy event."

I shake my head. "I haven't thought about it." I reach for my spoon. "I thought the guys didn't want to go to it? Leo practically ripped up the invite when it came."

She shrugs. "Beats me. They seem eager to go now, though. Vin called me this morning to tell me I was coming. I told him only if they have crème brûlée." She chuckles. Vin probably knew she wasn't joking, either. No one has a sweet tooth like Maddy. "But I also need to work on a Halloween costume for the annual party, so we should go shopping this week."

"You guys still throw the annual Halloween party?" I ask, remembering how much fun they used to be when I was a kid.

"Oh, yes. It's almost as grand as our Christmas party." She grabs a cherry and pops it into her mouth. "It's just one of the traditions we like to keep up with, especially because my dad always loved to throw a party. He'd find any reason to do it. Said it was the least we could do for the workers living on the property who have been loyal to our family over the years." I nod in understanding as her eyes appear slightly downcast. "He was a really good guy. Best Dad I could have ever wished for."

"You always had him wrapped around your finger. You could have asked him for the moon, and he would have figured out a way to get it for you," I say, making her smile. "He loved you and your brothers so much."

"Yeah, he did." She clears her throat, wiping at her eyes. "My mother won't be able to attend the party this year." She tips the ice cream container to its side. "She'll be jetting off to the south of France with her sister, but— Fuck."

"What?"

She scrapes her spoon against the inside of the now-empty container. "We need more ice cream."

Our eyes meet as we tumble over laughing, holding our stomachs tightly.

"I think I just peed a little," Maddy gets out.

The door to the pantry swings open, and two curious sets of eyes go from watching us with concern to amusement in a matter of seconds.

Maddy sits up, wiping her tears, still laughing. "I can explain. It's not what it looks like."

Leo arches a brow. "Really?" He looks to Eli, who's stifling a laugh. "Because it looks like you're hiding in the pantry like a couple of closet eaters, scooping ice cream out of the container...while on the floor."

I roll my lips to the side as I look around the small space, nodding. "I see how it might appear like that."

Leo grins, holding out his hand for me. "Let's go home, baby. It feels empty when you're not there."

My hand clasps his as he pulls me up to his side, placing a kiss on my temple. Feeling brave, thanks to the bottle of wine in my veins, I grasp his shirt and tug him against me, pressing my lips firmly to his.

"You guys are so cute it's sickening," Maddy teases.

"Oh, come on, Madeleine," Eli starts. "I'm sure you and Alastor are just as cute."

Her eyes narrow in on him, but she remains eerily calm when she says, "Of course we are."

Lie.

CHAPTER TWENTY-SIX

Leo

Lines of SUVs and opulent cars crowd the entryway drop-off, one after another, with chauffeurs depositing their guests and then driving away. Asher brings our SUV to a stop at the entrance, and Scarlett, Mauro, Madeleine, and I exit. Vin, Alex, and our mother make their way out of the following vehicle.

Vin straightens his jacket and rocks his neck from side to side. Looking between Mauro, Alex, and me, he asks, "Everyone ready?"

We all give a quick nod before Vin turns away, holding his arm out for our mother.

Coming around the vehicle, I find Scarlett smoothing down the satin fabric of her red dress. Her blonde waves cascade down her back as the tight fabric molds against every single one of her curves, stealing my breath. She's fucking stunning.

"How do I look?"

I lick my bottom lip, my hand reaching out to wrap around the side of her neck. My lips ghost over her ear, my tongue sneaking out. "You look like a goddamn queen." I press a kiss to the side of her neck. "*My* queen." I hear a small gasp slip between her lips and look closely to find her pupils dilated.

"Tonight?" she breathes.

"Tonight," I answer, tucking a piece of hair behind her ear before kissing her forehead. I intertwine our fingers and lead the way to the entrance with my family by my side. As we step through the archway, eyes land on us. Some are in awe. Some are in fear. But we don't have time to examine as we make our way toward the main room.

"Three o'clock," Alex mutters.

My eyes dart to my side, where I see Igor Vasiliev approaching along with a few of his guards. I tuck Scarlett closer to my side and notice Vin stepping in front of Madeleine.

A fake smile plasters its way onto Igor's decrepit face. "Ah, the Alaries. I did not expect to be seeing you tonight. You do not usually attend such events."

"We heard they have the best crème brûlée in the area and thought we would try for ourselves," Vin declares with an amused grin.

Madeleine snorts and quickly recovers, examining her manicured nails.

"Hmm..." Igor hums, his eyes resting on my mother. "Cecilia. It is always a pleasure." He puts his hand out, palm up, awaiting her hand as he does a slight bow.

She merely stares at it in disdain. "I wish I could say the same."

He straightens, quickly pulling his hand to his side. The corners of his lips turn down in displeasure. "Now, I see where your children get their manners from." His cold eyes dart between me and Vin.

"Oh, so you've noticed we don't care for you, yet you still make a show of yourself to gain my attention." She tilts her head, her smile growing.

"Well, I never," he mutters, appalled. "This doesn't appear to be the time or place to make a scene, so I will take my leave." He briskly walks away, his guards trailing closely behind him, appearing bored out of their minds.

"This way," Vin directs, leading us toward a table. We all take our seats, and I slide my arm around the back of Scarlett's chair as my eyes scope out the room. There is too much evil in one space. Political figures and billionaires all with hidden agendas and secrets that would destroy them if they ever got out. Secrets that many of them know we hold over them like a dog with its bone. How many of these fuckers have a *Blue Velvet Fantasies* card in their wallet?

But we brought the girls because we knew leaving them at home would make us look even more suspicious for being here without them. We didn't exactly tell them why we had decided to accept our invites, and I have no intention of unveiling that because I don't need to add any additional stress to Scarlett.

Just before the first course is served, we hear the familiar tapping of crystal glassware and look to the front of the room, where Governor Garrett Johnson stands proudly before his audience.

"Good evening." His conniving smile makes me sick, especially knowing how fucked up he is. The shit we've found on him... I grimace just thinking about it. "I'm so honored that you could join me and my wife tonight for what I hope is a night you will never forget." As he drones on and on about how successful his last four years in office have been and the promises he makes to the voters if he's reelected, I notice Igor slip from his seat, heading down a back hall toward the restroom.

"Alex." I tilt my head in that direction, and he catches the sight of Igor right before disappearing.

"On it." He discreetly slinks out of his seat, hiding in the shadows while he moves in the same direction.

I focus my attention on Garrett, who continues his ramblings as I try to appear as if my brother isn't in the process of dropping a tiny, undetectable microphone into the pocket of our enemy.

Scarlett places her hand on my thigh, and I bring my hand over hers. She leans closer to me, still keeping her eyes on the front of the room. "Is it just me, or does he like listening to the sound of his own voice?"

I laugh as I kiss the top of her head.

A few minutes later, Igor returns to his seat, but Alex is nowhere in sight. I check my watch, observing the seconds tick on, and just as I'm about to get up and search for him, he slides into his seat beside me.

"What took so long?" I ask, noting a hint of fury in his eyes.

He shakes his head. "Nothing." He straightens his tie and takes a deep breath before handing me a tiny earpiece. Inching closer, so only I can hear him, he says, "It's all set. I slipped it in his pocket while I reached over him for a paper towel. He wasn't too fond of my close proximity." He smirks. "Put this in your ear." He turns to his side and gives Mauro and Vin one as well. "Tap the button on the side when you're ready to listen."

We all give a slight nod, aware that the last thing we need is to draw attention to ourselves.

Garrett wraps up his speech and approaches his seat as servers appear, carrying the first course.

"Who's that?" Alex asks, his eyes narrowed in on a petite blonde walking timidly over toward Garrett and taking her seat beside him. Garrett gives her a hard stare, a flicker of anger taking over his features, but just as soon as it appears, it's gone. Once again, he's masked in a pleasant smile, making small talk with his constituents around him.

"That poor girl," Mother murmurs. She sighs, cutting into her salad. "That's his wife, Charlotte. Whenever I see her from afar with him, she appears afraid of her own shadow. I wish I could help her."

Alex's knuckles around his butter knife whiten. "He abuses her?"

Scarlett tucks herself into my side, her eyes downcast. I kiss her temple, running my thumb over the back of her hand.

"There's been no confirmation," Mother starts. "But it doesn't take an expert to spot the signs. Look at her."

"I am." Alex's eyes focus only on her back from across the room.

I snap my fingers before his gaze, and he blinks a few times, coming back to the present. "Remember, we need to stay discreet tonight."

He nods, looking down at his plate. "I know," he says, spreading the butter a bit too roughly on his dinner roll.

Madeleine takes a sip of her drink, her obnoxiously bright engagement ring flashing from the overhead lights. God, I can't wait until that ring is off her finger. I don't care if she pawns it or throws it into the ocean, but mark my words, that ring will be gone. Along with her fiancé.

Vin's eyes catch on mine as if thinking the same thing.

Mauro grunts, gaining our attention, and we follow his gaze.

Garrett heads our way with a beaming smile, most likely assuming that we're here to invest in his campaign. But he'll find out the second we leave that we only came for the free dinner.

"The Alaries." Garrett clasps his hands together, his eyes taking us all in. "What a pleasant surprise."

Mother plays her part perfectly. "Governor Johnson, we were so delighted to receive your invite for this evening. It has really been too long."

"It has," he agrees. "I've been so busy with the campaign and my new wife that the time has just slipped by." A greasy smile spreads over his face as he slides a hand over his slicked-back blond hair. "She's got a mind of her own, that one. Have to keep her on a tight leash," he jokes.

Alex drops his fork on his plate, his jaw clenching. I nudge his leg with my knee, and he relaxes, donning a tight smile. I'm sure the only thing making him smile is knowing how fast he can ruin this man's life from his computer.

"Understandable," Vin muses, appearing to agree with the idiot when he's merely just placating him.

"Ah." Garrett eyes Scarlett, his eyes darkening. "And who do we have here?"

A fire erupts within my veins, fury swirling beneath my skin.

Placing my hand on top of Scarlett's, my thumb resting over her wedding band, I clench my jaw. "My wife," I enunciate. "Scarlett Alarie."

Garrett's smile widens as he dips his head. "It's truly a...pleasure to meet you."

There's a hidden meaning in his words, and I fight the unrelenting impulse to jump up and strangle him until he's nothing more than a lifeless public figure.

Scarlett merely smiles, turning her hand over to intertwine our fingers. Catching me by surprise, she leans into me, slowly and seductively capturing my lips with hers. It instantly calms my bloodthirsty mind while also immediately making me unhinged with lust.

"Well," Garrett murmurs, clearing his throat. "Eat up. Enjoy the food and tonight's entertainment. I have some exotic dancers appearing soon to put on a show, which you won't want to miss."

"Oh, we won't." Vin gives him his smuggest smile, and we all watch as Garrett turns and makes his way from table to table before eventually reaching Igor's. The four of us discreetly tap our earpieces. A rustling sound floats over the voices, and I realize it's probably the fabric from his pocket. Thankfully, it's not enough to completely drown out their voices.

My eyes fix on the scene across the room as I eat.

"Everything all squared away for the auction?" Garrett murmurs. "No loose ends left untied?"

Igor grips Garrett's shoulder with one hand and hands him a familiar black card with the other. "Opening night is guaranteed to be a success. The fresh shipment will arrive that morning."

Garrett quickly scans the card and then slides it into his jacket pocket.

"All the information you need is on there," Igor says. "Shall we expect your attendance? I'm certain we'll have something that will meet your particular tastes."

Garrett nods as if listening to Igor tell him about the weather. "I will do my best. But what about the Alaries?"

Igor scoffs. "They won't be a problem. They have no inclination about what's been going on right under their noses. Too busy with their latest addition to the family. Especially Leonardo."

Garrett chuckles. "She is quite the looker. Can't say I blame him. Although, I would love a taste for myself." He rubs his chin, deep in thought. "Do you think he'd let me fuck her for the right price?"

Their laughter rumbles through the room.

And I lose all of my control, unable to stop myself.

I force back my chair and stand, the flimsy piece of wood with four legs collapsing to the ground, casting all eyes on me.

Vin puts himself between me and the aisle toward Igor's table, grasping a firm hand on my shoulder. "Don't," he warns gravely.

My chest heaves with too much force. I yank on my collar, needing air. I feel on the verge of a murderous rampage.

Something soft and warm touches my hand, and I glance down to see Scarlett looking up at me with furrowed brows. Her bright blue eyes latch onto mine, seeking answers I can't give her. At least not right now.

I let out a deep breath, bringing my hand to her cheek. Our eyes lock, a silent conversation occurring between us as we take our seats.

The voices in my ear resume, and my eyes latch onto the two most prominent monsters in this room. Garrett clasps his hand on Igor's shoulder. "We'll be in touch." And then he walks away, taking a seat at the following table to schmooze.

Fuck. We need that card.

My brothers and I look at each other. Deep in thought, Vin scratches a hand over his facial hair, his eyes moving to our sister. "Madeleine?"

"Yes?"

"Come with me. I need you to do me a favor." His eyes dip to the drink in her hand. "And bring that with you."

She rolls her eyes but places her napkin on the table and stands, trailing our brother with her drink in hand.

We intently watch as he walks toward Garrett's table, whispering something in Madeleine's ear. She looks up at him questionably but then gives a shrug and follows his lead. As they approach his table, the two of them wear wide smiles, letting out laughs as they strike up a conversation with Garrett. He falls into their trap as Madeleine places her hand on his shoulder, gifting him all her undivided attention and laughing at everything he says.

As Vin rears back in boisterous laughter, he swings his arms out and knocks Madeleine's drink onto Garrett, who looks aghast at his stained shirt. Madeleine grabs the closest napkin and starts dabbing at the liquid on his shirt, only making it worse. A few of the staff members block my line of sight. But after a couple of minutes, Vin and Madeleine walk away, heading straight for our table.

"I don't know why you had me go through all that trouble for this." Madeleine removes a black business card from the front of her dress and hands it to Vin. "But here."

Vin takes it, glancing at both sides, and then looks at me, Alex, and Mauro with a shit-eating grin.

"We have the address?" I ask.

"We have the address," he confirms triumphantly.

We have a location.

We have a date.

Everything is falling together just as it should be.

Scarlett peeks up at me. "Address for what?"

I brush her hair over her shoulder, admiring everything about her. From her sapphire blue eyes, soft pink lips, and sweet smile. "Nothing for you to worry about."

She purses her lips, her brows drawing together. "It has to do with...Le Diable, doesn't it?"

"It does." I won't lie to her. I'll never lie to her. But I'll only ever tell her what she needs to know. Nothing more than that, in fear of what it might do to her. "But I don't want you to worry about it." I glance at everyone around the table. "I'd say we got what we came here for. Is everyone ready to call it a night?"

Scarlett's bottom lip juts out. "But we haven't even had dessert yet."

"Yeah, I want my crème brûlée," Madeleine protests.

I place my lips next to Scarlett's ear so only she can hear me when I say, "The only dessert I want tonight is you."

Scarlett's porcelain cheeks turn a deep shade of pink, her eager eyes widening as her lips part.

Madeleine makes a gagging noise. "I don't even want to know what you just said to her."

"You're right," Vin starts, chuckling, rising from his seat. "You don't." He reaches a hand for Madeleine. "Come on. I'll buy you your very own crème brûlée on the way home."

Madeleine practically jumps from her seat, beaming like a child in a candy store, which makes me laugh.

Taking my wife's hand, I lead her out of this place of sin, intending to worship every inch of her body tonight.

CHAPTER TWENTY-SEVEN

Scarlett

I collapse onto our bed, still wearing my red satin dress. It hugs my body like a second skin, but I'm itching to get it off and throw on one of Leo's T-shirts.

"Tired, baby?" Leo removes his cuff links and slowly rolls up his crisp white sleeves. My eyes wander over his muscular forearms, covered in black ink, down to his thick fingers, knowing precisely what they can do.

I swallow hard and shake my head, suddenly feeling wide awake. My fingers glide over the soft fabric of my dress, every nerve ending in my body on fire. He steps beside the bed, looking down at me. His knuckles graze my cheek, traveling along my neck. "You did so well tonight," he praises. "Especially when you gave a little show in front of the governor."

I lick my bottom lip. "I wanted him to know who I belong to."

He lets out a guttural groan in approval, and my core erupts in need. His fingers trace my collarbone delicately and slowly. My breath catches as the pads of his fingers dip lower.

"I wanted to talk to you about something." He watches me cautiously as his fingers drift over the satin.

I blink back the lust I'm feeling, tightening my thighs together. "What about?"

He hesitates for a second before reaching inside his nightstand drawer, his hand sneaking in and coming out with a...*knife*.

My body tenses. Everything around me stills.

"W-what is that?" A cold shiver crawls over my skin.

"Please trust me," he says softly, sensing my trepidation. His free hand cups my cheek, his thumb gliding over my bottom lip. "Mauro suggested teaching you how to use a knife to protect yourself, and I agree." I start to shake my head in protest, but he continues. "He doesn't know your feelings on them. He doesn't know that part of your story because that's only between you and me." He places the knife on the nightstand and sits on the edge of the bed, twisting his body toward me. "If you're up for it, I think it would be good for you to take back the power Le Diable still holds over you because of this object." His eyes look off across the room and then back on me, something I've never seen before passing over him. "I want to know that you can take care of yourself if something ever happens to me."

My lips part, my heart rate accelerating in alarm. Why would something happen to him?

"I'm not going to live forever, baby." He smiles, but it's sad. Filled with regrets and fears. "You know as well as I do that what my family does is dangerous. Deadly even. And if something were to happen to me, well..." He pauses, his head dropping. "It destroys me thinking that I didn't prepare you better. That I failed you."

I sit up, grasping his face in my hands. "You've done more for me these past few months than anyone has in my entire life. You haven't failed me. You saved me." I crash my lips to him, desperate to be close to him. His lips move ravenously with mine, but for only a brief moment before he pulls back, searching my features.

"You're the bravest woman I know." His forehead rolls against mine. "And because of that, I know you can do this. So, let me help you." He pushes my hair back, holding my face as his eyes sear into mine. "Please."

I'm taken aback by his plea. This man has never asked anything of me before, but now here he is, asking, no, begging me to fight my demons with him by my side.

I nod, my breath heavy as I give in to his request. "What do you want me to do?"

"I want you to be able to look at a knife as your strength and not your weakness."

"How?"

He leans back, his eyes holding a command over me. "Lie back."

I nervously bite my bottom lip, blinking back any hesitations or fears I might have. Lying down, my head snug on the pillow with my hair pooled around me, I wait for what's to come with bated breath.

Leo reaches for the knife, gripping it tenderly. As he holds it above my heart, I feel a panic blooming within me. My chest heaves, my trembling fingers digging into the sheets.

"Who am I, Scarlett?"

"L-Leo."

He shakes his head, a mischievous grin growing. "Who. Am. I?"

"You're...you're my husband."

"That's right." He brings the tip of the knife only an inch away from my bare skin. "Would I ever hurt you?"

"N-no."

"Do you trust me?"

"With my life," I rush out, my pulse thundering.

"Good." The tip of the cold blade barely touches my skin, a shallow gasp escaping me. "Are you attached to this dress?"

I shake my head, my eyes never leaving his.

The blade travels down my chest, hitting the edge of the red fabric and slicing through it like butter. The bodice tears in two, revealing my breasts.

With precision, he glides the tip of the cold blade over my breast, circling it around my nipple. The peaks of both harden unbearably as he skims right across them, triggering an intense pulse in my core. His eyes darken, drinking in the sight of my desire.

Knowing my previous experiences with knives, I should be terrified. Shaking with fear and trepidation. Begging him to stop.

But I don't want to.

Not when I trust this man with every piece of my broken soul.

And not when my body is begging for more.

"Leo," I breathe, feeling more aroused than I ever have before. I grip the sheets, my fingers curling into the satin. The sensation of the deadly metal against my warm, soft skin is sinfully sweet.

He gradually drags the steel between my breasts and over my stomach. "Whose body is this?"

"M-mine."

"That's right, baby. And what do you say when you've had enough?"

"Stop."

One side of his mouth curves up. "Good girl."

As the blade coasts lower, leaving more of me exposed, my body thrums in...fear? No, not fear. But anticipation. I feel a stimulation awakening every nerve ending in my body.

Once he has the dress completely split down the middle, I feel a pounding between my legs, a rampant longing for him, and from the way his eyes trail over my body, taking in my flushed skin, he knows it, too. My thighs tighten together, trying to tame the wild need, but it's futile.

"Want me to help with that, baby?" Leo asks in a husky, silken voice.

I nod unabashedly.

The tip of the knife pokes at the lace covering me, and with a hard tug, he rips it off my skin. A moan escapes me as the fabric strains against my core with a delicious taste of friction, leaving me panting for more.

I'm suddenly aware of the fact that I'm lying here completely naked while he sits beside me, fully clothed.

And it amplifies the lust within me surging madly.

"Spread those legs for me," Leo orders. I do as he says, his eyes captivated between my legs, not daring to look away. "So fucking beautiful."

I feel wetness drip down my thighs. Embarrassment threatens to wash over me, but then his fingers snake out, two of them slowly caressing me back and forth between my slit.

"Leo," I whimper, my body begging for a release. An urge to rub against him, seeking the pressure I so desperately need, takes over as I scoot closer, but suddenly, his free hand lands firmly on my stomach, keeping me in place.

His eyes meet mine. "I'm going to need you to stay very still for me. Understood?"

My brows furrow. He's never asked this of me before, but I nod, waiting for what he has planned.

He keeps his fingers moving leisurely, temporarily distracting me as he replaces his fingers with the knife handle. I freeze up.

"W-what are you..."

He rips a piece of my dress and quickly wraps it around his hand like a bandage before taking the blade edge in his hand and positioning the handle right above my entrance. "I need you to keep your legs open wide, remain still, and trust me with what I'm about to do." There's a pleading look in his eyes as he waits for me. I hesitantly nod, my eyes bouncing from his to the knife. The anticipation is practically killing me as he drags it through my slit, my wetness coating it.

He gently pushes the smooth handle only an inch inside me, my pussy tensing around it.

"Relax, Firefly." His thumb finds my clit and provides a gentle stroke. Instantly, I melt under his touch, a content sigh leaving me. He pushes it in a little more, but instead of tensing, I relish the delicious stretch. The handle slides deeper until it's fully seated inside me.

Leo's grip on the blade tightens as he holds it still, letting my body adjust to the size. "How do you feel?" He circles his thumb over my clit, causing me to toss my head back, my hair fanning out over the pillow.

"Good. I want..." I moan. "More."

He takes that as his cue to begin moving the handle in and out, steadily building a rhythm of pleasure within my walls. He leans forward, his lips finding my hardened nipples, and a zap of electricity shoots down to my core as he nips and sucks, twirling the tips between his lips.

He increases the pace of his thrusts while his lips trail down my stomach. My pussy squeezes around the handle, grasping it tightly. "You feel that? That's your sweet pussy begging for more." His tongue slides over my skin, working its way up my body to my neck. He pulls back to look down at me. "You could stop this at any second with just one word, but you don't want that, baby. Do you?"

I shake my head, my eyes pinching shut as he hits that special spot inside me over and over again. A powerful orgasm is on the precipice, ready to overtake me. I can feel it in the curling of my toes all the way to the slight vibration in my fingers. The crescendo builds inside me as my body begs for more.

As if Leo knows my body better than I do, he rapidly swipes his thumb over my clit, back and forth, giving me that little something to push me completely over the edge.

"Come for me, Scarlett. Come for your husband."

He captures my scream with his lips as the earth-shattering orgasm rears its way through my body. I unravel beneath him, my back arching off the bed as stars explode behind my eyelids. My fingers clutch the sheets with all the strength I can muster, my chest heaving violently.

This is pure euphoria.

Eventually, my body and mind float down from the place between heaven and earth. Exhaustion seeps into every muscle and bone in my body. A languid smile takes over my lips as I peer up at Leo with droopy eyes, my heart feeling astonishingly warm.

Carefully, he slides the knife out of me, and I watch in fascination as he licks the handle clean, savoring every last drop.

"The best dessert I've ever had." He winks, making me blush.

As my heart settles into an acceptable rhythm, I sit up, my lips inches from his. "Thank you, Leo."

He reaches for my hand and brings it between us, placing the handle in my palm. "You're strong, Scarlett. Stronger than you give yourself credit for." He wraps my fingers around it. "I had this made for you. I thought if it felt like yours in every sense of the way, you might feel a connection with it instead of fearing it."

I unwrap my fingers, admiring the smooth silver blade. And right at the edge near the handle, the letters L and S are engraved. I look up at him, my eyes watering. "You never once judged me for my fear."

His eyes soften. "We all have fears."

My brows draw together. "Even you?"

"Even me," he answers.

"You're one of the most feared men in the world." My lips curve up. "What could you possibly be scared of?"

His eyes darken, his arms wrapping around my waist, pulling me against him. "Isn't it obvious?"

I shake my head.

"Losing you, Firefly." He presses a tender kiss to my temple. "That's the only thing in this world I fear."

CHAPTER TWENTY-EIGHT

Leo

An ominous, bleak sky greets us as we park our cars near the family's private plane.

"It's showtime," Vin says, adjusting his sleeves as he steps out of the car and strides toward the staircase.

I exit the vehicle, my eyes scanning for Dolion's car, which should have been here already. My phone vibrates, and I pull it from my coat pocket, seeing his name. I glimpse at Alex and Mauro and tell them to proceed as I take the call.

"Dolion, where the fuck are you?" I seethe. "The plane takes off in five minutes."

"Sir." Dolion hacks up a cough, causing me to pull the phone away from my ear. "I'm kind of under the weather. I think." *Cough.* "It's the flu." *Cough.*

I pinch the bridge of my nose. It's not his fault he's sick, but fuck, the timing couldn't be worse. We need as many of our best men available to put tonight's plan into action.

"Fuck, Dolion." I squeeze the back of my neck.

"I know, sir." He sniffles. "I can try to—"

"No. Get some rest. We'll manage without you."

"Thank you, sir." He coughs again. "Good luck."

I hang up and immediately dial Eli.

"Hey, boss," he answers.

"Dolion's not coming with us tonight."

He pauses. "What the fuck do you mean?"

"He's sick. Coughing up a storm on the phone. I told him to rest, so he'll be at his cottage tonight if you need backup for any reason."

"I was a goddamn Navy SEAL. I think I can handle a Halloween party," he murmurs.

I smirk, shaking my head. "How is everything?"

"Good. Alina just arrived, and the girls are getting ready for the party together."

"Where's my sister?"

He sighs. "Apparently, they're meeting there. She wants to surprise them with her costume." I can practically hear the eye roll in his tone.

"Don't forget," I say. "After tonight, we're dealing with the next problem on the to-do list. Understood?"

"Oh, don't worry. I'm very much prepared for that asshole."

I know he is. "Keep me posted. I'll call you when we're on our way home. We should be there before the party ends to make an appearance."

"Will do. And boss?"

"Yeah?"

"Make him pay."

"That's the plan." I slide my phone back into my coat pocket and walk up the plane's stairs.

"Everything all right?" Vin asks, already lounging in his favorite cushioned recliner. Several men find their places in the back of the cabin, mentally preparing for tonight's mission.

I nod. "Dolion will not be joining us tonight."

Alex looks up from his phone, arching a brow. "Why?"

"He's sick." I plop onto the free side of the couch beside him. "But we'll manage without him." My eyes scan the back, counting every available man with us. "We've got twenty men here, plus the four of us. That should be plenty to get the job done."

Alex opens his laptop. "How many does that leave at the estate?"

"Twenty-six," Vin answers. He lifts his drink, bringing it to his lips before closing his eyes and putting his chair into recline mode.

I stare at him. "In case you forgot, we're on our way to shut down an illegal sex-trafficking operation while also capturing Le Diable. This is not a fucking vacation."

Vin's eyes pop open. "Trust me, brother, I haven't forgotten. Merely getting ready for what we're about to face." A darkness sweeps over his gaze. He places his drink on the table beside him, blinking back whatever nightmares plague him. "You prepare your way, and I'll prepare mine."

Mauro clutches the arms of his chair, his eyes shut tight. I forgot he's not a fan of flying.

"Take this," I say, handing him a glass of liquid courage. It's not enough to interfere with tonight's mission but plenty to take the edge off.

He grips the glass forcefully, and I'm surprised it doesn't shatter in his grasp as he brings it to his lips. After a few sips, he relaxes into his chair, staring out the window beside him.

The plane begins rolling down the runway, eventually taking off into the air and soaring into an onyx sea.

"Arrival time for the city is expected to be nine p.m.," the pilot alerts us from the overhead speakers.

Alex keeps typing away on his computer, appearing distracted.

"What are you doing?" I ask, trying to peek at the screen.

He shakes his head. "I can't help but feel like I'm missing something. Just going over everything again." He shrugs. "There's a lot on the line. Mistakes would not be a good thing tonight."

I nod, turning my attention out the window. "It certainly wouldn't be."

An hour later, we arrive at the tarmac, a line of black SUVs waiting for us. After we all exit the plane, Vin stands strong, his gaze narrowing on every man who has come with us.

"We want this job done as swiftly as possible. In and out. To reiterate, Alex, Leo, Mauro, and I will enter the property on the pretense that we are there for the auction. Once inside, we'll scope out the place as discreetly as possible, and then Alex will search for the victims while Mauro searches for Igor. Leo and I will use our own methods to find Le Diable." His eyes scan the area until they land on three men in the back.

"Antonia, Mateo, and Lorenzo. You three will wait in the parking lot behind the building for Alex and will be responsible for escorting these women to either the closest police station or hospital. Drop them off. And leave. And I swear to fucking God, if I find out you laid even a finger on any one of them, you will be shoved inside a meat grinder and fed to my dog! Capisce?" He seethes. "Most of the women will barely be of age. These men are some sick fuckers with disturbing kinks." All three men nod earnestly, never wavering in their stance. "Good." He rolls up the sleeves of his shirt. "As for the rest of you, you are to wait in the SUVs around the corner until you receive my text. Only then will you enter the premises to finish the job and dispose of the motherfuckers inside."

They all nod like obedient soldiers.

Vin appears pleased, standing with his hands clasped behind his back. "Once our mission is completed, we will burn the place to the fucking ground until it's nothing but dust." He combs his fingers through his dark hair, pushing it to the side. "Now, let's go find this fucking Le Diable and make him regret ever messing with the Alaries." He turns, heading toward the first car, and Alex, Mauro, and I follow suit.

Every muscle in my body thrums in anticipation.

Because tonight, I will finally kill Le Diable.

But first...

I'll break him.

Pulling up beside what appears to be an abandoned Thai restaurant in a sketchy-as-fuck part of the city, we spot a few luxury cars covertly parked in a back lot. Coming to a stop, the rest of the SUVs trailing us turn off, finding a place to remain hidden.

"You're sure this is the place?" I ask with skepticism. The overhead lights flicker, dangling partially detached. The red paint on the outside is scraped off in sections. The massive window, looking into the seating area, is shattered, and shards of glass line the sidewalk.

"This is the right address," Alex answers, squirting a dollop of disinfectant on the palms of his hands and rubbing them together.

"Trust me, this is the place," Vin says matter-of-factly. "They don't want any unwanted guests like the feds to come sniffing around. So they choose a shit hole like this." Vin shuts off the car, and we step outside. As we approach the corroded door, there's an eerie chill in the air. "Be vigilant." Vin steps through the threshold first, and we are immediately met with four men stationed behind a counter, in front of a kitchen door, gripping rifles against their chests.

"Gentlemen." Vin shows them a bright smile. "I hear we're in for a treat tonight." The guards appear confused at our presence, unmoving.

"No entry without an invite," one of them murmurs, his voice hoarse from one too many cigarettes.

Vin smacks the front of his head. "I knew I was forgetting something." He reaches inside his jacket, and before they have a chance to move, we each pull out our handguns and shoot them dead on the spot, the silencers muffling any noise that might cause alarm.

We step over the dead bodies and pass through the swinging kitchen door with our guns tucked into our holsters, hidden beneath our jackets.

But what should be a kitchen is a far cry from it.

Walking through a dark hallway, lit only with subtle lighting from the trim on the floor, we inhale the scent of tobacco, leather, and sex that slams into us. Heady and unforgiving. Women line the entryway, wearing nothing more than what appears to be pieces of string wrapped around their bodies. These aren't the women we're here for, though. Most likely, these women work here, willingly or as willingly as one does in a sex club.

They're prostitutes. Not that I have anything against sex work. But I know there's a big fucking difference between these women who come here for a paycheck and the women hidden within these four walls, brought here against their will.

Fighting for their lives.

"Let's get this done quickly. This place is making me want to take a shower," Alex murmurs, brushing a woman's hand off his arm.

"Patience," Vin responds as we round the corner, finding ourselves in an open room.

Black leather couches are scattered throughout, facing a rather large stage. Several men are currently lost in lust as they receive lap dances. Scantily clad women walk around with trays in their hands, dropping off drinks to the patrons, who feel entitled to a squeeze or a grab as they take their beverages. Several hallways lead off to the sides where, I assume, there are private rooms for more discretion. Moans and grunts echo from behind several doors. A sleek black bar lines the far wall, and silver poles are stationed sporadically throughout the area.

"Fuck, this place is bigger than I envisioned." Vin's gaze takes in the massive space as he tugs on his collar. Many sets of eyes widen in our presence, knowing who we are. Fear commands them to cower further into their seats.

If they're scared of us now, well, they may not want to stick around for the finale portion of this evening's entertainment.

Too bad they're trapped here like the rats they are.

"Is this going to be a problem?" I ask him.

Vin's lips part, but a woman approaches. "Are you here for the auction?" she asks timidly. She stares down at her tray, waiting for one of us to answer.

"Yes," Alex confirms. "Would you mind showing us the best place to sit?"

She nods and turns, leading us toward the closest available sofas. "Would you like anything to drink?"

"No," Vin answers. "But can you tell us what time the show starts?"

She swallows hard. "In about fifteen minutes, sir."

Vin smiles. "And where might we find Igor? We'd love to give him our thanks."

The poor woman pales. "I-I... I'm not sure, sir, but I can ask around."

"We would appreciate that."

With that, she rushes away, turning down a dark hallway.

"Mauro," I state. He turns his head in my direction. "Follow her."

Mauro rocks his neck from side to side, rolls his shoulders, and then strolls off toward the same hallway.

"Come on!" an older gentleman on the couch closest to us yells. "Let's get this pussy show started!" He throws back his drink, and when a waitress walks by him, he grabs her by the waist, pulling her onto his lap.

She laughs nervously, shifting her body, trying to get out of his clutch. "I need to go get the next round of drinks, sir." She tries to stand, but he continues forcing her down.

His tongue snakes out, licking up the side of her neck. "You're going to stay right here and rub that pretty ass over my hard cock." He grips her hips, forcing her body to move back and forth on his lap.

Vin sighs, pinching the bridge of his nose. "This fucker is going to mess up tonight's plan." He stands, smiling as he walks over to the asshole. I watch as he bumps into the table, causing the man's glass to fall to the floor and shatter. "Shit. Did I do that?" He kneels down to pick up a piece of the broken glass and swiftly holds it against the side of the guy's abdomen. I glance around the room; everyone is too lost in their own worlds to notice what is happening. "You're going to let this pretty girl go. And you're going to do it right the fuck now cause if you don't, I will slice your pathetic dick off and shove it down your throat. Capisce?"

The man hesitantly nods, immediately removing his hands from the woman's waist, who abruptly hurries away.

"Good man." Vin stands and takes his seat back beside me, dropping the piece of glass to the floor. I don't miss the blood dribbling down the tip of it.

A blood-curdling scream has the three of us turning our heads to the left. Two guys walk by, amused. "Guessing that means the show is about to begin."

"Alex." I curl my hands into fists on my thighs, doing everything to stop myself from storming down that back hallway where the scream came from.

"On it." Alex gracefully stands and blends in with the crowds as he disappears down the hall.

Vin and I pull out our phones, waiting for the signal that we're good to start with our own show.

As five minutes turn into ten and then twenty, unease builds inside me.

"Do you think—" Our phones go off in our hands.

Alex

Clear. Twelve women.

I grind my back molars, my jaw clenching. Twelve women here against their will? About to be auctioned off like cattle to the lowest scum of the earth.

Vin pulls out his phone to send a text to the team, knowing we need to be quick.

"Three...two...one..." he murmurs just as a symphony of bullets ricochets near the entrance. Shouts and screams echo throughout the room as our men quickly advance inside, guns drawn. "Showtime." Vin and I stand, grabbing for our hidden weapons. "Ladies and gentlemen, there's been a slight change of plans in tonight's entertainment." His voice softens as he says, "Will the ladies working here this evening please exit out the front door? I promise no harm will come to you."

A few of the girls quickly run toward the exit, while some appear like deer caught in headlights. Eventually, they gather their wits and exit the building, leaving just us, our men, and the motherfuckers who came here tonight knowing they would be bidding on innocent women who were kidnapped and brought here to use for their own twisted pleasure.

Fucking sons of bitches.

I tighten my grip on my gun, aiming it at each man sitting on the nearby couches. The ones currently trembling in their own piss as sweat drips down their temples.

With all eyes on us, I let every bit of my wrath free. "Where is Le Diable?" I roar like a wild beast, sounding utterly unhinged, precisely how I feel.

A few men's faces pale, recognition of his name evident in their eyes. I spot one man trying to pull his phone out of his pocket discreetly, and so I aim the barrel of my gun right at his index finger, which is swiping animatedly across the screen.

Boom!

One second, the man is about to send a text, probably alerting the authorities for help, and in the next, he's hunched over in pain, screaming like a baby while holding a bloody hand with a missing finger to his chest. I take a few steps until I'm standing before him, pressing my gun into his head. "I'll ask one more fucking time, and that's as far as my patience extends. Where is Le Diable?"

The man shakes his head, muffled cries escaping him. "I-I don't know. I swear I don't know!"

"Who the fuck is he?" I growl. The man closes his eyes, shaking beneath his overpriced suit. "Give me his goddamn real name!" I shove the gun harder into his scalp.

"He only goes by that name!" His eyes pop open, terror glossing over them. "No one here knows his real identity. We were all invited by Igor because of our wealth and"—he swallows—"interests. But none of us know who Le Diable is." I lean all my weight into my gun. "He's the one who collects the girls based on our tastes, but that's all I know. I swear! Please, I have children!"

I scoff. "And yet, you're here. Preying on innocent girls." I whip the gun against the side of his head. "Sick fuck."

"How about this?" Vin takes a few steps to the center of the room. "We know Igor is the investor and the one who chooses which dickheads to invite to the auctions, and we know Le Diable kidnaps the girls, but can anyone in here tell us which dickless asshole owns this fucking hellhole?"

Silence.

"I see." Vin looks at me. A combination of fury, rage, and frustration is washing over him. "I wonder how many men I have to kill before someone in here eventually breaks." He aims his gun at the man from earlier in the evening who forced the woman down on his lap and shoots. Gasps echo in the room as the man falls to his side, blood pouring out of the hole in the center of his head.

Vin directs his gun at the next target, who raises his hands in surrender.

"Wait! Wait!" he pleads. There's sweat pouring down his face. Or are those tears?

"You have three seconds to tell me where the fuck Le Diable is hiding," Vin says calmly. "Three...two..."

"What the fuck is going on in here?" An angry Russian accent draws our attention. "Take your fucking hands off me!"

The two of us look over to the hallway, finding Mauro dragging a disgruntled Igor to the center of the room. Mauro tosses him to the floor, keeping a gun aimed at him.

As Igor kneels, his eyes take in the three of us, and fear flashes over his features.

"What... What are you doing here?" he stammers, confused by our presence. "You're not supposed to be here. You're supposed to be..." He stops talking, his eyebrows drawing together.

I get up in his face, gripping his jacket. "This is the last time I'm going to ask this question." I let out a deep exhale, pressing my gun into the side of his head. "Where the fuck is Le Diable?"

Igor's eyes widen. "He's..." His lips open and close. "But I..." Open and close. "I don't understand. They told me they were going to destroy you tonight. All of you. That they were going to be the new rulers of New York." He shakes his head, stilling. "You're supposed to be dead." His eyes calculate something within his mind, connecting dots. His face reddens as he says, "Those motherfuckers set me up!"

"What the fuck are you rambling about?" Vin asks.

Suddenly, Igor glimpses up and lets out a psychotic laugh. "You don't know. Oh my goodness, this is too good to be true." He pauses, stifling his laugh. "The world is about to see the fall of the Alaries."

Mauro clocks him on the side of his head with his gun, knocking him over. Tired of his games.

Leaning over him, I yank him up by his shirt. "You better talk right fucking now!"

Igor grasps his head; blood trails down the side of it. His lips curl up, a sinister smile taking over his entire face. "Le Diable isn't here. But I'll give you one guess where he is."

Vin arches a brow. "If he's not here, then where the fuck—" His words die on his lips as his eyes widen and lock onto mine.

It's the second time in my life I've had an out-of-body experience. Everything around me stills; the only thing moving is my heart, which races as fast as a hummingbird's wings. A ringing in my ears takes over as Vin shakes my shoulders, his mouth moving, but no noise is produced. Slowly, I hear a muffled sound as if underwater, and eventually, Vin's sharp words cut through my haze.

"Leo! Fucking hell! Snap out of it!" He shakes me one last time, good and hard.

"He knew we would be here," I breathe, my chest feeling unbearably too tight. "He knew we wouldn't be at the Alarie Estate tonight." The harsh reality of the situation hits me like a ton of bricks. "It's someone inside." My chest heaves with a relentless force, my body shaking with fury.

"We were played like fools, but especially you idiots who left your kingdom and your precious goods defenseless," Igor muses, enjoying this revelation a little too much.

And I've fucking had enough of it.

And him.

I lift my gun, aim it right between his eyes, and shoot. Igor's lifeless body drops to the floor. It doesn't take long for a pool of his own bright red blood to surround him.

"We need to go home. Now." I move, feeling numb to everything around me. The only thing taking over my thoughts is Scarlett.

Only Scarlett.

And my fear of losing her intensifies tenfold.

Agonizing pain radiates in the center of my chest.

My heart shatters with each passing second.

With shaking fingers, I reach inside my pocket for my phone and press Scarlett's name.

"Come on, Firefly," I plead. "Pick up the phone for me."

"Hi, you've reached Scarlett. Leave a message."

My heart comes to a crashing halt.

I failed her.

Vin calls over one of our guards as the three of us step outside. "Kill every man in here and leave nothing left behind. I want the whole place burned down until there's nothing but embers," he orders. "Make it look like a gas—"

Boom!

In only a second, the world around us burns.

Chapter Twenty-Nine

Scarlett

I t's showtime.

The massive, imposing doors swing open, and Alina and I enter the banquet hall, my lips parting in awe as my eyes take in the fully decorated space.

There are hundreds of carved pumpkins, servers dressed as skeletons, ghost silhouettes dancing across the walls, and at least a thousand candles burning brightly amid the extravagant space. The DJ in the corner is dressed as a vampire, blasting music from his speakers. And there's a ten-foot-tall cake depicting a different horror movie on each tier.

The Alaries sure know how to throw a party.

"Isn't this something else?" Alina beams, clutching my arm, careful not to get in the way of my wings. Her eyes trail down my white dress. "I love that you went as Juliet from the nineteen-ninety-six version. It's so romantic. We just need your Romeo to get here."

I chuckle. "Leo and his brothers had some work to do in the city, but hopefully, they'll return before the party ends. He said it was going to be a quick job. In and out." I give a half shrug, having no idea what tonight's job for them entailed.

Knowing there's a chance Leo might not make it to the party, I sampled my costume for him last night. To say he was pleased would be an understatement. A blush forms on my cheeks, just thinking about his reaction.

But he also insisted that I wear a holster strapped around my thigh under my dress to keep my knife in—the one I've been practicing using with Mauro in my self-defense classes and the same one Leo made me come all over...

God. I internally shake my head, tightening my thighs. This is not the time to think about that.

My eyes land on Alina beside me, who is dressed as, well, I don't exactly know.

"What are you again?" I ask, taking in her ensemble from top to bottom. She's wearing a black mini dress with tiny purple and pink balls attached all over her body and the word *Nerds* stitched across her chest.

She pushes her thick, black-framed glasses up the bridge of her nose. "I'm a box of Nerds." She tugs the top of her dress up, ensuring she doesn't spill out over the top. "But a sexy box of Nerds."

"Ahh, now I see."

"No, you don't.

"No, I don't."

We laugh as she reaches for my hand and leads us farther into the crowded room.

Without warning, Eli steps in front of us, pausing our movements. "Stay close tonight and keep your eyes open."

I frown. "We're on the Alarie Estate... This is the safest place in the world."

He nods. "Yes, I just..."

I cross my arms over my chest, drawing my brows together. "Is something going on, Eli?"

He glances around the room. "Nothing is going on." He smiles, but it doesn't reach his eyes. "Just doing my job to guarantee your safety is all."

Eli's never once lied to me, as far as I know. But right now, I know he's hiding something from me. Something that has him on edge. And if my bodyguard is on edge, so am I.

"Of course," I answer, subtly feeling the outline of my knife beneath my dress, which calms me. "We'll stay together."

He grins. "Enjoy yourself tonight. I didn't mean to worry you. I just want to ensure you're aware of your surroundings." He points to the entrance. "The only way in and out of this room is through those doors, so I'll post up there for the night to keep an eye on things."

Alina's arm tangles with mine. "I won't let her out of my sight, soldier." She gives him a mock salute and a wink before she pulls me along toward the bar.

Sidling up to the dark oak counter, Alina waves at the bartender, who quickly saunters over. His eyes are noticeably positioned on her chest before leisurely traveling to her face.

"What can I get you ladies?" He shows a harmless smile, but somehow, it feels off to me. Not right.

She looks over tonight's drink specials and says, "Two cranberry Moscow mules, please."

He winks. "Coming right up."

Leaning against the bar as we wait, I scan my eyes around the whole room, taking in everyone's costumes for the evening. There's a bit of everything from monsters and superheroes to movie characters.

I glance across the bar, noting the bartender on the other end, scooping ice into a shaker. His eyes catch with mine, a smirk appearing on his face, and I quickly look away. "Is it just me, or does something feel off with the bartender?"

Alina looks over her shoulder at the man making our drinks and then back at me. "He seems normal to me. Maybe a little extra friendly." She plucks an appetizer off one of the passing server's trays. "Should we get Eli?"

I shake my head. "No, you're probably right." I face her, giving a slight shrug. "I guess I'm not really a good judge of character anymore, seeing that all men give me the heebie-jeebies."

"All men except your husband." She waggles her brows as her shoulder playfully bumps into mine.

A slight heat spreads over my cheeks. "He definitely does not."

"You guys are so cute." She pretends to swoon. "I hope to someday find a guy who looks at me the way Leo looks at you."

I roll my eyes and smile. "Please, do tell, how does he look at me?"

She sighs dramatically. "Like you're his whole world."

A flush creeps up my neck. "Enough about me." I push my hair over my shoulder, suddenly feeling warm. "What about you and—"

"Here you are, ladies." We turn just in time as the bartender slides our drinks near us. "Enjoy."

"Thanks," Alina murmurs as she reaches for one, passes it to me, and then goes for her own. She grabs my free hand and starts leading us away from the bar. She takes a small sip, her lips curving up. "Damn, he makes a good drink."

I take a few sips of mine, savoring the sweetness. "Wow, this is good."

"Where's Maddy?" Alina asks, standing on her tiptoes to look over the crowd. But even in her heels, she's not tall enough to see much of anything. Her shoulders slump as her feet land firmly on the ground. "She said she'd be here by now."

I bite my bottom lip, worry gnawing inside me. Something's not right. Maddy's never late. "Maybe we should go find Eli?" I take a few more hefty sips of my drink as my eyes scan the room before placing the glass on the table beside us.

Alina reaches inside the top of her dress and pulls out her phone that's been hiding nestled in her cleavage. "Never mind. All good. She texted me ten minutes ago."

She turns her phone toward me, displaying the text.

Madeleine

Running late.

My brows furrow. *Running late?* Maddy's the type to put a thousand emojis in her text, along with countless exclamation points.

"Come on! Let's dance!" Alina places her drink on the table along with her phone and drags me to the center of the dance floor, where we sway our hips and move our arms in the air to the beat of the music.

We laugh as we jump up and down, shaking our hair around like we're groupies at a rock concert.

And it feels like two normal girls enjoying themselves.

Ten minutes into our dance, Alina grabs my hand. "Let's go to the bathroom. I have to pee so bad!" We just make it to the restroom door, down a quiet and empty hallway, when she abruptly stops. "Shit. I left my phone on the table." She looks in the table's direction and then back at me. "Don't move. I'll be right back!"

She takes off as fast as she can in her heels as I relax beside the wall. "I'll be right here," I say to no one, sliding down the wall and giving my feet a break as I sit on the floor. Searching my pocket for my phone, I curse when I realize I left it in my room.

My head rests against the wall, and my eyes close.

I'm having fun tonight, but there's one thing that would make this night even better.

"Hurry up, husband," I whisper into the air. "I'm waiting for you."

Suddenly, my attention moves to the main room, where the music cuts off, and the lights go out. Screams echo in the space as people panic, the candlelight not enough for them to see.

We must have lost power. But why hasn't the generator kicked on?

I brace the wall for support as I stand, about to step toward the room, when a spotlight turns on, aiming directly at the back wall, highlighting...

All the blood drains from my face.

Always mine is splashed across the wall.

Not with paint.

But with fresh crimson blood dripping down the wall toward its owner, a guard who's wearing the Alarie seal on his shirt.

I cover my mouth, my breaths coming out faster.

Blood-curdling screams happen all at once as others in the room finally see the lifeless body lying on the floor.

My throat dries up as my heart races beneath my chest.

"He's...here," I breathe, unable to hear my own words through my heart pounding.

My body trembles, curling in on itself as fear paralyzes me.

I knew this day would come.

But lately, I've been so delusional in my own little happy bubble with Leo that I thought maybe I could escape him.

I internally shake my head, trying to get a grip on myself.

Maybe this is just a bad dream.

But the image of chaos before me doesn't disappear.

And he's here.

For me.

Boom! Boom! Boom!

Gunshots from a military assault rifle fire off toward the ceiling, shattering chandeliers. Screams and shouts echo in the room, turning into pure madness.

"Nobody is to leave!" A Russian accent comes from a tall, muscular man who enters the room with a group of heavily armed men. Their eyes travel around the room as if looking for something or...

Someone.

Tears trail down my cheeks, knowing who.

Me.

"The Alarie Estate is under new management," the man says through a dark fit of laughter. "And our first task is to retrieve one person. Perhaps you know her." An audible silence takes over the room, everyone waiting for the name of this mysterious person to be said. But I already know the five syllables that are about to leave his lips before he says them. "Scarlett Alarie."

Alarming gasps leave a few people, hushed whispers swarming the air.

"Bring her to me and no one will get hurt." The man stands powerfully before everyone with a broad, sinful grin while the men with him begin combing the room, searching for me.

Cowering behind the corner, I search for any sign that it might be him, Le Diable. But his build doesn't match the man I became well acquainted with. He's too tall. Too muscular.

As I take a shaky step behind the closest column, a hand locks around my forearm, halting me. Before I can let out a scream, a second hand firmly clasps over my mouth.

"Relax. It's just me," Eli murmurs against my ear.

"Oh, thank God," I breathe into his palm before he drops his hand.

Eli towers over me, searching the area as he blocks me from being seen. His eyes darken with something new crossing over his irises. Fear. "We need to get you out of here." He doesn't hesitate as he tucks me into his side, dragging me down the hall.

But where are we going? Eli said it himself that there's only one entrance. One way in. And one way out. We're imprisoned in here.

"Eli, Alina went to get her phone," I rush out. "I don't know where she is—"

"I'll come back for her," he promises. "But we need to get you out of here. This was a trap."

"A trap?" I ask, my mind racing with this information.

He pauses, listening for any noise before we continue moving. "Leo and his brothers were trying to capture Le Diable tonight in the city."

"W-what?" My heart falters, and my breathing becomes difficult.

"I don't know what happened, but Leo called," he says. "So I tried to get to a space where I could hear him better, but his words were coming in muffled right as the lights cut out, and then his call disconnected. I tried calling him back, but there's no service." We come upon a small window hidden behind a pillar. "I'm going to help push you up and over. And then I need you to run to Dolion's house. It's the closest house nearby and has all the same safety features as the others. Get inside and lock the door."

"But...but what about you?" Pure fear causes me to stammer my words. "Won't you come with me?"

I can't do this alone.

He shakes his head, his chin jerking toward the window. "I can't fit. But I'll come find you as soon as I can." His hand clutches my shoulder. "You can do this, Scarlett."

I peer up at the window, taking a deep breath. "O-okay." I step out of my high heels, knowing I won't make it very far in these things.

Eli places his hands low and clasped together, waiting for me to step on them. I bunch the fabric of my dress around my knees as I lift my leg high enough so that my barefoot reaches the palm of his hand. My hand grips his shoulder as my other hand splays against the wall for balance.

"One, two, three." Eli guides me higher until I reach the ledge and pull myself up the rest of the way. I gaze out the window, ensuring no one is around, before I twist my body, angling my feet outside.

"There's going to be a slight drop. Relax your body and try to land on your side. Roll into the impact," Eli instructs me.

I nod as I inch out, the ledge of the window pressing against my stomach. Sliding out, I grasp the ledge with all my strength as I hang outside. I peek over my shoulder, noting the high drop.

Shit.

"You can do this," I say through tears. "Relax your body. Land on your side. Roll into the impact." I let out a rush of air, a chill sweeping over my shoulders.

Without taking a second to think about my predicament any longer, I release my clutch from the window and fall to the ground, landing on my ass and tumbling down the slight slope.

"Ow." I wince as I rub my thigh. That's for sure going to leave a mark.

"Scarlett, are you okay?"

"Yes," I whisper-shout, fearful that someone might hear me.

"Go to Dolion's. I'll find Alina and meet you there."

"Be safe, Eli."

"You too."

Quickly, I dash to the closest tree, hiding behind it. I peek around it, spotting Dolion's cottage nearby.

Relief fills me.

I'll be safe. I just need to make it there, and I'll be okay.

Inspecting my surroundings, I'm thankful to find I'm the only one on this side of the property.

Picking up the hem of my dress, I make a mad dash across the dark field, praying no one sees me. I hear men shouting in the distance and more bullets being fired, which pushes me to run faster. With every step I take in the cold grass, I feel a slight weight lift off my chest.

I'm almost there.

As I reach the steps to Dolion's house, I take two at a time and then pound on the metal door. "Dolion, it's Scarlett! Let me in!"

I grab for the doorknob, finding it unlocked, and quickly open and close it behind me, clasping the deadbolt in place.

"I'm safe." I close my eyes and rest my sweaty forehead against the door. My panting is the only thing I hear for the first few seconds as I wait for my heart rate to slow to a more acceptable rhythm.

Everything will be okay.

A deep mumbling noise catches my attention, and my eyes open wide. Standing perfectly still, I wait. And wait. Until suddenly, the sound occurs again, and dread fills me.

Because I know this noise.

Fear spreads through me as I gradually turn around, a gasp of horror leaving me as my eyes take in the sight in front of me.

"Maddy," I whisper.

Illuminated by only candlelight, she's tied to a chair in the center of the room with her hands and feet bound, her mouth covered in duct tape, and tears dribbling down her face.

Quickly, I rush to her. "It's...it's going to be okay." I kneel, reaching for the rope, trying to untie it. But with the tremor in my fingers, I'm struggling. Without a knife, I won't be able—

My knife.

"Don't worry." I stand on shaky legs, starting to raise my dress in search of my knife. "I have a knife I can use to..."

My eyes catch on a line of perfectly placed candles on the far side of the room, and my movements still.

I blink, praying that what I'm seeing is a hallucination.

Or maybe this is all just a bad dream I'm stuck in, and I need to wait for Leo to wake me up.

I close my eyes with a strong force before I open them again.

But the image before me is still present.

In a daze, I walk up to the wall, covered in printed photos, and reach for the one closest to me, bringing it inches away from my face.

It's...me.

Me when I was probably sixteen years old, sitting in a garden on the Alarie Estate with a book in my lap. The photo had to have been taken by someone watching me. I let the photo tumble from my fingers as I reach for another one. Except this one is of me when I was in college, wearing my school sweatshirt and studying in a library. I remember that night, but I thought... I thought I was the only one in there.

I let the picture fall from between my fingers as my eyes scan the entire wall, a tightness strangling my chest. There must be hundreds of photos of me—pictures of me as a child, me as a teenager, and me as a grown woman.

I'm staring at a shrine created for me.

I clasp my hands over my mouth.

No. No. No.

A lightheadedness takes over me as I sway on my feet, nausea invading me. Reaching for the closest hard surface beside me, my eyes flutter as my head drops forward, exhaustion swiftly weighing down on me.

"I don't... I don't feel...too good."

But why...?

Alina's words from earlier float through my mind. *Damn, he makes a good drink.*

The drink.

We were drugged.

My fingers seize the table's edge as I lean against it, trying everything I can not to fall to the ground, my muscles weakening with each passing second. My eyelids become heavy, and drift closed, but before they do, I spot a familiar object.

The final piece of the puzzle.

With a force of terror I've never felt before, I clumsily reach for the black devil's mask on the center of the table. "No...it can't...be." An unbridled fear overtakes every inch of my body, mind, and soul.

We need to get out of here.

Now.

"Maddy." I struggle to turn toward her, one hand clutching the mask to my stomach while the other uses all of my strength to keep me standing upright against the table. "We need...to get out...of here."

Her eyes widen as she screams against the tape, and I already know it's too late.

"Always mine," is whispered into my ear as fingers thread through my hair.

Blackness descends around me as my angel wings weigh me down, the devil's mask dropping to the floor beside me.

Le Diable won.

And I lost.

CHAPTER THIRTY

I t was a trap.

A fucking trap.

A high-pitched ringing sounds in my ears as I come to, groaning as pain lances my side beneath my ribs. I blink back the fog taking over me and press my hand on my temple where the throbbing is most intense. Blood dribbles down my wrist.

"Fuck," I breathe.

"Leo!"

I turn to my side and see Alex storming over, fury consuming his features. He crouches in front of me, looking me over. "Is anything serious?" he asks, noting the blood coming from the top of my head.

I shake my head, instantly regretting the quick movement. "Just some bruised ribs." I push myself to a standing position, unzipping my leather jacket. "Mauro and Vin?"

"They pulled you out of the debris, made sure you had a pulse, and now they're doing a head count on our men as we speak." He pushes his

303

glasses up the bridge of his nose. "They're both banged up pretty badly but refuse to acknowledge it, just like what you're doing."

I look around at the extensive damage. The club we were just standing in is completely gone, almost as if it was never here in the first place.

"What the fuck happened?"

"Explosion," Alex answers. "Apparently, this place was rigged to go off with us inside. Or it would seem that was the plan. But I was down the street with Antonio, Mateo, and Lorenzo, escorting the women off the property, and you guys had just stepped outside of the building when the bombs went off. The steel walls on the exterior must have protected you to an extent. When I realized what happened, I hacked the security cameras in the area, so whoever is watching them to survey the damage will see a continual loop of thirty seconds after the explosion." He runs his fingers through his hair, and I notice a slight tremble in his hand. "This was a trap."

"Yeah. I gathered that." I squeeze the back of my neck, feeling on the verge of eruption. My wrath is only growing every second that I'm standing here miles away from my wife. "I need to get home right the fuck now. Scarlett's in danger." I reach for my phone in my pocket, which, miraculously, is still intact. I press Eli's name, anxiety building in my stomach as the phone rings. "Pick up the fucking phone!" Fear takes over when it goes to his voicemail. I try again and again, getting the same fucking result.

Alex types into his phone, and two cars immediately pull up beside us. "I'll grab Mauro and Vin and meet you at the plane."

Ten minutes later, grinding my back molars, I step inside the plane, knowing one thing for certain. Le Diable knew we were coming here tonight, which means he's one of us. One of our most trusted men, as no one else was privy to tonight's plans.

Mauro and Vin are hot on my trail, looking worse for wear but with fierce determination in their eyes. Alex enters behind us with his phone pressed to his ear; frustration is evident in his demeanor. Our men, at least the ones who made it out alive, enter the cabin, taking their seats in the back.

Vin speaks with the pilot, doing everything he can to keep his composure. Mauro grabs the decanter filled with brown liquor and takes a large swig. And I feel like I'm about to combust at the seams; mania, unlike anything I've ever felt, filters through my veins.

I sit on the leather couch by the window with my phone in an iron grip, quickly press one in my emergency contacts, and hold it against my ear. "Pick up. Pick up. Come on, Firefly, please pick up." But after a few rings, it goes to Scarlett's voicemail. "Fuck!"

With a tremble in my fingers, I dial Eli for the hundredth time.

Pick up. Pick up. Pick up.

"Boss." Eli picks up on the second ring, sending a river of relief over me. I turn on speaker mode and place the phone between me and my brothers on the table. Loud music and several rowdy voices are heard in the background, indicating they're already at the party. "We keep losing cell service. It might be the rain, but—"

"It was a trap," I spit out. "Le Diable wanted us away from the Alarie Estate tonight to kill us. I need you to get Scarlett, Madeleine, and Alina out of there right the fuck now."

Static comes through the receiver. "What?" Eli asks, his voice muffled. "Fuck, the lights just went out."

"He's there," I breathe, my heart pounding erratically.

My brothers and I share a look. *We're too fucking late.*

"Get the girls the fuck out of there!" I roar.

"Leo, you're...cutting...in...out."

The line goes dead.

"*Cazzo!*" I reach for the phone, pressing Eli's name, but instead of Eli picking up, I get a robotic woman's voice that says, "I'm sorry. Your call cannot be completed as dialed."

"He's cut the cell service," Alex tells us, still holding his phone to his ear, before turning his head and speaking into the receiver. He paces the aisle, running a hand through his hair. "And you're sure?" He looks up to the ceiling of the plane, clenching his jaw. "Great, thank you." He snaps his phone shut and whips it toward the back of the aircraft. His hands grip the back of his neck as he faces away from us, breathing harshly.

"What the fuck is going on, Alex?" I rush out.

The plane begins moving swiftly down the runway, and I look out the window, seeing the tarmac disappear behind us.

Alex takes a deep breath. "On the way here, I ran a second round of background checks for everyone on the property. Only this time, there was one more than last time."

"Why would that be?" Vin asks. "We haven't brought anyone new on."

"Dolion," Alex breathes harshly, spinning to face us. "He wasn't here when my team ran the first batch because he was supposedly in Greece, tending to his dying mother."

"Supposedly?" I ask.

Alex removes his glasses and rubs one of the lenses between his shirt. "I received the background checks while you two were still inside, but when I saw Dolion's, well, something didn't feel right, so I've been doing some digging and just received the confirmation I needed from the Greek government."

"The Greek government?" Vin questions.

"I have connections." Alex rubs his temple.

"Spit it out," I demand. "I'm losing my patience here."

"Dolion's mother was murdered two years ago. Her body was found in the woods in her hometown of Greece. They never found who did it. But the point is...she's been dead for years."

It's like I'm in a fucking horror movie as all the pieces click together.

"So where the fuck was Dolion when he told us he was tending to his—" Vin's words trail off as he comes to the same realization. "Fuck." He sits up in his seat, leaning forward. "Dolion is Le Diable. He's who..." A muscle ticks in his jaw. "He's who fucking kidnapped Scarlett."

The blood beneath my skin boils with rage.

Black dots line my vision as I zone out, processing everything.

"Dolion." My fingers curl around my armrests, squeezing the leather. Closing my eyes, I picture all of the ways I'm going to kill him. All of the ways I'm going to make him pay for what he did to my wife.

Everything hits me all at once, and when I stand, ignoring the pain spearing down my side, my hand reaches out for the nearest glass cup. I slam it to the floor with so much anger, sending shards of glass flying everywhere.

"He wanted us away from the estate because he's on our fucking property! He has free rein to do whatever the fuck he wants! And I left him with exactly what he wants!" My chest heaves with each breath I take. My vision darkens. My head sways. I reach for the chair beside me, grasping the back of it. "I left him my wife on a silver platter," I get out in a hushed tone, my body shaking with an overwhelming amount of fury. "My wife!" My voice thunders in the cabin.

"He's one man," Vin surmises in a calm tone. He leans forward, resting his forearms on his knees. "We have an advantage over him because I assume he thinks we're dead. But as soon as we get to the estate, we'll take care of him."

"But he's not alone." I shake my head, pulling on the ends of my hair. "Igor kept saying, 'they.' He was talking about more than one person." I look up at Vin. "Dolion has to be working with someone, but who?"

A chime sounds from Alex's phone, and he retrieves it from the back of the plane. He runs his fingers through his hair and then looks between the three of us. "Things just got a lot more complicated." He slides his phone on the table, angling the screen so we can all see the footage.

We watch as Dolion strolls up to the guards on duty at the entrance, making small talk, and then shoots the four of them dead. He places his phone to his ear, and only seconds later, a line of at least twenty vehicles arrives. They drive inside the estate, and the moment the last car makes its way through, the feed cuts out.

Vin presses a button and speaks into the intercom beside him. "How much longer until we're back?"

"Fifty minutes, sir," the pilot answers.

"Get us there faster, or this will be the last plane you ever fly. Have I made myself clear?"

"Y-yes, sir."

I rub a hand over my face. "This wasn't just some kidnapping plot but a full-blown ambush to kill us and then take over the Alarie Estate! And we just gave it to them!"

Vin looks outside the window beside him, thoughts raging through his mind. He faces me when he says, "No, we haven't." He reaches for his phone in his pocket, brings it before him, and momentarily hesitates before hitting a contact I can't see. Placing his phone back on the table, we wait as it rings.

Who? I mouth as a familiar cold voice picks up on the other end.

"Well, if it isn't my least favorite cousin." Marco Marchetti's icy voice is not one I'd ever forget. He's as ruthless as they come. All of his siblings are. They make us look tame in comparison.

Vin rolls his eyes. "Cousin, it's been too long."

"Some might say not long enough."

"Now, now. Is that any way to speak to your family?"

Marco sighs. "What do you want, Vincenzo? I have a busy day ahead of me filled with torturing poor little souls."

Vin placates our cousin with a chuckle before his smile disappears, his expression turning cold.

I shake my head, but he stops me by raising his hand.

Vin stares up at the ceiling, making the sign of the cross, and utters four words that one should never say to a Marchetti. "I need a favor."

After Vin hangs up, we sit silently until he finally speaks. "It was the only way." Vin stares out his window, deep in thought. "I won't let our family or our home be destroyed."

A chime from Alex's phone has us all on alert as we wait for the next bit of information from Alex's team. Alex's eyes widen as he examines the screen, his head tilting to the side in confusion.

Vin twists the ring on his finger. "I don't think I can take one more fucking surprise, Alessandro."

Alex lets out a breath. "Then you're definitely not going to like this." He pushes his phone on the table before us. "When I went through the back rooms tonight, it took me a little longer than planned because I saw a computer just sitting there. No one was nearby, so I installed a bug to transfer everything over to my team." He rolls his lips, deep in thought. "This is security footage of the front entrance of *Blue Velvet Fantasies* about two hours before we got there. And..." He pauses. "It's Dolion getting into a car with..." He shakes his head and presses play, placing the phone before us.

Five seconds into the video, Vin, Mauro, and I rear back in shock.

"But he's dead!" Vin exclaims. "We fucking buried him."

Alex shrugs. "We buried someone."

Mauro grunts in agreement.

"The two of them have been working together this whole fucking time right under our noses!" Vin slams his hand into the side of the plane. His neck turns bright red as veins bulge from beneath his skin. "He's the fucking so-called ghost who owns *Blue Velvet Fantasies*?"

I hit pause on the video, zooming in on this fucker's face. A storm of rage unleashes inside me, one that no one would be able to tame. "That fucking son of a bitch is going to wish he stayed dead."

CHAPTER THIRTY-ONE

Scarlett

I feel like death as I come to, wincing from the pain radiating in my head. A groan rumbles through my lips as I bring my hands up to my scalp, my fingers massaging my temple. Trying to drop one hand to my side, they fall together, bound as one.

What happened?

My eyelids flutter open, and I try to take in my surroundings with blurry vision to recall where I am. Blinking a few times, I focus on the figure a few feet before me. It's hard to see much with only the candles providing a light source, but after a moment, the image becomes more prominent, and the memory of what happened rushes back to me.

The Halloween party.

The lights went out.

Men stormed the building, searching for me.

Eli helped me escape and instructed me to hide at Dolion's house.

Madeleine was bound to a chair in the center of the room.

Pictures of me covered every inch of the room.

Dolion's voice whispered in my ear right before I passed out.

My heart races as I try to get up to get to Maddy, but I find that not only are my hands bound with rope, but beneath the blanket wrapped over my legs, my feet are bound too.

Panic engulfs me as I whip off the blanket.

"Maddy," I whisper, her head slumped to the side, blood dripping down to the carpet.

She doesn't move.

"Maddy," I say with a little more force.

Nothing.

Sliding over to her, I nudge her thigh with my hands.

She stirs.

"Maddy, please wake up," I beg, my throat tightening.

Her eyelids flicker open, widening as she takes in the space.

"Maddy," I sob softly.

She tries to speak, but it comes out muffled against the tape.

"We'll be okay," I tell her. "Eli knows I'm here. I'm sure he'll be here any minute." I observe the sky out the closest window, unsure how to tell what time it is as darkness still reigns.

I don't know if I was out for minutes or hours.

And I have no idea how long it will be until Dolion returns, so I need to quickly devise a plan to get us out of here.

My eyes travel around the room, seeking anything that can help us. Anything that might—

My knife.

With my bound hands, I scrunch up the fabric of my dress to my thigh, where it reveals a gleaming silver knife attached to my black holster. Dolion probably assumed I wouldn't be armed. He thought I would be ill-prepared like the last time he took me.

But not this damn time.

I remove the knife from the holster and lean toward Maddy with it, but she shakes her head and tips her chin toward me, indicating to cut my ropes first.

I hesitate, wanting to help her, but eventually, I sit against the wall, my knees coming up to my chest. Maddy watches me with heavy lids as I place the knife between my knees, squeezing tight so it won't move. And then, I carefully move my wrists back and forth, fraying the strings one at a time.

I'm sweating by the time I get halfway through the binds, my muscles clenching in exertion.

"Mm-hmm," Maddy murmurs, and I know she's encouraging me to keep going.

I continue the back-and-forth motion, but suddenly, the knife slips, and I cut the palm of my hand.

I roll in my lips, holding in a scream. Blood spills onto the bottom of my white dress bunched around my thighs. My eyes water, but I shake my head, knowing I don't have any spare seconds to give in to the pain.

Placing the knife back between my knees, I keep going faster and harder, more determined than ever. String after string splits, and before I know it, the rope falls around me, freeing my wrists.

"Oh, thank God." I grab the knife and start working on the rope around my ankles, but suddenly I hear footsteps. Stopping, I reach for the blanket beside me and throw it over my legs as I lean against Maddy's chair, my hands hidden beneath it.

The footsteps get louder until suddenly Dolion appears in the room, a wide, dangerous smile on his face. "Oh good, you're awake." Frozen in fear, every part of my body seizes up. It's him. And although I've spent the past few months in his presence thinking nothing of it, now that I know who he really is, I can't move. Think. Breathe. All of the above. Because this is the man who tried to break me. The one who received pleasure by tormenting me night and day.

He stands in front of me, reaching down to pet my hair like his obedient puppy. Maybe when he first took me, I would have let him in fear of what might happen if I didn't obey. But now that I know the strength within me, the strength he underestimates, I flinch away, my eyes catching on the metallic handgun tucked into his waistband, directly in my line of sight.

"I was worried Jeffrey made your drink a little too strong for you," he admits. "You're so delicate. So fragile." He steps back, frowning. "You've been a bad girl, Scarlett." He plops down on the chair across from us, legs spread wide as he takes up the whole seat. "You betrayed me by marrying Leo. And no one is allowed to have what's mine." He pulls the gun from his pants and places it on his lap, sending a clear message to both of us.

Behave, or there will be consequences.

I need to keep cutting at the rope around my ankles, but his brown eyes won't look away from me.

Wait...Le Diable has green eyes. I'm sure of it. They were all I ever saw in my nightmares.

"Y-your eyes," I say, my voice breaking, giving away my fears.

"Oh." He reaches up to his irises. "Colored contacts." He pulls each one out, revealing his bright green eyes. "Irritating as fuck, but worth it."

All the air in my lungs evaporates as I find myself unable to look away, lost in his gaze. He's the monster of my nightmares. Only this time, he has a face and a name.

"Why?" I grip the leg of Maddy's chair for support with my free hand, my whole body trembling.

His brows furrow as he leans forward. "You were always mine, Scarlett. You just didn't know it." He drags a hand through his hair, deep in thought. "When we were kids, I would have given anything for you to notice me. To pay me the slightest bit of attention." He shakes his head, a muscle ticking in his jaw. "But you were so hung up on fucking Leo. He was the only one you ever had eyes for, and I never understood why!" He stands, towering over me. "What did he have that I didn't?" he roars. His whole body shakes. There's an unhinged fury I've never seen before flowing through him.

Tremors travel through me as I remain silent, swallowing down the fears keeping me rooted in place.

"No matter." He closes his eyes and takes a deep breath before sitting. "As promised, I knew you would be mine sooner or later. And once you were, I would need to do the only thing possible to guarantee you would never think of Leo Alarie again." A cruel smile spreads over his face as he says, "*Break you.*" My breathing escalates as I tighten my grip on the chair, my fingers practically going numb. "So I waited for years in the shadows until the day you would be mine. Body and soul."

Promised? What did he mean by—

"Aren't you going to ask me who promised you to me?" he asks with amusement. I don't say anything, so he lifts his gun, aiming it directly at me.

"W-who?" I stammer, sweat coating the back of my neck.

"I did," a familiar man's voice at the front of the house declares.

My heart drums violently in my chest as someone who should be dead saunters into the room, looking very much alive. And as he stands before me, my whole world turns violently upside down.

"F-father?"

"Hello, daughter." He grins triumphantly, watching me with pure maliciousness. His suit is ironed, his blond hair is styled, and his skin has a slightly healthy tan. This is not at all what a dead man should look like.

Shock causes me to drop the knife, thankfully landing silently on the carpet.

"W-what... I don't... I don't understand." My eyes fill with tears, blurring my vision. This can't be him. I shake my head, blinking, but when I open my eyes, he's still there, standing before me like a man who just got a second chance at life. "You're...alive?" I whisper, too stunned to say any more than that.

I'm no longer dealing with one monster but with two.

"You don't seem so happy to see me," he muses, taking the free seat beside Dolion. "But that can't be true because I heard you were crying over my grave." An evil smirk slashes across his face.

"Why?" My stare burns into him as I ask, "Why did you pretend to be dead?"

"Oh, Scarlett, you always were so naïve. One of the many things about you I couldn't stand." He leans back in his chair, rubbing his chin. "Where to begin? Where to—" His smile grows. "Ah, yes. The explosion."

"Explosion?"

"Yes, you dumb girl," he spits out. "The one I hired Dolion to set in the Alarie warehouse seven years ago." He glances at Maddy when he says, "You remember that day, don't you, dear? The day your father died."

Maddy's eyes widen, her chest heaving.

He nods. "I thought you might. You see, a few days before the explosion, your father had been sticking his nose where it didn't belong. And he somehow found out about my pride and joy." He looks wistful as he says, "*Blue Velvet Fantasies*." He smooths out his tie. "It was the best sex club in the country. One known for *special* auctions. And it was all mine."

My heart pounds wildly in my chest, my brows drawing together. "You were involved in sex trafficking?"

"Funny. You sound just as repulsed by the idea as Charles did." He feigns a frown. "When he approached me with his findings, the moral bastard wouldn't listen to my reasonings. He didn't give one damn for the abundance of money it would make us." He sighs. "So he destroyed it. Burned the place to the ground along with our business relationship, cutting all ties with me and telling me I had one week to leave his property, throwing away our twenty-year partnership."

He shakes his head. "The bastard even begged for me to let you stay. Saying you had always been one of them. Utter nonsense." He scoffs. "But he had no idea what he had done when he disrespected me by destroying my business." His hands, resting on the arms of the chair, clench into fists. "So I took matters into my own hands. I knew Dolion here couldn't take his eyes off you, always watching you from afar. But your head was in the clouds dreaming of that stupid Alarie boy, too distracted to notice the real prize."

He grips Dolion's shoulder beside him. "So, I made a deal with Dolion. Or should I say, the devil?" They both laugh. "He needed to set the explosion in the warehouse undetected, and if he succeeded by killing Charles, then when the time was right, I would hand you over to him."

My lungs cease to work as his words drown out around me. My father? My own father promised me to this psychotic man as payment for helping him kill my husband's father. He bartered me off like cattle to a psychopath.

Ice runs down my spine as my head begins to spin.

I knew he always hated me, but I never imagined...

I never thought...

How could he do this to me when I'm his flesh and blood?

"And oh, how the time was right." His malicious smile widens. "After the death of Charles, I fled with you that same night, stating that I wouldn't risk the safety of my daughter being associated with the Alaries anymore. But little did they know that your safety was of no importance to me. Just an excuse to keep me out of the clear of being a potential suspect. And for the past seven years, I've been busy building my own empire, preparing for this very moment to kill the Alaries and take over the Alarie Estate." He points a finger toward me. "And it's all thanks to you that we've succeeded."

"Me?" I ask, confused.

"Yes, you. Months ago, I needed something to distract the Alaries, and I knew just how to do that." He gestures toward Dolion. "It was time to give you over to Dolion as his reward for all his years of loyal service. So, we staged your kidnapping and my death, making the two appear connected. It was quite easy, really. All I needed was a man with a similar build to mine, and after killing him and placing my family ring on his finger, I left his body in my study before I set the place on fire." He tilts his head, studying me for a reaction. "With me dead, the Alaries wouldn't think to look into me. And with Dolion supposedly attending to his dying mother overseas, he was overlooked in the equation of your disappearance."

"That bitch deserved what she got." Dolion laughs.

"And with you taken," my father starts, looking directly at me. "They used all their time and resources to search for you. Just like I knew they would. Never once realizing what I was building in the shadows." His eyes dart to Dolion. "I admit, them finding you was not a part of the plan as you were meant to be the star in our next auction to help pay off some debts, sold to the highest bidder until they grew tired of you before returning to Dolion for good..."

Dolion lets out a frustrated breath. "For the tenth time, I was out doing my job, collecting women for your auction. It's not my fault one of the idiots you left me with fucked up by giving away her location. Besides, I never fucking agreed to sell her! And now that I finally have her back, I'm never letting her go. She's mine!"

My father's eyes grow darker, narrowing in on Dolion. "We'll see about that." A muscle tics in Dolion's jaw as my father's gaze turns on me. "Once the Alaries did find you, it turned out even better than I imagined because they spent the next several months continuing their hunt for Le Diable when he was here the whole time!" He lets out a boisterous laugh, slapping the arm of his chair like the true sociopath that he is.

"Never too far from you," Dolion says, his stealthy gaze on me.

Bile rises in my throat, and I swallow hard to keep it down.

"You see, child, *Blue Velvet Fantasies* has risen from the ashes once again, but this time, it was merely a decoy to be used for a greater purpose," my father states. "Your husband and his brothers followed the breadcrumb trail Dolion so kindly laid out for them and went there tonight thinking that's where Le Diable would be. They thought they had outsmarted us, but in reality, the place was extensively wired with hidden explosives that would destroy everything, including the precious Alaries."

A gasp leaves me, dread filling me. *No. No. No.* He's lying. I would know in my heart if Leo had died... Right?

"We had to make it look real by inviting several wealthy clients and obtaining a handful of girls. We even dragged in Igor Vasiliev to our little game, using him for his men we have now acquired. You know, the ones who stormed in here tonight," he muses. "But alas, Igor and everyone inside the club were killed to help me achieve everything I've ever wanted. Revenge on the Alaries. And I can truly say that revenge tastes fucking delicious!" He leans forward, his head tilting to the side as he examines me with disdain. "Tell me, child, how does it feel to be a widow?"

"You're l-lying!" I spit out, tears sliding down my cheeks. "They're not... They're not dead!"

He gives a slight shrug. "The bombs went off a couple of hours ago. There's nothing left but embers and scorched earth." He reaches into his pocket for his phone and turns it toward me. "See for yourself."

A black-and-white visual shows me a location of what appears to be mass destruction. There are pieces of metal and debris everywhere. Bodies lying lifeless. Some in pieces. Fires far and wide. It's an eerie nightmare.

"So, while you were partying with your friends tonight, enjoying yourself, your husband was most likely bleeding out slowly before eventually dying." He reaches out for me, placing a rough hand on my cheek. "I'm curious... How does that make you feel?"

Numb. That's how I feel as the image from the screen burns in my mind, knowing there's no way someone made it out of that war zone.

Let alone my husband or his brothers, who the trap was intentionally set for.

A sob breaks free from my throat as I shrink out of my father's touch and clutch the fabric of my dress. Pain spears me in the center of my chest, every section of my heart shattering into a million broken pieces.

Leo's dead. My husband is dead.

A hand crashes down on my face, whipping my head to the side.

"Don't fucking cry over Leo Alarie!" Dolion shouts in a violent outburst.

My father watches Dolion's cruelty with pleasure before his eyes move back onto me. "I've acquired business deals poor old Charles Alarie would have never had the balls to partake in. Ones that will make me richer than any king. And I've secured enough connections and loyal soldiers over the years to make this all a reality for me. Because tonight..." He steeples his fingers before him, his grin widening with each second. "The Alarie Estate will crumble. And it's time for a new era to begin with me as the ruler of this empire. It's finally all mine."

Dolion's brows furrow, his eyes latching onto my father. "Yours? You said it would be ours."

My father waves his hand around dismissively. "Ours in a figurative sense, not literal."

Dolion shakes his head, anger radiating off him. "No. That was not the plan we agreed upon." He slams his fist on the arm of his chair. "I did everything for you. I set the explosion that killed Charles Alarie. I gave you every piece of information from inside the estate you asked for over the years. I laid the fucking trail of breadcrumbs for the Alaries to uncover to ensure they met their demise tonight!"

"And I appreciate your dedication to the cause," my father starts. "But the plan from the very beginning was for me to take over the Alarie Estate. It was always the end goal. For me to lead. For me to conquer and rule. Not you." He smooths out his jacket. "I will forgo selling Scarlett in the next auction and give you her, and I will continue to allow you to work beneath me, but that is as far as my appreciation for your efforts extends."

"Beneath you?" Dolion's voice growls with fury. "You wouldn't have gotten your fucking revenge without me!"

As they continue to argue, my head slumps against Maddy's thigh, defeat weighing heavy on me. If Leo died...

Maddy's thigh bumps against my head, and when I look up, her big blue eyes, glossed over in tears, are pleading with me.

Don't give up.

"We lost," I whisper, my shoulders deflating. "You heard what he said. There's nothing we can do."

She nudges me again, and this time, when my eyes catch with hers, I can't ignore the vicious determination in her eyes.

And she's right.

We have to at least try.

Leo would be so disappointed in me if he knew I gave up and let these monsters win.

Cautiously, I reach for the knife on the ground between my legs and begin sawing the rope around my ankles with as much force as I can without being noticed.

"You should be honored to be one of my soldiers," my father remarks. "It is a privilege, not a—"

"Fuck that!" Dolion raises his gun and, without missing a beat, shoots my father in the stomach. Blood pools beneath his white shirt, seeping through the fabric. He gasps for air as he clutches his jacket before pressing his palms against the bullet hole.

I wait for the shock to course through me, but at this point, good riddance. One less monster for me to have to deal with.

"You...you son of a..." Blood spills from the corner of his lips as he slumps over, paling.

Dolion jumps up from his seat and paces. "Fuck!" He pulls at his dark hair. "This wasn't how things were supposed to go. We were supposed to rule together. And Scarlett and I were going to get married with your blessing. You promised me I would be rewarded for all my years of service with the only thing I ever wanted."

As Dolion continues to move, I feel the rope break free and fall to the floor. Glancing at Maddy, I lock eyes with her as I show a glimpse of the knife beneath the blanket. She closes her eyes and then nods, understanding what I need to do to try to get us out of here.

Suddenly, a symphony of bullets echoes outside the house, people screaming as the noise only intensifies. A nearby explosion causes the house to shake.

"What the fuck is going on?" Dolion roars, turning away from us to look out a window in the front of the house.

This is my moment.

Leaping to my feet, I take three giant steps, and then, with all my strength, I force the blade down on Dolion, piercing his skin. I had aimed for the side of his neck, but just as my knife was going down, the lights in the house turned on, and Dolion saw my reflection in the window and quickly twisted toward me, causing me to hit him in the shoulder.

He howls in pain, displeasure etched in his features.

"You bitch!" He reaches behind him, trying to pull the knife from his skin, but before he gets the chance, I get in my Ready Stance, bend my right knee, drive my right knee straight up, and then kick my right shin directly into his groin. Immediately, I return to my Ready Stance as Dolion groans and then collapses to the floor.

Mauro would be proud.

I turn to Maddy to free her, but just as I take a step, Dolion raises his gun. "Step away from her."

I still, unsure of what to do. I can't compete with a gun.

"I'll let you choose, Scarlett," he says, his lips curving up in delight. "You or her."

"W-what?" I stammer. He can't mean...?

"You get to choose who I'll kill. You or her?"

I shake my head, standing protectively before Maddy. "You're a monster."

He shrugs, pushing himself upright. "I've been called worse." He fires a warning shot inches away from Maddy, her body shaking in terror. "You have until the count of three, and if you don't make a decision, I'll make one for you."

"N-no..." I look to Maddy, our eyes locking.

"One..."

My breaths come out in fast pants.

"Two..."

I won't let him kill my best friend.

"Three."

"Kill me!" I scream, my chest heaving with each breath I take.

Without warning, the door to the house flies off the hinges as smoke fills the room and men stampede inside.

"Drop your weapon!" the soldier closest to us screams.

Dolion stares at me, pure evil in his eyes. "Oh, Scarlett. I was never going to kill what has always been mine."

"No!" I scream as he raises the gun, aiming directly at Maddy.

Something large crashes through the window behind her just as Dolion fires a shot. Smoke surrounds us everywhere, making it impossible for me to see what happened.

"Maddy!" I scream, shaking from head to toe.

Swiftly, I'm forcefully grabbed and yanked against a hard chest. The barrel of a gun digs into the side of my head, and I freeze.

"If I can't have you, then no one will," Dolion whispers against my ear.

"Drop your weapon, Dolion." Through blurry eyes, I see Vin standing only feet away from me with his gun aimed at Dolion. *He's alive.* His eyes have storms raging inside them as he looks between us. "It's over. Let Scarlett go."

His grip on me tightens painfully. "No. I don't think I will. In fact, I think we'll go together." I pinch my eyes closed. If this is my last moment on Earth, then there's only one face I want to see, and he appears as handsome as ever in my mind.

"Drop the gun!" Vin shouts.

Dolion takes a step back, trying to pull me back with him, but I keep my feet plastered to the floor.

A shot fires from behind me, and I'm positive it must have killed me until I hear Dolion scream in pain and collapse behind me, dropping his gun. Men quickly grab him, dragging him away. I spin on my heels, and the sight before me fills my eyes with tears of relief.

Am I dreaming?

"Leo," I breathe as little black dots take over my vision, and I collapse into a pool of complete darkness.

CHAPTER THIRTY-TWO

Leo

The second the plane hits the tarmac, a blacked-out SUV pulls up, its tires screeching to a halt.

I stride toward the driver's side in the torrential rain, yanking open the door. "Get out. I'm driving." The guard stumbles out of the vehicle as Vin, Alex, Mauro, and I hop inside. My foot slams down on the gas pedal, flooring our way out of the private airport. I look down at the GPS, which says we'll be there in fifteen minutes. My foot presses down harder, ensuring we're there in half that time.

As we come within a few miles of the property, I spot a familiar family crest on the line of awaiting vehicles.

The Marchetti men are here.

"Pull over." Vin points to the closest armored vehicle, and I pull up beside it without missing a beat. The four of us jump out and approach it.

Dressed like he's ready for battle, Cain, Marco's younger brother and the cousin I hate the least, steps out and advances toward us.

"Cousins," he greets us with a head jerk, clasping his hands behind his back. "Well, don't you look a little...disheveled."

Vin points to Alex, getting straight to business. "We need your men to get him inside first. Once he gets to his house, he'll be able to restore power and cell service."

"Of course." Cain nods, pushing back his wet hair. "Marco said the matter was urgent, and since I happened to be at our headquarters, I figured I would lend a helping hand." He smirks. "It's been too long since I've killed a man."

"Let me guess, two days?" Alex asks.

Cain shrugs. "Twenty-four hours."

Every second away from Scarlett is sending me into a furious tizzy. "What are we waiting for?"

Cain appears amused. "Someone's in a hurry."

I nearly snarl. "If your wife was inside those walls with the fucking devil himself, tell me, cousin, how patient you would be to get inside?"

Cain's eyes darken as he realizes the urgency of this matter. He signals to his men. "We move now. The tanks go in first—"

"Tanks?" Vin questions.

Cain points to the front of the line of armored vehicles, where a few tanks stand idle. Jesus Christ, we look like we're going into fucking battle. Well, technically, we are.

"You have tanks?" Vin's eyes widen in disbelief.

"Don't you?" Cain asks, arching a brow.

Vin wipes a hand over his face. "Looks like I know what I'll be getting my brothers for Christmas."

Cain smirks, shaking his head. "Alessandro, you get in the front tank, and Vincenzo, Mauro, and Leonardo get in the next one."

"Don't have to be so formal," Alex chides as he passes him, heading toward the front of the line. "We're related, after all."

"Let my men regain control of the estate, which won't take long, and then you'll be free to handle the situation however you please," Cain states over his shoulder as he approaches the third and final tank.

Vin, Mauro, and I make our way to the second tank, and within a minute, it begins moving toward the north side of the property where the front gates reside. My knee bounces as my neck and shoulder muscles tighten. My fingers drum on my thigh as I stare at the floor.

"We're going to save her," Vin says. "All of them."

I nod, lost in thought.

Because I can't even think about what will happen if we don't.

It's not an option.

The tank comes to a stop.

"What's going on?" Vin asks the driver.

"The first tank is making entry now, sir. We'll follow suit once they've cleared the way. Thirty men are at the gate entrance attempting to stop them, but..." He grins. "Nothing will be able to stop us."

Vin grasps his shoulder. "Now, that's the fucking spirit!"

An explosion thunders not far in front of us, and then our tank begins rolling. As we breach the gate, the driver asks, "Which way do you want to go, sir? The rest of the armored vehicles are divvying up throughout the property."

I lean forward. "When you get to the fork, take a hard left." I eye Vin. "They'll be at the banquet hall."

After what feels like hours but is only minutes, we arrive at the hall just as an explosion goes off by the entrance. The three of us quickly exit the tank and make our way over, finding our men and Marchetti's men working together to round up the intruders.

Vin grabs one of the assailants, pulling him up by the collar of his shirt. "Who the fuck do you work for?"

With blood spilling out the corner of his lips, he gasps, "Igor."

Vin drops him, letting the other men handle him. He scratches a hand over his stubble. "I'm guessing Igor lent his men to Anthony and Dolion, thinking he was a part of the team and not a part of the decoy."

Eli charges out of the front of the hall on high alert, and I feel immense relief, knowing Scarlett will be with him. But as he continues moving toward us, I see Alina by his side, not Scarlett.

Terror fills me.

"Where's my wife?" I roar.

"She's safe," he says reassuringly, temporarily easing me until his next words follow. "She ran to Dolion's house for help about an hour ago. I was trapped inside with Alina and the other guests until just now."

I gaze up at the sky and let out an unhuman-like growl as rain pellets my face. Thunder rumbles in the distance, echoing me.

"Dolion is Le Diable," Vin asserts. "And we're pretty fucking sure he's been working with Scarlett's father, Anthony Balcom, this whole time."

"What?" Eli snarls, his head snapping in the direction of Dolion's cottage. "I thought her father fucking died!"

"So did we," Vin answers, his eyes roaming around the property. "Wait, where's Madeleine?"

Eli's body stills. His eyes darken to almost black. "She's not with you?"

"Fuck," I rasp, calculating how many bullets I have left in my gun. Two. That's all I need.

Alina trembles, wrapping her arms around herself. Mascara runs down her cheeks as she stares at the ground, swaying on her bare feet. Mauro's arm promptly closes around her waist, holding her securely to his chest. She presses her face against him and sobs into his shirt as he runs his hands down her wet hair, calming her.

Suddenly, the lights throughout the estate turn on, and all four sets of men's eyes follow the path leading directly toward Dolion's cottage.

"I'm going to murder the both of them." I wipe a hand across my rain-soaked face. "They may not know we're here yet, but if they do, they'll get desperate, doing anything necessary to win." I look at Vin. "I need you to create a distraction at the front of the house while Eli and I case the back."

"You got it," Vin answers, motioning for a few of his men.

"No one is to touch Dolion. He's mine," I grit out as I glance around at each of them. "It's time to end this motherfucker once and for all."

I sprint toward the house with Eli, both of us veering right to sneak in the backway. Nothing but darkness surrounds us as we round the back with our guns drawn. A large window illuminated by lights catches our attention. Eli stands on one side of the window while I crouch under it and stand on the other side, hearing a man's voice. *Dolion.*

Eli and I peek inside, and horror fills me.

Dolion is standing with a gun aimed between Scarlett and Madeleine while Anthony is slumped over in a chair with blood covering the center of his shirt. Dolion's waving the gun in the air like an unhinged monster. His face is red with fury, his eyes jump erratically, and he quickly paces the room.

Fuck, this isn't good.

If he wasn't standing behind Scarlett, I could take a shot.

But my path isn't clear, and I won't risk it.

Looking over my shoulder, I spot the back door. I jerk my head, signaling to Eli what I'm doing, and quickly dash over to it. The door is locked, with one metal bolt keeping it sealed shut. I peer around in a panic for another point of entry, but there's nothing.

A gunshot sounds from inside, and I lose whatever is left of my sanity.

Aiming my gun, I shoot the metal bolt and then, lifting my leg, find all the force within me and kick the door open. As I step inside, an explosion erupts in the front of the house, and I hear men yelling as another shot is fired. It's complete chaos as I move swiftly through the halls, smoke filling the rooms.

When I reach the main room, I come to an abrupt stop as my heart malfunctions.

Eli is lying on the ground unconscious, with blood pouring out of his arm in front of a horrified Madeleine.

And Dolion is binding Scarlett before him with a gun pressed to the side of her head.

Please, God, don't let anything happen to her.

Dolion faces Vin and the other soldiers who have entered the front of the house, meaning he doesn't know I'm here. With stealth and precision, I work my way closer, seeing the tremble in Scarlett's body, which only drives the beast inside me crazy with the need for blood.

"Drop your weapon, Dolion!" Vin shouts with an authoritative tone, directing his gun at Dolion. "It's over. Let Scarlett go."

My fingers tighten around my gun, aiming at the center of Dolion's head, when I quickly realize that I don't have a clear shot. He's leaning down, his face right beside Scarlett's. It's too close to her. *Fuck.* I scan his body and note a few inches of space on his right shoulder that I can hit without risking the bullet passing into Scarlett.

"No. I don't think I will," Dolion responds. "In fact, I think we'll go together."

Scarlett whimpers as Vin roars, "Drop the gun!"

Dolion takes a step back, his feet stumbling as Scarlett stands her ground, giving me the one second of time that I need.

The shot echoes in the air as the bullet pierces him in the shoulder. He screams out in agony as he drops his gun to the floor and collapses to the ground, our men rapidly collecting him and his weapon.

Scarlett spins on her heels, facing me. Tears stream down her pretty face as relief washes over her features at the sight of me.

My wife.

My lifeline.

My reason for existing.

And she's alive.

"Leo," she breathes, suddenly paling and dropping to the floor. But just before her body lands on the hard surface, I catch her in my arms.

"I'm here." I look her over, ensuring there are no fatal wounds. There are bruises around her wrists and ankles, which I'm assuming were tied up, a red handprint on her cheek, and a cut on her hand oozing blood, which all makes me see red. I brush my lips against hers, breathing in her familiar floral scent. "Wake up for me, baby. Please."

Her eyes flutter open, and my heart squeezes in my chest.

"Thank fucking God." I kiss the top of her head, holding her closer to me.

"You're...alive." She lets out a sob, clutching my damp T-shirt, anchoring herself to me. "I thought... I thought..." She chokes on her words, rolling in her bottom lip. "I thought I was never going to see you again."

"Nothing would keep me away from you." I brush back her hair and wipe the tears from her cheek before she buries her face in the crook of my neck, and the sobs begin to wrack her body. I run the palm of my hand up and down her spine. "I'm never letting go of you."

"Sir." I turn to the side, my grip on Scarlett strengthening as I face Asher. "What do you want us to do with him?"

A few men drag over a barely conscious Anthony Balcom. The asshole who thought he was going to take over my family's home.

He's alive.

Oh...this is going to be fun.

"Take him to see Dr. Rose," I instruct.

"Sir?" Asher's brows furrow as he looks at me like I've lost my mind.

I grin. "He needs to be in perfect condition before he answers to me and my brothers."

Asher smirks and nods in understanding. "Of course, sir." He jerks his head, and the guards drag Anthony away. "And reporting that your sister and Eli are being transported now to the hospital. Madeleine was being held here, and she had a few cuts and bruises, but Eli took a bullet for her. He jumped through the window before the shot went off, and it got him in the arm. He's expected to be all right."

"Jesus Christ." I drag a hand through my hair, sighing. "Thank you for the update."

"Of course, sir." Asher clears his throat. "I'm... I'm sorry for not seeing this sooner. I should have known it was Dolion."

I shake my head. "None of us did." I look at Dolion, seeing him in a whole new light as a few guards detain him. My eyes wander over the space, pausing on a wall of pictures. I focus on the photographs, observing Scarlett in every single damn one. My blood boils with an unrelenting need for violence that I, somehow, keep contained so as not to scare Scarlett any further this evening. "I trusted him with my life, which meant I trusted him around the most important person in my life." My arms tighten around Scarlett. "We'll deal with the aftermath tomorrow. For now, I need to take care of my wife."

Asher tips his head and walks off.

I return my attention to Scarlett, who looks up at me as if I'm in charge of letting the moon rise and the sun set.

"Maddy's okay?" she asks.

"She's okay." I brush her hair back, my fingers needing to feel every part of her.

"And Eli will be okay?"

My lips curve up. "Eli will be okay. He's faced much worse over the years. A bullet to the arm is nothing to him."

She slumps against me. "I can't believe Eli took a bullet for Maddy."

"I guess they don't hate each other as much as they seem to."

"I guess not." She presses her forehead to mine, letting out a deep breath as we hold on to each other, neither believing the other is truly here.

I cup her cheeks in my hands, pressing my lips to hers. "Let's go home." She instantly relaxes in my arms as I lift her in the air. Her legs wrap around my waist as her head rests on my shoulder. "I've got you, Firefly. I've always got you." I brush my lips against her temple and carry her to the car, déjà vu hitting me.

But this time, I know she'll be okay.

Because this time, she knows she isn't broken.

She's strong and resilient.
Brave and beautiful.
And most importantly...mine.

332

CHAPTER THIRTY-THREE

Scarlett

After getting checked over by the doctor, with Leo by my side the whole time, and then soaking in the tub with him, retelling everything I remembered from tonight, he lifted me in his arms and walked us outside to my favorite spot.

Laying me down on the gigantic bed swing, he turns on the nearby patio heater and then takes the place beside me, pulling me against his chest.

His hold on me feels unbreakable.

We lie there in silence for a few minutes, listening to the lull of the water and the crickets nearby. The patio heater beside us keeps us toasty warm under the midnight sky. And as I take a deep breath, inhaling Leo's comforting scent, I feel genuinely at peace for the first time in a long time.

"I'm so sorry, Scarlett."

I sit up, taken aback at seeing Leo's sorrowful dark eyes. "For what?"

"For everything." He drags a hand over his face, closing his eyes. "I should have known. I should have paid better attention. I should have seen the signs." He shakes his head, frustrated. "Because of me, you ended up right back into the monster's hands, and he could have... He could have..."

He lets his words hang in the air, his face pinching together in anguish.

"But he didn't." I frame his cheek, grazing my palm against his stubble. "You can't keep me protected in a plastic bubble. That's not the kind of life I want to live."

"I would never—"

"I know." I smile, tracing his bottom lip. "Leo, you saved me in more ways than I can ever tell you." I look up at the stars when I say, "Every time I needed to mentally escape my surroundings when I was trapped with...Dolion." A tremor runs down my spine. I don't think I'll ever get over that Le Diable, a faceless monster, was merely just a man—a psychotic one, at that, but still just a man. "Well, I escaped here with you. To the Alarie Estate." I give a slight shrug. "I used to envision all those times we would run around the property, collecting fireflies. We wouldn't leave until we had a full jar, and then we'd open the lid and watch them fly around us. It was so beautiful. And I just remember being so happy in those moments." My lips curve up. "I assume that's why you call me Firefly, right?"

He shakes his head, his fingers threading through my hair. "No." A beautiful smile graces his face as his hand rests on my lower back. "I call you Firefly because you've always been my light in the dark."

My heart swells as butterflies swarm my stomach. I roll in my bottom lip, fighting back tears that want to escape.

"Take off your wedding band," he says softly.

My brows draw together. "Why?"

He tucks a piece of my hair behind my ear, his face softening under the moonlight. "Please."

I twist at the elegant platinum band engulfed in diamonds until it slides off my finger. It's the first time I've taken it off, and suddenly, I feel lost without it on. I hold it in the palm of my hand, careful not to drop it.

"Now, look inside it," he instructs.

My face scrunches in confusion until I bring the ring to my eyes and see an engravement. My eyes narrow in on the tiny print, and a gasp escapes between my lips.

"What does it say?" He slides his hands up and down my spine, caressing each spot, especially where the scars reside.

I clear my throat, no longer able to keep the tears at bay. The tip of my nose stings as my chest tightens. "My wife. My everything. My firefly." An onslaught of tears cascades down my cheeks, and Leo leans forward, pressing a tender kiss on each one. "The day you found me... I didn't want to be here anymore," I confess for the first time, my voice somber. His hand freezes in place, his chest beneath me stills. "I never imagined anyone would be looking for me, so I had given up on myself. I had lost all the hope in my heart."

"Scarlett..."

"But then you came for me," I say. "You never gave up on me. And at that moment in your arms, I had never felt safer and more loved in my life." I shake my head, my eyes downcast. "I didn't know at the time that it was you, but I did know whoever was holding me was never going to let go of me." My finger traces a circle on his bare chest. "So, when your mother came to me with the idea of marrying you for my safety, it was a no-brainer for me. Because Leo..." I meet his eyes and admit, "I've loved you my whole life. I never stopped. Not once."

I feel a weight lift off my chest from releasing those words. My heart swells, feeling so unbelievably full, all thanks to the man beside me.

His thumb runs across my cheek to catch each tear as he waits for me to continue. "After everything that happened to me, I thought... I thought I was destined for a lonely life—one where I would never feel...normal again. But you never gave up on me. Not once." I sniffle, blinking back tears. "You helped me heal with your patience and love. You showed me the strength I've had within me this whole time. I just needed some help to see it." I roll in my bottom lip. "So, I guess what

I'm trying to say is, there's no one I would rather spend the rest of my life with than you. My heart…" I let out a shaky breath. "It beats only for you."

Leo sits up, taking me in his arms. His lips crash against mine, consuming me whole. Raw and hungry. He pulls back, breathing hard as he rolls his forehead against mine. "I would search for you until my last second on this earth." His lips press to mine, gently this time, savoring every second. "You are the reason for my existence. You are the only one who keeps my heart beating. You are my whole world, Scarlett Alarie." He takes my ring from my hand and gently slides it on my finger where it belongs. "My wife. My everything. My firefly." His lips brush over my cheek and then glide down to my neck, grazing over my racing pulse. "There has never been anyone else in my heart but you. Only you."

A sob escapes me, an overwhelming feeling of emotions consuming me.

From the years we lost together.

From knowing everything this man would do for me.

From the love I feel for him, and he feels for me.

It's too much.

But at the same time, it's not enough.

"I love you, Leo," I whisper against his lips.

"I love you, Scarlett."

In one swift move, Leo rolls us over until he has me pinned beneath him. His lips trail down my neck, sucking, nipping, and kissing, sending me into a frenzy of lust. His hands grasp my waist as I wrap my legs around him, tugging him closer to me.

Feeling his hardened length rub against my center has me whimpering. My nails dig into his shoulders as I lift my hips, seeking more of that delicious friction. My clit rubs against him, igniting a rhythm of pleasure between my legs.

His fingers hook around the bottom of my nightie, pulling it up my waist and over my chest. My nipples instantly harden under his gaze, a cool chill in the air caressing my bare skin. Tingles spread over my skin as his tongue sneaks out, swiping over a nipple before he wraps his lips around it, sucking down hard.

"Oh God." I let out a breathy moan, my fingers curling in his hair. He repeats his ministrations to the other side, sending a shock of electricity to my core. I increase my pace, grinding harder and faster, feeling ravenous for him.

But it's not enough.

I need more.

"Tell me what you want, baby," he murmurs against my skin.

"You," I pant, feeling on the precipice of spiraling.

With ease, he removes my nightie over my head, tossing it to the side. His hand reaches between us, cupping my pussy over my panties, stirring warmth within me.

"These need to go," he breathes, sliding down my body.

My legs splay open for him as he situates himself between them, gazing down at me. There's no shame. No embarrassment. Only unrestrained want and desire. His lips press down on the fabric right over my slit, and I arch into him, silently begging for whatever he'll give me.

"My wife is so needy." His lips curve up into a devilish smile. "It's a good thing she has me to please her."

His thumbs hook under the lace, dragging it slowly down my thighs, around my knees and calves, and over my toes, leaving me completely naked.

My chest heaves. My heart thunders. And my pussy aches.

Suddenly, he leans down, pressing his face against my center, inhaling my scent before he licks one languid straight line, ending on my bundle of nerves with a flick from his tongue. My lips form a circle as my hands press down beside me.

"So fucking delicious," he murmurs before burying his head between my legs, feasting on me like a man who just found water in the desert. He sends my body into a state of euphoria, his tongue lapping up my arousal at a maddening pace, his hands grasping my thighs, keeping me in place as I shake against him. He doesn't bother coming up for air, not stopping even when my thighs strapped around his ears begin to tremble.

"I'm going... I'm going to...come!" I scream as his lips suck on my clit, sending a tremor of vibrations through me. My body arches off the cushion, exploding from pleasure, the orgasm rolling through me with no end in sight. Maybe it's minutes or maybe it's hours, but when I come to, I find Leo observing me, his eyes full of warmth.

"You're so goddamn beautiful when you come," he says, his knuckles stroking my cheek.

A flush spreads over my cheeks as I press my hand to his chest, his heart beating as fast as mine. "Show me who I belong to."

He doesn't hesitate as he stands, removing his pants. His cock bobs up, hard and thick. Precum drips from the tip, and my tongue swipes over my bottom lip, demanding to taste him.

My eyes wander all over him. From his chiseled chest. The intricate ink. His thick thighs. He's a god in his own right. Perfect. Magnificent. *Mine.*

Slowly, he strokes himself, and that satisfied arousal between my legs sparks to life, eager for more. Sitting up, I reach for him, my fingers wrapping over his.

"Let me," I say.

He removes his hand and steps closer. I kneel before him, placing my head level with his cock. His hand glides over the top of my head and down my neck, gently squeezing reassuringly.

I brush my lips across his tip and poke my tongue out to lick, savoring the salty taste.

"Fuck," he groans.

Without pause, I lean forward, wrapping my lips around his cock, sliding it down my throat as far as it will go. I place my hands on his thighs as I begin bobbing my head, sucking him off with just the right amount of pressure.

"God, that feels so fucking good," he praises me, sending a pool of wetness between my legs.

I use my tongue to massage under the head of his cock, twirling and swirling it around.

He looks down at me in awe, cupping my cheek. "You look so fucking pretty on your knees for me, baby." His thumb runs over my bottom lip. "But the only place I'm coming tonight is in your sweet pussy." He pulls out of my lips, leaving me panting and ready for more. "It's time to show you who you belong to, Firefly. Who you've always belonged to."

His lips crash down over mine. His hand presses into my chest, gently pushing me back down. I lie beneath him, my legs spreading wide open for him, watching as he positions himself at my soaked entrance.

For a moment, our eyes meet, and nothing else in the world exists. It's only him and me.

And then he plunges deep within me, sinking all the way inside. My eyes seal shut as I relish the feel of him. It's pure, unfiltered ecstasy. Everything my body craves and needs.

He begins to move, thrusting in and out, never letting up. I wrap my legs around him, latching my ankles together as I take everything he gives me. The tip of his cock hits that special spot, over and over again, and it doesn't take long for that familiar buildup of pleasure to overtake me.

"Look at me," Leo demands, his eyes boring into mine. "I want to see those beautiful sapphires when you come with your husband's cock inside you." He sneaks his hand between us, two of his fingers rubbing ferociously over my clit, giving me exactly what I need to unravel beneath him.

With his eyes on me, I scream his name, shattering into a million broken pieces. As I tremble deliciously, waiting to float back to the surface, the orgasm fades, leaving me in a state of blissfulness.

Leo slams into me faster and harder, groaning out in pleasure. His movements become jerky and unsteady as he spills inside me, coming with such intensity. He collapses against me, burying his head into the crook of my neck. Both of us pant wildly, sweat coating our skin. I turn my head to the side, his lips finding mine in an all-consuming, never-ending kiss.

And as we hold each other beneath the stars, fiercely and with so much love, I truly feel it.

I am his.

And he is mine.

My lids flutter open, and I find myself in our bed, which Leo must have brought me up to at some point during the night. As I sit up, holding the blanket to my chest, Leo walks out of the bathroom with nothing but a white towel wrapped around his sculpted torso. I bite my bottom lip, feeling heat tinge my cheeks.

"Good morning, Mrs. Alarie." He sits beside me, his hand lightly gripping my chin as he pulls me toward him and presses his lips to mine.

"Mmm... Good morning, Mr. Alarie."

"How are you feeling?" He eyes me, ensuring nothing was overlooked last night.

"Maybe just a little sore," I admit with a slight shrug. "But that's probably from other activities..." I arch a brow, showing a teasing smile.

"My apologies." He smirks, leaning in to kiss my neck. "I just can't get enough of your moans when my cock is buried deep inside you, making you come over." Kiss. "And over." Kiss. "And over again." I tilt my neck to the side, giving him plenty of room as his tongue snakes up my skin, sending a shiver over me. "I'll have to make it up to you."

"Yes, I think—"

Suddenly, voices filter into the room, sounding like they're coming from downstairs.

"Who's here?" I ask, clutching the blanket tighter to my chest.

Leo rolls his eyes and stares up at the ceiling. "Unfortunately, every-one."

"Everyone?" My eyes widen as a smirk takes root. "Even Maddy and Eli?"

"Even Maddy and Eli." He grins. "They're both fine. Eli got out of surgery only a few hours ago, so he might be a little groggy on pain meds, but he insisted on coming over. I think he wants to see for himself that you're okay. And Madeleine had a cut on her temple stitched up, but she's in good spirits, considering everything."

I roll in my bottom lip, placing my hand against his chest. "You mean to tell me you let your whole family into your house?"

"Against my better judgment." He grins. "And it's *our* house." He brushes back a loose strand of my hair, tucking it behind my ear. "But I knew it would make you happy."

I wrap my arms around his neck, pulling him toward me. "What did I do to deserve you?"

His lips press against mine. "It is me who should be asking that." His hand finds my bare thigh and skims up the inside. "Maybe we have a few minutes—"

"Don't even think about it. We are not having sex with your whole family downstairs." I swat at his chest as he playfully gathers me up in his arms and throws me on the center of the bed. He prowls over me, kissing his way up my naked body, revving up the engine between my legs.

He looks up at me as he presses a kiss to my core. "You're probably right, Firefly. Wouldn't want them to hear us." He stands, looking down at me with mischief in his eyes, knowing exactly what he just did to me.

My breaths come out uneven and choppy, my chest heaving. "Well, maybe if we're quiet and—"

It's the only invitation he needs before positioning himself on top of me, spending the next hour making me come over and over and over again.

After my morning wake-up call, Leo and I hurry down the stairs, showered and dressed, with Brutus by our side, to be greeted by a room filled with familiar faces.

Mrs. Alarie, Vin, Mauro, Alex, Maddy, Alina, and Eli.

"Scarlett!" Mrs. Alarie holds her arms out for me as she approaches, wrapping me up in her motherly embrace. "I'm so relieved that you're okay."

"I'm fine. Just a little shaken up," I confess.

She gives me a warm smile as we part, her eyes misting. "As soon as I got a call from Vincenzo, I headed straight home from France. I just needed to be with my family."

Maddy steps by her mother, attaching herself to me. I tighten my hold on her as she sobs into my shoulder, causing me to cry in return. We don't speak as we stand there, clinging to one another.

A throat clears, and we both turn our heads to see Alina. "Got room for one more?"

We laugh, making room for her to join. And as the three of us hold on to each other for dear life, I can't help but think how thankful I am to have these two back in my life.

Once we separate, I make my way to everyone else. Hugging Alex, Vin, and Mauro. Feeling unbelievably thankful that nothing serious happened to them last night. They're the brothers I never had but always needed in my life. And whether they like it or not, I'm officially their sister until the end of time.

Although, I'm pretty sure they approve of that.

"Got one more hug for me?"

I spin on my heels, finding Eli a little worse for wear. His left arm is in a sling with bandages peeking beneath his shirt, and his eyes appear exhausted.

He runs his fingers through his hair, staring down at the ground. "I can't begin to say how sorry I am for sending you straight into Dolion's hands." He shakes his head. "I never should have—"

I shut him up with a hug, careful to avoid his injury. "You did everything you could to keep me safe. And I don't want anyone to blame themselves for what happened, least of all you, who has been keeping a protective eye on me when Leo isn't around." I pull back, smiling. "I want to leave Dolion in the past. He doesn't deserve any of our time in the future. Don't you think?"

His lips curve up, his shoulders dropping in relief. "I couldn't agree with you more."

Leo's arm slips around my waist, tugging me to his side. His lips press down on my temple. "You're so damn strong."

Brutus nudges my thigh with his head, and I instinctively reach down to scratch behind his ears as he sits beside me.

I look around the room, a smile gracing my lips. I was raised as an only child with a mother who left me too soon and a father who terrified me. But now, here I stand, with not only a husband by my side but also a sister, a friend, four brothers, and a second mother.

"Only because of each and every single person in this room without whom I wouldn't be here today." My heart swells with a wealth of love that surges through me as I say, "My family."

Chapter Thirty-Four

Leo

"I expect this to be your top priority, Felix," I spit into my phone. "I want every diamond to shine so fucking bright that they can be seen from space. I'm giving you three weeks." I end the call and slide my phone into my pocket as I stroll down the hall. My knuckles tap against the partially open door. "You wanted to see me?" I ask as I step inside my mother's study.

She smiles warmly, gesturing to the leather seat across from her desk. "Yes." She shuffles some papers and then slides them into a folder. "How is Scarlett doing?"

I take a seat, placing my ankle over my knee as I lean back, letting out a heavy breath. "As good as can be expected. She hasn't seemed to let any of this set back her progress, which is good. But she'll need some time to come to terms with everything. Her father's involvement in all of this has stirred her."

"Understandable. It's been quite a shock for all of us. He was someone your father trusted immensely. It pains me to know that someone we let into our home, someone we treated as family, orchestrated your father's death." She shakes her head in disbelief. "I can only hope that time will help heal these new wounds." She leans forward, clasping her hands together. "And how are you doing?"

"Me?"

"Yes, you. You're my youngest son, and as your mother, I am allowed to worry about you."

"I'm fine," I respond matter-of-factly, looking away.

"You're fine," she says skeptically, her eyes glancing at the picture of her and my father, which she delicately picks up. "You found out who plotted your father's death, and you're fine." She nods deep in thought. "You found out a man you trusted for years was the one who kidnapped and tortured your wife while also working with her father, who planned on selling her off to the highest bidder, but you're fine."

My fingers tighten around the arm of the chair. "I will be fine. Right after I take care of them," I grit out.

She places the photo back in its proper place and studies me, a tenderness washing over her features. "I know this is hard for you, Leo, even if you won't admit it."

"I'm—"

"I'm your mother, Leo," she says abruptly. "And you're not fine."

Running a frustrated hand through my hair, I stare out the closest window. There are so many feelings brewing inside, but the biggest one of them all is guilt. "I should have known," I rush out. "I should have fucking known, and because I wasn't paying close enough attention, I failed both Dad and Scarlett by letting these monsters live and breathe in our home."

"You did no such thing, Leo." She brushes the wedding band on her finger—the one she refuses to ever take off. "Your father was so very proud of you. Of all of his children. Every night before bed, he'd tell me how lucky he was as a husband and a father." She wipes at her eyes. "He loved you very much. And he would never want you to blame yourself for what happened to him when it wasn't your fault. The only blame lies on two men who I assume are waiting for you to end their miserable lives as we speak." She lets out a breath, her features relaxing. "That is who is to blame. Not you. And as for Scarlett—"

I shake my head, ready to argue with her. "She never would have been taken if—"

"There's no ifs, Leo," she says firmly but gently. "You had no idea what Dolion was capable of. Who he truly was. None of us did." She rubs her temple. "You saved Scarlett. You brought her home—a place we never should have let her leave. And you have been nothing but an exemplary husband to her. I'm just... I'm just so very proud of the man you've become."

An invisible chain shackling me to the chair slowly unravels, a sudden ethereal feeling taking over me. I will always hold guilt for everything that has happened when it affected those closest to me. But I can at least try to move forward and do better. Be better. Because for her, my wife, there's nothing I won't do.

I clear my throat, uncomfortable showing emotions, even to my mother. "I should probably head to the warehouse. Vin, Mauro, Alex, and Eli are waiting for me."

She nods, her finger tapping her desk. "Of course. But speaking of Eli..."

I arch a brow.

"Well, now that we have Scarlett's perpetrator taken care of, I would like Eli to be assigned to Madeleine. Once he's fully healed, of course."

My brows draw together, confusion taking over. "Madeleine? Why?"

"As your mother," she emphasizes, squaring her shoulders, "just trust me on this."

I lean forward, resting my elbows on my knees. "We're already taking care of ensuring her wedding—"

Her hand shoots up, silencing me. "I don't want to know about any plans to ruin my daughter's wedding."

I roll my eyes, knowing she hates Alastor as much as we all do and is secretly elated that we won't let this wedding ever happen.

"But do this one thing for me," she says. "Call it a mother's intuition, but I would feel better knowing Eli is keeping a close eye on her."

I rub my chin, knowing neither Eli nor Madeleine will be happy about this. Not one damn bit. "Do you want to tell them the good news?"

She waves a hand dismissively.

I huff, pushing to my feet. "Guess I'll take care of it, then."

"Thank you." She shows an appreciative smile as I turn to leave. "And Leo?" I stop as I reach the door, peering over my shoulder. "Make them pay for what they did to the two people we love the most in the world."

A cruel smile tugs on my lips, the predator inside me clawing its way to the surface as I respond, "I will."

———

Pulling up in front of the warehouse, I find my brothers and Eli eagerly waiting for me.

"You said you'd be here ten minutes ago," Vin complains as he checks his watch.

I set the kickstand on my bike and pull off my helmet. "I had something I had to take care of." As I get up from my seat, Eli approaches, sporting a sling on his left arm. "Shouldn't you be resting?"

He gives a slight shrug. "Nothing would make me miss this. Besides, the doc's on standby in case my stitches come undone."

I smirk, turning toward the door, vengeance swirling within me. The only thing separating me from the monsters I'm itching to destroy.

To break.

Piece by fucking piece.

"Are you ready for this?" Alex asks, coming up to my side. He pushes his glasses up the bridge of his nose and grasps my shoulder.

"I've been waiting seven years for this. And I'm not willing to wait another second," I say. "It's time to make them pay for what they did to our family."

A hand grips my other shoulder. "We're in this together, brother," Vin states, his eyes staring straight ahead at the door as if he can see what lies behind it, waiting for us.

Mauro walks up to us, straightening his shoulders. He presses his fingers against his throat, swallowing hard. "F-for." He clears his throat. His voice brings a deathly silence around us, none of us wanting to miss a single word. "Dad...and," he rushes out in a hoarse whisper. His brows furrow as his hand presses into his skin. The pain is too much for him to finish.

"Scarlett," I say for him. He nods in agreement.

"And for you." Alex pats Mauro on the back.

We all stand there silently, glaring at the door.

"Well, what are we waiting for?" Vin strides across the pavement, his hands shoving the door wide open. "Let's kill these motherfuckers."

We follow after him, the five of us coming to a stop upon Dolion and Anthony gagged and bound to separate chairs in the middle of the room. As instructed, both have been patched up and left unscathed, leaving them ready to suffer at our mercy.

"Well, aren't you two a sight for sore eyes," Eli muses, crouching before Dolion with a malicious sneer. "I never liked you. Not one goddamn bit, arsehole." He looks back at us over his shoulder. "Fuck, that felt good to say out loud."

Vin dismisses the guards with a flick of his wrist, leaving just the five of us standing before these two who are about to repent for their sins.

I'm not even sure hell will welcome them after everything they've done.

Mauro whips out a knife from his pant leg and slices off the duct tape wrapped around each of their faces, his blade leaving a trail of blood across their skin.

And so it begins.

"Gentlemen." Vin widens his arms. "Welcome to the Alarie Estate. Oh wait... You're both well familiar with our home, which is why I'm curious why you ever got the silly little notion in your stupid fucking heads that you could take what is ours?" He looks between them with a lethal gaze. His arms cross over his chest, and his presence is that of a true leader.

"Your father," Anthony starts. "Was weak just like you fuck—"

Mauro's fist connects with Anthony's jaw, sending droplets of blood in the air. His chest heaves as he looks down upon him, rage contorting his features.

"I wouldn't talk badly about our father if I were you," Alex murmurs. "Not the best way to get on our good side."

"Or maybe we should just send you back to your good pal Igor?" Vin grins, smacking his forehead. "I almost forgot, we killed him. Just like we're about to kill you."

Anthony swallows, lifting his chin. "You're not going to kill me," he states matter-of-factly.

"We aren't?" Alex asks, amused.

Anthony shakes his head and stares right at me. "No. Because you would never kill your wife's father. It would be a dishonor to her."

I suppress my grin, crouching until I'm inches from his face, holding my hand open, palm facing him. "You abused Scarlett for years and threatened her with my family's safety." I curl in a finger. "You hired Dolion to murder my father." I tuck in the next finger. "You faked your death and had Scarlett kidnapped by a psychopath as a reward for his loyalty to you, and then he tortured her until she was seconds away from dying." My third finger drops. "You arranged an illegal auction for sex trafficking in our territory to lure us there with the intention of killing us. Not to mention you planned on selling off Scarlett at a future auction." My fourth finger curls in. "And then you tried but failed to take over the Alarie Estate like you were some fucking king in the Middle Ages." My thumb closes around my knuckles, and I slam my fist into his nose. A crunching noise is a clear indicator that it's broken. Blood gushes down the front of his face and over his lips as he groans in agony. I stand before him, using my T-shirt to wipe his blood from my hands. "Let's get one fucking thing straight right now. You will not be walking out of here alive."

Dolion laughs like a madman, watching the exchange. I realize now that I never actually knew him like I thought. The fact that I trusted him around Scarlett sends guilt slamming into me. I take a few steps until I'm right before him and grip his dark hair by the top of his neck, yanking his head back. "You find this funny?"

His laugh grows maniacally until altogether stopping when he notices Mauro placing Scarlett's knife into the palm of my hand.

"I heard my wife got you pretty good in your shoulder with this." I hold the knife between us, the sun casting through a nearby window, making it glisten. Dried flecks of blood coat the handle, and I know the blood belongs to Dolion. Warmth pools through me, feeling so damn proud of Scarlett.

"Your wife?" Dolion grits out, grinding his teeth. A bulging vein looks ready to pop on his forehead from the tension in his body. "She's mine!" he roars. "She was promised to me! I earned her! I fucking spent my life working for her!" His eyes widen as saliva pools at the sides of his lips, making him appear like a rabid animal.

"Yours," I repeat calmly, handing the knife to Vin as I look up at the ceiling, my breath quickening. Without warning, I get into his face, causing him to rear back as I grip his shirt in my clutches. "She has always been mine!" My voice rumbles in the room, nobody moving a muscle. "You fucking tried to break her but failed. So, guess what? Now I'm going to break you, over and over again, piece by fucking piece, until there is nothing left but a corpse that I will let the wolves feast on." A smile forms as I notice, for the first time, fear hovering over Dolion's green irises.

"Shall we get this started, gentlemen?" Vin adjusts a set of brass knuckles over his fingers and hands a set to Mauro.

I stand tall, remove my leather jacket, and toss it to the floor. Cracking my neck from side to side, I look down at Dolion. "You're going to regret ever laying a finger on my wife." I turn my eyes to Anthony. "And you…" I watch Mauro drag his chair away to the other side of the room. He rolls up his sleeves and then walks away, picking up a gasoline container from the corner. Anthony's eyes widen, and sweat drips down his temple as Mauro steps closer. "Burn in hell."

"Wait! Wait! We can talk about this." Anthony's eyes bulge out of his head; panic overcomes him. And rightfully so. "I can tell you where—" His words die out as Eli stuffs a gasoline-soaked rag into his mouth. He tries to move, but with his ankles and wrists bound to the chair, it's futile. Mauro pours the gasoline in a circle around him.

"An eye for an eye, don't you think?" Vin notes, observing Mauro's work. "You killed our father with fire, and now we'll do the same to you." He shrugs. "Seems only fitting."

Alex steps closer, holding out two lighters before me and Mauro. "Would you two care to do the honors?"

The two of us take hold of the lighters, flicking them to life—the small flames inching toward the gasoline.

"With pleasure," I answer.

Mauro and I lock eyes and, at the exact moment, toss our lighters toward Anthony. We watch intently as the fire rapidly grows before us, hypnotizing us with the hues of orange and a flicker of blue. Anthony's screams, even through the gag, bounce off the walls, and it doesn't take long for his cries to die out and for his charred body to slump over.

We all turn our attention to the next victim.

"Your turn." A dangerous smile takes over as the five of us get closer. "And I hope we didn't give you the wrong impression, but your death will be nowhere near as quick." I shake my head. "No." I examine the watch on my wrist. "My *wife* won't be home for hours. Something about helping Madeleine pick out flowers for her wedding."

Eli scoffs, rolling his eyes.

"So we have all day to play." I pound a fist into the palm of my hand, letting my eyes travel up and down Dolion's trembling body.

Mauro, Vin, Alex, and Eli stand side by side with me, preparing themselves as they stretch and roll up their sleeves. And it feels pretty damn good knowing these guys will always have my back just like I have theirs.

"I'll go first," I quip, stepping closer. Vin puts a hand on my shoulder, stopping me, and I look at him, confused.

"You're going to need this," he says, holding Scarlett's knife between his fingers.

I smirk, taking it, feeling like a predator about to devour his prey. My eyes latch on to Dolion as I think of all the ways I'm going to break him with this. "This is going to be so much fucking fun." I glance between each of them, a darkness sweeping over me. "For Scarlett." My gaze turns cold as my eyes lock with Dolion's. "For *my wife*," I emphasize just as the tip of the knife slashes across his chest, exposing a trail of crimson blood.

Revenge has never felt sweeter.

CHAPTER THIRTY-FIVE

Scarlett

THREE WEEKS LATER

My toes curl in the cool sand as I tug my jacket around me a little tighter, an icy breeze sweeping over me. Waves crash against the shore nearby, mixing with the sound of the crackle of the fire and boisterous laughter around me. But all the noise is a distant afterthought as my eyes become transfixed on the bright orange flames, with thoughts of my father and Dolion churning in my mind.

I knew my father despised me. Hated me with a burning rage merely because I wasn't the son he yearned for. The one who would make him proud, taking over the Balcom legacy. And because of that, I kept my distance and did as I was told like an obedient daughter. Trying everything in my power to make him proud of me. To make myself worthy of his love that he would never grant me. But I guess I never knew who he really was.

A cold-hearted monster.

One who was never capable of loving his own daughter.

To prove that, he gave me away to the devil himself. Offered me up to him as his reward for years of loyal service before he planned to sell me in an auction.

But because my heart had always belonged to another, Dolion's tirade of jealousy sought punishment. Revenge. Unimaginable pain. And above all, he wanted to break me.

A shiver runs through me as dark memories begin to resurface. *The devil's mask. A knife. Blood. Screams.*

Quickly, I blink them back, wrapping my arms around myself.

I know how close Dolion was to truly breaking me. To snapping my soul in two. But he failed. Not even coming close. All because of one man.

Leo Alarie.

My husband.

Warmth rushes over the glacial chill sweeping throughout my chest.

Leo made it his mission to find me, to save me from the monster's clutches. And he didn't stop until he slayed the demons that haunt me.

He took my shattered pieces with patience and love and made me whole again. And because of that, and so much more, I love him with everything I am.

"Hey, you." Maddy's voice disrupts my thoughts, and I internally shake my head as she plops herself on the seat next to mine with two glasses of white wine. "You looked a little lost in thought," she says, handing one to me.

"Was just thinking," I admit with a half shrug. I take a sip and enjoy the crisp, peachy taste that slides down my throat.

"I can understand that." She looks over at the ocean and then back at me. "Mom told me you're taking on more at the women and children's center. Starting with building a library?"

"Yeah. I thought it might be nice to give them a place for their minds to escape when things are a little too much."

Maddy smiles. "I think that's a great idea. And I'd love to help if that's okay."

I snuggle my side into hers, resting my head on her shoulder. "I'd love that."

She places her glass in the sand. "Leo wanted to talk to me about something tonight. Any idea what that might be?"

I purse my lips, shaking my head. "No, he never mentioned anything to me. Maybe it's just about your wedding."

Her eyes look downcast as she gives a half shrug. "Maybe."

"Here he comes," Eli says, peering across the fire.

Maddy and I turn to see Vin trudging through the sand, making his way toward us with a glass of whiskey. He looks tired as he combs his fingers through his hair.

"What took you so long?" Maddy asks.

He walks up to her and rubs the top of her head, making her scowl. "Just had to take care of some business, but I'm here now." He sits on a chair between Mauro and Eli, throwing back a hefty sip of his drink. Mauro and Alex share a look Vin notices, causing him to shake his head. "Not now," Vin mutters.

Voices behind me by the patio cause me to look over my shoulder, where I find the staff setting up a feast for dinner. "Are we celebrating something tonight?" I ask. Large space heaters are positioned by the table, lights are strung around the quaint space, and pink flowers in vases are stationed in the center of the long table. I narrow my eyes on the flowers, realizing they're the same kind that were left in my room while I recovered at Mrs. Alarie's house, gladioli.

Maddy shrugs. "Beats me." She brings the glass to her lips, looking across the fire, and I swear I see a fleeting moment when her eyes connect with Eli's before she averts her gaze and stares across the water.

"I made it!" Alina approaches with a contagious smile, marching through the sand. Her sweater comes undone against the wind, and her long brown hair flies over her shoulders.

"Hey, I didn't know you were coming today!" I start to stand, but she motions for me to sit as she bends down to wrap her arms around me.

"Of course! I was so relieved I could finish my finals early. Besides, there was no way I was missing this!"

My brows furrow. "Miss what?" I look over at Maddy, who quickly starts guzzling her wine.

Suddenly, Mauro comes over and places his chair beside Maddy's for Alina to use.

"Thank you," she says and signs at the same time. Her cheeks grow a soft shade of pink. He gives her a slight nod and then walks back to his spot, taking a seat on the sand.

"I don't understand…" I peer over at the grand table being arranged, watching as Mrs. Alarie directs the setup of all the food. My eyes then travel around the group, jumping from person to person who all seem to be avoiding eye contact with me, their eyes glancing anywhere but at me. "Is something going on?"

A hand lands on my shoulder, and I peek up to see my favorite pair of dark whiskey eyes staring down at me. Leo's expression softens, a slight smile forming. "Want to take a walk, Firefly?"

Butterflies swarm my belly. As I stand, he removes his jacket and places it over my shoulders. Holding out his hand, I instinctively take it, intertwining our fingers. His thumb glides smoothly back and forth across the back of my hand, tiny goose bumps erupting over my skin.

That overwhelming happy feeling in the pit of my chest takes root, spreading over me like English ivy.

We walk silently for a few minutes, wandering farther away from the group until we lose sight of them and approach a quiet spot with a sizable log. Leo sits and pulls me down to his side, wrapping an arm around me. The sun in the distance is just beginning its descent—beautiful hues of orange and pink shimmer across the sky.

"It's so beautiful here," I say, burrowing closer to Leo's side.

His arm tightens around me, his lips landing on the top of my head, softly pressing gentle kisses. "No sunset could ever compare to you."

I chuckle, shaking my head. "That was pretty corny."

"What's wrong with corny?"

I look up at him, my lips curving up. "Not one damn thing." I lift my chin, waiting for his lips to find mine in a gentle, sweet kiss.

One that feels like home.

He brushes back my hair, sweeping it over my shoulder. His forehead rolls against mine, his warm breath caressing my skin. "I love you."

I grin, cherishing those three little words that hold so much power. "I love you."

He smiles and pulls back, staring off at the ocean. "You know, I was thinking it was a shame we never did everything the right way."

I gaze at him, confused. "What do you mean?"

"Just that I never had the chance to propose to you. I never got you an engagement ring. And we never had a proper wedding or a honeymoon. We missed out on all the good parts, don't you think?"

I stare at our joined hands, the platinum bands on our fingers catching my attention. "When I was a little girl, that's all I ever dreamed about. An elaborate engagement. An over-the-top wedding. But now that we're married, I've realized those things aren't as important as I thought they were. They're nothing in the grand scheme of things."

He nods, deep in thought. "I guess you're right." He reaches into his pocket and pulls out a small black box. "Guess I should just toss this in the ocean then, huh?"

He lifts his arm, and before I even comprehend what I'm doing, my fingers snatch around his wrist. "Leo." I blink a few times, my eyes glued to the box. "What... What is that?"

His lips curve up as he sends my heart into overdrive, kneeling on one knee before me. He's at eye level with me, and I see the nerves dance across his irises as I try to contain my emotions.

"Scarlett," he breathes. "You are and have always been the only woman in my heart. You brought light back into my life when I was so accustomed to darkness. And now that I have you, I'm never letting you go." Tears glide down my cheeks and a broad smile blossoms across my face. "I promise to love you every day for the rest of my life. I promise to wake you up from every nightmare and hold you in my arms until you fall asleep. I promise to always keep the fridge stocked with precut vegetables and fruit. And I promise to always leave the nightlight on for you." A full-on sob takes over me, my throat tightening with a vise-like grip.

He opens the box and a gasp escapes me as he plucks out the delicate engagement ring, holding it before me. Two thin platinum bands intertwine, covered in little diamonds looking like vines, and they meet at the center, where a beautiful pink diamond is attached to two white diamonds on the sides that look like wings. "Will you, Scarlett, my firefly, please make me the happiest man in the world by marrying me...again?"

I vigorously nod, holding out my trembling hand and watching as he slides the ring on my finger. I stare at it in disbelief for only a second before jumping into his arms, my limbs wrapping around him as we roll in the sand, both of us laughing.

I lie on top of him, pressing kisses to the side of his neck. "Is this why a fancy dinner is being set up at the house?"

He grins. "Yes. I wanted everyone to be able to celebrate together."

I arch a brow. "And how were you so certain that I would say yes?"

"Maybe because..." He places the palm of his hand on my chest. "Your heart." And then places my hand on his chest. "And my heart." He presses his lips to mine. "They beat for each other."

I roll in my bottom lip, biting down as my eyes water.

He sits up, embracing me in his arms. "Thank you." His hands cup my cheeks, his thumb gently wiping away my tears.

"What are you thanking me for?" I brush sand off his shoulders, trying to distract myself.

"For breathing light back into my darkness."

An onslaught of tears builds behind my eyes. "Without you, there would be no happily ever after for me." I brush my lips over his, anticipation building between us. "Without you, I would be broken in the dark." My lips crash onto his as his hand slides behind my neck, tugging me closer to him, our hearts truly beating as one.

Epilogue

SCARLETT - SIX MONTHS LATER

Deep breath in. Deep breath out.

I stop at the top of the marble stairs, my heart tripping over itself as nerves get the better of me.

What if I trip and fall? I inwardly groan, counting the abundance of steps I'll need to take in my four-inch heels. When I chose the New York Public Library as our wedding venue, I never considered all the steps it would entail.

My fingers anxiously twist on the silver chain around my neck before quickly smoothing out the pendant so that it lies flat against my skin and the blue diamond is perfectly centered.

With the stone archway blocking me from being seen by anyone, I take a moment to calm my beating heart. Gently, I push back the cathedral-length veil, ensuring it glides gracefully down my backside. My hands slide down the front of my ivory lace bodice, resting on my stomach, where I feel the movement of each rushed breath I take.

Beautiful music performed by the string quartet drowns out the voices of the three-hundred-plus guests, and the smell of thousands of books eases my racing mind.

"You can do this," I breathe, not feeling as confident as I should be for someone who is about to have a room full of eyes on them. I'm starting to regret not taking Maddy up on her offer to accompany me down the stairs.

As I lift my trembling foot, ready to take my first step, my eyes catch on movement beside me.

"Thought you might want some company." Vin strolls up to my side, looking every bit the part of the perfect gentleman in his black three-piece suit. He smiles warmly at me as he braces his forearm out for me to take. "You look beautiful, Scarlett."

"Thank you." I smile as I loop my arm with his, my hand resting on his forearm for support.

"Don't forget, there might be hundreds of people waiting for you, but there's only one person in that room who would burn the whole goddamn world down for you." He squeezes my hand with his free one. "And I've never seen him so nervous in my life, so why don't we put the poor guy out of his misery and get this show started?"

I laugh quietly, nodding. "I'm ready."

"Of course you are." Vin straightens his shoulders. "You're an Alarie, after all." He gives me a wink and leads us down the stairs. My heart thunders in my ears as I focus on each step, careful not to trip and make a damn fool out of myself.

"He's only got eyes for you," Vin whispers.

"What?" I ask, glancing up. He tilts his head toward the far side, and just as we take the last step down leading to the aisle, I look over, and my heart stills.

Everything around me fades into the background as my eyes latch onto Leo. And all the nerves bundled inside me wash away to a distant, faraway place.

My heart thrashes in my chest as I see my knight in black armor. His perfectly tailored black suit fits him like a glove, showing off his taut chest and thick thighs. His dark eyes travel over me with so much adoration and love, as though he is engraving this moment into his memory.

He rolls in his bottom lip, his eyes watering. *I love you*, he mouths.

I swallow hard, my throat tightening. *I love you*, I mouth back.

The quartet begins to play our chosen song, and everyone in the room stands, turning my way.

Vin uses his hand to cover my own, resting on his forearm. He leads us down the aisle, white roses lining the way with lavish white flowers draped like vines throughout the space.

It's truly a fairy tale come to life.

I see Maddy and Alina standing beautifully at the left side of the altar in their satin soft-pink dresses. They're both blotting their eyes with tissues, making my eyes water even more. Alex, Mauro, and Eli are standing to the right in their matching tuxes, all three of them displaying warm smiles. And Mrs. Alarie sits in the front row, a broad, beautiful smile overtaking her face as tears tumble down her cheeks.

My eyes stray back to Leo, and I notice an urgency in his demeanor. He rocks back and forth on his heels as if waiting for me to get to his side is absolute torture for him.

Just as much as it is for me.

The moment I reach him, Vin quickly places my hand in Leo's and grins at us as he takes his spot beside him.

"You look perfect, Firefly," Leo whispers in my ear. I shift to face him, coming only inches away from him. The officiant's words blur in the background as Leo brushes his lips against mine. "I have a proposition."

"And what is that?"

As the officiant continues speaking, his words echoing across the grand room, Leo leans closer to me. "Seeing that your husband so generously rented out the whole library for the entire day, I say we make the most of it," he whispers, ensuring his words are only heard by me. A mischievous smile forms on his handsome face. "You. Me. Naked. In the romance section, with a bottle of champagne to celebrate." A flush crawls over my skin as I begin to fantasize about this scenario. "I promise not to get the books wet." He brushes his lips against my ear. "But I can't make the same promise to you."

My tongue runs across my bottom lip, wishing he would close the space between us. It's taking every ounce of self-control I have not to wrap my arms around him and tug him against me, devouring him before everyone in here. I tilt my chin up, his breath caressing my face as I lean in, needing a taste.

He ghosts his lips across mine, not pressing down. "I can't wait to lick the champagne off of every inch of your body."

My cheeks instantly flush as I roll in my bottom lip. I was going to wait until tonight to tell him the news, but I guess now is just as good of a time as any. "It's too bad I won't be able to enjoy any of it," I say softly, not wanting anyone in the room to hear what I'm about to tell him.

He pauses, his brows furrowing. "Why not?"

I give a slight shrug and a mock frown. "Unfortunately, pregnant women can't drink alcohol." I bite down on my bottom lip, stifling a smile.

Leo's eyes widen, his lips parting. "You... You mean?"

I give a little nod, unable to contain the smile blossoming across my face.

Without a second of hesitation, Leo pulls me against him, crashing his lips down onto mine. I savor his taste, his demanding touch, and the love seeping into my bones.

Not only is he my first love. My husband. My everything.

But now, he's the father of our child.

The room erupts in hollers and cheers as the officiant clears his throat, appearing confused by our early kiss.

Pulling back, I look up at him, my heart swelling. "I take it you're okay with this?"

"No, Firefly." He cradles a hand over my cheek, his thumb brushing away any loose tears. "I'm over the fucking moon about this." He rests his forehead against mine. "We're having a baby."

"We're having a baby," I repeat, savoring being in his hold. The one place in the world I have always felt most at home.

"I may not be much of a reader, but without a doubt, I can say that this is my favorite story," Leo says.

My brows tug together. "Which story?"

"Our story." His lips curve up, my eyes watering as warmth caresses my skin. "The one where we made our way back to each other and fell in love all over again."

I bite down on my bottom lip, holding back tears. "And what happens next in our story?"

"Well, that's the best part." He frames my face in his hands, his dark eyes latching onto mine. "We get to find out together. Because it's you and me until the end of time." His nose rubs against mine. "My wife. My everything. My firefly."

His lips meet mine in a tender kiss as the world stops moving and everything around me disappears. I stand on my tiptoes, wrapping my arms around his neck. He deepens the kiss, his hands grabbing my waist, pulling me flush against him. And as my heart thrashes beneath my rib cage, it hits me.

I'm living out my very own happily ever after.

The end.

Thank you for reading Broken in the Dark!

If you enjoyed this love story, I would be forever grateful if you could leave a review on the platform of your choice. Your support means so much to me and helps spread the word to other readers!

Acknowledgments

To you, the person who decided to give my book a chance—Thank you! I am a relatively new author and hope to learn and grow with each book release, so thank you for your support.

To my twin sister, Amanda—Thank you for always being my biggest fan. I love you.

To my mom and dad—I appreciate your love and support, but please don't read any of my books. Just trust me on this.

To Grace—I don't even know where to begin. But let's see... Thank you for your unfathomable support and encouragement during the writing process. Thank you for the continuous back-and-forth messages I always look forward to listening to. Thank you for dissecting the stories and characters with me and helping me create something I'm proud of. But most of all, thank you for being an amazing friend from over nine thousand miles away.

To Amanda—Thank you for always believing in me! I hope you know how much I genuinely appreciate your support and friendship. And thank you for always letting me send horrible rough drafts of my manuscripts your way without judgment!

To my beta reader, Ashley—Thank you for always saying yes when I send another book your way! I truly appreciate your continuous support and feedback!

To my beta reader, Steph—Thank you so much for all of your help! So glad we found each other on Bookstagram!

To my editor, Erica Russikoff—Thank you for taking such great care of my story. As always, it was an absolute pleasure working with you!

Thank you to all my readers who share their love for my books on social media! Your kind words help spread the word to more readers, and I am forever grateful for your support.

About the author

Ashley Elizabeth is an author of steamy contemporary romance. Her books will always tell a love story with just the right amount of spice and, most importantly, end with a happily ever after. When she's not reading a romance novel or overthinking everything, you can find her at Starbucks, keeping them in business, or watching Jurassic Park for the thousandth time with her fur baby, Bailey.

ALSO BY ASHLEY ELIZABETH

Before I Tell You
Before I Saw You
Before I Loved You

KEEP IN TOUCH WITH ASHLEY ELIZABETH

WEBSITE: ashleyelizabethauthor.com
INSTAGRAM: @ashleyelizabethauthor
TIKTOK: @ashleyelizabethauthor
GOODREADS: goodreads.com/ashleyelizabeth